"I'll help you get Liz's place ready for sale."

Abby shifted in the passenger seat to stare at Hunter. "Seriously? You're not teasing me, are you? You're really going to help me?"

"Yeah. I'm really going to—"

Before he realized what she was up to, Abby launched herself over the console and threw her arms around his neck.

"What the—" As Hunter turned his head to give her hell, she kissed him.

On the mouth.

In the middle of Main Street.

In the middle of rush-hour traffic.

PRAISE FOR DEBBIE MASON

"Debbie Mason writes romance like none other."
—FreshFiction.com

"I've never met a Debbie Mason story that I didn't enjoy."
—KeeperBookshelf.com

"I'm telling you right now, if you haven't yet read a book by Debbie Mason, you don't know what you're missing."
—RomancingtheReaders.blogspot.com

"It's not just romance. It's grief and mourning, guilt and truth, second chances and revelations."
—WrittenLoveReviews.blogspot.com

"Mason always makes me smile and touches my heart in the most unexpected and wonderful ways."
—HerdingCats-BurningSoup.com

"No one writes heartful small town romance like Debbie Mason, and I always count the days until the next book!"
—TheManyFacesofRomance.blogspot.com

"Wow, do these books bring the feels. Deep emotion, heart-tugging romance, and a touch of suspense make them hard to put down..."
—TheRomanceDish.com

Summer on Honeysuckle Ridge

DEBBIE MASON

A Highland Falls Novel

FOREVER
New York   Boston

Copyright © 2020 by Debbie Mazzuca

Excerpt from *Christmas on Reindeer Road* © 2020 by Debbie Mazzuca

Cover design by Elizabeth Stokes. Cover illustration by Rob Hallman. Cover copyright © 2020 by Hachette Book Group, Inc.

Forever
Hachette Book Group
1290 Avenue of the Americas, New York, NY 10104
read-forever.com
twitter.com/readforeverpub

First Edition: May 2020

Forever is an imprint of Grand Central Publishing. The Forever name and logo are trademarks of Hachette Book Group, Inc.

The publisher is not responsible for websites (or their content) that are not owned by the publisher.

The Hachette Speakers Bureau provides a wide range of authors for speaking events. To find out more, go to www.hachettespeakersbureau.com or call (866) 376-6591.

ISBNs: 978-1-5387-1694-6 (mass market), 978-1-5387-1693-9 (ebook)

Printed in the United States of America

OPM

10 9 8 7 6 5 4 3 2 1

This book is dedicated to the memory of my grandfather Dudley Copland, who encouraged my love of reading, storytelling, and all things Scottish.

Summer on Honeysuckle Ridge

Chapter One

♥

You know, this doesn't look anything like I pictured Honeysuckle Ridge Road. There's not a honeysuckle in sight. Or a farm. Or any sign of civilization at all, for that matter. All you can see for miles and miles is trees. Ginormous trees," Abby Everhart said to the Uber driver while holding her eight-pound gold-and-tan Yorkshire terrier close.

The man didn't so much as blink. He'd barely spoken the entire four-hour drive from the airport in Charlotte to Highland Falls, North Carolina. At least she assumed they were close to the town. She'd seen a sign a few miles back, peeking out from a stand of trees.

With her nose pressed to the window, her dog growled. Obviously as impressed with the view as Abby. Or maybe Bella had spotted a wild animal lurking in the dark forest that practically swallowed the narrow dirt road winding its way up the mountain.

Abby refused to think about what was crawling around on the forest floor. The past two days had been stressful enough.

If it wasn't for her ex's longtime housekeeper, Elinor, Abby wouldn't have known about the registered letter that had been delivered to his Bel Air mansion days before their divorce was final. She'd have no idea that she'd inherited her great-aunt's farm in Highland Falls or that Chandler (the aforementioned ex) had been having an affair with the head of his legal team, Juliette Devereaux. Or that he planned to marry her.

But as much as Abby appreciated Elinor standing by her, she could've used at least a day to wallow in her misery—some sympathy also would've been nice—but Elinor wasn't having it. She'd decided the inheritance was a sign from the Universe that it was time for Abby to get out of Dodge, or in this case, LA.

Abby slouched down in the backseat of the car and lifted her cell phone to take a picture of the Uber driver, the dark woods up ahead, the dark woods on her right, and the dark woods on her left.

What had she been thinking?

She never should've listened to Elinor. She should've contacted the lawyer in Highland Falls and had her sell the farm and wire her the money. But as Elinor had pointed out, Abby was homeless, almost penniless, and mostly jobless.

At least in Highland Falls, she had a home. Just because the idea of living in the mountains with not a soul in sight wasn't her cup of tea didn't mean everyone felt that way. There had to be a reclusive dot-com millionaire somewhere who wanted nothing more than to drop a pile on a mountain hideaway.

She swiped to her notes on her phone and created a

list of potential buyers to target. Then she texted Elinor and attached the photos.

If you don't hear from me in twenty-four hours, look for this man, and look for mine and Bella's bodies in these woods.

But instead of the *swoosh* of the message being sent, the text just hung there. Abby's eyes went wide at the thought that she was so far from civilization she was in a texting dead zone. It would be weeks before Elinor sent up an alarm. Abby swiped back to her potential buyer list, deleted *dot-com millionaire*, and added *serial killer or person on the run*.

She glanced at her driver, prayed he didn't fit into either category, then leaned forward in case he was hard of hearing, which would explain why he'd ignored her questions for almost the entire drive.

"Stan, I don't want to be one of those know-it-all passengers... Trust me, I've dealt with them before and totally understand how annoying it is. There were a few of them I would've happily mur..." She cleared her throat. Better not to put ideas in his head just in case.

"Anyhoo, you might want to check your GPS. I called mine Chandler. That's my ex, and he was as much an annoying know-it-all as my GPS. It was also wrong thirty percent of the time. I'm not the only one who's experienced a GPS fail, you know. There was this woman I heard about whose GPS directed her into a lake. I still haven't figured out why she actually drove into the lake. She had to have seen—"

Stan cut her off, grumbling, "We're here," and turned off the main road.

"Oh, wow. That's so...awesome." She tried to sound enthusiastic, but even reminding herself that she was still alive and breathing didn't help. And then she kind of stopped breathing when a log farmhouse came into view—a rustic log farmhouse in need of some TLC. And that TLC needed to be provided by a professional, she thought, her head listing to the side as she followed the crooked line of the covered porch that appeared to wrap around the entire house.

Elinor was wrong. The Universe hadn't been giving Abby a sign to get out of Dodge. The Universe was giving her the middle finger.

Sensing the driver watching her in the rearview mirror, clearly waiting for a reaction, Abby forced a wide smile. She never should've told him the farm was worth a small fortune. She hadn't done it in a braggy sort of way. It was more like a positive-thinking kind of thing. As in, if she put out positive thoughts, positive things would happen in return. She glanced at the rusted green tin roof. Clearly, she was doing something wrong.

"Look at our new home, Bella Boo. It's...charming."

Abby got out of the car, her gaze moving from the meadow to the woods that bordered the extensive property, and the dusky-blue shadows of the mountains looming up behind the forest.

A shimmer of light caught her eye to the right. "Oh, look—there's a pond, and a barn."

Her fake smile fell when she spotted an outhouse near the yellow barn. Surely the farmhouse had indoor plumbing. Her upper lip trembled from the effort of forcing a smile back on her face. "You know what, with a little money"—more like a small fortune—"this place will be so amazing, I'm not sure I'll be able to bring myself to sell." Ha! If she wasn't broke, and she didn't need money to finance her comeback in LA, she'd give the farm away.

"Word of advice: keep a close eye on your dog," Stan said as he set the suitcase beside her.

Since Abby had been living out of her car for the past six months, Elinor had lent her the Burberry suitcase. And probably because she'd looked so pathetic, Elinor had also insisted on taking Abby to her friend's beauty salon before she flew off on her new *adventure*.

Thank goodness she had, because while Abby might be completely out of her element, she at least looked somewhat like the woman she used to be (and hoped to become again), and that gave her a small measure of comfort. Although instead of her signature long, straight blond hair, she was now a redhead with long, curly locks. And instead of her designer-store wardrobe, her current wardrobe came from the consignment store.

But the faded denim shorts and white boyfriend shirt she wore looked fab with the four-inch wedge sandals and her hot-pink-painted toenails.

"Thanks for the advice, Stan. I won't let her out of my sight." Abby gave him a genuine smile, appreciating his thoughtful concern, especially since he hadn't been happy to discover she had a dog in her pink-patent-leather Louis Vuitton bag.

Bella had sensed his fear right away and used it to her advantage, snarling and growling so Abby would keep giving her doggy treats.

Abby took out the flat fee she and Stan had agreed upon and added a generous tip, even though she couldn't afford it. She and Stan shared a bond, after all. They didn't always get the respect they deserved driving cars for a living. She'd also leave a nice comment about her experience. Although she did wonder if she should give Stan some pointers.

Not to toot her own horn or anything, but her passengers rarely left her anything below a five-star review. And she didn't have to bribe them or fake that she'd enjoyed their company. She was a people person, and if it wasn't for the glamorous life she'd led before Chandler and Juliette had destroyed it, she would've enjoyed her Uber gig. She glanced at the farmhouse. Who was she trying to kid? She so wanted her Hollywood life back.

Stan nodded his thanks and stuffed the money in his pocket. As he walked around the hood of the car to the driver's-side door, he added, "Hawks and eagles would just as soon eat her as look at her. Same goes for coyotes and wolves."

Abby decided she preferred the non-speaking Stan to the speaking one. "Okay, then. Thanks so much for sharing that with me." She gave him a smile that stretched her cheeks. "Good thing we don't have to worry about bears."

"No, you gotta worry about them too. But they're more likely to go after you. Same with mountain lions, so have an eye." He opened the car door. "Watch out for snakes and spiders too. There are some deadly ones in this neck of the woods."

She'd been wrong. Serial killers and criminals on the run were the least of her concerns. It was wildlife with murder on its mind that she had to worry about. "Um, you know, maybe I should..."

She was about to suggest he drop her off in town but that would feel too much like giving up on her dreams. Besides, it wasn't like she had money to burn. And no matter how high the odds seemed to be stacked against her at that moment, she'd beaten seemingly unsurmountable odds before.

In her tween years, this kind of challenge would've been her jam. Her favorite pastime had been hiking in the woods with her father. They hiked every weekend in good weather and bad. The girl she used to be wouldn't have been afraid of spiders or snakes or deadly wildlife of any kind. Back then she'd been fearless, the more physical the adventure the better.

She waved goodbye to Stan, putting on a brave face as he drove away. She was all alone in the middle of no—Her jaw dropped. What had she been thinking? Her cell phone didn't work, she didn't have any means of transportation, and she had no food!

"Stan!" Abby took off at a run up the gravel road with Bella in her arms. "Look in your rearview mirror!" She waved her free hand, crying out when she skidded across the loose gravel and nearly fell on her face.

The time it took to regain her footing cost her, and she broke into a full-on sprint. Or as much of a sprint as four-inch wedge heels allowed. "Stan!" she called out, her voice strained from lack of oxygen. Her legs protested as she ran up the hill (okay, so it might have been more of a jog), and sweat trickled down her face. A muscle knotted in her side, and she stopped, bending over to wheeze. "I think I'm going to die." Then hope surged through her at the sound of Stan's car slowing at the top of the hill, and she lifted her head...only to see the taillights wink goodbye as they disappeared from view.

She fought the urge to sit on the gravel road and cry. "Suck it up, buttercup," she told herself. She'd faced far worse and survived. All she had to do was stay positive. If worse came to worst, she'd change her shoes and walk to the main road. As she turned to make the trek back to the farmhouse, Bella gave her a doggy kiss. "Thanks, Boo. I'm okay."

But so out of shape it wasn't funny. She supposed that's what happened when you made your living sitting on your butt. "It looks like you might be sharing your treats with me." They wouldn't last a week.

A sudden image of her hunting for their food made Abby laugh despite the worry that they might actually starve to death. "Maybe Aunt Liz left something in the cupboards."

Except the lawyer handling the estate said she'd had a difficult time tracking down Abby, and Liz Findlay had died months before. Which made it unlikely there would be anything edible left in the house. That animals hadn't already gotten into, Abby thought, when two gray squirrels appeared on the rooftop.

Holding up her phone in hopes of getting a signal, Abby made her way through a jungle of bushes and overgrown shrubs to the front porch. Pushing aside the greenery that was encroaching on the stone path, she nearly missed the *swoosh* of a text being sent. She froze, praying it wasn't her imagination as she shielded her eyes from the sun to squint at the screen.

"We're saved!" she cried at the sight of three bars. She set a squirming Bella at her feet and hurried back to her bag on the stone path. As Abby reached inside to retrieve her wallet and the lawyer's number, her phone rang— FaceTime. She smiled, thinking it was Elinor checking for proof of life after the text Abby had sent.

She pressed Accept. "Yes, I'm alive ... " Her eyes went wide. Instead of Elinor, Abby's gorgeous blond mother and her equally gorgeous blond stepsisters appeared on the screen. *Crap!* That would teach her to check the number before accepting.

She swallowed a panicked *eek* when she realized they'd see the rundown farmhouse in the background. Her face frozen in a smile, Abby shuffled to ensure they had a view of the trees and mountains. Then she positioned the phone at just the right angle—as far as her arm would stretch out and up—while trying to look perfectly natural. And unfazed.

Her mother and stepsisters had no clue what was going on in Abby's life. If they had, they would've dragged her back to the small Southern town they called home and she called social purgatory. But even worse than that, they'd know she was a failure.

After years of being voted the Everhart most unlikely to succeed, she refused to let them discover she'd lost everything. Even if it meant pretending that she still lived in the mansion in Bel Air and that her husband still adored her.

"Hi!" She waved at her mom and stepsisters. Bella cocked her head, looking up at her as if to say *What the hay?*

She was nervous. She knew it was weird to be nervous talking to her own family, but she kind of dreaded these phone calls. Her mom had married the twins' father when they were four and Abby was fourteen. Haven and Haley were everything Abby would never be. Brilliant and beautiful, they excelled at whatever they set their minds to. And while Abby was positive her mother didn't do it on purpose, the calls were usually a litany of the twins' recent successes.

"Happy belated birthday, darling! I'm sorry we didn't call from India but the time difference is horrendous." Her mother blew her kisses, and so did the twins.

"Happy birthday, Abs! Your hair is totally lit! It makes your green eyes pop," her stepsisters said at almost the same time.

Abby self-consciously touched her hair. "It does look like it's on fire, doesn't it?"

Haven, the youngest twin by five minutes, laughed. "No, silly, lit means awesome."

She really was getting old.

Elinor and her hairdresser friend, Kate, had decided that Abby needed to change things up and do something completely different. She'd tried to explain to them that red was her natural color, and it had never been a good look for her. It was also a color that reminded her of a time in her life when everything had gone from bad to worse. But blond? She'd totally rocked blond. Poker-straight, long blond locks were her Hollywood look...Now that she thought about it, she probably should've gone with brown or black.

"I don't know," her mother said. "It makes you look a little peaked, don't you think?"

"Mom, stop. She looks fantastic."

And that's what made the calls difficult. Her stepsisters were sweet and kind, and Abby always came away feeling like a horrible person because she resented them for being perfect.

"Of course she does." Her mother smiled at the twins. "Who wants to tell Abby your news?"

"Mom." They both groaned, sending apologetic glances at Abby.

"What? You should be proud of yourselves and shouting your accomplishments to the world. Abby's as proud of you as I am."

She was, because she adored Haven and Haley as much as they adored her.

Ignoring the twins' second groaned *Mom*, their mother shouted their latest accomplishment to Abby. "The mayor is hosting a dinner in your sisters' honor before they leave for college. They're being given the key to the town for all they've done to make Shady Mills a wonderful place to live. Can you imagine? They're only eighteen and being given such an honor. I swear, they're setting the bar too low for themselves. They should set their sights on the White House."

Right, because a supreme court judge and neurosurgeon were setting the bar too low. Abby could only dream of being as smart as her sisters. They'd graduated high school a year early with scores of 4.0, and were given full rides to Stanford. But first they'd taken a gap year to travel and volunteer with non-profits.

Abby had been lucky to have graduated high school at nineteen with a 2.5, and the only college to offer her a scholarship was the University of Hard Knocks. She'd headed for Hollywood the day after graduation. And while she didn't have the looks or the talent to make it as an actress, she did have an eye for the next big thing, whether it be in makeup, hair, fashion, or the Hollywood social scene. More important, she had passion and drive.

"If it wasn't for Abby, the mayor wouldn't be honoring us," Haven said.

"It's totes true, Abs," Haley said, no doubt responding to Abby's pained smile. "When you gave up your YouTube channel to focus on philanthropy and giving back, you inspired us."

It took everything Abby had to keep the smile on her face. She was a fraud. She didn't deserve the twins' love and admiration. She hadn't given up her YouTube channel to focus on philanthropy. She'd given it up because Chandler and his attorneys (i.e., Juliette) had wanted her wiped off social media.

And that was a truth she couldn't bear her family to hear. She couldn't stand the idea of Haley and Haven looking at her like her Hollywood friends now did.

"I'm sure Chandler is as proud of you as we are," Haley continued. "Did he spoil you like he always does on your birthday?"

He hadn't spoiled her for the past two years. She'd just pretended that he had for all their sakes. Just like she'd pretended he still loved her, ignoring the signs that he was having an affair.

"Yes, darling. Tell us what he bought you." Her mother craned her neck as though looking for another five-carat pink diamond ring, which was the last birthday present Abby had received from Chandler. He'd demanded it back as part of the settlement. "You look like you're at a resort. It's not a spa-slash-rehab resort, is it?"

"Mom! Of course it isn't. Why would you even think something like that?"

"You do hang around with all those Hollywood types, darling. And you are a little gaunt." She leaned into the screen. "You don't look like you've been sleeping either. You've got black circles under your eyes."

Abby leaned in to peer at herself. "It's mascara." She licked the tip of her forefinger and ran it under her bottom lashes.

Haven's and Haley's eyes rounded.

Thinking they were shocked that she no longer wore lash extensions, Abby swallowed a sigh to say, "I've heard that lash—"

"No! Look, Abby! It's Bella."

She frowned and looked down. Bella wasn't there. Following her stepsisters' pointed fingers and their squeaks of terror, she turned, emitting a terrified squeak of her own. Her teeny-tiny dog was racing across the field toward a huge white...wolf! In her panic, she dropped her phone and ran.

"I'm coming, Boo! Mommy will save you!" She raced across the meadow.

Bella stopped about fifteen feet from the wolf to snarl

and bark at the animal. The wolf tilted its head to the side, appearing confused. Maybe because most animals were smart and ran at the sight of it. Or maybe it found the bow and dress her dog wore confusing.

"Bella, do not annoy the big, bad wolf. Come here, baby. Come to Mommy." Abby's heart hammered as she closed the distance between her and Bella. The wolf did the same. Slowly, lethally, he padded across the grass. "Shoo! Go away! Argh." Abby growled in hopes of scaring him off, waving her arms over her head to make herself appear bigger than five-foot-four.

The wolf stopped, and she thought her attempt to scare him away had worked. But then, over the frantic pounding of her heart in her ears, she heard a deep voice shout, "Wolf!"

A huge man with longish hair and a short beard walked out of the woods carrying a tree stump on one broad shoulder and an ax over the other. Abby prayed he was a lumberjack and not an ax murderer because he looked a little scary.

"I know it's a wolf!" Abby cried out as she bent over on the run to scoop Bella into her arms. "Do not fall. Do not fall," she told herself as she veered to the left at an all-out sprint, praying the lumberjack took care of the wolf.

"Stop running!" the man yelled.

She glanced over her shoulder to see the wolf loping after them and screamed.

"Wolf!" the man shouted again, but this time, Abby noted that he'd put down his huge log and his big ax and was jogging toward them. Jogging!

"I know it's a wolf!" she shouted at the lumberjack. "Do something! Go back and get your ax!"

"Watch where you're going!"

"Watch where I'm going?" she yelled back at him, furious and terrified at the same time, afraid her legs would give out at any minute. "That's as helpful as you shouting—Argh!" she cried as she fell face-first into a weed-filled pond.

Chapter Two

♥

Hunter reached the pond just as the woman rose from under the murky water like a creature from the Black Lagoon. Big green eyes peered at him from under a hat of slimy weeds. A toad jumped off her head and into the cattails behind her. Focused on holding her pocket-sized dog over her head, she didn't notice.

He figured it was a good thing that she hadn't—she had big city written all over her. No doubt she was staying at Three Wild Women Winery. The resort was not far from here and attracted women like her. He assumed she'd gotten lost on one of their organized hikes.

She spat out water and then said to the dog, which looked like a drowned rat, "Are you all right, baby?"

Okay, so that explained why the rat was wearing a bow and a dress.

"Give me your hand." He leaned forward, extending his own.

Her lips flattened as she eyed him from under the weeds. "Maybe if you'd yelled *Watch out for the pond* instead of *Watch where you're going*, I wouldn't be drowning in..." She scrunched her small, upturned nose and shuddered.

"You're not drowning. At most, the pond is four feet deep in the middle." He didn't know why he felt the need to stand on the edge of the pond arguing with this woman. He'd probably said more to her in the last few minutes than he'd said to anyone in months.

"Really? Have you spent much time in here, Mr...." she began as she waded toward him and reached for his hand.

He noticed the leech on her arm and drew an irritated breath through his nostrils as he wrapped his hand around hers. No matter how much he wanted her gone, he couldn't just haul her out and send her on her way with a bloodsucker attached to her smooth skin.

Those moss-green eyes of hers went wide, and he opened his mouth to tell her to relax—there was no need to get worked up over a leech—but he didn't get a chance. She screamed, knifed out of the water, and yanked on his hand, putting the weight of her curvy body behind the hard tug. He slipped on the mud-slicked grass and, with a shout of surprise, fell face-first into the pond, swallowing a mouthful of swampy water.

As he got to his feet, he wiped his mouth with the back of his hand while looking around to give the woman hell. She wasn't there. He must've fallen on top of her. Searching the murky water with his hands, he came into contact with something full and soft...He swore under his breath, moving his hand to grab an arm instead of a breast. She burst to the surface sputtering and panicked.

"I'm sorry. I didn't mean to grab your...I couldn't see. The mud and the weeds..." But his muttered apology and halting explanation for the inappropriate contact was lost in her splashing and thrashing as she turned in frantic circles.

"Bella! Boo, where are you?" She froze. Then, with her mouth opening and closing like a fish out of water, she stabbed her finger at the other side of the pond, where her dog hung by its white dress from Wolf's mouth.

Hunter placed a firm hand on the woman's shoulder when she snapped out of her shock and made a move toward her dog. "Wolf, drop it." His dog lifted his pale-blue gaze. "Now."

Only when Wolf stretched out in a submissive position on the grass did Hunter relax his grip on the redhead's shoulder. His dog was part wolf. The instincts to hunt and kill for survival were deeply ingrained. Every animal was the same, even the rat in the dress. Wolf nudged the dog with his nose as though trying to figure out what the hell it was.

"Do something! He's going to eat her!" the redhead cried as she waded through the water, apparently willing to take on Wolf despite her fear.

He felt a reluctant admiration for her, which might explain why his warning came out on a growl. "Don't move." These days the only things Hunter allowed himself to feel anything for were his dog and his wood-carving. "If he was going to eat your dog, he would've eaten her five minutes ago."

Hunter nudged the woman out of the way and hauled himself out of the pond, moving to sit close enough to grab the rat if Wolf changed his mind. It's not like they got a lot of visitors around here—domesticated animals or humans. Hunter was good at keeping them away.

He felt the redhead's stare as he pulled off his steel-toe boots and his socks. Even though he wanted to ignore her, he looked up. Somewhere inside him was a remnant of the man he'd been raised to be.

She pushed the weeds off her head. "That's your dog, isn't it?"

He nodded as he glanced at Wolf to see whether the rat, who was shaking the water from her dress, was amusing or annoying his dog. *Still confused,* he thought at the sight of Wolf's cocked head. Hunter took the opportunity to pull off his T-shirt, looking up at the woman's gasp. Her eyes were riveted on his bare chest. "Don't worry, lady. I'm leaving my shorts on."

"Oh." She clutched the corner of her bottom lip between her perfect white teeth, then gave her head a slight shake. "I mean, I should hope so. Now, are you going to help me out of here or not?"

"Not." He lifted a shoulder at her shocked expression. "What do you expect? You tried to drown me."

"I was trying to save you! I thought you'd scared off the wolf but then I saw him sneaking up behind you." She crossed her arms as though realizing her white shirt was molded to her chest and didn't leave much to the imagination.

He was right there with her. He'd been trying to ignore her chest since she'd stood up in the pond.

"And you know what," she continued. "You calling your dog Wolf when you knew I was terrified wasn't the least bit funny. If you ask me, it was really immature of you."

"That's his name."

"Your dog's name is Wolf?" Not waiting for an answer and obviously taking him at his word that he wouldn't help her out, she waded to the edge of the pond. It took a couple tries for her to get a grip on the muddy grass and pull herself out of the water.

"Yeah." He averted his gaze. He might've been celibate for the past couple years and this woman wasn't even close to his type, but that didn't mean he was immune to a body that would have a priest rethinking his vows.

With his eyes on his dog, Hunter came to his feet. "Okay, Wolf, the rat's entertained you enough for one day." An outraged gasp came from behind him, and he pinched the bridge of his nose. He should've known better than to offend her *baby*.

"That's a horrible thing to say. You've hurt her feelings. Don't listen to him, Bella Boo. You're Mommy's beautiful girl." She talked to her dog in one of those high-pitched, annoying voices that women reserved for babies. Real babies.

"Lady, she's not a kid. She's a dog. She doesn't know what a rat is."

"You have no idea what you're talking about. No idea what she's been through. She...*Argh*. "Get it off! Please, please, get it off me!"

She'd seen the leech. "Calm down, and I'll—" He glanced over to see her doing a panicked dance on the side of the pond while pulling up her shirt. At the sight of her bare stomach and a glimpse of a lacy white bra, it took a minute to regain his power of speech. Long enough that the woman was seconds from ripping off her shirt.

"Stop! You're not covered in leeches. You have one on your—" Okay, so they'd multiplied in the last few minutes. "If you stop stripping and stop moving, I'll get rid of them."

He wished Liz were here so he could foist the crazy redhead on her. No doubt his old friend was up there having a good laugh at his expense. Liz and Honeysuckle Farm had saved him. They'd given him a reason to live after his last tour of duty had taken him to hell and beyond.

In the beginning, Liz probably would've agreed that she and the farm had saved him. But a few months before she'd died, she'd told him she hadn't done him any favors giving him a place to hide. He'd been worried she'd ask him to leave. Maybe she would have if she hadn't gotten sick. Then she'd needed him as much as he'd needed his reclusive life on the ridge.

He pulled a pack of waterproof matches from his cargo shorts pocket and took a step toward the woman flapping her arms and running on the spot while making small bleating noises. A couple yards away, Wolf and the rat sat side by side watching her with their heads cocked. If not for the task that awaited him, Hunter might've been amused by the sight. But all he could think about was having to deal with a hysterical female when he'd rather be carving the eagle he'd seen in his dream.

"Keep your eyes on the prize," he murmured as

he closed the distance between them. The sooner the leeches fell off her pretty, soft skin, the sooner she and the rat were gone.

With that in mind, he gentled his voice, talking to her like he would a frightened animal caught in a trap. He relaxed a bit. He might not be good with people, women like her in particular, but he was good with wounded animals.

Except a wounded animal wouldn't look at him with pleading moss-green eyes when he crouched at its feet, and it wouldn't have kissable pink lips that trembled when it tried not to cry.

She sniffed. "The Universe hates me. My life is a disaster. I'm a disaster."

He couldn't speak to her and her life being a disaster, but he was pretty sure, in this instance, it was him the Universe hated.

Seeing her mistress's distress, the rat raced to her side, barking and snarling at Hunter. From behind him came his dog's warning growl. Hunter held up a hand. "Wolf, stay." Then he looked at the rat. "Bella, sit." And to her mistress. "Lady, close your eyes and stay still. I don't want to burn you."

"Burn me?" she squeaked, moving her leg out of reach.

He held up the match. "Faster than salt." Then he wrapped his hand around her slender ankle, drawing her leg between his thighs. He stroked the skin just above her calf with his thumb, and she settled a bit. He struck the wooden match along the side of the box. It flared to life, the smell of sulfur filling the air. He held the burning ember to the leech attached to the back of her knee. All the while ignoring the thought that her skin was as soft and as silky as he'd imagined.

She shuddered when the leech shriveled up and fell at her feet. "Please hurry up and get the rest off me."

"They're harmless." It was true, but she had more than one attached to her delicate skin, and they'd been living in the pond, which was no doubt a cesspool of bacteria. Since he didn't want a crying female on his hands, he highlighted the positive. "They've been using leeches in medical therapy since medieval times. They improve blood flow and keep tissue from dying. They're good for fishing too."

The leech Hunter had first noticed on her arm plopped off, and her eyes went wide. "Does he not like my blood?"

He held back a smile at her question. She sounded offended. "Pretty sure he does. He just got all he could handle."

"How much blood are they taking from me?"

She'd gone pale so he lied. "Barely a gram." More like fifteen.

"Oh, okay. I can't donate blood anymore. I get woozy and faint. Even when they give me double my allotted cookies and juice. It's a shame because I'm a universal donor and have really rich blood." She looked down as a leech fell off her inner thigh. She sighed, sounding relieved.

So was he, until he looked up and spotted one attached to the top of her left breast.

She followed his gaze. "He's probably almost done." Her voice rose with what he assumed was hope.

He struck another match and handed it to her. "I don't think so."

She handed the match back. "You do it. I need to hold my top closed so he doesn't fall inside."

"Right." Hunter came to his feet, keeping his eyes focused on the leech in a valiant attempt to ignore the valley between her breasts. It wasn't easy, nor was this leech easy to detach. It finally succumbed to his second attempt, and she bent at the waist as it fell from her chest. Then she straightened and shook out her hands, turning in circles while asking, "Are they all gone?"

"Yeah. You're good." He was about to add *to go*, but he couldn't in good conscience let her leave before dealing with the possibility of pond scum infecting the tiny wounds. "Probably best if you grab a shower sooner rather than later. I can hunt you up some clothes to borrow." If Liz was still here, she would've offered.

"I'll do that, thanks. But don't worry, I have my own clothes." She lifted her hair off her neck, then her eyes went wide and her hands dropped to her sides. "You don't think they're in my hair, do you? I swear, I felt something move."

"It's just your imagination."

"Maybe, but I'd really appreciate it if you checked. And you kind of owe me, right?"

"How exactly do you figure I owe you?" he asked, then, remembering the toad, he motioned for her to turn around with his finger.

"I wouldn't have fallen in the pond if it wasn't for your dog."

"You wouldn't have fallen in the pond if you looked

where you were going or listened to me. So no, I don't owe you," he said even as he moved her long spiral curls aside.

"But I thought I was in danger, so yes, you do owe me. You should have your dog on a leash, you know. And if you don't mind me saying, you should also change his name before some other poor woman has to go through what I did."

"I'm not changing my dog's name."

"Don't forget my traumatic experience with the leeches," she said as if he hadn't said anything. She made a face, and her shoulders went up to her ears. "There aren't any in my hair, are there?"

He ran his fingers over her scalp and then shook out long curly locks. "You're good."

She turned with a smile and offered her hand. "Thank you. I'm Abby, by the way. Abby Everhart. And you know Bella. Wow, she really seems to like your dog. She doesn't usually play well with others."

"Hunter Mackenzie." He shook her hand and glanced at the rat, who was offering Wolf a stick. There was a small pile building in front of his dog.

"Come on, Boo. Mommy needs a shower." She crouched and patted her thigh, obviously not anxious to get closer to Wolf.

Hunter walked over and scooped up her dog, who looked like she was about to bite his arm. Until she got a look at his expression. She whined, glancing back at Wolf. "You won't get any help from him. He knows who his master is."

"Are you implying she doesn't?"

"Oh, I'm pretty sure she knows exactly who the alpha is in your relationship. Her." He laughed at Abby's annoyed expression, surprising himself. His laugh was gruff, rusty from disuse. It was past time the rat and the lady left. "Word of advice: if she doesn't listen to you, you need to keep her on a leash when you go for a hike." He gave her sandals a pointed look. "You might want to get yourself a pair of hiking boots in town."

She snorted a laugh. "Do I look like someone who hikes? Yeah, I didn't think so," she said in response to his *not in this life* look. She made a face when he handed her the dog. "We both need a shower, Boo." Then she looked up at him. "Do you think it would cost a lot to drain the pond? It has to be a health hazard."

"Come again?" She couldn't seriously be suggesting he drain the pond because she fell in.

"The pond. I'm thinking of draining it."

"You're serious?"

"I am, and I don't know why you're looking at me as if I have two heads."

"Because you're talking about draining *my* pond. I don't know how things are done where you come—"

"Oh, okay. I get it now. You're a squatter." She gave him a sympathetic smile, and he knew it was sympathy he saw on her face because he'd gotten enough of it when he'd come back from his last tour to last him four lifetimes.

"I'm not a squatter. I . . ." He trailed off as an alarming thought hit him, and he turned to look at the farmhouse. A suitcase and a pink purse sat on the stone path. *No, she couldn't be.*

"You don't have to feel bad about it or apologize. Trust me, I totally understand what it's like to have your whole life implode. The people you thought were your friends abandon you, you end up on the street, never knowing where your next meal is going to come from or how you're ever going to get back on your feet."

She gave him an apologetic smile. "I wish I could give you more time. But a couple days is all I can afford, then I really do have to insist you leave. I'm putting the farm on the market."

Her words wiped away his desperate hope that she was simply a lost tourist and not Liz's long-lost greatniece. He crossed his arms and stared her down. "Ah, no you're not. Half the farm is mine, and I'm not going anywhere."

Chapter Three

♥

At the sound of voices coming through the open bedroom window, one voice in particular, the deep, gravelly one that belonged to the man who seemed to have the deluded idea that he owned half of Honeysuckle Farm, Abby inched the bathroom door closed. She didn't want to wake up Bella, who was out cold in a doggy bed made of towels on the bathroom floor, bundled in her favorite pink-hooded bathrobe.

Abby tiptoed across her great-aunt's guest bedroom to avoid the creak of the ancient floorboards. At a drawn-out squeak, Abby froze with her foot poised an inch above the threadbare area rug. The stress of the past few days ensured she lost her balance, listing to the side, arms pinwheeling in an effort to keep herself upright. The towel she'd wrapped turban-style around her wet hair after her shower unraveled and took out the mug on the dresser. It fell to the floor with a loud *thunk*, and she swallowed a groan.

She strained to hear if the men stopped talking. They had, and that made her mad. At herself, because this was her home now. They had no business being here. It's not like she'd invited them.

When they picked up their conversation where they left off, she was about to stomp to the window to send them on their way but stopped herself in the nick of time. Not only was she clad in just a towel, but announcing her presence would ensure they didn't pick up where they left off, and she'd have no idea what she was up against. There was no doubt in her mind that Hunter Mackenzie would do everything in his power to block the sale of Honeysuckle Farm.

She'd been right when she saw him coming out of the woods; he was a killer—a killer of hopes and dreams.

Just let him try. She wasn't going to take it anymore.

"Do you hear that, Universe? I'm not going to take it anymore," she whisper-shouted the words at the white, wood-planked ceiling and noticed a yellow water stain the size of the bed that made her want to cry. Instead she grabbed her phone off the avocado-green dresser and flipped to where she'd started a list of work the farmhouse needed. The length of the list made her want to cry too.

And it wasn't because she was afraid of getting her hands dirty or of learning how to repair water-damaged ceilings or the hundred and one other minor repair jobs on her list—Google and DIY videos would be her new best friends. The problem lay in paying for the supplies and in the length of time it would take for her to tick off every last item on her list.

"I don't know what I ever did to deserve all the crap you're raining down on me," she muttered at the ceiling, then thought about the woman whose house she was standing in. "It's not like I wished my great-aunt dead, you know."

When Elinor had informed her that she'd received a registered letter from a lawyer in Highland Falls, North Carolina, Abby had been positive there'd been some kind of mix-up. She didn't know anyone in Highland Falls, let alone North Carolina. But after puzzling over the connection for hours, she'd remembered her father talking about an aunt who lived in a small mountain town in North Carolina.

The only reason Abby remembered the conversation—she'd pretty much blocked out anything to do with her father after he'd left her and her mom—was the older woman's reputation as the black sheep in the family. Abby had found that intriguing.

But not intriguing enough to look up her great-aunt when she was old enough to do so. She'd closed the door on the Findlay side of the family a week after her thirteenth birthday. It had taken a month to realize her mom was telling her the truth and that the father Abby adored wasn't coming back.

She looked around the bedroom, thinking her circumstances weren't any better here than they were in LA. If anything, they were worse, she thought as she added the guest room ceiling to her to-do-before-putting-on-the-market list. She'd had ten items on her list even before she'd broken into the farmhouse through the front door. There'd been a tiny crack in the glass so she hadn't felt too bad about breaking it. Except replacing the window now ended up on her list too.

She'd decided not to wait for the lawyer to arrive with the key, and she hoped it didn't come back to bite her as hard as breaking into Chandler's cosmetics company had. If not for smelling like rotten eggs and her skin being coated in pond scum, Abby would've waited for the lawyer to arrive. Then again, putting a locked door between her and Hunter Mackenzie had seemed like a good idea at the time.

Securing the towel at her chest, Abby ducked to climb onto the big brass bed that was framed by two windows. She winced when the headboard clunked against the log wall, waiting a second before leaning across the mountain of pillows to get a look at the men.

Without window coverings, she had to be careful of leaning over too far. She imagined that her great-aunt felt curtains were unnecessary since the farm was in the middle of absolutely nowhere. If Liz Findlay was as big a nature-lover as the paintings in the farmhouse suggested, the older woman probably enjoyed her unfiltered view of the trees.

Obviously, she and her great-aunt had nothing in common, Abby thought as she looked down at the two men on the patio below.

She gasped. Hunter Mackenzie had called the police! She recognized the older man as a policeman from his navy uniform, shiny gold badge, and big gun. Still, he was way less intimidating than the man sprawled on the chair opposite him. Hunter looked to be about thirty years younger than the gray-haired man with the handle-bar mustache. He also had at least six inches on the older man and a good deal more muscle.

Unbidden, an image of Hunter shirtless came to mind. The way the sun had shone down on his thick, wavy chestnut-colored hair, bringing out the copper highlights. How his golden-bronze skin had glistened. The way his muscles…Okay, that was enough of that. She tried blinking the image away. But, like the man, it was a very stubborn image and seemed destined to remain on her visual keeper shelf.

Not that she was into men who belonged on the cover of *Men's Health*. Some women went crazy for the hot lumberjack type, but not her. She preferred men who were long and lean. Pretty boys, her father would've said. She frowned. For years, she hadn't spared her father a passing thought but in the past few days, he'd been on her mind a lot. It was only natural, she supposed. Liz was his aunt, after all.

Abby refocused on the man sprawled on the red Adirondack chair. Hunter had changed into an olive-green T-shirt that hugged his wide chest, hinting at the eight-pack beneath. There was a military insignia she couldn't make out on this left pec. Given his bearing and the way he liked to bark orders, it wouldn't surprise her if he'd been a ranking member of the armed forces. He probably knew a hundred ways to kill a person, she thought with a glance at his big, powerful hands. They were steepled on his chest as he watched the man across from him light a cigar.

The police officer blew out a tendril of sweet-smelling smoke. "I don't know what possessed Liz to leave the place to that girl. Before you came along, she'd promised it to me, you know." He nodded, looking around before refocusing on the man in front of him. "If it wasn't for you, Hunt, I'd take the city gal to court. Fight her for this place. I'd probably win too."

Abby buried her face in the pillow to cover her gasp upon learning another man might stand in her way.

"You probably would, Owen."

Abby lifted her head to frown down at Hunter. He certainly didn't seem to mind if this Owen person inherited the farm.

"Yep, probably." The older man nodded again and chewed on the end of his cigar. "At least with me, you know I wouldn't be selling the place. You'd always have a home here. But as much as I want to, I can't bring myself to go against Lizzie's last wishes. She must've had a reason for leaving it to the girl. You sure she never said anything to you?"

"Not a word."

Panic loosened its grip on Abby's chest, and she breathed a little easier. At least they weren't going to try and steal her inheritance away.

"She promised the place to you, didn't she? And not just the meadow and barn."

Hunter nodded, then leaned forward to rest his elbows on his knees. "A couple months after I'd been here, Liz started making noises about leaving me the farm. I told her she'd probably outlive me and to stop talking about it. I had no idea she'd left me the land and barn until Eden called."

"Eden gave me a bunch of bull crap about lawyer-client confidentiality, but as far as I could tell, Liz changed her will a couple months before she died. You think she was of sound mind when she did?"

Abby held her breath. Owen was still looking for a loophole. And worse, Hunter wasn't lying. He really did own half of Honeysuckle Farm. A lucrative half, given that the barn appeared to be in better condition than the farmhouse, not to mention the amount of land he owned.

Hunter raised eyes that Abby knew were the color of the summer sky at the man sitting across from him. From Owen's defeated sigh, she imagined the older man had been on the receiving end of an icy, penetrating stare similar to the one Hunter had leveled at her earlier.

"Fine. I won't contest the will. But by the time I'm finished with her, that city gal will be begging you to take the farm off her hands."

Abby gasped, then slapped a hand over her mouth.

"Careful now, Owen. You never know who's listening, and that sounded like a threat. You're chief of police for another few weeks." From the way he glanced up, Abby could've sworn Hunter had heard her gasp.

"No harm in showing Miss Fancy Pants what she's getting herself into, now is there? You told me yourself she was going to be a pain in your ass. So the way I see it, the sooner we get her gone, the better. In all these years, she didn't so much as pay Lizzie a visit or give her a call. And now she waltzes in here and steals the farm out from under us? Seems only fair we give her a taste of Highland Falls retribution."

"I'm a pain in your patootie, Mr. Lumberjack? Well, let me tell you something," Abby shouted out the window. She went up on her knees on the mattress, leaning over to grab the window frame. She wanted to make sure they heard her loud and clear and saw that there wasn't a speck of fear on her face. "You—"

Her towel let loose. With a panicked *eek*, she grabbed the edge of the fabric and scrambled backward, only she went too far and fell off the bed.

* * *

Hunter was beginning to think Abby Everhart was the most accident-prone person on the planet, or the clumsiest. Either way, Owen might be doing her a favor with his plan to frighten her away. Except she hadn't looked scared up in that window a few minutes ago. From the glimpse he'd gotten of her expression before her towel fell off, she'd looked angry. He couldn't recall her face once she lost the towel but the view had been spectacular.

His lips twitched as he recalled the muttered curse words that followed her yelp and the thud of her falling off the bed. She had a creative way of expressing herself.

At the squeak of the back door opening, Hunter said to Owen, "Not a word."

The older man looked up with a frown. His hearing wasn't what it used to be. His eyesight wasn't either, which Hunter imagined Abby would be happy to hear. But that wasn't something he'd tell her. He couldn't without giving himself away.

He heard her whispering something to her dog before he saw her. It sounded like she was warning Bella away from Wolf. He found himself bracing for the moment

Abby came into view and wasn't exactly sure why. He was attracted to women who were strong and determined. Women who didn't want or need a man to make their life complete. Women who were happy with the simple things in life.

So when Abby Everhart sashayed onto the patio wearing a cherry-printed dress that matched her dog's, the last thing he should be feeling was heat low in his belly. He should be snorting a sardonic laugh at her mile-high shiny red heels, not craving the feel of her lush curves filling his hands.

Hunter shifted in the chair. Owen was right. Abby Everhart had to go, and she had to go now. But when he looked into her eyes, he couldn't say the cutting words that would help send her on her way. He didn't know why. He had no problem saying the words that kept his family and friends at bay. The only explanation he had for his reluctance to hurt her was that there was something he recognized in her eyes.

"Hello, gentlemen. I don't see a housewarming present so I'm assuming you're not here to welcome me to the neighborhood." She went to set Bella—who wore a leash—on the ground, searching the sky before doing so. "Would one of you like to share?"

Her lips flattened as Bella sniffed around Wolf, who looked up at Hunter as if to say *Do I have to?* He knew how his dog felt. He felt the same way about the rat's owner.

"Well?" Abby asked with a boatload of attitude, hands on her hips.

Feisty, Hunter thought. Wondering if it was an act or

a characteristic of the red hair. She'd braided her long, curly locks and the braid hung over one shoulder, leaving a damp circle on her left breast. Hunter forced himself to look away.

Owen stared at the rat. "What the hell is that?"

She narrowed her eyes at Hunter before saying to Owen, "She's my dog. And she isn't a *that*." Hunter heard the unspoken *or a rat*. "She's a Yorkshire terrier, and her name is Bella. She can be vicious, so don't say I didn't warn you."

Owen looked at Abby like she wasn't the sharpest tool in the shed. Hunter had thought the same, but he was beginning to think he may have misjudged her.

In her next breath, she proved she'd misjudged Owen. "And, Mr. Chief of Police, don't think you can scare me away. My great-aunt left me the farm. Not you. Or you." She looked at Hunter with fire in her eyes. "So you both can take your sour grapes on out of here and leave me alone. I have work to do."

Hunter grimaced. In his old friend's eyes, she'd just thrown down the gauntlet. Owen wasn't a bad guy but he'd loved Liz, and he was still hurting over her loss. He didn't just resent that Abby had been left the farm instead of him or Hunter; he didn't feel she deserved it. Not only was she an outsider, she'd never had anything to do with Liz. Hunter understood where Owen was coming from. He felt the same way.

"Don't worry, Fancy Pants. We'll leave you to your work as soon as Eden arrives with the paperwork for you and Hunter to sign." He looked up at the farmhouse. "Word of advice: you might want to start with the roof.

You never know what sort of animals found their way into the house."

Hunter sighed at the shadow of panic that crossed Abby's face. It was all well and good for Owen to scare her—he wouldn't be the one who had to deal with her. Then, as though to cover her reaction, she struck a confident pose, flipping her braid over her shoulder, cocking her hip, and thrusting out her chest. The watermark from her braid had rendered the white part of the dress see-through, reminding him of the view from the bedroom window a short time ago.

His fingers curled into fists when the image that was seared into his brain caused the muscles low in his belly to tighten with desire. All bets were off now. Self-preservation overrode his ingrained need to protect her.

So he met her challenging stare with one of his own. "Owen's right. I know for a fact you've got mice; spiders are a given. But I wouldn't be surprised if you've got squirrels and raccoons. Hope your rabies shot is up to date."

"There better not be squirrels or raccoons in the house or you two have some explaining to do," Eden said as she stepped onto the patio with a large cellophane-wrapped basket in her arms. Hunter's younger brother's wife was a beautiful woman with wavy, caramel-colored hair. And like the rest of Hunter's family, she could be a pain in his ass when she wanted to be.

"Don't you go giving us crap, Eden. You're the one who told us the farmhouse was off-limits after Lizzie's funeral," Owen reminded her.

She had, but other than today, he and Owen had steered

clear of the place anyway. It wasn't the same without Liz. There were too many reminders of her here.

Ignoring Owen, Eden handed Abby the basket. "Welcome to Highland Falls. You mentioned you were taking the red-eye from LA so I figured the last thing you'd want to do is go to the grocery store. I had them put extra muffins, sausage, crackers, cheese, and fruit in the basket. It should tide you over until tomorrow afternoon at least."

"Oh my gosh. That was so nice of you. Thank you so much." Abby hugged the basket, clearly touched by the gesture.

"It was my pleasure," Eden said with a smile as she removed her purse strap from her shoulder and walked to the table. "We'll get the legal stuff over with, and then we'll get better acquainted. I'll give you the lowdown on who's who in Highland Falls."

"That'd be great," Abby said as she put the basket down beside Eden's purse.

Hunter's sister-in-law pulled out a stack of papers and two pens. "You probably know by now that you share Liz's inheritance with Hunter."

"Yes. He says he owns most of the property and the barn?" She said it in a way that suggested she thought he was lying. Or at least hoped he was.

"He does. I can walk the boundaries with you later, but you own the farmhouse, the property behind it, in front of it, up to the main road—which you share—and then to the top of the meadow, or hill, you could say."

Abby cast a self-conscious glance from him to Owen, then squared her shoulders. "Did my aunt happen to leave any money for repairs? There's quite a lot of work that needs to be done."

Owen clamped his cigar between his teeth, speaking around it. "Don't you go changing a thing. Lizzie loved the old place just the way it is. She didn't change anything when her grandmother left it to her, and her grandmother didn't change a thing when her mother-in-law left it to her."

Hunter imagined there was some truth to what Owen said, but there'd been repairs that he'd offered to take care of for Liz that had nothing to do with the aesthetics of the farm, and she'd always refused. She'd gotten downright ornery when he'd taken it upon himself to repair the porch. Threatened to throw him off her property if he didn't leave it be, so he had. He'd thought maybe her putting things off had to do with lack of funds and pride, but during the six months before she'd died, he'd begun to suspect something else was at play. He just hadn't figured out what.

Eden cast Abby an apologetic smile before saying to Owen, "Would you mind going to my car and getting my tape measure for me? I want to mark off the property line for Abby."

Owen got to his feet muttering about knowing when he wasn't wanted. He'd know as well as Hunter did that Eden wanted to get rid of him.

His sister-in-law waited until Owen disappeared around the side of the farmhouse to say, "Please don't be offended. Owen adored Liz, and he's having a difficult time dealing with her death. My brother-in-law is too, though he'd deny it under torture. You're not fooling anyone, Hunter. We all know how much you loved Liz. She felt the same way about you. She adored him," Eden told Abby. "Hunter took care of your aunt the entire time she was sick."

Okay, he'd heard enough. "I've got things to do. Call me when you want me to sign the papers."

As he walked away, he heard Eden explaining that while there was no money for repairs, Liz knew what a softie Hunter was, and she'd been sure he'd lend Abby a hand.

Eden brought the papers over for Hunter to sign before she headed for home, repeating what he'd overheard her telling Abby earlier. Liz would expect him to lend her great-niece a helping hand. And his sister-in-law expected him to be a good neighbor.

It was after midnight when Hunter heard his *neighbor* scream. He was sitting on a tree stump, leaning against the barn, the logs burning in the open fire pit filling the warm night air with the smell of wood smoke. The moon was high and bright above him as he sketched his vision for the eagle that had come to him in a dream.

Wolf sat up and nudged his thigh. Hunter ignored him just like he ignored Abby's second and third screams. As much as they'd teased her, other than spiders, a mouse or two, or possibly a bat, she wasn't in any danger.

Chapter Four

♥

Abby stood bleary-eyed and exhausted near a small patch of grass sipping a cup of coffee while she waited for Bella to do her business. Birds flitted from tree to tree nearby, twittering and chirping. Abby squinted into the early morning sunlight to ensure they were little birds and not birds big enough to carry off her dog. While searching the branches, she caught a glimpse of canary yellow just beyond the trees and glared at the barn.

She'd found a mouse on the foot of her bed at midnight. Then, as if her screams had opened the gates of the wild kingdom, a bird dive-bombed her. And while she and Bella hid under the covers with the flashlight on her phone, she came face-to-face with a giant spider.

She shuddered at the memory of the terrifying encounter. She'd spent the rest of the night sitting in the rocking chair in the living room with a blanket pulled tent-like over her and Bella.

But if Hunter thought he could scare her off, he'd learn soon enough that she didn't scare easily. Well, she kinda did, but her perfect Instagram-worthy life would remain just a dream unless she got the funds from the sale of Honeysuckle Farm, so she wasn't going anywhere.

He was deluded if he thought he could get rid of her that easily just because she was a city girl. She was made of sterner stuff and had a few tricks of her own up her sleeve. She'd take a page from his book. She couldn't afford to buy him off so she'd scare him off instead.

And not with mice or spiders or the terrifying sounds of wild beasts that came around two in the morning. She highly doubted that anything in the great outdoors would scare the former Special Forces solider. That unsurprising Hunter Mackenzie tidbit had been provided by his sister-in-law, who was so much nicer than her brother-in-law and Owen.

Abby raised the mug to her nose, inhaling all that caffeinated goodness. Along with the rich, nutty fragrance she detected a hint of lavender. She took a sip and hummed with pleasure. She could see herself becoming addicted to the exclusive cup of joe from Highland Brew. Eden's best friend was one of the owners, and the place sounded exactly like something Abby would've been all over before Puppy-Gate.

Located in an old mill, Highland Brew served their exclusive brands of coffees by day, and their craft beers at night. They also featured live bands on weekends and had an open mic. It sounded like fun, something Abby hadn't had in months. But high-end coffee beans and fun weren't exactly in her budget and wouldn't be until the farmhouse sold.

The hope that she'd be putting Honeysuckle Farm and Hunter and Owen in her rearview mirror by the end of next week had gone out the window when her to-do list hit fifty. Her revised goal was to have it on the market in three weeks and sold by the second week of July, which was four weeks away. After that, she imagined the housing market would die off until September. If she had to stay that long, she was pretty sure she'd die too.

Tackling the to-do list on her lonesome would probably lead to her untimely demise, but that's where Hunter and her plan came into play. While nothing in the great outdoors would scare the six-foot-four manly man, she was betting that a helpless city girl who was afraid of her own shadow and who could talk until the sun went down would have him running for the hills. Better still, doing whatever she asked him to do to get rid of her.

She smiled at Bella, who was doing her impression of a baby bull, pawing at the grass with her hind legs, and scooped her up. "Time for us to get our girly girl on, Boo. We have a mountain man to terrify."

She froze at the warm tingle low in her stomach. Surely she wasn't excited at the prospect of seeing said mountain man again? She brushed the thought aside, telling herself not to be ridiculous. It was the idea of Hunter taking care of her to-do list that had brought on the warm tingle.

But the image that immediately popped into her head suggested it was the former rather than the latter. In her mind, Hunter appeared shirtless. His drool-worthy sculpted back was to her, his golden skin glistening, his muscles flexing as he hammered the ceiling above her bed. When a wanton redhead who looked uncomfortably familiar appeared in said bed, Abby quickly blinked the image from her mind before it became not just uncomfortable but X-rated.

Any further thoughts about hot times with hunky Hunter and his hammer ended when her cell phone rang and she picked it up to check the screen—a FaceTime call from her mom. Obviously, Abby's texts reassuring her mother and her stepsisters that she and Bella were fine and enjoying the spa treatments at the resort hadn't been enough to alleviate their concerns.

She looked around for a suitable location to take the call and caught a glimpse of a flowering bush with sweet-smelling trumpet-like flowers of orange and yellow at the side of the farmhouse. She hurried over to pose in front of the picture-perfect bush.

As she pressed Accept, she realized her lack of sleep had messed with her thinking (her first clue should've been her hot-contractor fantasy). She should've been focusing more on what she looked like than the backdrop. Although both could trigger an over-the-top reaction from her mother.

Abby forced a wide smile. She'd blame the bags under her eyes and her pasty-colored skin on a spa treatment that had gone wrong. She raised her hand to her head as the call connected. She wasn't sure what she'd blame for her hair. It looked like she'd stuck a wet finger in a light socket—either that or the wanton redhead in her fantasy had had some off-the-charts sexy times in bed. It seemed no amount of hair product could tame her wild curls today or the wild fantasy she couldn't stop thinking about.

Her stepsisters appearing on the screen without their

mom took care of it right away. "What's going on? Is everything okay?"

The only time Haven and Haley called without Abby's mother was when they needed her advice. As perfect as they were, they were still teenagers, and there was stuff no teenage girl wanted to talk to their mother about. Especially a mother who thought the sun, moon, and stars rose in you. Not in her, obviously, but in her sisters.

Haven and Haley stared at her. "What happened to you, Abs?" Haley asked, as she was the more direct of the two.

Abby touched her face. "You're not going to believe this, but I'm allergic to seaweed. Maybe it happens when you eat as much sushi as I do. Who knows?" She shrugged. "Anyhoo, they tried to counteract the hives with a soothing milk treatment, and that didn't work either. And my hair..." She looked around and lowered her voice. "I swear the woman must've had shares in Chandler's cosmetics company. Can you believe...?" She trailed off at the expressions on their faces. "What is it?"

They shared a glance, then Haven nodded at Haley. "We know, Abs. We know everything."

Abby's heart dropped to her feet. They couldn't know everything she'd been telling them was a lie. "What are you talking about?" She tried to force a confused look onto her face but was able to manage only a strained smile.

"Everything. We know that Chandler sued you and that he divorced you."

As though she read the panic on Abby's face, Haven

interrupted Haley, "Mom doesn't know. We didn't tell her, and we won't." She touched her baby finger to the screen. "Pinky swear."

Abby let out a slow, leaky breath. She could get through this. The worst hadn't happened. Her mom had no idea what was going on, and Haven and Haley didn't know she was broke or that she'd been homeless.

"I'm sorry. I should've told you guys but you were out of the country, and I didn't want to worry you."

"We're not babies anymore, Abs. We're your sisters, and we want to be there for you as much as you've been there for us. If it wasn't for you, we wouldn't have been able to take a gap year or travel the world with Mom and Dad."

"It wasn't like I footed the bill for you guys to jet around the world staying in five-star hotels. You lived in remote villages, helping to make a difference for girls, and I was honored to be able to play a small part in that." It was because they'd been living in remote corners of the world for the better part of a year that Abby had held on to the hope that they wouldn't find out what happened to her.

"Are you sure you're okay, Abs?" Haven asked.

"Of course I am." She pointed at her hair and made a face. "Despite what it looks like, I'm fine. Honestly, you guys don't have to—"

Haley cut her off. "They said you lost everything. That you're broke."

So they knew more than she'd given them credit for. "Okay, listen, I'm not going to lie to you. The last few months have been pretty awful, but things are looking up now."

She stepped away from the bush, let Bella down to explore, and turned the phone toward the farmhouse.

"I know it doesn't look like much," she said as she took them for a tour of the grounds. She didn't want to take them inside in case she ran into a mouse or a spider or a rabid racoon. Plus, if they thought the outside needed work...

"Did your great-aunt leave you enough money to hire a contractor?" Haley, ever the practical one, asked.

Both girls looked at her, and she couldn't bring herself to lie to them, at least about this. Besides, it was a teachable moment. They could be on this journey virtually with her as she got back on her feet and reclaimed her dream. Everything came so easy to them—she was as much to blame for that as her mother (not to mention they were blessed in the beauty and brains departments)—but one day their luck might change, and her journey would provide them with a road map.

"No, she didn't. But I'm resourceful, and I have it all figured out. You're not going to recognize this place once I'm finished with it."

"But, Abs, you have no money, and you don't know anyone there," Haley said.

"Uh, do you remember who you're talking to? I didn't know anyone when I moved to LA and I barely had any money. All I had was passion and persistence, and look how well that worked out for me." The reminder was good for her. She had to stop thinking about all she'd lost, let go of the past, and focus on the future.

"You still would've been living the life if you hadn't married Chandler," Haley said.

"I know. I should've listened to you guys. But you were fourteen and in love with Justin Bieber, so I didn't really trust your taste," she teased. Her mother had loved Chandler, but Haven, Haley, and her stepdad hadn't been fans.

"You can joke all you want but it's not fair you lost everything because of him. If it weren't for you, Chandler's company would still be experimenting on animals with no one the wiser. You saved Bella. And now you're living all by yourself in the middle of nowhere." Haven chewed her thumbnail. "Are you sure you're going to be okay? Haley and I can come stay with you. We can help."

She had no doubt they could—they'd built schools in Africa and India. And the nights would be less scary with them there. But as much as she could use their help and company, she didn't want to ruin their summer. "You guys haven't seen your friends in months, and I'm sure you have a list of volunteer projects in Shady Mills as long as my repair list. I want you to enjoy your summer. Besides, I'm fine. I'm not alone."

She told them about Hunter, leaving out the part that he'd most likely terrorized her last night. In her version, he was the neighbor of every woman's fantasy instead of what he actually was: the neighbor from hell.

Haley and Haven grinned at each other and then at her. "You like him," Haven said, leaning forward and fluttering her eyelashes.

"No. I don't," Abby said, then realized she'd

contradicted herself. "I mean, yes, I like him as in he's a kind and helpful neighbor. But I don't like him the way you're implying. Stop making googly eyes at me. The last thing I want is another man in my life. Take it from me, girls, you don't ever want to have to depend on a man. So don't let yourself get distracted at Stanford."

If Abby had an education, if school had come as easily to her as it had to her sisters, she wouldn't be in the mess she was in. But even if she'd known what she did now, it wouldn't have mattered. She had difficulty reading. The words jumbled up and didn't always make sense. It's why YouTube had been her medium of choice. "You keep your eyes on—"

Bella, who'd been happily trotting after her, now darted past her, growling and snapping. "Hang on a minute, Boo. You'll hurt your throat," Abby told the dog straining against the leash. She moved forward to loosen the tension. As soon as she did, she saw what Bella was trying to reach.

A snake was coiled and ready to strike.

Bella lunged.

"No!" Abby cried and, thinking only to protect Bella, darted forward to scoop her up. She wasn't fast enough. The snake's fangs locked on her forearm. She cried out, jerking her arm away.

"Abby, what happened?" Her sisters' voices came through the phone in her hand, startling her from her shock. "A snake bit me." She stumbled backward as it slithered beneath the house.

"What kind of snake? What did it look like?" Haven asked.

"Big, light brown with a reddish head. It's under the house." She glanced back with a shiver as she put distance between herself and the snake.

"Abby, don't panic or anything. But, um, I just looked up snakes in North Carolina, and there are some poisonous ones."

She swallowed, remembering that the Uber driver had said the same thing. "It can't have been poisonous. It doesn't hurt. Much." She looked down at the red mark on her forearm. "I feel faint. My legs are shaky." Bella whined and licked her cheek. "It's okay, Boo. I'm fine."

"Abby, stop saying you're fine when you are absolutely not fine!" Haven yelled at her.

"Go, Abby. Go right now and get Hunter. And don't you dare drop us. We're coming with you this time," Haley said.

Abby did as her sisters told her, running across the meadow. Her heart pounded, her ragged breath searing her dry throat as she raced for the barn with Bella tucked under her good arm. Panting, she could barely get Hunter's name past her lips. When she did, it was at the level of a normal conversation, as if he was standing right in front of her.

And then he was there, and she thought he might be yelling at her again but she couldn't hear him over the buzzing in her ears. He slid an arm behind her back and bent to put his other arm behind her knees, scooping her up and into his arms. He was strong, solid, and safe, and the panic that had her chest muscles and vocal cords in a stranglehold relaxed a little.

"Abby, calm down. Just breathe slow and easy. You're gonna be fine." His eyes went to the red mark on her arm as he strode toward the barn. "Can you describe the snake? Its color, markings?"

When she told him, he didn't say or do anything other than search her face and nod.

She heard her sisters crying and went to pick up the phone tucked between Bella and her chest.

"Hang on." He shifted her in his arms, reaching around her to retrieve her phone. At the feel of his strong fingers brushing against her breast, the breathing she'd managed to slow down seconds ago hitched, and her cheeks heated. Embarrassed by her reaction, surprised that she had one when she could very well be dying, she focused on the screen he held up for her. Her sisters' faces were red and blotchy, and their eyes were tear-filled.

"Thank you," she murmured, wondering if he heard her when he stared straight ahead.

"Don't cry. I'm not going to die," she told her sisters, looking up when Hunter shouldered his way into the yellow barn. It was cavernous, with very little light, and smelled like cedar. Two large fans hung from the ceiling, their gentle *whoop whoop* swirling the warm air. "I'm not, am I?"

"No, not from the snake bite."

It sounded like he wanted to kill her though. She thought better of asking why and instead said, "Did you hear that? Hunter says I'm not going to die."

"You promise?" they asked him.

He glanced at the screen. "Yeah. I do."

She noticed his tone wasn't as brusque as the one

he used with her. She wasn't surprised. Haven and Haley had that effect on people. They had that effect on her too.

"See, everything will be all right. I'll call you later, okay?"

"No. We're not leaving you alone, Abs. And if you hang up on us, we're telling Mom everything."

"Yeah, we'll tell her you're broke and that she was wrong about Chandler, and we were right."

Oh my gosh, she had to get them to stop talking. "Okay. I won't hang up, but—"

"I bet Mom wouldn't think Chandler was so wonderful if she found out he was having an affair with his lawyer while he was still married to Abs."

Abby gasped. "Where did you hear that?"

Haven clapped a hand over her mouth, and Haley made a face. "You didn't know?"

"Yes, but I just found out a few days ago." She told her sisters what had happened at the mansion in Bel Air. How Elinor had felt bad about Abby's circumstances and offered for her to have a shower and hot meal and how Abby had ended up hiding in the pantry when Juliette and Abby's once-best friend, Tiffany, had shown up unexpectedly at the mansion.

The last thing Abby had wanted was for Juliette to discover her there and have her thrown in jail. Sitting on the pantry floor with Bella in her arms, Abby had learned about her inheritance and that Chandler was marrying Juliette after having an affair with her for the past year and a half.

Caught up in the moment and her story, Abby had

forgotten about Hunter until he lowered her onto a bed. He looked down at her, and there was something other than the annoyed expression she was used to seeing on his face. She wondered if perhaps she wouldn't have to pretend to be the ditzy city girl who was afraid of her own shadow (she definitely didn't have to pretend to be afraid of snakes) and talked from sunup until sundown. Maybe all she had to do was tell him the truth.

Chapter Five

♥

Hunter brought his cell phone to his ear as he watched the snake slither away along the forest floor. He wasn't particularly fond of carrying the phone but it was a concession he'd made to his family and friends. They'd leave him alone as long as they were able to call and check on him every couple of weeks.

"Gotta tell you, son. I reach for my anti-acids whenever I see your name come up on my screen. Usually means someone died or I've got bad guys to go after," Owen said.

The last time Hunter had called the chief was to tell him Liz was gone. "I just removed a copperhead from under the farmhouse. You wouldn't happen to know anything about that, would you?"

"Come on, you know me better than that. Snakes give me the heebie-jeebies. All I did was howl under her window some. Which you also know since you were there, sitting in that chair, watching me. Just about gave me a heart attack."

As much as Hunter hadn't wanted to check on Abby, it

wasn't in him to sit there and do nothing when someone was in distress. Even someone who was turning out to be a major pain in his ass. So he'd walked over to check things out. Other than Abby, everything was quiet. Nothing to set off alarm bells. As far as he could tell, she'd gotten spooked. Not really a surprise. Still, he'd decided to stick around and parked his ass in the Adirondack chair for the night, thinking that until he got rid of Abby Everhart, he wouldn't get his eagle carved.

He had the same thought not more than a few hours ago when she'd come running across the meadow screaming his name. Her hair was a mass of curls, a fiery red cloud framing her pale, feminine features, her eyes so big they'd practically swallowed her face. He imagined his eyes had gotten pretty big too. Backlit by the morning sunlight, she might as well have been running toward him naked for all that her calf-length white nightgown hid.

"Snake get her or the dog?" Owen asked with a wince in his voice.

Hunter scrubbed a hand over his face, clearing away the image of Abby in the meadow. "Her. She was protecting the dog."

"Good thing, I suppose. Size of the dog, it wouldn't have made it. She okay?"

Unlike what most people thought, a copperhead's bite was rarely deadly to a human. Tissue damage was more of a concern than the venom. Same couldn't be said for animals, especially animals the size of the rat. Someone needed to take the dog in hand before it got itself or its owner killed.

"Yeah. She's fine. It was a dry bite." A dry bite was a bite from a venomous snake without venom being released. About twenty to twenty-five percent of pit viper snakebites were dry. Still, he'd called Doc and had him come over to check her out to be on the safe side. "I think we may have misjudged her."

"How's that?"

"She's not some rich Hollywood type who has no in interest in keeping Liz's legacy alive. Sounds like she needs the money. She's divorced. Her husband was cheating on her with his lawyer."

"You know what it sounds like to me? It sounds like Fancy Pants has caught your interest."

"Then you better head over to Doc and get your hearing tested. I'm not interested. In her or anyone else."

"Here's the problem. First off, you're fooling yourself thinking you're happy living out there all by your lonesome with nothing but Wolf and your woodcarvings for company. After you came back from Afghanistan, me and Lizzie thought you just needed time to heal. Never expected you to become a hermit."

Hunter looked at the phone—cursing the woman who'd had him making the call in the first place—as he headed down the trail to home. He didn't like leaving her alone in his place for long. She'd been talking to her sisters when he'd left. Haley and Haven had promised to keep an eye on her, and they had his number. But he didn't trust Abby not to snoop. She seemed the type.

Nosy, just like Owen. "I'm not—" he began to protest the chief's accusation that he was a hermit.

But his old friend talked right over him, which was

par for the course. If Hunter hung up on him like he wanted to, Owen would keep calling back until he'd stated his case so Hunter decided to let him talk and get it out of his system.

"...Second off, I'm not blind. I saw the way you looked at that girl, and it was obvious you liked what you saw. My pops would've said she has the look of the fairies about her. I'm thinking a wood nymph with her big green eyes and long red hair. So you'd best have a care or she'll put you under her spell, and there'll be no help for you then."

"You've been hanging out with Aunt Elsa again, haven't you?" Hunter's aunt had been best friends with Owen and Liz for as long as he could remember. Along with another of their childhood friends, Ina Graham, Liz and Elsa had owned Three Wise Women Bookstore on Main Street for decades.

"Don't say I didn't warn you. Your generation ignores the tales from the old country at your own peril."

"If I happen upon a wood nymph or a sprite, I'll be sure to let you know. Now, if you don't mind, I need to get Abby back to the farmhouse to find a ginormous spider. Her words, not mine," he said as he walked into the clearing.

"Oh, come on now, son. Do you hear yourself? She's already halfway to getting you under her spell, and you don't even know it. But you better break the hold she has over you quick, because she's not the one for you. Sloane is, and she always was. And once you move past your grief and guilt, you'll remember what you two had together, and you'll want it back."

He supposed it spoke to Owen's concern for him that he brought up Hunter's ex-fiancée. Sloane was off-limits. Everyone knew it—his family, friends, and Owen. Hunter hadn't spoken to or about her since the day he'd broken their engagement. There was no going back.

"I gotta go," he said. "Let the rangers know that there's a black bear and her cubs moving toward town along Willow Creek."

"You do realize it's their job to track that sort of thing, don't you?"

"Yeah, just like I realize it's your job to make sure that Boyd doesn't have his still running on the ridge."

"You've gotta be shitting me. Boyd's running shine again?"

"If it wasn't shine, it had a pretty powerful kick for cider."

"Dammit, Hunter, you're not supposed to be shooting the breeze with him and drinking shine."

"You can't have it both ways, Chief. You're always on me about getting out and socializing more."

"Well, I can't say I'm impressed with your companions of choice these days, so maybe you should lay off the socializing for a while."

"Happy to oblige. Enjoy your pancakes at Dot's."

"How did you know I was at Dot's?"

"You're predictable." And he'd recognized the older woman's voice in the background.

Abby was predictable too. He walked into the barn to find her hugging a life-size carving of a black bear. She shot a panicked look over her shoulder. "Hurry! I can't hold him up much longer."

He jogged to her side. "What the hell were you doing?"

"To be honest, I kinda thought he was real at first, and Bella was sniffing around him, so..." She lifted a shoulder.

"So what? You decided to attack a bear to save your dog?" The woman needed a keeper.

"No. Once I realized he was a carving..." She wrinkled her nose, admitting sheepishly, "I was petting him."

He swallowed a sarcastic *Why am I not surprised?* and placed a hand on the bear's head, nudging Abby out of the way. Then he crouched to rebalance the carving. He rarely invited anyone into his space, and if they did come, they knew better than to touch his woodwork. The bear had been one of his first large pieces.

At a shift in the air, he glanced over his shoulder. Abby was turning slowly in her bare feet in the middle of the barn. Her head was tipped back to look at the wooden geese suspended in flight from the ceiling, her fiery red curls brushing her lower back and her gauzy white nightgown swirling around her calves.

If Owen saw her now, he'd give Hunter a smug but concerned smile. Abby looked like a wood nymph surrounded by Hunter's carvings. Except wood nymphs were supposedly ethereal. Abby was curvy, cute, and clumsy. Which meant he didn't have to worry about his old friend's prediction coming true. Abby didn't have him in her thrall.

Or so he thought until he tried to take his eyes off her. "Stop spinning. You'll make yourself dizzy and fall on your face. You're the clumsiest woman I've ever met." A touch of pink darkened her cheeks, and he dragged his gaze back to the carving, feeling like a jerk. "You were supposed to stay in bed until I got back."

"You were gone too long. I got bored."

He stiffened at the feel of her moving behind him.

"Did you kill the snake?"

"No. Why would I?"

"Uh, because it bit me."

"It felt threatened. It was just protecting itself." He knew how the snake felt. Hunter straightened, taking a step back to gauge the steadiness of the carving before turning to her. "You have to be more mindful of your surroundings, Abby. You're not in the city anymore."

"I think I know that. I've been sucked on by leeches, bit by a snake, dive-bombed by a bird in the middle of the night, and I was chased from my bed by a big-butt spider." Her eyes jerked from her forearm to his face. "You don't have black widow spiders here, do you?"

He scratched the back of his neck, debating whether to tell her the truth. Since he'd just finished telling her she had to be more aware of her surroundings, he went with the truth. Although he kept the fact that the bird she thought had dive-bombed her was in all likelihood a bat. "Yeah, we do. Brown recluse too. But if it's as big as you claim, it's probably a wolf spider."

She looked like she might faint, and he rested a hand on her shoulder. "They're big, but their venom isn't deadly. You're okay."

"No, I'm really not. If I don't hurry up and sell the farm, Bella and I will die here." She wrapped her arms around herself, then winced and released her right arm. "I thought living on the mean streets of LA was scary but it has nothing on Highland Falls. I'd take gangbang-ers and drug addicts over venomous spiders and snakes any day." Her eyes filled. "I really hate it here. I'm not meant for this kind of life."

He wanted to ask her what she meant about living on the mean streets of LA but he could tell she was minutes away from a breakdown. He didn't blame her. Didn't mean he was onboard dealing with a hysterical woman though. He'd never been good at it. But the way she was looking up at him, her bottom lip trembling between her teeth, he had to say something before the situation got worse.

"You just have to hang on for a month, two at most." He gave her shoulder a comforting squeeze.

"Two months?" Her voice rose on a high-pitched note. "I can't. I can't do it." She looked around the barn. "I'll sell you the farmhouse right now. As is, for a hundred thousand dollars. It's worth at least double that, probably triple."

"I can't. I don't have any money."

"You have to have money. Look how you live, and your carvings are incredible. They're works of art." She looked at the bear and then glanced at the moose on the other side of the barn that he'd captured in mid-charge. "I mean, they're a little scary. Mostly because they look so real...and angry. I guess ferocious would be a better word." She returned her gaze to his. "But I bet your work is in high demand."

"I don't sell my carvings." Ever. To anyone.

"What? Why the heck not?" She looked truly shocked.

"I do them for me."

"Okay, but if you sold just a few of them, you could buy the farm. I could help you. I featured an artist on my channel and turned him into an overnight sensation. He's successful and rich now. You could be the same. You'd never have to worry about having crazy neighbors with wild kids."

He couldn't resist. "How about a crazy lady with a wild Yorkie?" Then he frowned and looked around. "By the way, where is your dog, and my dog?"

"I don't know where Wolf went, but Bella's on a time-out in your room." She lifted her hand to her mouth, mumbling something around the thumbnail she chewed.

"Say again?"

She sighed and lowered her hand. "She was humping Wolf."

He laughed, then sobered at the look she shot him. "What did Wolf do?"

"He snapped at her and pushed her away. I think it hurt her feelings. It's hard to be rejected, you know. I felt bad putting her in time-out but she needs to understand she can't go around trying to have sex with every dog she meets."

"She wasn't trying to have sex with Wolf, Abby. She was trying to dominate him. I talked to you about this yesterday, but you obviously weren't listening to me. If you don't show her who's boss, you're going to be in trouble. She thinks she's a hundred-pound mastiff, not an eight-pound Yorkie. And the first things that have to go are her bows and dresses."

She waved him off. "You're just saying that because you're a guy. And not just a guy. You're a guy-guy. Like one of those alpha guys. Lumberjack man." She nodded and made a fish face, pointing at him. "That's what this is all about. You're projecting."

"Really? I'm projecting on a dog? All right, I've heard it all now." He ducked to look her in the eyes. "You're treating your dog like a baby. She's not a baby. She's a dog. And if you don't want her to get eaten, you better start treating her like one."

She slapped her left palm to her chest. "That's a horrible thing to say. Do you not think I've suffered enough? I've been—"

He held up a hand. "Yeah, I know. Leeches, snakes, mice, spiders, and bats all have it in for you."

"Bats? I never said anything about... The bird wasn't a bird, was it?"

"Ah, no, it wasn't, but don't worry about it. I'm going to take care of it."

Her face lit up. "You're going to buy the farmhouse?"

"What? No. I told you, I don't have any money."

"But your carvings are... Okay, fine," she said, no doubt catching a glimpse of his *not happening* expression. "Eden said you were in the military. Like some crazy elite force. So you must have a good pension. Unless you got dishonorably discharged. You didn't, did you? Eden said you were a hero and that you were awarded the Purple Heart."

"I wasn't dishonorably discharged." In his mind, he should've been. He shouldn't have been given a medal for an operation that cost two men their lives. "Still doesn't change anything. I don't have the money to buy the farmhouse."

"What do you do with your money?" She looked around the barn as if drawing some unsavory conclusions.

So he told her the truth. "I give it away. And don't ask me to who because it's none of your damn business. Now go get your dog, and I'll get my toolbox."

"I have a better idea. Why don't Bella and I stay here while you take care of my animal issues?"

"No."

Her mouth fell open. "Why not?"

"Because I said so." He walked away. She was giving him a headache. Probably because she talked too much. Or it might've been because he'd talked more in the past twenty-four hours than he had in months.

"That's not an answer," she called to his back.

He turned. "Do you want my help or not?"

"Yes, but I—" She lifted her hands in a gesture of frustration, and it was then that he realized the true root of his headache.

It was from the strain of keeping his eyes on her face. "There's a shirt hanging on the back of my door. Put it on."

"But it's like seventy degrees out…" She followed the direction of his gaze. "Oh. Oh!" She whirled around and, cradling her arm, ran for his room.

Chapter Six

♥

The next afternoon, Abby knocked on the door to her bedroom with one hand while holding a plate of blueberry muffins from the gift basket in the other hand. "Hunter, I brought—"

"Don't you dare come in here, Abby. You nearly took off my head last time."

"I told you I was sorry. I didn't mean to turn on the ceiling fan. I had no idea the switch was behind me when I leaned against the wall." To ogle his muscles.

"I don't have time to talk. And if you don't stop bugging me—"

"Bugging you? I was trying to help. And just so you know, I was going to feed you. But if you don't want the blueberry muffins—"

· The door opened, and he took the plate. "Thanks." He closed the door in her face.

Her mouth fell open. Honestly, he was the rudest man she'd ever met. But he was reframing the window in her bedroom to seal a newly discovered animal entry point so she decided to keep her opinion to herself.

Her cell phone rang with another FaceTime call from her family. She walked down the stairs as Hunter renewed his hammering in her bedroom. She sat on the second-to-the-last step and accepted the call. Staring at the phone, she prayed it was her sisters and not her mother.

"Thank goodness," she said when Haven and Haley appeared on the screen. "I was afraid you were so worried about me that you'd broken your promise and told Mom."

Haven scrunched her nose, looking confused. "Why would we be worried about you?"

Abby stared at her and raised her arm. "Uh, bitten by a snake, remember? A ginormous snake. A deadly snake."

"Abs, it wasn't a deadly snake. Copperheads just get a bad rap."

Peeved that Haley was dismissing her trauma so easily, Abby said, "Really? And when did you become the snake expert in the family?"

"I'm not a snake expert. Hunter is. He said you'll be fine, and he was right. You look so much better now than you did yesterday morning." Haley smiled.

"Where's Hunter?" Haven asked, looking past her.

"In my bedroom." He'd spent yesterday afternoon and evening working in the attic and her great-aunt's room, which were supposedly worse than hers. Except last night the bat had come back, and he'd brought friends.

At her sisters' wide-eyed stares, she corrected herself. "Hammering. He's hammering in my bedroom to ensure that I won't be sharing my room or my bed with any wild animals tonight." She narrowed her eyes at the two of them as they tried to suppress their grins. "Do not even go there."

"Why not? He's sooo hot. He looks like Thor. I mean, he looks like Chris Hemsworth playing Thor. If I were ten years older, I would totally do—"

"Haven Helen Everhart, I don't ever want to hear you talk like that again."

Her sisters laughed. "You sounded just like Mom."

"Yeah, well, you better be careful or I'll tell her you're not the innocent little angels she thinks you are."

"Oh, come on, admit it. He's off-the-charts gorg, Abs. If we were the type of girls who ranked men by numbers, we'd give him a twenty out of ten. He's in a class all by himself," Haley said.

"Of course he is, because no one would want to be in the class with him. He's overbearing, bossy, and grumpy." And he'd hurt her feelings when he'd said she was the clumsiest woman he'd ever met, even if it was kinda true.

"Please don't turn into one of those women," Haven said.

"What women?"

"You know the ones. Their husband leaves them for someone else, and they turn into bitter and angry women who shut themselves off from love," Haven said.

"Yeah, don't do that, Abs. We want you to be happy. You deserve to be happy. And you deserve to have someone who loves *you*. The Abby we know, not"— Haley glanced at Haven, who nodded as though giving her permission to say whatever was on her mind—

"the Abby Chandler and your Hollywood friends wanted you to be."

Abby rested her head against the wall, stunned. "I tried really hard not to let the fame and the fortune go to my head or change me. Honestly, I didn't think it had. I'm sorry. You guys should've said something."

"No, it's not that. We loved your fame and fortune. You spoiled us, and we couldn't have been prouder of you. We were always bragging about you to our friends."

Abby forced her smile to stay in place as Haley confirmed her worst fears. She'd lost her sisters' admiration and respect. She was nothing now. Just a penniless woman living in the middle of nowhere whose risk of dying before she was thirty had increased exponentially because she didn't have what it took to survive in the mountains of North Carolina.

She felt like the loser the mean girls in high school had proclaimed her to be.

"But you weren't really *you* when you were with Chandler, especially the last couple of years. Abs—"

Afraid she might cry, Abby interrupted Haley, "I promise, I won't become bitter and shut myself off from love."

"Great. Because we think Hunter is perfect for you," Haven said.

"You can't be serious. This is why you called, isn't it?"

"Yes, and before you list a hundred and one reasons why it won't work—"

"Besides the man having absolutely zero interest in me, you mean?" Abby interrupted Haley. "Which, by the way, is mutual. I have no interest in him either. And, yes, I'm not blind, so I do realize he is an incredibly good-looking man. Although totally not my type."

"Just saying, but maybe you need to rethink your type because your type sued you and then dumped you."

"That's not nice, Hal," Haven said, then smiled at Abby. "We just don't want you to rule Hunter out because you think he's not your type. The same goes for Highland Falls. It might be just the change you need. It probably doesn't feel that way because of the snake and everything, but maybe you need to give it a chance. Hunter too, because he—"

"Fine. I promise to keep an open mind. I'll just ignore Hunter's tendency to bark at me. Yell at me. Grunt instead of answering my questions. Look at me as if I'm a blonde instead of a redhead. And instead of focusing on his domineering, bossy 'tude, I'll focus on his rugged masculinity."

At her sisters' amused smiles, she hammed it up, moving her hand through her hair in a sensual way. Except her fingers got caught in her curls, and she had to yank them out, which kind of ruined the effect. She continued anyway. "His thick wavy hair and his piercing blue eyes, that mouth with the full bottom lip and that thick neck and bulging muscles that make you want to...Ummm." She closed her eyes, doing her best impression of Meg Ryan's fake orgasm in *When Harry Met Sally*.

There was a reason Abby never made it as an actress, but she'd made her sisters laugh, and that made her smile. Until she opened her eyes and saw the *oh, crap* expressions on Haven's and Haley's faces.

"He's right behind me, isn't he?"

Her sisters nodded, giving the man standing behind her finger waves.

Abby groaned. "Shoot me now."

"Gladly." Hunter stepped around her to head for the side door onto the porch. He was shirtless, and a tool belt rode low on his hips, his khaki shorts and heavy work boots showing off his muscular calves. But it was his smoothly muscled back that caught and held Abby's gaze. As though he sensed her lustful attention, he slung the T-shirt he had bunched in his hand over his shoulder.

"Abs, do something! He's leaving," Haley whisper-shouted over the line.

"Go after him, Abs. You need him. Just apologize. Blame us."

"Okay. Okay." She didn't want to chase after him, but her sisters were right. She needed him. She'd been waiting for a good time to ask him to help her with the rest of her to-do list. She just hadn't figured out what to offer him in return. Now she'd be lucky if he finished sealing the gates to the wild kingdom for her.

She heard her mother calling for her sisters. "Is she asking if you've seen her phone?"

"Yeah, we kinda gave our phones away, so we—"

"Why would you..." She blew out a breath. "Right. I told you I'd buy you new iPhones when you got back." Abby's mother and stepfather didn't have a lot of money for extras, and Abby made sure her sisters never went without. She knew what it was like to be the kid wearing the neighbor's hand-me-downs, the kid who didn't have a cell phone or laptop. She'd been the one to buy Haven and Haley the latest tech gadgets, and the latest trends in clothes and shoes. Whatever they'd wanted, Abby bought. "I promise, as soon as I sell the farm, I'll buy you new phones."

"No. We can take the money from the school accounts you set up for us. That's really why we called. We talked about it, Abs. We want you to take the money. You can pay Hunter to fix the house and buy whatever you need. We can work our way through school. We don't mind, honest," Haley said, with Haven nodding beside her.

"Absolutely not. I want you guys to focus on school." She didn't want her mom to feel like she had to help them either. And Abby knew she would. Her mother had always worked hard, but after Abby's dad left, she'd had to work two jobs just to keep them afloat. She'd never complained, but Abby had heard her crying herself to sleep at night and had vowed that one day she'd pay her back. She'd made several attempts over the years, only for her mother to refuse the money. So instead, Abby spoiled her sisters, mom, and stepfather at birthdays and Christmas. And with a gap year that had turned into a family trip of a lifetime.

Her mother and stepfather had been worried sick about the girls traveling to remote parts of the world on their own (as had Abby), but they understood their desire to help others. It was something they aspired to themselves. So after first clearing it with Haley and Haven, Abby presented them with the trip as a retirement present.

Her stomach clutched at the thought that she might never be able to spoil any of them again. Outside she heard a truck's door slam. "I gotta go. Hunter's leaving.

Don't forget to erase the phone's history before you give it back to Mom."

"We love you, Abs," the twins cried in unison.

"Love you guys too." She made kissy faces at them as she ran for the door...and tripped over her shoes.

* * *

"Hunter, wait!" Abby flew out of the farmhouse, waving her arm to flag him down.

"You see, this is what happens when you take too long taking a leak, Wolf. Next time I tell you we're leaving, you better get your ass in the truck ASAP." He turned to look at Abby, who was pounding on his window. He lowered it. "What?"

"I'm sorry. I didn't mean any of what I said or, you know, the fake orgasm thing." Her cheeks pinked, and her eyes lowered to his chest. He was wearing a clean T-shirt, but he suddenly felt naked under her stare. As though she sensed his eyes on her, she lifted her gaze to his.

"You sure it was fake?" *Way to go, Mackenzie.*

"Was what...Oh, that, yeah. I'm not very good at it. I couldn't fake an orgasm to save my life. It became a bit of an issue with my ex. I..." She wrinkled her nose. "You really didn't need to know that, did you?"

"Nope." He frowned and tapped his finger against his forehead. "What happened there?"

"Here?" She pointed at the red mark, and he nodded. She glanced away, saying something under her breath.

"Come again." She looked at him, and he bowed his

head. "No. I didn't mean literally. I meant what did you just say?"

"I ran into my phone."

"How is that even…" He held up his hand. "Never mind. I've gotta go."

"No!" She reached through the window and grabbed his arm. "Please, don't go. I'm really sorry. I shouldn't have objectified you that way. I didn't mean anything by it. It was Haley and Haven's fault. They're just looking out for me, and they think you…Never mind. I won't ever talk about you like that again. I'm truly sorry. Please tell me what I can do to make it up to you."

She looked like a lost puppy with her big pleading eyes, and he opened his mouth to tell her he was going to finish her room once he got back from town, but she just kept talking. He'd never met a woman who talked as much as her.

"I really need to sleep tonight, and if you don't finish animal-proofing my room, I won't. Unless you stay with me." She held up both hands, palms out. "Not *with me*, with me. I mean in the other bedroom. Or if that's too close, on the couch."

"Are you done?"

She nodded, clutching her bottom lip between her teeth. It had taken him less than two days to be able to read her tells. She was trying not to cry, and why that caused something to move in his chest, he had no idea. He did know he didn't like it.

"I'll be back in about twenty minutes to finish up. I just have to go to town and pick up a couple things at the hardware store."

"Town? You're going to town? I need to go with you."

"No. I don't have time. The hardware store closes in fifteen minutes," he lied. He needed time away from her before he lost his ever-loving mind.

She was already halfway to the house. "I'll be two minutes. I just have to grab my shoes and Bella."

"No way. Dog stays. She's in the crate."

"I can't leave her by herself. I've never left her alone before."

"That's fine. You don't have to," he said and started the truck.

"Okay, okay, but can you leave Wolf to protect her?" She walked back to the truck. "I know you think I baby her, but what you don't know is I rescued her from my ex's cosmetics company. She was subject number three. They were testing a new hair-care product line on her. A lot of people don't know this but a Yorkie's hair is almost identical to humans'. When I took her from the lab, most of her hair had fallen out, and she had open sores on her skin."

Now what was he supposed to do after hearing that? He scrubbed a hand over his face and leaned over to open the door for Wolf. "Sucks for you, buddy. But that'll teach you to be quicker next time. Don't whine. At least she's in the crate."

"You're a good dog, Wolf. I promise, I'll buy you a treat at the grocery store." Abby gave Wolf some love, and Hunter's dog glanced back, looking as if his sacrifice might've been worth it after all.

"I don't recall saying anything about a grocery store run." Hunter might as well have saved his breath. Abby was already in the house. She might be uncoordinated but the woman could move when she wanted to. The thought had him thinking about her on the stairs, faking an orgasm, which led to him thinking about her ex.

Only moments ago, he'd agreed she'd shared too much so he didn't understand why the curiosity now. *Why indeed?* he thought when she ran out of the house wearing leopard print shorts and a matching top with a deep V, her lips as shiny and as red as the hair she pulled on the top of her head in a mass of messy curls.

"See, I told you I wouldn't be long." She gave him a blinding smile as she climbed into the seat beside him.

He sat there looking at her for a minute, trying to figure out what was different about her. She looked the same but there was an energy about her now. She seemed vital and... happy. She was happy. That's what it was.

"This is going to be so much fun. People to see, places to visit. Maybe I can stop in and say hi to Eden. And I definitely have to stop in at Home Sweet Home. The local Realtor," she said like he wouldn't know.

He rolled his eyes. "I did grow up here."

"Yes, but you live in the woods. So there's probably a lot that goes on that you know nothing about."

"There's not."

"I'm sure." She smiled. "So, I was thinking, you're so good with wood and construction that maybe you could help me get the farmhouse ready for sale? I have a crazy-long to-do list, but I'm hoping the Realtor will be able to help me wheedle it down some. It shouldn't take you more than a week—"

"No," Hunter said and turned onto the main road.

"Why not? It's not like you have a job. I'm sorry, that sounded rude. What I meant is you don't have a boss you have to answer to. You can take some time off if you wanted to. Eden did say Liz would want you to help me, you know."

"Okay, let me tell you again in terms you might understand. No. N. O. No way. No how."

"You're a very rude man, Hunter Mackenzie. And let me tell you, when I was driving for Uber, I met some winners. There was this one—"

"Abby, if you don't stop talking right now, I'm going to pull over and you can walk to town."

"You wouldn't."

He pulled onto the shoulder.

"Okay, okay. Gosh. You should probably get something to eat. You sound hangry." She glanced out her window, crossed her arms, winced and uncrossed them, and then said, "Fine."

He pulled back onto the road and drove in blessed silence the entire way to town. She started moving around in the seat as they passed the WELCOME TO HIGHLAND FALLS sign.

As the town came into view, out of the corner of his eye, Hunter watched Abby open and close her mouth. He had to work to hold back a laugh. It was killing her not to ask questions, but he had no intention of putting her out of her misery. She craned her neck to look at the falls as he drove across the bridge.

Brightly colored summer flowers and plants lined either side of the walking path, leading to gardens on either end of the bridge. It was a tradition started by the owner of the local garden center, Winter Johnson, who was the mayor of Highland Falls. She also owned a shop in town called Flower Power.

On the left side of the bridge, down from the falls, was the old mill that had been converted into Highland Brew. As Hunter drove along Main Street, he caught sight of Owen getting out of his patrol car in front of the police station and prayed the old man headed straight for the door. He didn't. Someone called to the chief from across the street. He lifted his hand to wave... and spotted Hunter. His jaw dropped in shock.

Hunter hadn't been in town since the day he'd returned from his last tour. If he'd needed anything he couldn't grow or hunt, Owen or Liz picked it up for him. When Liz got sick, his family stepped in, leaving him food and supplies whether he wanted them or not.

Owen noted Hunter's passenger, and his shock turned to disapproval. He wasn't the only one. Just up the street, Hunter spotted his aunt, and she spotted him. Abby too.

So did his sisters' friends, and a couple of guys he'd grown up with. Unlike Owen and Hunter's aunt, they all got *Praise be to Jesus, Hunter Mackenzie has come back to the land of the living* smiles on their faces. No doubt his mother and his sisters would be receiving phone calls later that night. It wouldn't take them long to start planning the wedding.

"I'll help you get Liz's place ready for sale."

Abby shifted in the passenger seat to stare at him. "Seriously? You're not teasing me, are you? You're really going to help me?"

"Yeah. I'm really going to—"

Before he realized what she was up to, she launched herself over the console and threw her arms around his neck.

"What the—" As he turned his head to give her hell, she kissed him.

On the mouth.

In the middle of Main Street.

In the middle of rush-hour traffic.

Chapter Seven

♥

Oh my gosh! Abby's lips were pressed to Hunter's mouth and not to his cheek, where she'd fully expected and intended for them to be. She hadn't meant for them to land on his perfectly delectable lips, no matter how warm and firm they were. He tasted delicious too, like summer and blueberries.

Her eyes popped open. They'd been closed? A more important and urgent question took precedence over that one: What the heck did she mean he tasted like summer and blueberries? She hadn't slipped her tongue into his mouth...Oh my gosh, she must have! How else would she know he tasted like blueberries?

She lifted her gaze to his as his whole body (at least the parts she was pressed against) went rigid. He stared at her for one terrifying second while lifting his left hand from the wheel to remove her arm from around his neck before turning his gaze back to the road. Her lips brushed his beard as he did so. It was much softer than she expected it to be.

"Do you mind?"

The anger beneath his coldly clipped question pene-
trated her shock, and she jerked back. "I'm so sorry. I
didn't mean to kiss you."

He stared straight ahead. His profile looked like it
had been carved from granite—a study of rugged male
perfection. Albeit furious male perfection.

When he'd pinned her with his glacial stare before
returning his gaze to the road, she'd gotten a glimpse of
the warrior his enemies must have faced. It had been a
tiny bit scary.

"I meant to kiss you, just not on the lips," she continued to explain. "I was so grateful and relieved that you
agreed to help me get the house ready for sale, I kinda
lost my mind." Please, dear God, don't let him change
his. "But if you hadn't turned your head, I would've
kissed your cheek and not your mouth."

She really, really didn't want to bring up the whole
slipping-him-the-tongue thing, but she had to try to
explain and apologize. Because accidently slipping him
the tongue was way worse than accidently kissing him
on the lips. She glanced at him to see if her apology had
softened him at all.

He still looked stone-cold furious as he turned in to
the hardware store parking lot.

No doubt the conversation he'd overheard on the stairs
earlier hadn't done her any favors. He probably thought
she wanted to jump his bones. She didn't blame him.
Haven and Haley were perfect examples of his wide-
spread appeal so she imagined he'd been the recipient of
unwanted female attention in the past.

Even she wasn't immune to his appeal, as evidenced

by the warm tingles low in her stomach whenever she was around him. And he wasn't her type. Though her stomach muscles clearly disagreed with her, because they'd clenched a couple of times. As far as she knew, nerves didn't cause warm tingles and clenching muscles; excitement did. And, um, arousal. Which, if she was being completely honest with herself, after the initial shock of her lips landing on his, her tummy may have clenched with a tiny bit of desire.

There was a completely innocent explanation though. She was an affectionate person who enjoyed kissing and cuddling, and other than Bella, she hadn't had anyone to kiss and cuddle with in more than a year. Long before Puppy-Gate, Chandler had brushed aside all her overtures with a perfunctory kiss on the cheek. It should've been her first clue that he was getting his kisses and cuddles elsewhere. Although Juliette didn't strike her as the kissing and cuddling type.

No more putting it off, she thought when Hunter parked the truck and shut off the engine.

"So, about the tongue thing, I don't have any excuse for it. Other than your mouth must've been open to yell at me, because we both know how much you love to do that." She smoothed down her leopard print romper, which must've ridden up when she threw herself at the man currently staring at her like she had two heads.

She nodded. "You're absolutely right. There's no excuse for what I did, but I promise it was unintentional. And not only didn't I mean to, I didn't enjoy it even one little bit." Lately, the Universe had been kicking her in the butt hard so lying probably wasn't the smartest thing to do if she wanted a reprieve. Karma and all that. "I might've enjoyed it a tiny bit. I'm sure you did too. Just a little?"

His scowl said it all. He didn't enjoy the kiss even a little. Though she supposed it didn't qualify as a real kiss so there was no reason she should feel the least bit offended.

"You're damn right I was gonna yell at you. You threw yourself at me in the middle of rush-hour traffic, Abby. I could've lost control of the truck and hit someone."

She glanced at the six cars parked at the stoplight. "I don't think that qualifies as rush-hour traffic. But I get your point, and I really am sorry. Please forgive me for kissing you and slipping you the tongue?" *And please, please, don't renege on your promise.*

"What? You didn't slip me the tongue."

"If I didn't slip you the tongue, and trust me, I'm so glad that I didn't, why did I taste blueberries?" She left out the summer part.

"I finished off one of the blueberry muffins you gave me as I was coming down the stairs. I must've had a crumb on my mouth." He moved the tip of his tongue over his bottom lip and made a face. "I don't taste blueberries. I taste cherries."

"My lip gloss." She smiled and dug the tube out of her purse. "Isn't it delish?" She pulled down the sun visor. As she reapplied her lip gloss, she felt his eyes on her and slanted him a sideways glance. He was staring at her mouth. Kinda like he might want to kiss it. *Oh no,* she thought as her stomach tightened in response to the thought and his steady gaze.

He rubbed his palm over his lips. "No, it's not *delish*," he said, then muttered, "You have got to be kidding me."

"No. I'm serious. It's cherry-flavored." She went to hand him the lip gloss tube, but he was lowering the window to an older woman.

She had strawberry blond hair cut fashionably short with white bangs framing her face. Her eyes were as vivid blue as Hunter's, and she was staring at Abby. But not in the same way Hunter had been staring at her seconds ago.

"You've got Liz's eyes, and now you've got her house. It should've gone to my nephew, you know."

"Aunt Elsa, let it go. Liz would expect better of you, and so do I."

So much for Abby's idea to ask Elsa Mackenzie for a job. Eden had filled her in about her husband and Hunter's aunt and the Three Wise Women Bookstore that she'd owned with Liz and their mutual best friend Ina Graham. It didn't matter that the last place Abby wanted to work was in a bookstore—she needed money for supplies and food.

When Abby leaned across the console, Hunter pushed back against the driver seat as if he was afraid she was going in for another kiss. She rolled her eyes at him while extending her hand to his aunt. "Hi, Ms. Mackenzie. Eden mentioned that you and my aunt were close. I'm so sorry for your loss."

It grew awkward the longer Abby's hand hung out all by its lonesome in midair, but just as she was about to pull it back, the older woman clasped her hand.

"It was a great loss for all of us in Highland Falls. The town isn't the same without Liz. She was the lifeblood of this community. The best friend I could've asked for." She gave Abby's hand a vise-like squeeze that left little doubt how she felt about her. "But you wouldn't know any of that because you didn't know Liz. For the life of me, I can't understand why she left you the farm."

"Okay, Aunt Elsa, if there isn't anything you need from me, you should probably head back to the bookstore and lock up."

"Oh, there's something I need from you, all right. I need to know if you've lost your mind or if I need to have my eyes checked. So please tell me I didn't just see you kissing the woman who stole the farm from you?"

"I didn't steal the farm from him! He stole it from me."

Why? Why hadn't she learned to think before she opened her mouth? She didn't need this woman as an enemy, and she desperately needed Hunter Mackenzie's help.

"You need your eyes checked, and I need to get into the hardware store before Ed closes up for the day." Hunter motioned his aunt back and then opened the door, easing his long, lethal frame from the truck.

Abby did the same with her short, soft frame, but with far less grace than Hunter. At least she didn't trip and fall on her face. How was that for looking at the bright side of life on a particularly crappy day? She might actually get the hang of this positive-thinking thing. Earning some good karma might come in handy too. When someone had had as much bad luck as she'd had recently, every little bit helped.

"Ms. Mackenzie, I really am sorry you feel I stole your nephew's inheritance." Abby rounded the truck to Hunter's side. "I'm not sure why Liz left the farmhouse to me either. But I am grateful. Truly, I am."

"If you were the least bit grateful, you wouldn't be selling the place. Liz always meant for Honeysuckle Farm to be kept in the Findlay family. When Liz's father disowned her, his mother, Mary Findlay, took her in. She left Liz the farm, just like Mary's mother-in-law left it to her. But I bet you didn't know that, did you? You don't know Liz's history or the farm's. And looking at you, I can't say I'm surprised. It's too bad your father died. He at least knew the value of family."

"If you believe that, you didn't know him very well," Abby said and walked away.

After having words with his aunt, words Abby couldn't make out, probably because—along with her face—her ears were burning, Hunter caught up with her.

"Sorry about that. You okay?" He stopped her with a hand on her arm.

Even though she was far from okay, she nodded but didn't meet his eyes. Elsa Mackenzie's words had hit home, and they hurt, because she was right. Abby didn't deserve any of this. She knew nothing about her great-aunt and the farm and what they'd meant to the people in this town.

Maybe it wasn't entirely her fault. She'd been a kid when her father left them. She had good reasons for losing contact with his side of the family. But it didn't make her feel less ashamed. Or unworthy. "Your aunt's not very nice."

"She's having a hard time dealing with losing Liz, but you're right. She wasn't very nice." He held open the door to the hardware store.

"From what I've heard, you loved Liz too, and I *stole* the farmhouse from you, but you're nice to me... Well, sometimes you're nice to me. Like when you handle pest control and offer to help me with repairs." She gave him a tentative smile as she walked into the store. "You are still going to help me, aren't you?"

"Yeah, just don't let my aunt or anyone else around here know."

She stopped to stare up at him. "You mean Elsa isn't the only one who feels that way about me selling the farm?"

"Seems to be the general opinion around here."

"Then why are you helping me?" She narrowed her eyes at him as the answer smacked her in the forehead. "You want to get rid of me, don't you?"

He lifted a broad shoulder. "Nothing personal. I like my space and my quiet, and there's not been a lot of that with you and the rat around."

"Stop calling Bella a rat. And it's not my fault that—" she began, hooking her purse over her shoulder with a bit of attitude because he actually did want to get rid of her. It was too late by the time she realized she'd put a little too much attitude into the move to stop her purse from hitting a display of paint cans. Several of which would've fallen onto the cement floor if not for Hunter's quick reflexes.

"And then there's that," he said as he returned the paint cans to their rightful places. "You can't survive here on your own. You're a city girl through and through."

She opened her mouth to defend herself because it wasn't fun to be considered completely useless and inept, which he didn't say but his *for the love of God* expression totally implied. She cheered herself up with the knowledge that, as much as he didn't want her here, she didn't want to be there. And now that she knew how the entire town of Highland Falls felt about her, the sooner she got the farmhouse sold the better.

"I am a city girl, and I'm darn proud of it." Instead of adding the *so there* that was on the tip of her tongue, she tossed her hair, added some more attitude—this time to her hips—and walked ahead of him.

Pulling up her list on her phone, she squinted at the towering rows of pumpkin-orange metal shelving to her left. The store could use some lighting and signage, she thought as she headed for an aisle that looked like it might contain tile. The linoleum on both the farmhouse's kitchen and bathroom floors had started to curl up at the edges where the glue had given way. She pulled up the farmhouse board on her Pinterest page.

"Abby, watch out!"

She looked up from her phone to see a gorgeous, bare-chested man wearing a kilt coming her way. Which would've been okay if the man was real but he took center stage on a ginormous sign, and it wasn't made of paper.

Before Abby did a face-plant in the highlander's kilt, a muscled arm wrapped around her waist and whisked her out of harm's way. Then Hunter let her go and lunged for the huge wooden sign. "Ed, you can let go. I've got it."

The man did as he was directed, and Hunter lifted the wooden sign as though it weighed nothing at all and walked it to the sales counter.

His face red and sweaty, the older man in the black apron wiped a hand across his brow. "Sorry, lass. I didn't know there was anyone about." His eyes went to Hunter—who propped the sign against the counter—and they got wide. "I thought I recognized that voice but didn't believe my own ears. Hunter Mackenzie, as I live and breathe. It's good to see you, lad." Ed smiled at Abby, his eyes twinkling. "I take it we have this lovely wee lass to thank for bringing about this miracle?"

It was a miracle? Oh my gosh, how horrible to think something as simple as Hunter coming into town to shop was considered a miracle. She wondered what had happened to him that he preferred to live his life alone in the woods with only his dog for companionship. Her heart ached for him. It had to have been something horrendous. No one would choose to live that way.

As though Hunter sensed her sympathy (and curiosity), he scowled at her and said, "This is Abby Everhart, Ed. She's Liz's niece, and we're here to pick up supplies. She's paying me to help her get the farmhouse ready to put on the market."

The twinkle in the man's eyes dimmed. "You can't be serious?"

He seemed like such a nice older man that Abby resented Hunter for intentionally turning him against her. She hurried over to the sales counter and whisper-shouted, "You said not to say anything! And since when am I paying you to help me?"

"There's worse things to have the man thinking. Me being with you is one of them. And I never said I was doing the job for free."

"You're such a jerk." But because she was tired and flustered, *jerk* came out sounding like *flerk* with a lot of tongue action. She tried again, and this time it came out as *twerk*.

Hunter looked down at her, and his lips twitched.

"Jerk," she said again, relieved when it came out exactly as she had intended. "A really big one."

He started to laugh, which might've been why he missed Ed's "Well, I'll be."

When the older man noticed her watching him, he cleared the smile from his face, but he no longer looked at her like she was a traitor to the entire human race.

She'd like to keep it that way, and hoped by sharing with Ed, he'd share with everyone in Highland Falls that she wasn't a horrible person. "I'm really sorry you're all disappointed that I'm not keeping the farm in the family, but I can't afford to, and I have a job in LA." She gave Hunter an eyelash-fluttering smile only because she was pretty sure it would tick him off, and told Ed, "I offered Hunter the farmhouse at a really low price, and I'd be willing to do the same for anyone from Highland Falls that might be interested in buy—"

"You'll not get anyone from town or the next county to make on offer on Liz's place, lass."

Abby's stomach dropped to her feet. "Wh—" She concentrated hard so her words wouldn't come out jumbled. "Why's that?"

"Liz would haunt them, is why. And if she didn't, the

rest of the Findlay women who'd gone before her would. Honeysuckle Farm was a Findlay farm, and that's how it shall remain. It's why Liz left the farm to you, a woman she never knew and who'd never bothered to know her, instead of Hunter here. It's a Findlay tradition."

"I'm an Everhart," she said as her hope she could get Ed or anyone in Highland Falls on her side dwindled.

"Blood tells and so do the eyes. You're a Findlay, all right." His phone *ping*ed, and he pulled a pair of glasses from his apron pocket and read the screen. "Just like I suspected. You won't be able to give the farmhouse away. Elsa Mackenzie has just posted an edict on the town's social media, as well as the bookstore's. Anyone who makes you an offer will have to deal with her. And trust me, not many folks around here will risk getting on Elsa's bad side. Isn't that right, Hunter?"

Abby pressed a hand to her chest, shocked. "She can't do that. That's . . . I don't know what it is but there must be a law against it. I'll call . . ." Remembering the conversation she'd overheard between Owen and Hunter, she went with a lawyer instead of the police. "Eden." She raised her phone to her ear.

Hunter took it from her and ended the call. "You're not calling Eden. I'll talk to my aunt. But for now, let's get what I came for. Do you have a list of what you want to get done?"

"Yes, but I can't . . . " She leaned in to him and lowered her voice. "I can't pay you. I hardly have any money."

"You just get what you need, Hunter. I'll open an account for you. I know you're good for it. Besides, in Highland Falls we take care of our men and women who served. Hunter here was a member of Delta Force, a unit so elite that even the defense department doesn't acknowledge its existence," the older man shared with Abby, beaming with pride at Hunter. "He was team leader, and he—"

"Appreciate the offer to put the supplies for the farm on the books, Ed. I'm sure Abby's good for it." Hunter's affable tone belied the tension she saw in his eyes. "I'll take an IOU," he told her.

"You're still going to help me? I don't have to pay you anything upfront?"

"No, I—"

She threw herself into his arms and hugged him tight. After everything Ed had said about Elsa, Abby had needed some positive news. She felt Hunter stiffen and tipped her head back to smile up at him. "Don't worry, I won't embarrass you by kissing you again."

"Too late," he muttered, looking over her head.

She turned to see what he was looking at and dropped her arms from his waist. "Oh my gosh, are they real?" she murmured as three extremely well-built and extremely gorgeous men walked their way wearing white T-shirts and kilts. One of the men looked like a slightly younger version of Hunter, only without the beard. She looked from the man to the sign behind her. "That's you," she said, touching the photo of him on the sign.

His lips quirked. "It is. And you must be Abby Everhart, the woman who's managed to do what none of us have been able to." His startling blue gaze moved from her to Hunter. "Nice to see you in town, big brother."

Hunter grunted in response, then asked, "Why are the three of you wearing kilts?"

"Interview and photo shoot for *Highland Falls Herald* to advertise the games."

"So why are you here, then?"

His brother held up his phone. "You're trending on social media." He grinned at Abby. "Something about you kissing a cute redhead in the middle of Main Street."

Hunter followed the direction of his brother's amused gaze and sighed. "Abby, do you mind?"

"Mind what?"

He nodded at her hand stroking the sign. "You're patting my brother."

Chapter Eight

♥

As Hunter loaded the last of the supplies into the back of the truck, he glanced at the hardware store for some sign Abby was actually going to listen to him this time and get her butt out here. But no, the woman couldn't drag herself away from a conversation if her life depended on it.

She was a social butterfly. Flitting from one man to the next, one conversation to another at warp speed. She was exhausting, and his brother and his cousins weren't helping. They were happy to keep her talking. Even happier to pump her for information—about him. He should've dumped her off on the side of the road.

He slammed the truck's gate and was about to head back in and drag her out when she appeared at the door, laughing at something his brother, Shane, said. She had a great laugh, a warm laugh, big and genuine. Like her smile. As mad at her as he was, it surprised him that he could appreciate her laugh. And that blinding white smile.

But when he glanced at his brother and found Shane

watching him closely, a slow, knowing smile tipping up his brother's lips, any positive thoughts Hunter might've been having about Abby and her laugh vanished.

His brother thought he was interested in her. Which Shane would no doubt share with Eden, who would then share with the rest of the women in the family. Which meant that, thanks to Abby Everhart, Hunter was about to have his world turned upside down.

Because no matter how much he objected, they wouldn't believe him. They'd see Abby as the answer to their hopes and prayers of the last two years. The woman who'd save Hunter from himself and drag him back to the land of the living. They didn't care that he had no desire or need to be saved. He was content with his life exactly the way it was.

He got in the truck, slammed the door, then powered down the window. "Abby, move it or you can find another way home." She had no idea how close he was to peeling out of the parking lot and leaving her behind.

"One sec, I promise!"

"You have got to be kidding me," he muttered when she held up her phone, taking a selfie with his brother and cousins.

What had he been thinking agreeing to bring her with him? He racked his brain trying to figure out what she'd done or said to make him agree. Oh right, he'd felt sorry for her and the rat. That'd teach him to let sympathy overrule common sense.

He revved the engine and put the truck into Drive. Abby's eyes went wide while Shane's and his cousins' narrowed. Good, that's more like it, he thought when their narrowed gazes turned to scowls. He'd just proven to them that he had no interest in the tiny redhead whatsoever. So when Shane shared with the women of the family that Hunter had left Abby stranded in the hardware parking lot staring after him, they'd realize the same thing.

A glance in the rearview mirror proved him wrong. The damn woman wasn't standing staring after him, she was running after him, calling, "Hunter, wait! Don't leave me. I need you!" And she, the clumsiest woman on God's green earth, was running in sky-high heels.

Cursing under his breath, he braked hard, the smell of burned rubber filling the cab. He bowed his head as Abby ran into the back end of his truck.

The woman was a walking disaster. But she wasn't whiney, he thought when she responded to his brother's and cousins' concern with a big smile and a cheerful wave. The woman was resilient. And determined. He admired the former and worried about the latter.

"Gosh, you're impatient," she said when she opened the passenger-side door to hoist herself awkwardly into the truck.

"Impatient? I was impatient the third time I told you to get out of the store and into the truck. That was the fifth time."

She rolled her eyes and powered her window down to stick her head out. "Don't forget to bring your wives and kids to the farm for a visit! I'd love to meet them. That goes for you and Eden too, Shane!"

Hunter stared at her. "You can't invite them to the farm."

"Why not?"

"Because I said so." He glanced at his brother and cousins in the rearview mirror. The three of them were waving and laughing—at him, no doubt. He stuck his middle finger out the window.

"'Because I said so' isn't an answer. Besides, I can invite whomever I want to visit the farm. It's not like I invited them to the barn."

"They're my family."

"A family you rarely see, from what your brother and cousins said. Why is that? Don't...Hey, the grocery store is that way." She pointed to the sign that was visible from the parking lot and grabbed his arm. "Where are you going?

"The farm."

"No." She shook his arm, which she still held on to, her long fingernails a cherry red. "I have to go to the grocery store, remember? The only food I had was in the gift basket from Eden, and you ate it all."

"I didn't eat it all. I had a couple of blueberry muffins." Unconsciously, his eyes went to her mouth, and he thought about the conversation they'd been having just before his aunt interrupted them.

Abby had thought she'd slipped him the tongue. She hadn't—her lips had been soft and sweet. As far from a kiss with tongue and heat as you can get. But for a second, tongue and heat was all he could think about and exactly what he wanted when he stared at her glossy red lips. He bet she tasted like cherries. She'd probably swiped on another coat of her lip gloss for her selfie with his brother and cousins.

"You don't have to glare at me. I'm not asking you to come in with me. I swear, it'll hardly take any time at all. You don't want me to disappoint Wolf, do you? I promised him a bone for looking after Bella."

"Trust me, Wolf has no problem getting his own bones."

She gasped. "That's a horrible thing to say. He's babysitting my baby, and now all I can picture is him eating her."

"Relax. He's not going to eat her, but he also doesn't need a bone."

"Wolf might not need a bone, but Bella and I need food. You'll feel guilty if you come over tomorrow and find us lying on the kitchen floor dying of starvation."

"It takes more than three weeks to die of starvation, and you've got water. Liz kept a garden behind the farmhouse. Carrots, potatoes, and beans should be about ready to harvest now. There's strawberries and blueberries back there too."

"That would be wonderful if Bella and I were vegetarians and fruitarians, but we're not. I also need chocolate, ice cream, and…" She gave him a smug smile. "Tampons."

Hunter pulled a U-ie on Main Street, cars honking as he headed in the opposite direction toward the grocery store. "You have ten minutes," he growled at Abby.

"Thank you." She smiled and went back to her phone.

"What are you doing?" He regretted asking the question before it was even out of his mouth.

She held up her phone, showing him the selfie she'd taken in front of the hardware store. "I'm sending it to my mom to show Haven and Haley, and now I'm sending it to Elinor. She's my ex-husband's housekeeper. For another few days at least. Elinor's going to print off the photo and leave it out for Juliette and Tiffany to see. Tiffany is a member of the Bel Air Babes. We used to be besties. Until they turned on me after my ex dumped me. Now I call them the Bel Air Bs on account of how they acted toward me. But they're in love with anything and everything Scottish, especially men in kilts. They'll die of jealousy when they see this."

He stared at her, wondering what the hell she was even talking about.

"Honestly, I don't really get it. I mean, obviously, I understand the appeal of hunky highlanders. I'm just not really a fan of men wearing skirts. And that whole wondering what's under the kilt gets kinda old."

"Really? That surprises me since you asked my brother and cousins what they were wearing under theirs at least three times."

"I was just having fun with them. But Tiffany and the Bel Air Bs would have been all over them. They're seriously addicted to *Outlander*. It's a television series set in Scotland. They have a viewing party once a week. I used to go to them. Only because I can never turn down a social event. But I wasn't into the whole historical-time-travel thing like they are. They even went on an *Outlander* tour in Scotland last fall. I bailed, of course."

He gave his head a slight shake to clear the information overload. "Is there a reason why you're telling me all of this?"

"You asked what I'm doing, so I told you."

"A simple *I'm texting my sisters the selfie* would've sufficed."

"Don't forget Elinor. You know, without her, I never would've known about my inheritance. Come to think of it, I probably wouldn't have made it to Highland Falls at all. I owe her a lot."

"Yeah, me too," he said dryly.

"Ha-ha. But you will when I make her scones for you tomorrow morning." She held up her phone. "She just sent me her recipe, and they're to die for."

"You don't have to make me anything, Abby."

"Yes, I do. And really, they're as much for me as they are for you. A hangry Hunter is not a fun Hunter to be around."

"Cute, but I can bring my own food. And you know how I said we can defer payment of your IOU? I'm collecting on it now."

"But I barely have enough money to buy groceries and to pay for—"

"Cancel the invite to my family, and we're square."

"But that would be rude. I don't understand why you've shut them out of your life. They seem so nice. And they love you. They're worried about…Fine. I'll visit them at their houses."

He'd make sure she was too busy to visit anyone. He'd keep her tied up at the farmhouse if he had to. Turning in to the grocery store parking lot, he searched for familiar SUVs and trucks. When it looked like he was in the clear, he said, "You've got ten minutes."

Twenty minutes later, slouched in the driver's seat of

his truck so no one would see him, Hunter watched as the doors to the grocery store slid open and a woman walked out. It wasn't Abby. He glanced at his phone, debating whether or not to text Eden for Abby's number. He decided against it. He'd have to jump through hoops to get her number, and somehow either Eden or his brother would spin it in a way that made it seem there was more going on between him and Abby than there was.

"Dammit." He glanced around to be sure the coast was clear before getting out of the truck. He'd ignored five text messages from his aunt and three from Owen.

Hunter strode across the lot and through the sliding doors, getting hit by a blast of cool air and the smell of fruit when he entered the store. Above the sound of pop rock playing over the speakers, he heard a familiar laugh. He followed the sound to the deli, where Abby was talking to an attractive black woman with vibrant blue shoulder-length hair.

If Hunter wasn't mistaken, the woman had bought the local beauty salon a few years back. And since she was a local, he didn't understand why Abby was acting like they were lifelong friends.

"Abby, we've gotta get going. Hey." He lifted his chin at the other woman, relieved that he didn't know her well enough that she reacted to his presence like it was the Second Coming. He took Abby by the arm to drag her away but she shook him off and did the air-kiss-cheek thing with the woman, whose name he learned was Josie. Abby promised to call her and meet for coffee before returning to his side.

"Hunter, that was so rude. Josie was just telling me

the latest gossip about my ex's cosmetics company. She attended a beauty conference in New York last month." She touched her hair. "Which reminds me, I have to book an appointment before I go back to LA. Anyhoo, Chandler's company's latest shampoo is frying customers' hair. It's true," she said, obviously mistaking his stare as disbelief instead of what it was—a bleed in his brain.

He needed to get her out of there and back to the farm before he lost his mind.

A couple with a little boy walked by, and Abby smiled. "Hi. I love your hair," she said to the woman. "Do you go to Josie's?"

"Thanks. Yeah, I do. Your hair is great too."

"You're so sweet, thank you. I—"

She looked like she was settling in to have herself another twenty-minute chat so Hunter took her by the arm and dragged her toward the cash register. "You folks have a good night."

"Hunter! I'm not finished." She showed him her basket, which held a raw meat bone the size of her arm, a package of cold meat, and a brick of cheese.

"You're not finished because—" He broke off when a man wearing coke-bottle glasses walked over with a bag of dog food in his hand.

He greeted Hunter with a nod—someone else he didn't know, thank God—and greeted Abby with a hundred-watt smile. "The manager said it'll take him about a week to get the brand you want, but he called his sister—she's a vet—and she said this one is almost as good, Abby."

"Really? That was so sweet of him to go to all

that trouble. Make sure you thank him for me, Walter."
She gave the fiftysomething man's arm a friendly
squeeze. "And don't forget"—she leaned in to him and
whispered—"no more black hair dye. Silver is where
it's at, Walter. Trust me, the ladies won't be able to
resist you."

"You think so?"

"I know so." She winked, then looked at Hunter and
sighed. "I better go. Hangry man."

"Would you stop calling me hangry," Hunter said
when the other man was out of hearing range.

"Stop acting like one. Now, I just need a few more
things, and we'll be on our way." She looked at her
phone. "Do you know where—"

"Give me your phone. It'll be faster if I do it." When
she shook her head, he plucked it from her hand.

"Hunter! Give me my phone. That's private."

He held the phone out of her reach as he tried to read
her grocery list. He frowned, unable to make out half the
words on her list. He looked at her. Her cheeks matched
her cherry-red lips, and he figured that was as good an
answer to the question he wanted to ask as any. Still,
he wanted to know for sure, which should concern him.
"Are you dyslexic?"

"Something like that," she murmured, taking her
phone back.

"What do you mean?" He followed her down the
bread aisle, thinking about her creative cursing the other
night and earlier today at the hardware store when she
called him a *flerk*. "Abby?"

She stopped to peruse the bread, then glanced at him.

"If you tell me why everyone, well, everyone who knows you, acts like it's a miracle you came to town. What happened two years ago, Hunter? Why do you hide away at Honeysuckle Farm?"

Someone would tell her if she stuck around long enough. But none of them knew the whole story. "I'll get the flour, eggs, ice cream, milk, and butter." Those were easy enough to figure out. "You get the rest."

He didn't know whether she was relieved to be let off the hook or not. He knew he was. He hit the dairy aisle, picked up what he wanted, grabbed a bag of flour, and went back to find her talking to Walter in the same aisle where he'd left her.

"What? There's too many to choose from." She glanced down as he placed the dairy items in her basket. "Umm, chocolate ice cream. Nice."

He took her by the arm. "Read the rest of your list to me," he said, then proceeded to move her up and down the aisles at a more reasonable pace.

"Oh my gosh, you're going so fast, you'd think I was an A-list celebrity and you'd spotted my stalker on aisle five."

"Six. Walter is following us."

"He's pretty protective of me, and you're acting—"

"You met him twenty minutes ago!" He raised a finger when she opened her mouth. He couldn't take another one of her long-winded, convoluted explanations. "Are we done now?"

"Yes."

"It's about time." He'd never been happier to reach the checkout line.

"You act like I've been in here an hour when I've hardly taken any time at all. In LA, it would've taken me longer to find a parking spot than it's taken me to shop today," she said, digging around in her oversized pink purse. "Sorry, it'll just take me a minute," she told the cashier, who'd rung her purchases through.

Five minutes later, his patience completely gone, Hunter pulled his wallet from his back pocket. He handed the cashier the money, gathered up the bags, and headed for the door.

Behind him, he heard Abby thanking the cashier and apologizing for him being so cranky. At the sound of her heels clicking on the tiles as she hurried to catch up to him, he said, "Slow down." He put his back against the door to hold it open for her. His eyes went over her head, and he groaned. He thought his day had been bad, but it had just taken a turn for the worse.

"What did I do now?"

"Nothing. Just avoid eye contact with the Betty White look-alike coming our way, and whatever you do, don't let her touch you."

Chapter Nine

♥

Abby frowned at Hunter as she stepped out of the grocery store. Watch out for Betty White look-alikes? She must've heard him wrong. Maybe the embarrassment caused by Hunter asking if she was dyslexic had messed with her hearing. It was definitely messing with her head. She kept replaying the moment in her mind, wishing she'd handled it differently.

She could've said *Darn that auto correct* or that it was her version of shorthand. But she found it hard to lie or think up a believable excuse when she felt like a deer frozen in the middle of the road, headlights burning into her retinas as a car barreled toward her. *Splat.* Just like that, her secret was exposed.

The only consolation was that, other than Hunter, no one here knew her secret, or at least part of it. But really, in the whole scheme of things, what could it hurt? Hunter had already seen her at her worst—over and over again—and he avoided people as though his life depended on it, so it wasn't like he'd tell anyone.

Hunter's face appeared in her line of vision. It was a very handsome face, even though, the majority of the time, when those crystal-blue eyes looked at her, they were filled with irritation or frustration. Except that one time in the truck when he'd looked like he'd wanted to kiss her.

"Abby, snap out of it. We've gotta go."

He definitely didn't want to kiss her now, she thought at the irritation in his gruff command.

"Sorry, your talk about a Betty White look-alike threw me." If she'd heard him right, that was a pretty good comeback. She glanced across the parking lot, relieved to see a white-haired woman who did indeed look like the actress. Beside her, a twentysomething woman with amazing chestnut-colored hair tucked the older woman's arm through hers.

"You're right," Abby said. "She does look like Betty White, and the woman beside her looks like Nina Dobrev's twin. Elena on *The Vampire Diaries*," she explained at Hunter's blank look.

Well, it was either a blank look or he'd gone from irritated to angry. She'd noticed that his whole demeanor took on a glacial aspect when he was angry. It was crazy how well she'd come to read this man in such a short time. His eyes—wow, she hadn't noticed until just then how long and lush his lashes were. But his eyes still had that blank thing going on so she added, "It's another television series that the Bel Air Bs were obsessed with. It was before my time though. And I'm not into any of that supernatural stuff like time travel and vampires. You have to believe it to be able to—"

"You think I'm joking about not making eye contact with her, don't you?" he interrupted, and she now knew why she'd just then noticed his eyelashes. He was totally in her space. "You'll find out soon enough. Don't say I didn't warn you." He strode off, lifting the bags higher as if to hide his face.

If his arms weren't full of her groceries—groceries that he was not only carrying but that he'd paid for—she had no doubt he'd be dragging her to his truck just like he'd dragged her up and down the aisles. Despite her curiosity about Betty White's look-alike, she hurried after him. "Okay, okay. I'm coming. Thanks for paying for my groceries, by the way," she said when she reached his side. "I must've left my wallet at the farmhouse. I'll pay you back though."

He glanced to his left, muttered what sounded like a not-so-nice word, then said, "You can pay me back by getting in the truck without saying one word to—"

"Hunter Mackenzie, is that really you?"

He dragged a deep breath through his nostrils before turning with what he probably meant to be a smile but looked more like a pained grimace. "Hey, Granny MacLeod. It's good to see you."

Abby gasped. "That's your granny and you were trying to sneak away from her without saying hello? Hunter Mackenzie, you should be ashamed of yourself. I don't know what your problem is with—" She gave the older woman an apologetic smile for her grandson's anti-social behavior.

"She's not my granny," he said through what sounded like clenched teeth.

The older woman smiled at Abby and lifted a crooked finger. "I ken that face and those witchy green-gold eyes. You'd be a Findlay, wouldn't you, lass?"

Betty White with a Scottish accent threw her as much as her comment did, but Abby regained her composure and smiled, offering her hand. "Yes, I'm Abby Everhart."

Hunter's sharp intake of breath had her glancing his way. Oh crap, he'd warned her not to let the older woman touch her. But just as Abby remembered his warning, a blue-veined hand with dry, crepe-paper-thin skin closed around hers. And while the hand looked and felt delicate, Granny MacLeod's grip certainly wasn't.

"A month from now, in the forest deep, you'll die as you came into this world—alone. The fear and shame that led you on the path will die as well. This I see, so it will be."

Abby stared at the woman, who'd had a vacant expression on her face only seconds before and was now smiling.

Granny MacLeod released Abby's hand and glanced from her to Hunter. The older woman's smile faded, no doubt in reaction to the glacial expression on Hunter's face and the shocked-spitless one on Abby's.

"I did it again, didn't I?" She gave Abby an apologetic smile. "I'm sorry if I frightened you. It's beyond my control. I have the second sight, you see. A gift passed down to the eldest female MacLeod of every generation." She looked at Hunter with compassion in her kind, wise eyes. "I'd not have you hurt again, lad. I hope whatever I've prophesied won't cause you more pain."

"I'm sure it won't. He'll be only too happy to get rid of me, although dying seems a little extreme." Abby forced a laugh that sounded completely fake.

Hunter turned away to load the groceries in the back of the truck.

"Granny, you promised you wouldn't touch anyone today," the younger woman said as she reached them. She made a face, then offered her hand, laughing when Abby stared down at it. "It's okay, I don't have the *gift*. My older cousin is supposedly in line for the honor. Bless her. I'm Sadie Gray, by the way," she introduced herself when Abby shook her hand. "And don't let Granny's prophecies freak you out. Yesterday, she told me I was pregnant and that I was going to be arrested on suspicion of kidnapping, if you can believe it."

"I wouldna be so quick to make fun of your granny's gift," Betty White's look-alike said with a pointed glance at Sadie's stomach.

The younger woman's jaw dropped. "Gran!" Then she looked down at her tight white T-shirt and denim shorts and grimaced. "Have you never heard of stress eating? I'm entitled to gain a few pounds after what I've been through."

"Hey, Sadie. Everything okay?" Hunter asked.

"Hey, Hunter. It's been awhile." She looked like she wanted to hug him but held herself back, raising a shoulder instead. "You know my brother. He's off to make his fortune and left me holding the bag. Again. This time he left me to run Highland Tours, his latest get-rich scheme that's barely breaking even. But who knows, I might sell out this weekend's farm tours." She held up a stack of flyers. "Walter called and said they need more. That's a good sign, right?"

"Do you mind?" Abby asked, holding out her hand for a flyer.

"Not at all. It's a shame Honeysuckle Farm can't be on the tour this year. It was always a popular stop."

"Really? Do people pay admission?" Abby asked, thinking this might be the answer to her money problems. At least enough to cover everyday expenses like food and cell phone bills.

* * *

Hunter leaned against the headrest of the driver's seat before starting the truck. He needed a minute to regroup. Granny MacLeod's prophecy had shaken him. As much as he'd like to follow Sadie's lead and brush it off as nothing, he couldn't.

Three years ago this past April, there'd been a party at Highland Brew before they'd headed to Fort Bragg to prepare for their upcoming tour. It had been loud, the beer flowing and music playing. They were all on a high. They were adrenaline junkies, addicted to the adventure, to making a difference. He'd been steering Sloane into a quiet corner to get five minutes alone with her when he'd felt a tug on his hand. It was Granny MacLeod, come to wish him well.

Every word of the chilling prophecy she'd uttered that night had come true.

Out of the corner of his eye, he watched as Abby went to buckle up. She stopped, her hand frozen in midair with the seat belt hanging from it, her eyes going wide.

Here it comes, he thought. He'd been wondering how long it would take once they were in the privacy of the truck for her to break down. He was surprised she'd held it together this long.

"My ice cream!" she cried. "It'll be melted. Would you mind if I went in and got another carton? Please." She made prayer hands. "I promise I won't be long. I'll even share it with you."

"Not five minutes ago you were told you have one month to live, and you're worried about your ice cream?"

"I wanted my ice cream before, but because of Granny MacLeod's prophecy, now I need it. Not that I really believe in that sort of thing. It's like I said earlier— I don't buy into the whole supernatural, vampire, time-travel kind of deal."

"She didn't say anything about time travel or vampires. She said you were going to die in the woods."

She stared at him.

"Sorry, that was stupid. The last thing you need is to be reminded of what she said. But you're right, you know. It's pseudo-science. There's no evidence that supports it. Scots are superstitious, especially the older generation who didn't grow up here."

He'd said the same to Sloane that night three years ago. He'd believed it then but he didn't now. He had to get Abby out of Highland Falls before the month was up. "Don't worry about your ice cream. I put it in a cooler. You're good."

"That's great, thank you," she said as she snapped her seat belt into place. "And there's no need to apologize. It probably looked like I was going to freak out because you brought up Granny MacLeod's prophecy, but it was actually the exact opposite. By repeating it the way you did, in that lovely blunt manner you have"—she grinned at him—"I figured it out. She wasn't seeing my future. She saw my past. I already died in the woods."

"Say what?"

"Okay, you'll have a hard time believing this, but I used to love the great outdoors. Maybe not as much as you, because you're extreme, but I really did enjoy traipsing through the woods. My dad and I used to hike every weekend. It didn't matter what the weather was like. We'd head out at first light and wouldn't make it home until the sun had disappeared on the horizon."

She looked out the passenger-side window as though remembering. "I was twelve. It was late September, and time had gotten away from us. It was getting dark when we began heading back down the trail. I'm not sure how it happened. I'd run ahead of my dad, and then, all of a sudden, the ground gave way beneath me. I don't remember anything after that. I was told I hit my head on the rockface before my twenty-foot free fall was broken by a tree. I had a stroke when search-and-rescue were carrying me down the trail. For a few minutes, my heart stopped. I slipped into a coma and didn't regain consciousness for two weeks."

The clumsiness, the spelling, the times where she rambled and lost focus all began to make sense.

She glanced at him. "You're putting it together now,

aren't you?" She lifted a shoulder. "It took a lot of doctors and nurses to put me back together again. A lot of money and time too."

"And a lot of grit and determination on your part, Abby. You don't recover from that type of injury without it." He knew that firsthand. One of his men had suffered a traumatic brain injury after an IED blew up their Humvee.

"It took two years for me to learn to walk and talk and function normally again. Or as close to normal as I'll ever be," she said with a self-deprecating laugh.

"Hey." He hesitated, then reached for her hand. It felt small and soft in comparison to his. He gave her fingers a gentle squeeze before releasing them. "Don't do that. What you've overcome is nothing short of a miracle, Abby."

"I know. It's just sometimes I wonder what my life would've been like if I hadn't fallen and had a stroke. Believe it or not, I was smart. Top of my class. Straight As. In spelling and reading, no less. And now...well, you know."

"You taught yourself to walk and talk again."

She smiled. "I had some help."

"But you did the work, and you didn't give up. Seems to me you can do whatever you set your mind to."

"I hope so. I told Sadie I'd have the farm ready for the tour this weekend."

"You didn't."

"I did. And why are you looking at me like I lost my mind?"

"Because..." Now that he knew her history, he'd be

more careful what he said to her. So instead of saying she had to have lost her mind to think putting the farm on the tour was a good idea, he said, "People take the tour to see a working farm, Abby. And in case you haven't noticed, Honeysuckle Farm is no longer a working farm. Liz used to sell pots of honeysuckle and products from her bees."

"She was a beekeeper?"

He nodded. "You didn't know?"

"No, I didn't. Weren't you listening to your aunt? I'm a horrible niece who had nothing to do with her great-aunt and was undeserving of her legacy."

"Right. And when Elsa said at least your father knew the value of family, you said she didn't know him very well."

"Obviously you don't have a problem with your memory."

"No, I don't. So what did you mean? I take it you and your dad had a falling-out."

"You could say that." She shrugged. "I might as well tell you. I've told you everything else. Maybe if you know the whole story you won't judge me so harshly. Don't bother denying it," she said when he opened his mouth. "I know you think I'm as bad as your aunt does. Only you keep your opinion to yourself. I mean, you don't say what you think of me out loud, but I can see it in your eyes sometimes."

"Yeah, I kinda got that when you told Granny Mac-Leod that I'd be happy to get rid of you. For the record, I wouldn't want to see you hurt in any way, Abby. And that's the truth."

"That's nice to know. Although I notice you didn't say you'd be sad to see me go."

"No, I didn't." He smiled.

She rolled her eyes. "Sometimes honesty is overrated, you know. Anyway, here's the truth: I do feel like a horrible niece. But after my dad left me and my mom, I didn't have anything to do with the Findlays. He disowned us so I guess you could say I disowned them. He left the day before my thirteenth birthday. I was going to surprise him. I could take a whole five steps without using my walker. It was silly to think he'd be proud of me. He loved the Abby I used to be, and he knew as well as I did that I'd never be that fearless, adventurous girl again. Then there were the hospital bills. I used to hear him fighting with my mom about them. If it weren't for me, they'd probably still be together."

He wished he'd never asked. "I'm sorry."

"No, I'm the one who's sorry. I shouldn't have dumped all of that on you."

"I asked. And, Abby, I think Liz would be glad she left you the farmhouse."

She sniffed and ran a finger under her eye. "That's the nicest thing you've said to me since we met. Thank you."

He leaned across her to open the glove box, patting inside for a package of tissues Liz had left in there on the last trip they'd made to the hospital for her chemo treatment. She'd gone fast, faster than any of them had expected. None of them had been ready for her to go. Least of all him.

He handed Abby the package, and she looked up at

him, her green eyes shiny. "You're not going to say anything else that will make me cry, are you?"

"Thinking about it. It's not really my business though."

"From my admittedly short time in Highland Falls, I couldn't help but notice people here don't seem to have a problem sticking their noses in everyone else's business. So lay it on me."

"It seems to me you have more in common with them than I do. My SOP—standard operating procedure—is to steer clear of everyone and their business. But I'm going to break my own personal rule." He seemed to do that a lot with her. Something he'd think about later. "You sound like you're blaming yourself for your dad walking away from you and your mom, Abby, and from my experience, I don't think that's the case. He blamed himself for your accident. Every time he looked at you, every time he saw you in pain and struggling to relearn what had once come easy to you, it ripped out another piece of his heart. I'm not saying it's right what he did but it sounds to me like the guilt was killing him and he thought you'd be better off without him. I know it's hard to hear, but as difficult as it was for you, you probably were."

Hunter knew he was right, and he knew that because he'd done the same thing himself.

Chapter Ten

♥

Whoever said confession was good for the soul was wrong. Abby had a list as long as her arm of the mistakes she'd made over the years, but confessing to Hunter ranked in the top five. He didn't bark at her anymore or look at her like she made him want to pull out his hair or roll his eyes. Or if he did, he was quick to cover his frustration with a solicitous smile, at least as solicitous as Hunter Mackenzie could be.

Yesterday was a perfect example. He'd been up on the ladder painting the living room ceiling, and she'd tripped on the tarp on her way to the kitchen, which sent her flying forward. Thankfully, not into the rungs of the ladder where Hunter stood but into the metal shelf where the paint tray sat. The paint tray tipped over and onto her head. She'd stood there, dripping in white ceiling paint, waiting for him to lose his mind.

No, not just waiting, hoping and praying that the Hunter she'd come to know and apparently really liked came back. Instead, she got the new Hunter. The one who helped clean her up enough to then carefully guide her upstairs because some of the paint had gotten into her right eye.

Once they reached the bathroom, he not only started the shower for her, he made sure the water temperature and pressure were just right. Then he laid out towels and shampoo. After which, he gave her one of his newly minted attentive smiles and suggested she have a nap. A nap! She'd never been more tempted to pitch a fit than she had been at that moment.

But how could she, right? He was being sweet and patient and kind. She'd have to be an ungrateful biatch to throw a temper tantrum. "And I'm not a biatch, am I, Boo?" she said as she filled Bella's water dish at the kitchen sink. She crouched to place it beside the pink princess food dish that was still full of food, then fixed the red bow on Bella's head.

This morning, Abby had decided to ignore Hunter's directive of not babying her dog and treating her as if she were a human child, dressing Bella in her adorable cherry-printed sundress.

Today was the farm tour after all, and she wanted Bella to look adorbs. Abby wore her sundress with the same cherry print as Bella's, but she'd added the white frilly apron she'd found in the kitchen drawer. She wanted to look farm-girl-ish.

She'd tied her hair back with a white kerchief to complete the look, and she was barefoot instead of wearing heels. As someone who was vertically challenged and had a slight shoe addiction, it was a huge sacrifice on her part to go barefoot. But she had a lot riding on today, and she wanted everything to go absolutely perfectly.

She kissed the top of Bella's head and reached up for a doggy treat on the counter. "This is the last one until you start eating your food, Boo. I know you miss Wolf, but you can't get yourself worked up over a man." As the farmhouse was now a construction zone, Hunter didn't want Wolf around.

Bella looked up from rooting around in her dog dish for her treat that Abby had hidden underneath the food in hopes of enticing her to eat. Her dog appeared to be as perturbed with Abby as Abby was with Hunter.

She sighed. "I know I'm one to talk, but it's different in my case. You have a crush on Wolf, and I don't have one on Hunter. Okay, so I'm not entirely immune to the man. Please, I have eyes. But I never should've told him about the accident and the stroke, or my dad. I never should've cried."

It had colored the way he treated her. He thought of her as a pathetic invalid now. Her mother, stepfather, and even Haven and Haley, despite being ten years younger, had coddled and pampered her and made excuses for her. It's why she'd never told anyone in LA about the accident, not even Chandler.

They just thought she was an uncoordinated klutz whose phone had the worst auto correct on the planet and that every so often she slurred her words, which they put down to the cocktails they had typically consumed at the time.

In LA, everything was superficial. It was all about who you were with, who you were wearing, what parties you attended. Who was in, who was out, what was in, and what was out. And for years, Abby had been one of the in-crowd. No one felt sorry for her there. She'd made it. She'd been someone. Until she wasn't.

She pushed the depressing thought away and washed her hands in the farmer's sink, distracting herself by focusing on the happy fact that the sink no longer leaked. She'd thought she'd have to replace the faucet and sink but Hunter had ticked it off her list two days ago. He'd fixed the stove too. Really, it was incredible how much he'd accomplished in such a short time. If she didn't know better, she'd think he was anxious to get rid of her.

The thought startled her. She was surprised and a little horrified to discover that a part of her actually believed these past few days that she and Hunter had spent in close quarters, working side by side toward a common goal—okay, maybe not so much side by side as she supervised and he worked—had changed the way he felt about her. Of course it hadn't. His true feelings for her were just one more thing he'd kept hidden from her the past few days.

At the sound of gravel crunching and then a truck door closing, Abby's stomach took a little dip. It was Hunter. She glanced at Bella. She hadn't dressed her up to get on his last nerve, but she kinda hoped it did. At the heavy clump of his boots on the porch, Bella perked up and moved to sit at the door, anxiously waiting for it to open. Which is why Abby hurried over to the oven to take out the doughnuts she'd made, even with three minutes left on the timer.

She didn't want to look as pathetic as her dog. Abby had been baking half the night and all morning in hopes of not disappointing the people on the tour. She'd used berries from the bushes behind the farmhouse in all the recipes. The kitchen table was covered in baked goods that she planned to sell today in order to raise some much-needed funds. Last night, she'd also put sale stickers on the furniture and knickknacks that she thought could legitimately pass for antiques.

She turned off the timer and opened the oven, rewarded with the enticing smell of vanilla and sugar filling the kitchen. She'd been a little worried that she'd misread the recipe when it called for her to bake instead of fry the doughnuts. But not only did they smell delicious, they were perfectly round and golden brown. She hadn't known she had a knack for baking until she'd made Elinor's scones for Hunter the other morning. But more than a knack, she actually enjoyed it. She found it relaxing and satisfying.

When she'd said as much to her mother on what seemed to have become their nightly FaceTime call, she'd given her a sad smile before reminding Abby they used to bake together all the time when she was young. But then Abby had the accident and they didn't have time to do the mother-daughter things they'd once loved. Her mother had been too busy working to pay the bills, and Abby had been putting all her time and effort into relearning to walk and talk so that her mother's sacrifices wouldn't be for nothing.

The side door opened as she was placing the tray on the cooling rack on the counter. She steeled herself for Hunter's reaction to her dog dancing at his feet. Beneath the black T-shirt that was molded to an upper body she couldn't keep her eyes from caressing, his chest expanded, and hers filled with hope. This was it, the moment they'd get back to normal.

But he didn't say anything. His hand stalled above Bella's head, and he turned his head to look at Abby's cherry-red painted toenails. Inch by inch, his eyes traveled up her body until his gaze met hers. They held for a brief moment, then he turned to pat Bella's head and say as he straightened, "Relax, rat."

Still feeling the effect of his slow perusal, that brief moment when his eyes held hers and butterflies took flight in her stomach, she didn't call him out for calling Bella a rat. It was a missed opportunity. Except now when he called her dog rat, it sounded more like a pet name than a curse word.

Without looking at her, Hunter lifted his chin at the doughnuts on the tray. "You've been busy."

"Do you want one? I just need to fill the center with the berries." She reached for the bowl of raspberries and blueberries that she'd tossed with granulated sugar.

"I'm good, thanks."

"Don't pretend you don't like my baking. You were humming when you ate my scones the other morning."

"What are you worked up about? I never said I didn't like your baking." He glanced around the kitchen and must've spotted the trays of baked goods covering the table because his eyes got the tiniest bit bigger before darkening with a flare of emotion that he quickly shut down. Which meant he was either angry or worried or just plain frustrated with her. He wasn't the only one. She was getting more ticked by the minute.

His eyes came back to hers. "I get your...*the* problem now."

She wanted to scream at the way he'd just edited himself.

"What did you do? Stay up half the night baking?" His eyes searched her face. "This is nut—You have enough pastries to open a bakery. Why don't you grab a nap before—"

She couldn't take it anymore. She tore off her oven mitt and tossed it on the counter, then put her hands on her hips. "A nap? You think I need a nap? Do I look like I need a nap, Hunter? Because I think I look pretty darn good. We both do, don't we, Bella Boo? Don't you think Bella looks cute, Hunter? Oh right, I'm not supposed to dress her like a human anymore. Why was that again?" She tapped her lips with her forefinger and then held it in the air. "Right, because she was dominating me."

She turned her back to him and blinked back angry tears. "And no, I don't plan on opening a bakery. I'm hosting the farm tour. You know the farm tour you were dead set against me taking part in but have barely said a word about since I told you I had a stroke!"

She turned to see him watching her with his arms crossed, his impressive biceps almost enough to stop her mid-rant, but then she caught sight of his raised eyebrow and marched to the fridge. She flung open the door and grabbed a container filled to the brim with blueberries. "I had to do something with all the berries you picked for me. Remember when you took over for me yesterday because two hours was all you deemed my fragile body able to handle?" She slammed the container onto the stove. "I'm not an invalid, Hunter."

He walked to the stove and picked up the container of berries, putting them back in the fridge.

"Don't you dare tell me I need a nap." She sniffed. "I'm not crying," she said when he pulled a tissue from the box on top of the fridge and handed it to her.

"I know." He leaned against the fridge, obviously waiting her out. "Let me know when you're ready to talk."

"I don't want to talk to you anymore. I told you everything, and you told me nothing, and it came back to bite me." She meant it, but she lost her resolve when she looked up at him. She didn't know what it was about Hunter that made her tell him things she'd never told anyone else. Even when her last confession had turned out so badly. "You changed after I told you about the accident. You're not being yourself with me."

"Maybe I am. Maybe this is who I really am."

She thought about that for a minute. "No, it's not. You're holding back. You're treating me like there's something wrong with me, and I hate it. I can look after myself. I've been doing it for years. I moved to LA when I was nineteen and made a life for myself, a really good life. And when that all fell apart, I lived in my car on the streets of LA for six months. I might not have thrived, but I did survive. And trust me, that's not easy to do when you have no one to turn to. I don't need your pity or your protection. I don't want either."

"What do you want?"

"I want you to be real. If I annoy the heck out of you or frustrate you or irritate you, I want you to tell me."

"You sure about that? Seems to me you didn't appreciate it when I did that either."

"Okay, so maybe you don't have to tell me every time I annoy you, because I seem to do that a lot."

"Not so much anymore."

"Really? Are you just saying that because you feel bad you made me cry?"

"No. I have no reason to feel bad. Seems to me you cry pretty easily. And all I was—"

"Hunter, that's a horrible thing to say! I rarely cry, and let me tell you, I've had plenty of reasons to cry. Besides, crying doesn't mean you're weak." She narrowed her eyes at him. "I know what you're doing. You're giving me exactly what I asked for, aren't you?"

"Yeah, I am. So be careful what you ask for, Abby." He moved into her and rested his big calloused hands on her shoulders. "And just so you know, I don't pity you or think of you as an invalid or as fragile. But now that I know you've suffered a traumatic brain injury and had a stroke, I'm going to tell you if I think you're pushing yourself too hard and when you should take a break."

"The accident was sixteen years ago, Hunter."

"Doesn't matter. You start having issues when you're tired or stressed. You have to listen to your body."

He might not like it if she listened to her body because sometimes, when she looked at him, her body suggested she do some very naughty things. She crossed her arms. "You went too far. You were smothering me and being overprotective."

He dropped his hands from her shoulders and crouched to gently tug his bootlace from Bella's mouth. "Fair enough. I don't think I was, but if that's how you feel, I'll back off."

"Really?"

"Yeah, and since we're being open and honest, I'll tell you again, the farm tour is a bad idea, and it's going to come back and bite Sadie, not you."

Abby walked to the kitchen counter. "I have things for them to look at and buy. I even dug up and potted some honeysuckle plants to sell. And I found a few jars of honey and some soap in the pantry."

"The honeysuckle plants you potted are already dead. You cut off the roots. And the honey's straight from the hive." At her blank look, he explained. "It's unprocessed, and it's been in there for at least a year, so it's probably gone bad."

"Really?" She shook her head, refusing to let him discourage her. He just didn't want a bunch of people traipsing around the farm. "They can pick blueberries and strawberries. You couldn't have picked all of them. And I have antiques for sale and my baking too. I have enough ingredients to make another batch of scones. I can do a baking demonstration." She should've thought of that before.

"It doesn't matter. It's too late for you to back out now. Sadie bumped Owen for you so I can't see him being willing to take your place."

"Owen as in Police Chief Owen?" she asked as she lifted the doughnuts from the baking sheet.

"Yeah. He owns the property adjacent to this one. He runs a Christmas tree farm."

"Does he sell Christmas stuff too?" she asked, thinking that if he did Sadie should've bumped her instead.

"No. Liz was always after him to diversify, but he said he was waiting until he retired."

Abby felt a little better about bumping Owen but not by much. She didn't want to let Sadie down. If Hunter would just let her show his carvings, the tour guests wouldn't care that Honeysuckle Farm was no longer a working farm. But she knew he wouldn't. He changed the subject every time she brought it up.

He gave Bella one last pat before standing and walking over to give the doughnuts a sniff. "They smell great. Save me one."

"Why don't you have one now? I have coffee on."

"Can't stay. I'm heading into town."

"Wow, twice in a matter of days. People are going to faint." She smiled and started spooning the berry filling into each doughnut's cavity. Some fell off, and she pushed it back in with her finger. "They'll think I worked my witchy Findlay magic on you."

He snorted. "Yeah, right. Thanks to you, my mother and sisters have arrived in Highland Falls. I have to be at Shane and Eden's in twenty minutes."

"You should've invited them here. I'd love to meet—" He didn't hide his grimace from her. "Sorry, I don't know what I was thinking." She ignored the twinge of hurt that he obviously didn't want her to meet his family and went back to spooning the filling into the doughnuts.

"You should probably put Bella in her crate. Safer for everyone that way."

She hated that he was right, hated it more that he didn't try to make an excuse about why he didn't want his family to visit. It was because of her. She'd seen how he reacted the other day in town when people assumed they were an item. Her throwing herself at him hadn't helped. She supposed she didn't blame him. "Okay, bye. Have a nice visit with your family."

He gave a noncommittal grunt as he opened the door to leave. "Abby." She looked up. "You were right, you look good."

She smoothed her hair back. "Really?"

"Yeah," he said, then started to laugh. "Except you just dragged blueberries through your hair."

Two hours later, Abby conceded that Hunter had been right. The tour of Honeysuckle Farm was a bust. She blamed it on the man wearing the Hawaiian shirt and orange Bermuda shorts. Out of the eight people on the tour—two seventysomething sisters, a mother with her daughter and two grandchildren, and Hawaiian Shirt Guy and his wife—he was the most vocal in venting his displeasure. He'd also just threatened to leave a one-star review for Highland Tours.

His wife gave Abby and Sadie an apologetic smile while waving her husband away.

They were standing in the strawberry patch, their berry-collecting baskets empty. Hunter must've picked every last ripe berry within a mile radius. Abby had spotted a bush of green berries and had triumphantly held up a branch, thinking she'd saved the day, but Sadie had slapped it out of her hand. The berries were poisonous.

"Oh no, the two sisters are looking from Hawaiian Guy to their phones," Abby whispered. "Wait, we have a chance. They're looking at us now. Smile and wave like they're your best friends in the world."

Abby nudged Sadie, who stood there with her arms crossed. She wore a red T-shirt with a yellow-and-green-plaid kilt with red lines, rolled-down wool socks, and cool black boots that had a Doc Martens vibe.

"I'm serious," Abby said, noting the expression on Sadie's heart-shaped face. "They have to feel like they have a personal connection with us and want us to succeed, or they're going to be sheep and follow Hawaiian Guy's lead. They'll leave . . . They're doing it right now," she said when they wouldn't make eye contact. "I can't believe they did that. They loved my berry doughnuts and my scone-making demonstration."

"Hawaiian Guy did too. He was like a vacuum, hoovering up every doughnut, scone, and cupcake in sight. I'm really sorry, Abby. I know you were hoping to make some money off the sale of your baking. I should've explained things better. I really suck at this tour operator thing."

"You absolutely do not. You're awesome. You're fun and knowledgeable and great with everyone, even Hawaiian Guy."

"I'm used to dealing with jerky men. Especially my baby brother, who once again conned me into helping him out. I always fall for his sob story."

Hunter had filled Abby in on Sadie's brother. He didn't have a lot of good things to say about Elijah Gray. Hunter didn't understand why Sadie always came back to Highland Falls to bail him out. She lived in Charlotte and had a good job as a graphic designer. Although she'd shared with Abby a little while ago that she'd quit her job because her boss had wanted more from her than her designs and didn't take kindly to the word *no*.

"You're a good sister, and you don't want to see him lose his business."

"He can't lose this business. If he does, he'll blame me like usual, and then I'm the one who has to bail him out. I've got enough to worry about."

Sensing genuine panic in Sadie's voice, Abby patted her arm. "Don't worry. We're going to turn this around right now and make sure Highland Tours gets rave reviews."

"Let them leave as many one-star reviews as they want. No one looks at them anyway."

"I hate to be the bearer of bad news, but as much as you don't think reviews matter, they absolutely do. Trust me. I drove an average car for Uber in LA when everyone else was driving Beemers and luxury SUVs, but my reviews were fantastic, and I got a ton of repeat business."

But this was way out of her wheelhouse. Not that she'd tell Sadie. Abby clapped her hands to drag the seventy-something sisters' attention from their phones, while at the same time racking her brain for an activity to wow the group. "All right, everyone. Let's put our phones away. We have a very special treat for you today."

"The bees! We're going to see the bees!" the little boy and girl cheered. "Can we wear the suit again? Please. Liz let us."

The children, their mother, and their grandmother took part in the tour every year. They were almost as vocal about Abby's failure to live up to their expectations as Hawaiian Guy. The grandmother, who apparently owned an antiques store, had given her professional opinion on every item Abby had for sale, ensuring that the only things Abby sold today were the apron she'd had on and a miniature oil painting to the two sisters for ten dollars.

Although the antique lady's daughter wanted to buy Abby's pink-patent-leather Louis Vuitton, and she hadn't been happy when Abby refused to sell, even when she offered her three hundred dollars. Abby knew she should've accepted the offer, but she just couldn't bring herself to part with the bag.

It would've felt too much like giving up on her dream. The pink-patent Louis Vuitton had been the first purse Abby had bought that wasn't a knockoff. She'd barely been able to afford knockoffs until she'd featured a day in her Hollywood life on her then six-month-old YouTube channel and it had gone viral. For her, the purse was a talisman, a tangible sign that if she'd made it once, she could make it again.

"I'm so sorry, but the hives are off-limits. We've had an infestation of killer bees." She fake-shivered. "Scary, right? But don't worry, this is way better and not as dangerous." Thankfully, an idea came to her just in the nick of time.

They'd go on a nature walk. She'd make a game out of it. Whoever spotted the most wildlife would win. She'd figure out their prize later.

"What is it? What are we going to see?" the little boy asked. Then something caught his attention in the meadow, and he pointed. "I want to go to the barn too."

Abby turned to see Hawaiian Guy opening the barn door.

Chapter Eleven

♥

Hunter stood beside his brother on the gravel drive, waving goodbye as his mother and sisters drove down Mirror Lake Road on their way back to Charlotte. It would take them four hours to get home. He wouldn't relax until he'd gotten the text that they'd arrived safely.

He filled his lungs with the warm air, laden with the sweet smell of the birch trees that populated this part of the forest, their pale green leaves rippling in the breeze. As far as he was concerned, there was nothing more peaceful than listening to the wind move through the trees. In the distance, he made out the low buzz of a chain saw and the faint smell of cedar mingling with pine. Someone was building a house on the Suttons' old property, he surmised from the direction of the sound.

Could be wrong though. It was the first time he'd been back here since leaving for his last tour. He'd bought a three-acre lot just up the road from Shane's. Hunter had planned to build a log house for him and Sloane, with plenty of room for the three kids they'd eventually hoped to have. He should've known better. If war had taught him anything, it had taught him not to plan for the future.

The day he'd come home and ended his engagement to Sloane, he'd signed the lot over to her and her mother. From what he could see, they hadn't made use of the property. He thought that was a shame. It was a beautiful piece of land set in a grove of old-growth pine and had a spectacular view of Mirror Lake.

His brother clapped him on the back as the black SUV's taillights faded from view. "That wasn't so hard, was it?"

"Easy for you to say. You sat back laughing and drinking beer while I was interrogated for two hours by our mother and our two sisters, who've grown up to be even bigger pains in the asses than when they were teenagers." He rubbed the heel of his palm against his chest. "They gave me heartburn and a headache."

"That's what happens when you avoid them for almost a year."

He stopped rubbing his chest to look at his brother. "It hasn't been that long."

"Yeah, it has."

He thought back over the past year. He'd spent months looking after Liz and then months helping Owen through his grief. The year before that, he'd rarely seen anyone. It was Owen and Liz who'd slowly coaxed him back into society, if only a society of three. Not that his family would think the past year was an improvement over the last one.

Guilt caused the muscles in his chest to tighten, and he tried once again to rub the ache away. They deserved better. "You wanna remind me why I accepted the invite to this get-together?"

"You knew if you didn't, they'd track you down at the farm, and they wouldn't care if they couldn't find you. As long as they had some one-on-one time with your new girlfriend, they'd be happier than pigs in—"

"Yeah, and I wonder who told them about Abby. Your job isn't keeping you busy enough if you have time to spread..." He trailed off at Shane's shocked expression. "What?"

"I didn't realize you guys were really a thing. Wow, that's probably the best news I've had—"

Now it was Hunter's turn to stare at his brother. "What are you talking about? We're not 'a thing.' I'm helping her with the farmhouse. Nothing more." The last words he'd said to her mocked him.

She had looked good. Better than good, if he were being honest. But that's not why he'd told her. She'd been disappointed that he hadn't been onboard with her meeting his mother and sisters—so not onboard as to rate a *no way, no how*—and she'd read that on his face because she'd asked him not to hide his feelings from her. She wanted to keep it real so that's what he'd done.

But he couldn't make himself walk away knowing he'd put the hurt in her eyes, so he tried to make her feel better. Which made him wonder if he didn't have a bit of a thing for Abby Everhart after all.

He tried listing everything about her that drove him crazy—the woman never shut up, she talked to perfect strangers as if they were long-lost friends, she never stopped asking questions, she was overly affectionate and upbeat—but all he saw was the smile she gave him today.

It was a smile that could light up the world, and these past few days that smile had been lighting up his. And when she messed up and got that look in her eyes, it messed with his head and made him want to take her in his arms and kiss the hurt away. But no way was he getting that close to anyone again. He wasn't cut out for relationships. He wouldn't allow himself to be responsible for someone else's happiness.

He sensed his brother watching him and decided it was time to leave. He glanced up at the sky. "I should probably get going. We're in for a storm."

"You're so much like Dad it's scary."

"Come on, I'm not like Dad." He'd loved his father. There'd been a time when he'd been honored to be compared to him. Like Shane, their dad had worked for the USDA Forest Service. No one knew the woods like him or could track like him, although Hunter thought the past two years had put his skill level close to their father's.

"Maybe you don't drown your guilt in a bottle but you hide away on Honeysuckle Ridge letting it eat away at you. Don't kid yourself, big brother. You blame yourself for Danny the same way Dad blamed himself for Robbie. The old man didn't think he deserved to be happy after that, and neither do you. It's bullshit. There was nothing any of us could've done that day to save Robbie."

He held Hunter's gaze, a hint of fire in his navy eyes. Shane didn't lose his temper often, but he was close, so Hunter kept his mouth shut and let him talk. He figured he owed him that much.

"Don't think I don't know that you've taken on some of that yourself. I get it; there was a time when I thought I could've saved Robbie too. We can't help it. It's in our DNA. Every Mackenzie comes out of the womb believing they're meant to save the world. But Danny? Come on, Hunt. There was nothing you could've done differently." Shane put his hands on Hunter's shoulders and leaned in to rest his forehead against his. "It's got to stop, big brother. You can't go on like this. It's killing Mom."

Hunter jerked back. "What the hell are you talking about? Don't try to guilt me, Shane. I was here today. She's fine. She's happy. She's got Sam, the girls, grandbabies on the way, and you and Eden."

"You ever heard the saying *You're only as happy as your least happy child?*" Shane's lips quirked, and he shrugged. "Okay, I know it's corny, but Eden said it, and she's usually right about this kind of thing. I have an incredibly smart wife."

His brother was so in love with his wife that it was almost painful to be around them. "I don't know about that. She married you."

Shane laughed, then sobered. "I miss you. The guys do too." He opened his mouth to say something else but closed it when he saw Eden walking toward them.

She smiled and slipped an arm around Shane's waist. "What are you guys doing hanging out here? You're missing out on a great view down by the lake. A group of women hikers have decided to go skinny-dipping."

His brother laughed. "That's very thoughtful of you,

honey. Should I be worried that you're encouraging me to check out naked women?"

"They're not for you to check out. They're for your brother to. Come on, I have a bottle of Highland Brew's latest craft beer on ice for you, Hunter."

"Hey, wait a minute. I thought that was for me." His brother grimaced.

Something was up. If Hunter wasn't mistaken, Shane grimaced because his wife pinched his waist. "What's going on? Don't lie to me, Eden. You're easy to read."

"I'm not that easy to read. Just ask your brother."

Hunter crossed his arms, fully intending to stay there all night if he had to. He noticed Eden's white-knuckled grip on her phone. "Who called you? What's going on that you're trying to keep me from leaving? It's Abby, isn't it? It has to be. I haven't known a moment's peace since—"

"No, it's not... Well, yes, indirectly it involves Abby, but she didn't do anything wrong." She glanced at her husband and raised her shoulders. "I couldn't stop them. I tried."

Hunter's eyes went wide. "Oh no, do not tell me my mother and sisters are on their way to the farm."

"I'm sorry. But honestly, it's your fault, Hunter," Eden said.

"How is it my fault?" he shot over his shoulder as he jogged to his truck.

"You actually talked to them."

He turned to look at her. "I always talk to them. I mean, I might take a while to answer their messages, but I eventually do." Unless he heard something in their voices that concerned him, and he called right back.

"No. I mean you gave more than your usual mono-syllabic answers. You hardly grunted or snorted. Hunter, you carried on an actual conversation. And you...you smiled." Eden looked like she might cry.

Hunter shook his head as he got into his truck. When his brother joined him, he said, "There's something wrong with your wife."

"She's a little more emotional than usual," his brother said as he powered down the passenger-side window. "Don't worry, honey. Everything will be fine. Why don't you have a nap? Lie down on the chaise on the deck."

"You've done it now," Hunter said, thinking of Abby's reaction earlier today. "I thought you'd be better at this. How long have you been married now?"

"What are you talking about?" Shane said, smiling when Eden nodded and mouthed, *I love you*.

"Forget I said anything." He should've known Abby's reaction wouldn't be the same as most people's.

"No way. I have a feeling this'll be interesting. Come on. Tell me."

"It's just that Abby hates it when I tell her to have a nap." He glanced at his brother. "She thinks I'm being overprotective."

"So, what's wrong with that?"

Hunter was about to say *I know, right*, but then his brother added, "It just shows you care." And Shane was clearly fighting back a laugh.

Hunter scowled at him "Let it out before you hurt yourself."

"I'm sorry, but come on. You have to admit it's pretty funny that you've fallen for a woman like Abby."

"Just because I'm concerned about her getting enough rest doesn't mean I'm falling for her." He went off-road in hopes of cutting off his mother at the pass. "And what do you mean *a woman like Abby*? She comes off as a bit flaky, but she's not. If you knew what she's dealt with—"

"Once again, you prove me right. *Oaf.*" He put a hand on his head. "Seriously? Are you so worried about Mom and the girls meeting Abby that you're willing to risk our lives?" At Hunter's raised-eyebrow glance, Shane said, "All right, so maybe not our lives but definitely your shocks. Anyway, Mom and the girls will love Abby. She's warm and sweet—"

"Not helping."

"She is, and that's what I was getting at. I wasn't dissing her. It's just that she's all bubbly and light and super friendly and chatty, and you're...not." He laughed. "She's your exact opposite whereas Sloane was the feminine version of you. The you before your last tour."

He didn't want to talk about Sloane. Anytime he did, the guilt and shame became unbearable. He'd failed her and Danny. They were twins—Sloane the older by ten minutes. They'd moved to Highland Falls in grade school, and within days, the three of them had been inseparable.

He'd heard Sloane had left town a couple weeks after he'd broken their engagement. She'd been a cop and transferred to Charlotte. Rumor had it her mother blamed

Hunter for the loss of both of her children, as Sloane rarely came home.

"Just stop, okay, Shane. I—" he began as pulled onto Honeysuckle Ridge Road.

"Right, we're not supposed to talk about Sloane or Danny or Afghanistan or how damn lucky we are that you came back alive. We mourn the men and women who didn't come back as much as you do, but don't expect us not to celebrate the fact that you did. You wanna know why Mom and the girls risked you disowning them over this? Because they saw in your eyes what we've all seen since Abby arrived in Highland Falls. Life, brother, and there was no way they were leaving town until they met the woman who put it there."

Hunter turned onto the road leading to the farm. At the sight that greeted him his hands strangled the steering wheel and his blood pressure skyrocketed. Beyond the tour bus and the black SUV parked near the farm, people crawled in and around the barn like ants, invading his space.

"I'm going to kill her," he muttered. He pressed on the gas, dust and stones kicking up under the tires as he sped down the gravel road. The truck bounced when he went over the small rise on a rutted path to the side of the meadow. Everyone turned, including his mother and sisters and the woman who'd just finished hugging them. Their eyes went wide when he slammed on the brakes, and the truck rocked back and forth.

He left the door hanging open as he strode from the truck and his brother staring at him whispering, "What the hell?" And then as though Shane's shock cleared and he'd figured out who Hunter was about to kill, he shouted, "Hunter, wait! Let's talk about this."

"No." He jabbed his finger at Abby, who held up her hands.

"I'm sorry. I'm sorry. Please, just let me explain."

He bent at the waist to put his face in hers. "This is mine. My space, my barn, my meadow, and you were warned what would happen if you let anyone in here." He caught a flash of Hawaiian print coming out of the barn and turned his head. "Get the hell off my property now." He straightened. "All of you." Then he stabbed his finger at Abby again. "Don't you or your dog set one foot or one paw on my property ever again. We're done."

"But, Hunter, you don't understand. Everyone hated the tour, and they were going to give Sadie one-star reviews, and she can't afford one-star reviews. No matter that she thinks she can, she can't. I can't tell you why Highland Tours' success is so important to her because she told me in confidence—"

"Stop. I don't care. I don't care about you or anyone else. Just get the hell out of here."

"Hunter Mackenzie, that is enough," his mother said, placing a protective arm around Abby's shoulders. His sisters, who used to look at him like he was their hero, shook their heads and joined their mother to support Abby. His brother did the same.

"I know you're mad, and you have every right to be. No, he does. He really does," Abby said to the murmurs of disagreement coming from his family and the small crowd gathered outside the barn. "But your art, your incredibly gorgeous and ferocious work, deserves to be seen." She gestured to their audience. "You and your woodwork saved the tour. Everyone is in awe of your talent, Hunter. I've had four offers for the bear alone. They're good offers. I mean really, really good. You could make a—"

He pulled his cell phone from his back pocket, punched in Owen's number, and brought the phone to his ear. As soon as the chief answered, Hunter held Abby's gaze and said, "I need you to come to the farm and arrest Abby Everhart for trespassing, breaking and entering, and whatever else you can charge her with."

Chapter Twelve

♥

Late that same afternoon, feeling dejected and defeated, Abby trudged back across the meadow toward the farmhouse, inadvertently crushing the fragrant wildflowers beneath her feet. Hunter's truck was where he'd left it earlier, but he didn't answer when she'd knocked and called through the barn door. She didn't dare open it. She was nervous just being there.

Nothing about today had gone the way she'd hoped. After sharing earlier with Hunter how he was making her feel and him seeming willing to change his solicitous ways, she'd had pie-in-the-sky hopes for the day.

Riding high on Hunter's *You look good* compliment and the fact that her berry doughnuts were so delish, she'd eaten two instead of the one she'd allotted herself. She'd even gone so far as to believe her luck had finally changed.

Just minutes before the tour bus had arrived, she'd done a visualization exercise. She'd imagined herself waving goodbye to the enthusiastic and happy tour guests with fistfuls of money in her hands. The reality didn't even come close. She hadn't been able to wave goodbye to Sadie and the terrified tour guests because her hands were handcuffed behind her back, and there wasn't a single dollar bill in either one of them. Not even the two sisters' ten-dollar bill.

At the last minute (like no exaggeration—they were standing on the tour bus steps), the two sisters decided they didn't want either the white ruffle apron or the tiny oil painting and demanded their money back.

Abby sighed as a cool wind swooped down from the mountains to swallow the warm, fragrant breeze and whip her hair around her face as she continued her trek back to the farmhouse. Unable to use her hands—she had Bella in one arm and a container of berry doughnuts in the other—she tried shaking her hair off her face but it was stuck to her tears. Like literally stuck because the glue she'd used to apply the fake eyelashes had somehow run down her cheeks along with her tears. So much for her hope that the eyelashes would mask her swollen eyes.

She tripped over something in the meadow and whimpered "Please be a stick. Please be a stick" but it was soft and a little squishy and felt nothing like a stick. Still, she didn't hear it hiss so there was that. She did a nervous dance anyway and then picked up her pace.

Lifting her right arm, she used Bella to push the hair from her eyes. "Thanks, Boo." She sniffed, and Bella went to lick her. Abby held her away from her. "Sorry, baby. I appreciate the love, I really do. But those were cheap fake eyelashes, and I don't want you to get sick on the glue." She blinked her left eye, trying to get the

narrow black strip of eyelashes that was obscuring her
vision to fall off as she walked on.

A gust of wind swirled by and nearly blew her off her
feet. Once she'd regained her balance, she glanced at the
ominous dark clouds chasing each other across the sky.
"We might end up in Oz before the night is over, Boo.
I'm sure Hunter would be thrilled." She had a flashback
of him yelling at her and sniffed back more tears as
everything he'd said and everything she'd felt in that
moment came rushing back.

But no matter how much he'd hurt her feelings,
he had every right to be furious at her. She never
should've allowed his space to be invaded. In her
defense, it hadn't been entirely her fault. Except she'd
been almost glad when Hawaiian Guy had opened the
barn door and introduced the tour group to the wonders
of Hunter's magical world. She'd wanted the tour to
be a success for Sadie's sake...and, yes, indirectly for
hers. She didn't like to fail at anything, and her portion
of the farm tour had definitely been a bust until then.
But in the end, all her good intentions were for nothing,
thanks to Hunter.

She supposed she shouldn't be surprised at the out-
come. With her, good intentions were often tied to her
gut instincts, which inevitably led to trouble and, the last
two times, the threat of jail time. She needed a T-shirt
with the saying THE ROAD TO HELL IS PAVED WITH
GOOD INTENTIONS stamped on her chest as a reminder. Maybe then she'd think twice before embarking on
another crusade.

The only reason she wasn't in jail was because

Hunter's mother and sisters and brother had intervened. They were really nice, and Abby appreciated them sticking up for her. Except she had a feeling they might've indirectly made matters worse. But really, how much worse could they get? Hunter hated her, and he wasn't going to help her with the house anymore.

At the reminder, her gaze flitted from the crooked porch to the tin roof rattling in the wind. Hunter had done a temporary fix to the roof on account of her lack of funds. He'd suggested she talk to the Realtor at Home Sweet Home to see if putting on a new one was worth the time and the money she didn't have. She'd called and left a message but still hadn't heard anything back. She was pretty sure she knew the reason why—Hunter's aunt Elsa.

Abby imagined the older woman was thrilled that her nephew would no longer have anything to do with her. Then again, maybe Abby didn't have to worry about Hunter's aunt putting up roadblocks anymore. Now Elsa Mackenzie probably considered Abby selling out worth it to protect Hunter. It was funny, but right then, Abby wasn't as worried about the work that needed to be done or selling the farmhouse as she was about Hunter never forgiving her.

Drops of rain splattered on her nose and cheeks, and she took off at a run, certain with the way her luck had been of late that those swollen black clouds were about to unleash a rainstorm of biblical proportions.

No sooner had the thought popped into her head than the heavens opened in a torrent of wind and rain. Tucking Bella close, she used the container of berry doughnuts to protect her dog, wondering why she couldn't be right about something other than the weather.

In the few minutes that it took for her to reach the porch, Abby was soaked. Her hair was plastered to her head, her sundress to her body. And Bella, well, she kinda looked like a drowned rat. "At least Hunter won't be around to tease you, baby," she said as she juggled Bella and the container to open the door.

As soon as she got inside and closed the door, Abby put Bella down. Big mistake, she thought when her dog shook her way through the living room to the kitchen, spraying water as she went. Abby hurried over to the floral couch to grab a couple of towels out of the laundry basket.

She'd assumed her great-aunt didn't have a washer and dryer and hadn't thought to ask Hunter, who hadn't thought to share when he saw her doing laundry in the kitchen sink yesterday. She'd found the almost-new stacked washer and dryer in a closet earlier today when she'd been on the hunt for another platter. Except she'd forgotten her clothes were still on the clothesline. It wasn't until the little boy and his sister pointed out her underwear and bra flapping in the breeze during the tour that she remembered.

How did the pioneers do it? she wondered as she towel-dried her face and hair with the scratchy, hard towel. It smelled nice though. She turned on the kitchen light and mopped up the floor, then used the other towel to dry off Bella.

Once she was finished, Abby took them to the laundry closet. "Okay, Boo, I need a hot shower," she said when she returned.

The *ping* of an incoming message stopped her mid-stride. Praying it was Hunter, she hurried back to the kitchen counter. She looked at the screen. Elinor had texted her. She'd received the pictures of Abby's baking that she'd sent hours before.

I must say, I'm terribly impressed, Abby. You did a marvelous job. I'm sorry I didn't respond sooner. We've just unloaded the last of my boxes at Kate's.

Instead of responding by text, Abby called. A text seemed so impersonal. She felt horrible that she hadn't checked to see how Elinor was doing today of all days. "I'm so sorry!" she said as soon as Elinor picked up. "I totally forgot today was your last day." And she'd honestly expected Chandler to come to his senses and keep Elinor on. She'd worked for his family since he was a little boy, and she'd lived in the guesthouse on the property for just as long. But it seemed like whatever Juliette wanted, Juliette got. "Are you okay?"

"I am. Thank you for asking, dear. But truthfully, it would have been harder if not for Juliette being an absolute horror the entire week."

"I'm sorry she was so awful to you." And sorrier that Chandler had let her get away with it. Honestly, Abby didn't know what was wrong with him. "After your decades of loyalty and service to the family, you deserve better." It probably didn't speak well of Abby, but she was secretly pleased Elinor didn't like Juliette. "I hope Chandler gave you a huge retirement bonus."

"I would have settled for a small one, but, as I understand it, the company is having financial difficulties. I gather there's a problem with the new shampoo and conditioner upon which they've built their ad campaign. Chandler promised that, as soon as things turned around, he'd fulfill the agreement his parents made with me. But Juliette told him he wasn't legally obligated so I'm not counting on it."

Abby imagined that the company's financial difficulties were responsible for Juliette being an absolute horror. "I can't help but feel I'm to blame for you not getting your bonus. If not for me, the company wouldn't have had to create a new shampoo and conditioner and ad campaign in the first place. I'm so sorry, Elinor. These days I can't seem to do anything right."

"What happened? Did the furniture and bake sale not go well?"

"It was a bust, actually, and worse, I messed up badly with Hunter."

"Is that the handsome man with the beard?"

"Yes, he's the one who's been helping me get the house ready for sale, remember?" She'd snuck a picture of him the other day when he'd been painting the living room ceiling and sent it to Elinor. Now that she thought about it, that may have been the reason she'd tripped over the tarp and ended up covered in ceiling paint.

"Of course. How could I have forgotten? Kate was quite entranced with the man. But speaking of forgetting, I've been meaning to tell you that, when Juliette had Tiffany over for drinks yesterday afternoon, I left out the photo of you with the men in kilts. Tiffany spotted it straightaway and was pea-green with envy. So bravo, your plan worked exactly as you'd hoped. She couldn't stop talking about the photo. She wanted to know where exactly it had been taken and how you'd met the men."

No, that wasn't exactly what she'd hoped would happen. She didn't want Tiffany asking questions. "You didn't tell her the truth, did you?" Abby tried to push down the panic that she heard in her voice and felt in the pit of her stomach.

"I may have embellished a tad. I told her that while you were no longer living the life in LA, you were certainly living it in Highland Falls. I'm surprised you haven't heard from her, actually. Although Juliette made it clear she wasn't happy about Tiffany's interest in you or how well I said you were doing. No doubt Tiffany doesn't wish to find herself on Juliette's bad side. Which I'm afraid I can relate to, as no doubt you can too, Abby."

She nodded, then remembered she was on the phone. "Sadly, I can."

As someone who'd been on Juliette's bad side for almost a year, Abby totally understood how Tiffany felt. And if the new lines weren't doing well, Abby was most likely still on Juliette's bad side. So the last thing she wanted was to draw the attorney's attention. Abby didn't trust Juliette not to mess with her life. It was already messy enough, thank you very much.

Honestly, she didn't know what had possessed her to ask Elinor to print off the photo and wave it under Tiffany's nose. *Oh, please, of course you know.* She rolled her eyes at herself. She'd done it to make Tiffany jealous. What she didn't understand is why her once-best friend's opinion mattered to her.

Okay, so she knew that too. She just wished those

feelings from back in her high school days weren't so deeply embedded in her psyche that she couldn't get rid of them. It was almost a decade since she'd graduated. You'd think she'd be able to let it go. She was no longer the girl who didn't fit in or have any friends...Oh my gosh, she was so that girl! She no longer fit in in LA, and she didn't fit in here, as today had so clearly shown.

And friends? Other than her sisters, who she wasn't sure counted because they were family, and maybe Elinor, the one person she'd begun to think might be a friend had tried to have her arrested. And, as Puppy-Gate had proven, Tiffany and the Bel Air Bs weren't her true friends either. Right then, she realized just how incredibly hurt she'd been when they'd chosen Chandler and Juliette over her. Sometimes it really did feel like the people who she cared about abandoned her when she messed up.

She returned her attention to Elinor and the reason Abby had called her in the first place. They talked about the older woman's plans for the future. Elinor sounded upbeat, which alleviated some of Abby's guilt. She was carrying around so much of it right now that her shoulders sagged under the weight.

"Kate's yelling at me so I'd best go and get some of these boxes unpacked. Just remember, Abby, it's only when it's dark that you can see the stars. I'm sure your young man will forgive you."

"He's not really my young man, but from your lips to God's ears that he forgives me, Elinor. Don't you and Kate overdo it."

Abby had barely gotten out her goodbye when Haven

FaceTimed her. Her sisters had decided to buy one phone and share it. Gorgeous, brilliant, kind, and fiscally responsible? No one should be that perfect. She accepted the call without thinking, and she knew she should've thought when Haven and Haley appeared looking absolutely stunning in the matching Tory Burch ivory silk maxidresses Abby had bought them last summer.

They stared at her, crying out at almost the same time, "Abby, what happened? You look like—" They glanced at each other as though searching for a word that wouldn't make her feel worse than she obviously looked.

There was no way she'd tell her sisters what a mess she'd made of things. "Nothing serious. I just touched something in the garden that I'm allergic to, and my eyes swelled."

Her sisters leaned forward as Abby inched back and nearly tore the muscles in her arm holding the screen as far away from her face as possible. Sometimes she hated FaceTime. Why couldn't her family have a normal phone call anymore?

"Oh, wow, Abs. That's really bad. Your eyes are almost swollen shut. They look—"

"Not good, I know. It didn't help that I got caught in a torrential downpour." She was losing the battle to keep her cheerful smile in place so she turned the phone in the direction of the dining room window. At least the weather outside was backing her up, she thought. Although she could've just as easily held up the phone for them to listen to the wind and rain battering the tin roof.

"Um, Abs, that storm looks pretty bad. Did you listen to the weather report?" Haley asked.

Haven nudged her sister. "I'm sure it's fine. She doesn't need a weather report. She's got Hunter." She smiled at Abby. "Now tell us, how was the farm tour?"

"It—it was..." Her bottom lip began to tremble, and she clutched it between her teeth to make it stop.

"Aww, Abs, don't cry. It can't be that bad," Haven said, sounding like she might cry too.

Her sister's sympathy broke the last of Abby's control over her emotions, and she sobbed out her story. Ten minutes later, curled up on the couch with Bella in her lap, she dabbed at her eyes with a pillowcase from the laundry basket.

"So I've ruined everything. I have no—" She stopped herself from saying she had no money because they'd feel guilty and offer her some. "No one to help with the house now." She rubbed her cheek against Bella's head and waited for the pep talk she was sure would follow. No doubt her sisters would tell her how awesome she was and that Hunter had overreacted and would come around. And she'd soak up every ounce of their sympathy because she could really use some right now. It had been hard retelling the story to her sisters. She'd relived every horrible, embarrassing moment of it.

"Abs, how could you? After everything he's done for you."

Stunned, Abby stared at Haley.

"You know, just because you think his woodwork is incredible and deserves to be seen doesn't give you the right to invade his space."

"Hals—" Haven tried to interrupt her twin.

"No, I won't stop. Can you imagine how Hunter felt

seeing all those people going into his home without his permission? Just think about it from his perspective, Abs. Not yours. You're crazy-outgoing, a total extrovert. You love people and parties, the bigger the better and the more the merrier. In Hunter's shoes, you would've been over the moon that someone thought your work was so fabulous it deserved to be seen by the whole world, but he's the exact opposite of you."

Abby continued to stare at her sister but not in shock. "You're absolutely right," she whispered. "I did feel horrible for what I'd done, but honestly, I didn't truly understand his reaction until just now. Thank you, Hales. It's not easy to hear that I'm a horrible, unfeeling biatch from my sister, but I'm glad you told me. I really did need to hear it."

"You're not a horrible, unfeeling biatch, because we wouldn't love a horrible, unfeeling biatch as much as we love you, but you have to make him understand how sorry you are."

"I will. I'll figure out a way. Somehow." Because as much as she wanted to, he didn't want anything to do with her. And she had a feeling that, if Hunter Mackenzie didn't want to be found, he wouldn't be. "And now that the farm tour was a bust, I have to figure out how to make money." She held up her hand when her sisters opened their mouths. "No. We've already had this conversation. I just have to find someone in Highland Falls who'll hire me."

"What about the tour bus lady?" Haven suggested. "You said she was really nice."

"Sadie's great, but she's hardly making enough money

to pay herself. And after today's fiasco, she's not going to get any referrals from the tour." She was just one more person Abby owed. "And honestly, given the influence that Hunter's aunt Elsa seems to hold over this town, I doubt very much that anyone will hire me."

"So do what you did when you moved to LA. You were only nineteen. You didn't know anyone, and you had nowhere to live and barely any money. With everything you've learned in the past nine years, you should be able to make money on a new YouTube channel almost right away," Haley said.

"It's a great idea, but first, as part of the settlement with Chandler, I'm legally not allowed, and second, I'm stuck in the middle of nowhere. It's not like people are going to tune in to watch me bake scones and fix up this place."

"Haley's right. This is exactly what you need to do. And you can. No, just hear me out," Haven said when Abby went to object. "First, Abby Everhart is not allowed to use social media to profit in any way."

"Um, Haven, the NDA, remember?"

"I'm pretty sure no one is taping this conversation, but anyway, it's kinda easy to figure out why you disappeared from social media. All anyone had to do was put two and two together. But you don't want to be Abby Everhart, anyway."

"I don't?"

"No, you told us you have to reinvent yourself and here's your opportunity."

"I meant I had to reinvent myself for LA, not here."

"When life gives you lemons, make lemonade." Haven

smiled. "You said that when we spilled yellow paint on your green dress."

Abby laughed. "I remember; you were ten. But it was easier to turn the yellow blobs of paint into lemons than it will be to turn Honeysuckle Farm into something YouTube worthy."

"No, it won't. You always thought that the reason you became a YouTube sensation was that you can intuit what the next big thing will be, and you absolutely can, but that's not why over forty million people subscribed to your channel and watched your videos. It was because of you, Abs."

"Haley's right. Abby Everhart Does Hollywood didn't go viral because people wanted to see the highlights of LA. They wanted to see them through your eyes. You're funny and fun, and it helps that you're cute and klutzy too. People can relate to you. They were cheering you on when you dragged your butt up the hillside to the Hollywood sign wearing the Marc Jacobs wedge sneakers you declared would be big the following year. But they didn't tune in because you were absolutely right. They tuned in because when you posed by the sign you tripped on your shoelace and rolled down the hill."

Haley laughed. "That was the best, and your day making sushi at the food truck you were promoting was a close second."

"But your fall in the pond and being bitten by a copperhead snake could totally outdo either one of those," Haven said.

"They were not funny!" Abby protested, then thought back to the day she met Hunter, and her lips twitched.

"Okay, so mine and Hunter's first meet was kinda funny. But there's no way I'm reenacting it for a video."

"But that's the thing, the farm and Highland Falls are rife with opportunity for you," Haley said.

"If you mean rife with the opportunity to be stung by a venomous spider or snake or eaten by a bear, then you'd be right."

"Any good story has to have an element of death, so people will be *dying* to follow your adventures." Haley laughed. "You can call it City Girl Goes Country or Abby Does Highland Falls instead of Abby Does Hollywood."

Haley might not be laughing if she heard Granny MacLeod's prophecy, Abby thought. Although it could make for an interesting opening. She could do a teaser trailer to get people interested. The thought surprised her. She was actually considering doing this. "There's one problem. I'm only here until I sell the house."

"Well that could take some time, which is a good thing because you can make a ton of videos and then you'll have all the content you need to keep your channel going when you're back in LA," Haley said.

"Or you might want to stay. What?" Haven said at the face Abby made. "You might. You haven't given it a chance. Anyway, Haley's right, death sells, but so does sex and sexy highlanders. We showed our friends the picture of you and the guys in their kilts, and they were ready to pack their bags and come for a visit. Which we totally are, by the way. We're coming for the Highland Games, and don't say you won't be there. It's like a month away."

"That's it." Abby straightened on the couch, feeling a tiny sliver of optimism and excitement. "I couldn't see the hook, but now I can."

"You're going to do it! She's going to do it!" The twins squealed at almost the same time, then high-fived each other.

"I'm going to do it." She smiled. "And it's thanks to the two of you. I mean, I have to figure out my new persona, find some equipment, and I probably should have someone else register it. No, not you guys," she said when her sisters raised their hands. "You'd be too easy to trace back to me."

"What about Sadie?" Haley asked. "You said she's a graphic designer, and you like her."

"I do, and I owe her, so this would be the perfect opportunity to repay her for ruining today's tour. I can promote Highland Tours and she can help me with the channel. I'm going to call her right now."

As soon as she got off the phone with her sisters, she called Sadie. It took her no time at all to get the other woman onboard. She even gave Abby the perfect event to video and to make some money at.

Every year the town celebrated Summer Solstice on the Village Green. According to Sadie, Liz always had a booth where she sold her products from Honeysuckle Farm. Sadie checked the vendor listings for this year, and Abby's aunt was still listed. So she could use her booth and sell her baked goods to earn some money. Better yet, Sadie even had some of the equipment Abby would need and knew of a place where she could rent the rest.

After she disconnected, Abby held up Bella and

kissed her nose. "I don't want to jinx it, Boo, but maybe Elinor's right. Maybe I had to go through all the crappy stuff this past year to get me here."

Abby had barely gotten the words out of her mouth when a jagged flash of lightning out the living room window was followed less than a second later by a violent boom of thunder that rocked the house. The kitchen lights blinked out, and she was left sitting in the near dark with her dog. She hoped it wasn't a sign of things to come, or the Universe's commentary on her new idea.

Chapter Thirteen

♥

Another bolt of lightning and roar of thunder sent Bella off and under the couch.

"It's okay, Boo. It sounds worse than it is." While praying that was the truth, Abby turned on the flashlight on her cell phone. The rain now sounded like hail as it hit the tin roof, and the wind whistled through the cracks and crevices of the old house. The one comforting thought was that the farmhouse—built more than a century ago—must've survived storms much worse than this.

Abby got down on her knees in front of the couch to coax Bella out. "We'll get nice and cozy in the bed and snuggle. Maybe Wolf and Hunter will come check on us." Wishful thinking on her part, she knew, but at least the mention of Wolf drew Bella from under the couch.

Abby gathered her into her arms and headed for the kitchen pantry. The shelves didn't have much in the way of food, but there were three flashlights and two large battery-operated lanterns on the bottom shelf. Their presence seemed to validate her thought that Honeysuckle

Farm had survived its fair share of storms. Though her aunt was undoubtably much better prepared to do so than Abby.

Unhooking a reusable shopping bag from the back of the door, she gathered up two flashlights and a lantern, then collected supplies to get them through the night. A bag of cookies, ice cream (she couldn't let it melt and go to waste), a spoon, two bottles of water, and the last of Bella's dog treats.

As Abby turned toward the back staircase, the wind gave a ghoulish howl, and she ran as though her life depended on it. She took the stairs two at a time, breathless when she reached the landing. She turned toward her bedroom, but with windows on either side of the brass bed, she decided her aunt's bedroom would be safer.

She'd taken a peek at the master bedroom the day she'd arrived. The room was much bigger than the guest bedroom, with a reading nook at the far end. There were two comfy-looking chairs with a window behind them but the windows were far enough away from the bed to offer a measure of comfort.

When she opened the door, Bella didn't whine or act strange. Abby took that as a good sign. She wasn't superstitious, but still…She glanced out the window as she walked to the bed to put down her supplies and held back a nervous shiver so as not to worry Bella. Abby was worried enough for both of them. She'd never been in a storm like this before.

"We'll just get you all cozy," Abby told Bella around the phone she'd stuck between her teeth, the flashlight shining down on the bed. She placed the bag on the floor at her feet and then pulled back the heavy white comforter to tuck Bella underneath, ensuring she piled the down pillows high enough around Bella that she couldn't see out the windows. Once Abby had unloaded the supplies, she gave Bella a treat before setting the lantern on the bedside table and turning it on.

"Look at that, it lights up the whole room, Boo." She didn't know about her dog, but she felt a little better with the room lit up like it was two on a sunny afternoon.

Now to take care of the view that was ruining her attempt to stay positive, she thought, and walked to the reading nook. She leaned over the chair to close the heavy green drapes. Then, turning to do the same at the other end of the bedroom, she noticed a book on the floor.

She went to the bookshelf and crouched to pick up the book. Instead of returning it to the shelf, something, call it a gut instinct, made her open the book. Which was a little weird for her. She rarely picked up a book of her own volition. She didn't enjoy reading. She found it tedious and difficult and it brought back memories of her struggles in school: the teasing she'd endured at the hands of the high school mean girls. It was why she'd never joined the Bel Air Bs' book club.

Still, she looked down at the floral-covered book in her hands and turned the page. She knew right away it wasn't just any old book. It was a journal written by her great-aunt Liz in 1972. She wrote in a loopy style of cursive that made it more difficult for Abby

to read. She studied Liz's penmanship, sounding out
the words.

> The wind was howling and whipping around the trees
> when my father pulled up to the farmhouse. Inside, I
> was howling too, but my father didn't care. He didn't
> want me anymore. I was an abomination. That's what
> he said. I had to look up the word. I wish I hadn't.
>
> I don't think my grandmother wants me either. She
> probably thinks I'm an abomination too. Except she
> gave me this journal when she heard me crying yesterday
> afternoon. I don't know what I'm supposed to write.
> I'm fifteen years old and stuck in the middle of nowhere.
> I miss my friends, I miss my family, not my father, but
> my mother, my brother, and my sisters. I miss riding my
> bike in Central Park, going to the New York Public
> Library, window shopping on Fifth Avenue....I just
> want to go home.

Bella whined, pulling Abby's attention from the book.
She didn't know how long she'd been sitting there
reading, but she'd known almost from the first line that
this was a book she'd complete. Until that moment, she
hadn't felt a connection to her great-aunt. She hadn't felt
anything for the woman Hunter, Elsa, and Owen loved.
But now she could almost hear her voice, and she wanted
to know more about the girl who'd been banished from
her home in the big city to the mountains of North
Carolina. She was almost tempted to skip ahead, but
something told her she needed to read every line of her
great-aunt's story in order.

Abby closed the book and tucked it under her arm. As she went to stand up, she noticed four more books with similar covers and of a similar size sitting on the fourth shelf from the bottom. A book for every decade, she surmised. She pulled out the first book in the row and opened it. Sure enough, it had been written in the 1980s.

Abby set the book on the end of the bed and went to close the other set of drapes. Her thoughts were still stuck in the pages of her great-aunt's journal so she didn't look out. Though it didn't escape her notice that her aunt had arrived on what was probably a night much like this, and she'd survived.

With that comforting thought in mind, Abby walked over to give Bella a cuddle. "I'll be right back, Boo." After offering Bella another treat, Abby went to her bedroom to retrieve her nightie. She decided that when she had some extra money, she'd replace the nightwear with something more suitable for farmhouse living.

She stuck her head out into the hall to make sure Bella wasn't crying before ducking into the bathroom for a quick shower and to change. When she came out of the bathroom, the shirt Hunter had lent her caught her eye. It was hanging on the back of the chair by the bed. She'd forgotten to wash it and give it back to him. Maybe tomorrow she'd use it as an excuse to see him. Remembering what Haley had said, Abby thought she'd wait a few days.

She went over to the chair and picked up the soft denim shirt, slipping it on to ward off the damp chill in the air. It still smelled like Hunter, like cedar and clean

mountain air. She inhaled again, deeper this time. There
was something calming about the smell, which surprised
her. Calm wasn't an emotion she attributed to Hunter.
He certainly didn't make her feel that way.

Although the drama of their encounters probably
didn't help. Neither did his sheer size and the testoster-
one that seemed to ooze from his pores. Or his cranky
demeanor. It was no wonder he made her nervous, she
thought, remembering the warm tingle she'd get low
in...She sighed. As she'd clearly established earlier in
the week, the warm tingles Hunter gave her had nothing
to do with nerves.

And maybe because she'd thought of Hunter just
before crawling into bed with Bella, Abby woke up to
hear him calling her name. The room was dark. Some-
time in the night she must've turned off the lantern. She
strained to hear above the howling wind and the creaks
and groans of the house. It sounded like it moaned as the
wind tried to tear it apart.

She was just about to berate herself for having the
thought when she heard a man's voice and what sounded
like the pounding of heavy boots coming down the hall.
Then the door flung open at the same time the wind
roared and the house shook. A shadow raced from the
doorway to throw itself on Abby. The solid, muscular
weight of the body covering hers forced the air from
her lungs. Her pained grunt morphed into a scream as
chunks of the ceiling fell and a tree limb ripped through
the roof.

As quickly as the terrifying noise had filled the room,
it faded. The bedroom grew eerily still and quiet as she

stared at the thick, leafy tree limb that stabbed the hard-wood floor just inches from the side of the bed. Then she turned her gaze to the rain-soaked man who covered her body with his, and thought the Universe worked in mysterious ways.

* * *

She's all right. Hunter silently repeated the statement a couple times in an effort to calm his jackhammering heart. The thought that she wouldn't survive the storm had been forefront on his mind as he raced the black clouds back to Honeysuckle Ridge. He was having a hard time moving past the scenarios that had played out in his head.

Within minutes of Abby walking across the meadow to the farm, SAR (search-and-rescue) had called to ask Hunter for his help in finding a missing five-year-old who'd wandered from one of the campsites. The storm had just unleashed its fury, making a difficult job even more difficult. Hunter had found the little boy down by Willow Creek. The grateful parents had no idea the danger their son had been in, and not only from a flash flood but also from a protective mama bear.

As Hunter headed back to Honeysuckle Ridge from the search staging area, he had no intention of stopping at the farmhouse. He didn't want to see Abby; didn't think he'd ever see her again. And he'd been more than all right with that. But that was before he spotted the wall of dark clouds and the green tinge to the sky. Tornadoes were rare in the area, but he knew the signs.

Hunter reached for the lantern on the bedside table and turned it on. He lifted his gaze to survey the damage, checking to see if they were in immediate danger of the roof caving in. Water poured through the opening but then slowed to a trickle as the wind died down and everything quieted. He followed the length of the tree limb to where it jutted out from the hardwood floor. Unable to keep from asking himself the inevitable *what if*, he dragged his gaze to Abby's swollen, bloodshot eyes.

He opened his mouth to ask if she was okay but didn't get a chance because she threw her arms around his neck.

"Thank you, thank you for coming to save us. I'm so glad you don't hate me." She sobbed into his chest. "You tried to have me arrested six hours ago. I thought you'd never want to see us again." She sniffed, then withdrew her arms from his neck to draw a whimpering Bella close.

"Seven hours ago."

"Pardon me."

"I tried to have you arrested seven hours ago. I shouldn't have let my family talk me out of it. You would've been safer at the station than here."

"But you forgive me, right? You're here so that must mean you forgive me."

"The reason I'm here is to make sure that you and the rat aren't hurt in the storm." As he pushed himself off the bed and offered her his hand, he once again looked up at the ceiling. Now that she was okay and the adrenaline rush had started to fade, anger was beginning to take the place of relief. "Come on. You can't stay here."

She ignored his hand and sat up. She wore his shirt over her nightgown, and she scooped a trembling Bella into her arms. "So you were worried about us, but you still hate me."

"I don't hate you, Abby."

"Somehow you make that sound worse. Like I'm not worth the effort it would take to hate me."

"So you'd rather I hate you?" He gave his head a slight shake and picked up the lantern. He'd never understand women. No, he'd never understand this woman. He offered his hand again. "Come on. I'm taking you to the barn."

She lifted a shoulder. "I guess it's better than having you feel nothing for me at all."

At a long, drawn-out creak from the ceiling, he grabbed her hand and yanked her off the bed and against his chest. "Trust me, Abby. I feel plenty for you."

He did, and it wasn't just annoyance or frustration or fear. He wanted her. He wished he didn't but he did, and somehow he had to wrap his head around the why and the how of it and what he was going to do about it. But right now, he had to get them out of there.

She searched his face and gave a sad little nod. "I know. I'm a pain in your butt."

He glanced up at the bulging ceiling. "At the moment, you are. We have to get out of here now." He pulled her after him.

A chunk of plaster hit the bed seconds after they cleared the door.

"Wait." She pushed Bella at him, then ran back into the room. "Go. I'll catch up with you."

He sent her an exasperated stare, tempted to leave her there. Instead he backtracked to follow her into the bedroom, watching in frustrated disbelief as she posed for a selfie with the tree. Then she grabbed a book and a package of dog treats and placed them in a shopping bag.

"Seriously, you'd risk the ceiling caving in on you to take a picture of yourself?" he said as he grabbed her and the bag.

"The selfie was an afterthought. I'm starting a new YouTube channel, and the picture will show just what my life in Highland Falls is like. It would've been better if I'd thought to capture the moment as it was happening, but... You wouldn't be interested in reenacting it, would you?"

"I'm going to pretend you didn't just ask me that." He dragged her down the hall, quickening his pace.

"Just so you know, I'm not all about me. I went back for Bella's treats and Liz's journal." She pulled her hand free.

Afraid she'd trip, he slowed his pace on the stairs to keep an eye on her. "I didn't know she kept one," he said once they reached the kitchen.

What he didn't say was that he appreciated Abby wanting to keep Liz's book safe. He glanced at her bare feet and went to the cupboard under the stairs, grabbing a pair of Liz's rubber boots and a rain poncho.

"I didn't know that cupboard was there. Thanks," she said when he handed her the boots and poncho. As she pulled on the boots, she raised an eyebrow at him. "Just like I didn't know there was a washer and dryer in the closet."

He held back a smile. "I didn't want to spoil your fun." Or his, because it had been pretty amusing listening to her complain while hand-washing her laundry in the sink.

"Thanks." She glanced at him as he helped her pull the poncho over her head. "And thank you for coming tonight, even if you haven't forgiven me." She moved to the kitchen counter and picked up a container. "I made you a fresh batch of berry doughnuts."

"I know. I heard you."

"You were there the entire time I was pouring out my heart to you, begging for your forgiveness, and you didn't say a single word? Do you have any idea how that makes me feel?" She grimaced. "Sorry. I shouldn't have said that. It's not about how you made me feel. It's about how I made you feel. I honestly didn't think what I did was that horrible. Until I looked at it from your perspective with some help from Haley." She offered him the container. "I know it doesn't come close to making things right, but I truly am sorry, Hunter. If there's anything I can do, anything at all to make it up to you, please tell me, and I'll do it."

She stood in front of him wearing an olive-green rain poncho, her curly red hair a tangled mess, her eyes bloodshot and swollen, and the first thing that he thought of asking her for was a kiss. He must be losing his mind. And since the one thing that Abby Everhart did that was guaranteed to make him lose his mind, especially with her staying with him for the night, he said, "Don't talk for the next eight hours."

"But—"

"Not a word."

"Wait, wait. I just need to get this straight. So you'll really and truly forgive me if I don't talk for eight hours? You won't hold a grudge and throw it in my face every day? And you'll still help me with the house?"

"Yes, I'll forgive you. I won't hold a grudge. And I'll help you with the house. Your time starts—"

"Just one more. I promise. It's the last one."

He nodded, and she smiled. "Okay, just because the tree made a hole in the master bedroom doesn't mean the entire roof has to be replaced, does it?"

"Afraid so." Her face crumpled, and he slid an arm around her shoulders, tucking her close as he guided her from the house. And not just to comfort her. He didn't want her to see that half the covered porch was gone. He'd wait until tomorrow to tell her the full extent of the damage.

Chapter Fourteen

♥

I can hear the wheels turning in your head," Hunter muttered from where he lay on top of a sleeping bag beside the bed that he'd given up for Abby last night.

She rolled onto her side and stared down at him with pleading eyes. He had no idea how hard it was for her not to speak.

His eyes were closed, and she found her own drifting to his mouth. To his full, beautifully shaped lips that she'd wanted to kiss last night out of gratitude and relief, and maybe, just maybe, a little want and need.

"It's six in the morning," he said, and she gave a guilty start. Praying that his eyes were still closed and he didn't see her staring down at him. They were, thank goodness.

"You have thirty more minutes to go." He continued. "Six hours if I counted the times you talked in your sleep."

She winced and was glad he couldn't see the face she'd just made. She hadn't been talking in her sleep; she'd been talking to him when he'd returned in the middle of the night. Then, remembering their agreement, she'd mumbled some nonsensical words and pretended she was asleep.

The poor guy must be exhausted. He'd dropped her and Bella off, left Wolf to look after them, and then headed back to put in several hours on the house. Supposedly to mop up the water in the master bedroom and repair whatever other leaks he found, but she got the feeling there was something else he was concerned about that he wasn't sharing.

She lay on her back and bit down on her bottom lip to keep from talking. Hunter could probably go days on end without speaking to anyone. It would drive her insane. She tossed and turned on the double-size bed. She had no idea how he fit on the mattress. Surely his feet hung over the edge. As far as being comfortable? It was hardly comfy and cozy.

Like the rest of the space, the bed was basic and plain and appeared to be handmade, which didn't surprise her. The former Delta Force soldier was an extremely talented and resourceful man. But what did surprise her was the lack of family photos, of anything personal, for that matter. Then again, it probably shouldn't.

She glanced at the bedside table. He did have books though. A lot of them. That was just one more thing they didn't have in common; he obviously loved to read, and she hated it. Although her aunt's journal might prove to be the exception. Abby shifted in the bed, stretching out her legs and feet to see if Hunter could fit. Just like she thought: he wouldn't.

At the drawn-out sigh coming from the floor, she

decided she'd make a cup of coffee and head outside before she drove herself and Hunter nuts. Inch by careful inch, she pushed herself upright on the bed so as not to disturb him.

He cracked one eye open. "Where do you think you're going?"

She pointed at the coffeepot on the small counter near the woodstove and mimed making herself a cup and taking it outside to drink. He opened his other eye to stare at her. She had a feeling he found her miming as annoying as her talking.

She stood up and nodded at the bed. When he gave her a blank stare, she silently acted out him getting up and crawling into the bed. She glanced over her shoulder to see if he'd gotten the idea and noticed that Wolf and Bella were now sharing the large dog bed in the corner. She went to say *aww* but then closed her mouth and pressed her hands against her chest, looking at Hunter to see if he'd noticed the heartwarming sight.

He gave his head a clearly frustrated shake. "You're as annoying not talking as you are talking, so just talk."

She opened her mouth, then clamped it shut. There was no way she was going through that torture and not having him forgive her. She tried to act it out silently, but at his increasingly exasperated expression, she mouthed *Will you still forgive me?*

"For . . . Yes, I forgive you. Just don't ever do it again."

"Thank you, thank you, thank you. That's the hardest thing I've ever done. And I swear, I'll guard your privacy with my life. I won't let anyone—"

"Abby."

"Yes?"

"Technically, you haven't spoken for a total of forty-five minutes. You were asleep the rest of the time."

"That's crazy. I can go without talking way longer than that. You've been working at the house with me for days..." He crossed his arms, and she corrected herself. "Okay, so you've been working, and I've been helping. Fine, overseeing. But I have been tidying up. You have to give me that at least."

"I'll give you that, but you've just proved my point. I've spent a couple of days under the same roof with you, and, trust me, you're always talking. And if you're not talking to me, you're talking to the rat."

She looked at him and made a *zip it* motion with her finger across her lips. She had to unzip them almost immediately and made a face.

He laughed, then looked surprised that he had. It wasn't the first time she'd made him laugh, and he'd had the same reaction each and every time. It made her sad to think he hadn't had occasion to laugh in quite some time. Even though her life had been kind of crappy for the past several months, she was pretty sure she'd found something to laugh about every day, or if not to laugh, at least to smile about. She smiled now, though inwardly because she didn't want Hunter to know that she was happy she'd made him laugh.

"I'll zip right back up. I just didn't want to go through the whole acting-out thing again." She nodded at the mattress. "You should grab a couple hours' sleep in your bed. I'll go outside and have my coffee, get organized for my day."

He sat up and scrubbed his hands over his face. "I'm good, thanks. I'll just grab a shower and then go up to the house with you. Don't go without me, okay?"

"I won't." She smiled at Wolf, who'd lifted his head when Hunter stood. When Wolf lay back down, Bella snuggled closer. Abby could've sworn Wolf sighed, but unlike every other time, he didn't nudge her away. "Aww, did you see that? Bella's growing on Wolf."

"More like she's tenacious, and he recognizes when he's in a battle he can't win."

"Aww, they're like me and you."

He gave her a dark look.

"I'll, ah, just get my coffee now and go outside." It wasn't exactly a big space, and he was a big man so Abby brushed against him as she shuffled to the counter. "Sorry." She smiled and made a *zip it* motion across her lips again. This time he didn't laugh. But she wasn't sure if he didn't because it wasn't funny the second time around or because he'd felt the same jolt of awareness that she had when her chest brushed against his.

Not wanting to tick him off further, Abby focused on her phone as she waited for the coffee. He was in the shower by the time she filled her mug with the dark, aromatic brew, so she didn't make one for him. She left Wolf and Bella sleeping peacefully and went outside on her own.

She walked to the side of the barn where she assumed Hunter kicked back to relax. She'd noticed the spot yesterday. Sitting beneath a gorgeous old shade tree there were a couple of big stumps, a fire pit, and a silver-gray log stripped bare of bark. On the other side of the tree, there was a pretty brook and beyond that a farmer's field with rolled bales of hay.

She had a feeling the stumps were where Hunter sat so she walked around to take a seat on the log beneath the tree. It was early, the sun's butter-colored rays not yet strong enough to burn away the morning mist. The mountain air was cool and damp and carried with it the scent of pine and the smells of hay and of honeysuckle.

A far cry from the smells she'd woken up to in LA these past months: car exhaust, sun-baked asphalt, and rotting vegetables from the garbage bin overlaid with the smell of frying bacon and onions from the greasy spoon she parked behind. The June heat wave had made everything worse.

Other than yesterday, the temperatures here hovered around the mid-to-high seventies, and there always seemed to be a light breeze. A welcome change from a hundred degrees in the shade.

But the weather and the smells weren't the only difference. Here she was awakened by birds singing, crickets chirping, and a babbling brook. In LA, it was horns honking, engines roaring, and tires screeching.

Putting her mug of coffee on the ground, she took her phone from the pocket of Hunter's shirt, then swiped the screen to her lists. She was a list addict. They kept her focused and organized, something she struggled with. So far she had nothing under the heading *Second Act*.

Her life had been in such turmoil the past six months that the stress and worry had blocked her creativity. There hadn't been time to think about her future when her present was such a mess. It was all she could do to keep a roof over her and Bella's heads and food in their bellies. She didn't have time for daydreaming and creating. The most she'd hoped to do here was eke out some time to map out her next steps so she'd have a running start once she got back to LA. But now, thanks to her sisters' suggesting she get an Abby Does Highland Falls YouTube channel up and running, she had that and then some.

Movement caught her eye, and she looked up to see Hunter rounding the barn. A whispered "Oh, my" escaped from her parted lips. There was something very appealing about a man fresh from the shower, his thick, wet hair brushed back from his handsome face. The white T-shirt he wore with faded blue jeans only added to the appeal as they showed off his hard, muscular build. The work boots he wore and the tool belt slung over his shoulder didn't hurt either.

Abby forced her lips into a welcoming smile while praying he hadn't heard her whispered comment. But the way his piercing gaze held hers suggested he might have, either that or he was reading her mind, which would be way worse.

She waved because she didn't know what else to do and then calmly asked, "Where's Bella and Wolf?" in hopes of ridding herself of the self-conscious nerves swirling around in her stomach—she subscribed to the *fake it until you make it* maxim. She swallowed a groan when she realized it wasn't nerves swirling around in her stomach. The darn warm tingle was back.

Hunter shook his head as though she'd managed to

annoy him simply by raising her hand and asking about their dogs. He pressed a finger to his lips. At least he managed to get rid of the annoying warm tingle for her, she thought as he approached. She frowned when he pointed to the meadow. Was he actually telling her to go back to the farmhouse?

But then she saw what he was pointing at, and an *aww* escaped before she could stop it. She pressed her own fingers to her lips when, in reaction to her *aww*, the deer feeding in the meadow with two fawns at her side lifted her head.

Abby came slowly to her feet and raised her phone to capture the moment. Absorbed in the mommy and her babies, she didn't realize Hunter had come to stand behind her until he reached over her shoulder and snagged her phone.

She opened her mouth to give him crap but he pressed two fingers to her lips. "Shh."

She crossed her arms, ticked that he'd ruined her video, but her anger faded as she watched the fawns frolic in the meadow while their mommy stayed close by. The mist slowly burned away as the sun rose higher in the sky, the streaks of purple and pink giving way to a clear, crystal blue.

"That was so beautiful," she said when the fawns scampered into the forest with their mother following behind.

"They're here every morning. At dusk too."

"I've never noticed them before."

"I'm not surprised. You've been so focused on what you don't like about this place while you get the farmhouse ready to sell, you haven't opened your eyes to its beauty."

She could argue that point with him. After all, she saw him. But he was right. If it wasn't for Hunter, she would've missed the doe and her fawns playing in a meadow dotted with rainbow-colored flowers. And maybe he was right about something else. Maybe she had purposely been walking around with blinders on because she resented being stuck in the middle of nowhere. Just like her aunt had, and look what happened to her. Abby almost laughed at the thought that, like Liz, she'd come to love Highland Falls and choose to spend her life here. Not in this lifetime. "Why did you take my phone?"

"You were missing out on being in the moment."

His chest against her back felt warm and solid, and he smelled like fresh laundry off the clothesline with a hint of the woods. "I'm not missing out on it now." She tipped her head back to smile at him. "This...that was a very nice moment, thank you."

* * *

Hunter managed to retrieve his chain saw from the master bedroom without Abby realizing he was in the house. If she hadn't shut the rat in the guest bedroom with a boatload of toys, he wouldn't have made it this far undetected. She'd been worried the dog would make herself sick eating the scraps Abby had a tendency to drop on the kitchen floor while baking.

Now Hunter just had to get back down the stairs and out the side door without her noticing. If she spotted him, he'd lose another thirty minutes, and he'd already lost enough time with her. She'd either want him to sample her latest batch of berry doughnuts or help her fill the damn things.

He never should've told her about the bushes on his side of the farm but he couldn't hold out on her. She'd been upset she wouldn't have enough berries to make doughnuts for her booth at Summer Solstice. And he'd just given her a rough estimate of what the roof and porch repair would cost and felt the need to soften the blow.

There was only so much he could do on his own. Her jaw had dropped at his five-figure guesstimate, and her pretty green eyes had gone wide. He'd expected an even stronger reaction when he'd told her she'd be lucky to head back to LA by early August. Surprisingly, she'd taken the news in stride. She'd said the time line worked well for this new venture she had going with Sadie.

But her reaction had set off his internal warning system. It was a sixth sense that had saved his ass in the past, and this time it had him wondering if there wasn't more to Abby being okay with sticking around. And that *more* was him.

He hadn't missed her slip about them having a nice moment watching the deer together or the way she'd smiled up at him. Both her comment and that smile worried him. But more concerning (and disconcerting) than her reaction was his own. Instead of being ticked that he'd have to put up with her for at least another six weeks, he apparently was completely okay with it, because he'd had no reaction at all.

He stopped to listen and heard her singing. Something

about it being her fight song and that she was going to take back her life. The way her voice was going in and out, she was probably dancing around the kitchen, which wouldn't surprise him. She didn't stop moving or talking or thinking or planning. She was... He settled on *exhausting* instead of a half dozen other adjectives that popped into his head. Some like *adorable, fascinating*, and *sweet* that had him questioning his own sanity again.

She also had excellent hearing. Either that or she'd sensed him watching her because she turned with a baking sheet of golden, blueberry-scented pastries in her oven-gloved hands. Her face lit up. "Just the man I wanted to see. I need your opinion on my blueberry-lavender hand pies."

"You can't sell those at Summer Solstice, Abby." He placed the chain saw on the floor by the door.

She laughed. "You just want them all for yourself, don't you? I know how much you love blueberries. They smell delish, don't they?"

"If delish means delicious, then yeah, they do. But it has nothing to do with me. Bites of Bliss, the local bakery, sells small bites of desserts. Tarts, cheesecakes"— he glanced at the cupcakes with pink-swirl icing and dipped strawberries sitting on the dining room table— "and cupcakes. So you can't sell those either." He lifted his chin at the table.

"But they're amazing. They're strawberry and white chocolate." She put down the tray, took off the oven mitts, and went over to the table to pick up a cupcake.

"It doesn't matter how good they are, Abby—" he

began as she walked back to him. She shoved the cupcake into his open mouth.

Once he'd swallowed the last mouthwatering bite, he said, "Okay, so you're right. They are amazing. But it doesn't matter. My aunt has the booth beside yours, and once she sees that you're selling the same as Bliss, she'll lose her mind."

"Oh my gosh, why does that woman hate me so much?"

He didn't think she needed him to repeat the issues Elsa had with her. "Bliss is Ina Graham's niece. Ina owns part of Three Wise Women Bookstore, and both she and my aunt are protective of Bliss. From what I've heard, the bakery hasn't been doing well."

"I'm sorry to hear that. I don't want to hurt her business, but I really need... Wait, I have the perfect solution. I'll just call Bliss and make sure we're not selling the same stuff. And it's not like I'm planning to open a bakery, right? This is just like a one-time thing to make some money to help offset the cost of my everyday living expenses and so I can rent the equipment I need. Oh my gosh, I can totally promote her on my new YouTube channel." She smiled. "Now all you have to do is come with me and smooth things over with your aunt."

"No way. You couldn't pay me to set foot on the Village Green. I'm going fishing Friday." He needed a day on his own, and so did his dog.

"Please, Hunter. Please." She made prayer hands. "If you're there, you can at least stop your aunt from embarrassing me in front of everyone. Just imagine how I'd feel if she talked about me like she did the other day."

"You'll be fine. Sadie will be with you. And if Elsa gets out of control, the mayor has the booth on the other side of yours. She'll..." He trailed off.

Winter Johnson was his mother's best friend. They were thick as thieves, and the last thing he needed was Winter pumping Abby for information about him—and them. As he well knew, everyone became Abby's best friend within minutes of talking to her, and the woman had a habit of oversharing.

"Okay. I'll go with you. But—"

Abby threw her arms around his neck and was just about to lay one on him when she drew back and gave him a self-conscious smile. "Sorry. I'll just hug you instead." She removed her arms from around his neck and slipped them around his waist, resting her cheek against his chest. She sighed. "You smell really good."

So did she. She felt good too. He stepped back before he did something stupid like kiss her senseless.

Chapter Fifteen

♥

When they pulled into the parking lot beside the Village Green to set up for Summer Solstice early Friday morning, Hunter was given a preview of what the day held in store for him and decided his worst expectations of how this would play out weren't even close.

"Careful, Ed! Stay there, and Hunter will come help you with the sign as soon as we find a parking spot," Abby yelled out the passenger-side window. "Okay. Thanks, Walter!" She waved at the silver-haired grocery clerk, who was directing traffic in the lot, and pulled her head back inside. "Walter says there are a couple spots open on the other side of Sadie's tour bus."

"How many cups of coffee did you have this morning?"

"Two. Why?"

"You need to switch to decaf," Hunter said as he drove across the gravel lot. "And stop volunteering me to help everyone."

"I offered your help to two people, Hunter. Josie and Ed." She gave him a teasing smile and reached over to squeeze his bicep. "That's what you get for having big muscles. Wow, they really are big and hard, aren't they?"

"Do you mind?" he asked with a pointed look at her hand stroking his arm.

She pulled her hand away. "Sorry. Oh, there's Eden and your brother. It looks like he's having a hard time—"

Hunter powered up her window and locked it. She shot him an irritated glance before turning to pound on the window and wave. He knew the moment his brother and Eden registered his presence in the truck because their mouths dropped.

"Eden and Shane look surprised to see you so I guess that means you don't usually attend Summer Solstice?"

"No. I don't."

She leaned over and kissed his cheek as he pulled into an empty spot beside the tour bus. She smelled like vanilla and the woods at night, and the sexy scent turned him on almost as much as the warm weight of her breasts pressed against his arm. He drew in a long, frustrated breath when she moved away. It was all he could do not to wrap an arm around her waist and bring her tight against him.

"Thank you for coming with me. I really appreciate it, and I won't volunteer your muscles to anyone else. Promise." As though she couldn't help herself, she gave his bicep another squeeze. "I'll help Josie if you help Ed."

"I'll take care of them both, Abby. You get everything organized for me to take to the tent."

"Thank you." She leaned toward him.

"Abby, you don't have to kiss me or thank me every time I do something for you."

She frowned, twisting at her waist to grab her purse from behind the seat. She held it up. "I was just getting my purse. But I'm sorry, you're absolutely right. I shouldn't be kissing you like that. It's totally inappropriate. I promise, I won't do it anymore. Not thanking you will be a harder habit to break. My mom kind of—"

He slid his hand under her long hair, wrapping his fingers around the back of her neck, drawing her close, breathing in her sexy fragrance, savoring the feel of her body pressed against him. He'd wanted to shut her up but now he wanted nothing more than to feel her mouth under his.

She blinked up at him, her lips slightly parted as though she'd lost her train of thought, and he'd definitely lost his. He gave her a second to realize what he was about to do and pull away if she wanted to. He didn't know if it was him or if it was her who made the next move, but he didn't care. She tasted like cherries, and her lips were warm and soft beneath his. *She* was warm and soft, and his fingers flexed in her silky curls, aching to explore the body pressed against his side.

He deepened the kiss, exploring her with his tongue and his teeth instead of his hand that was wrapped around her waist, rubbing the silky fabric of her hot-pink-and-bright-yellow jumpsuit between his fingers. She moaned against his mouth, and he dragged her across the console, so completely lost in the kiss that he forgot where they were for a moment.

Until a horn broke through the sexual fog, and he

jerked away from her to look around, panicked that someone had seen them. Panicked that he had gotten so lost in the taste and feel of Abby that he'd forgotten the cost that came with caring for someone. It was a cost he refused to pay. He wouldn't put anyone through that kind of pain again, especially her. She'd been through enough.

"Sorry, I—" he began, but she shook her head as she drew back to straighten her clothes.

He looked away, the temptation of her body too much to bear. He hadn't quite gotten his desire for her under control, and for a man who prided himself on his ability to control his emotions, that told him everything he needed to know.

He was a soldier, once lauded for his skills on the battlefield, his ability to be in absolute control of his emotions, to read the danger in any given situation. He read the situation in his truck just as easily as he once had on the battlefield before his life had gone to hell, and he knew without a single shred of doubt that Abby was dangerous.

"No, it's okay. You kissed me to shut me up."

He heard the question in her voice and grabbed on to the excuse like a lifeline. "Yeah. Good to know it worked."

Kissing her had been one of the biggest mistakes he'd ever made, even bigger than agreeing to come to the festival in the first place.

"Okay, well, you know how I asked you to be honest with me?"

He sighed. He couldn't win with this woman. But

maybe that was good. Maybe this was just what he needed to hear because he really was having a hard time getting his desire for her under control. "Yes, Abby. I do."

She nodded. "Right, so I figure it's only fair that I'm honest with you. 'Cause, you know, I think honesty is really important in a relationship. Not that I think we're in a *relationship* relationship. But it's important even in a friendship. We're friends now, aren't we?" She must've seen something in his expression to override the impression and said, "Okay, but we are neighbors."

"If you don't soon get to the point, Ed is going to walk into the side of a car with the sign and Josie will have her tent set up." And Hunter was thinking about kissing Abby again.

"All right, it's just that kissing me to shut me up is a really bad idea."

"I'm kinda getting that it doesn't work."

"Well, this is me being totally honest with you despite also being embarrassed to admit it, but, Hunter, you kissing anyone wouldn't be considered a punishment. It's almost an incentive to keep talking so you'll keep kissing me. You're a very good kisser."

"Abby, shut up."

"That's really rude but much more effective. Aren't you glad we talked about this? Honesty really is the best policy. I'm going. I'm going."

* * *

By the time Hunter got back to the truck after helping Josie cart her boxes to the tent, Ed attach the sign advertising the Highland Games to the entrance gate, and his brother set up his equipment on the center stage— Shane and their cousins' band, Culloden, was providing the entertainment for the festival—at least thirty minutes had passed, and Abby was nowhere to be found. But everything for her bake sale was still sitting in the back of the truck.

Hands on his hips, he looked around, only to see Sadie and Abby talking animatedly as they crossed the parking lot. Sadie nudged Abby, and she looked up.

She ran toward him waving. "Sorry, I'm coming. Crap." She hit a pothole and her arms went in the air. He was too far away to reach her, but Sadie grabbed Abby in time to keep her from falling on her face.

"Good thing you made me wear my sneakers or I probably would've broken my ankle," she told him when she reached his side.

"Next time, try walking instead of running." He lifted his chin at the woman beside her. "Hey, Sadie. Where have you been?" he asked Abby as he hopped into the bed of the truck.

"Sorry, that was my fault. I had to hide the unicorns in the gardens and asked Abby to help," Sadie explained.

"Oh my gosh, Hunter. You won't believe the gardens, they're magical. And the unicorn stuffies are so cute. The kids will go crazy. But it's too bad dogs are banned from the festival because Wolf could've filled in for Granny MacLeod's Minnie. That's Granny MacLeod's white horse that usually plays the role of the real-life unicorn, but she threw a shoe. And the white donkey that some-times fills in for Minnie was being extra contrary.

"Still, I can already tell the event is going to be a hit with my subscribers, especially when I get your grandmother on film telling her story about seeing a unicorn after being struck by lightning, Sadie. She doesn't only look like Betty White; she acts like her too."

Hunter, who'd tried to tune Abby out at *magical garden*, got the table, chairs, and coolers filled with baked goods out of the back of the truck. He knew all about Granny MacLeod's claim to fame and her contribution to the festival. She owned I Believe in Unicorns on Main Street. If it had a unicorn on it, Granny MacLeod sold it in her shop, and like most of the businesses in town, she used the festival to promote her store. But the festival wouldn't be complete without a unicorn hunt in the garden maze.

It was also a big draw at the Highland Games. Not a surprise since unicorns were Scotland's national animal. In Celtic mythology, a unicorn symbolized purity and innocence. The animal also represented masculinity, power, and chivalry. And nowhere were courage and honor more admired than in Highland Falls.

"I better get going," Sadie said. "I have to make sure my brother made it home last night. If he didn't, I need to make arrangements to get Granny here in time for the opening ceremony."

"I'm sure Hunter...won't mind lending me his truck to pick her up." Abby gave him a look that said she should earn points because she hadn't volunteered him for the job.

In her dreams. "No one drives my truck but me, and that goes double for you."

"Are you insinuating that I'm a bad driver?"

"I'm pretty sure I can guarantee that you are."

"Then you should probably read these." Sadie tapped her cell phone screen and handed him her phone. "Nearly every review commented on Abby's driving, how safe they felt with her compared to other drivers, how she never yelled or honked her horn, and weaved expertly in and out of traffic."

Hunter lifted an eyebrow as he read the glowing five-star reviews, then raised his gaze to Abby. She'd crossed her arms and was watching him with a smug smile. "Did you pay them?"

Her jaw dropped, and Sadie rolled her eyes.

"You're such a guy. Women can drive just as well as any man."

"So maybe I should check out your reviews?" Everyone in town knew how often Owen had pulled over Sadie for speeding in her teens.

"Okay, that's not fair. I never said *I'm* a good driver." Sadie smiled and put an arm around Abby's shoulders. "That's why Abby's agreed to drive the tour bus, starting tomorrow."

"What about the farmhouse?" Wondering as he asked why it bothered him so much, because it did. And it wasn't because Abby obviously assumed he'd handle the repairs—he was doing that anyway. It was because she wouldn't be hanging out with him during the day. And if that wasn't a strong enough reason for her to take the job with Sadie, he didn't know what was.

"Never mind. I can handle it. It's not like you do anything anyway." Okay, he might be unhappy with the evidence of just how far and how deep Abby had gotten under his skin, but that was no excuse for him hurting her. "I'm teasing, Abby. It's fine."

"You're sure? I didn't think—"

"I'm sure." And because he felt guilty, he told Sadie, "If you need someone to pick up your grandmother, just text Abby, and we'll figure it out."

"I really am sorry, Hunter," Abby said when Sadie backed out of the parking space, waving as she pulled away. "You've already done so much for me, and it's taken time away from your carving. I'm hoping that, between the tours and my YouTube channel, I'll have enough money to pay someone to repair the roof and porch. If this works out the way I hope it will, I'm going to pay you too. The plan is to get the channel up and running this week—"

"Right now, how about we focus on the bake sale?" He'd been around her long enough to know that it didn't take much for Abby to get off track. The woman was as easily distracted as Wolf had been as a pup. And just as it had worked with his dog, Hunter found that patient redirection worked with Abby too.

She laughed and picked up the two chairs. "I know what you're doing, you know. You do the same thing with Bella."

He avoided looking at her and piled one cooler on top of the other. "I don't know what you're talking about."

"Of course you do. And I honestly don't mind. At least you don't yell at me like my ex did or make me feel stupid." She grinned up at him. "Are you going to beat him up for me?"

"Someone should've," he muttered, wondering how anyone could..."I've yelled at you."

"You have, but I've yelled at you too. And it's not the same. I might not have appreciated it, but I understood why you did. You didn't do it to hurt me. Chandler did. But I allowed him to, and that's on me." She glanced at him. "What?"

"Earlier, you said we were friends, and I might've made you feel otherwise. I don't play nice with others anymore, Abby. But I'll be there for you if you need me, and if that makes me a friend in your book, then I guess that's what I am."

"You're lucky my hands are full, Hunter Mackenzie, or I'd hug you."

* * *

Three hours later, Hunter wasn't feeling so friendly toward Abby. The damn woman had left with his truck more than an hour ago to pick up Granny MacLeod, and as far as he could tell, neither one of them had put in an appearance at the festival.

He felt his aunt and the mayor glancing his way from their tents on his left and his right. He sat behind a table surrounded by baked goods under a yellow tent painted with Liz's signature honeysuckle and honeybees. It's where he'd spent the last three hours. Stuck between the two older women, who were watching his every move. It had actually been worse when Abby was around so he supposed he shouldn't complain that she wasn't there.

"You might as well start giving away the cupcakes

and hand pies," his aunt said. "No one is going to buy them."

He dug his wallet out of his back pocket, pulled out a ten-dollar bill, and put it in the cash box. It looked lonely in there so he pulled out two fives and tossed them in. "Maybe if you'd stop glaring at people when they came over, they would."

"No, what Elsa needs to do is lift her edict on Facebook," the mayor said. "Abby talked to Bliss and cleared what she was bringing with her. So I don't know what your problem is, Elsa."

Winter Johnson was an attractive woman in her early sixties. Her Cherokee and Scottish roots were evident in her tan skin, high cheekbones, and blue eyes. She wore her jet-black hair long and straight. Although today she sported a sparkly purple streak, courtesy of Josie. Who knew fairy hair was a thing?

"I'm selling books, Winter, and you're selling your beauty-and-wellness products," his aunt said.

Winter sold natural products derived from plants and flowers that were raised on her farm.

Hunter was pretty sure he knew where his aunt was going with her comment. "Abby doesn't know anything about bees, Aunt Elsa. She's been here for just over a week. And it's not like she hasn't had a lot on her plate. She..." He trailed off at the sour look on his aunt's face and the knowing one on Winter's. He couldn't win. And people wondered why he preferred the company of his dog.

His brother sauntered over. "You look like you're having fun. Hey, Winter. Hey, Aunt Elsa. How are sales going today? My brother entertaining you with his scintillating conversation?"

"It was very entertaining when Abby was here," Winter said with a twinkle in her eyes.

"Is that so? She should be back any minute now. She's just wrapping up her interview with Granny MacLeod," Shane said and picked up a cupcake.

Hunter grabbed the cupcake on its way to his brother's mouth. "That'll be ten bucks."

"Be serious. We've been performing for Abby's YouTube channel for the last twenty minutes. I'm starved."

"Are you kidding me? She's been back for that long and didn't come here?"

"You missed her, didn't you?"

His aunt and Winter leaned so far over to get a good look at him that he was surprised they didn't fall out of their booths. "No, I didn't miss her. I didn't sign up to man her booth for the day. I need to check on the dogs."

He got up from the chair and came around the table to see if he could spot Abby in the crowd. The vendor tents were set up to the left of the stage, the gardens and unicorn maze to the right.

"She already did. She stopped by Penelope's Pet Emporium and bought them some treats."

That explained why his ten-dollar bill had looked lonely. She'd absconded with the cash. "It would've been nice if she told me where she was going and when she got back."

"You know, you sound like a concerned boyfriend."

He was going to kill his brother. He dragged Shane away from his aunt's and the mayor's earshot. "Stop trying to stir up crap. You know as soon as they get home, Winter will be on the phone to Mom and so will Aunt Elsa. And then my phone will start ringing." Which meant he'd turn it off for the night. And that reminded him that he already had. He pulled out his phone and turned it on. He owed Abby a mental apology. She'd texted him three extremely long and detailed messages.

"Can you blame us for wanting to know what's going on? It wasn't that long ago that you were having her arrested. So what, did you guys kiss and make up?" Shane choked on the cupcake he'd just taken a bite of. As far as Hunter was concerned, it served him right.

"Whoa, you did, didn't you?"

"No." *That didn't sound the least bit convincing,* he thought as he handed his brother a bottle of water. And the reason it didn't sound convincing was because the kiss he'd shared with Abby was getting too much air time in his head. Which just went to prove that it was long past time that he got laid. In response to the thought, his mind provided him with an image of Abby. Clearly, he was spending too much time with the woman.

"She's had a lot to deal with," he told his brother in an effort to sound more convincing as well as to find a way to get her out of Highland Falls before the summer was over. "I'm just giving her a hand. The storm hit the farmhouse hard. There was a lot of damage to the roof and porch. Everyone I've called is either booked until August or doesn't return my calls."

"Sounds like Elsa is at it again."

He glanced at his aunt, who was serving an older gentleman. "I don't see why she'd put up roadblocks to getting the roof and porch repaired."

"True, and Honeysuckle Farm wasn't the only place that got hit, from what I've heard. I might know someone though. I'll give them a call."

"Appreciate it." He leaned back to see if Abby was close to wrapping it up.

Shane pointed to the gardens. "She must've finished her interview." His brother nodded in approval when Abby went to hug Granny MacLeod, dropped her arms, and stepped back. "Someone must've warned her."

"Oh yeah, I warned her, but she didn't listen. Granny MacLeod prophesized that Abby would die in a month in the woods. Less than a month now, I guess."

Shane stared at him. "How can you be blasé about it? You know as well as I do that Granny MacLeod's prophecies come true." Unlike Abby and Hunter, some people, like his brother, received a good prophecy. Except Shane hadn't thought so at the time.

"Abby thinks Granny MacLeod saw her past, not her future." He explained to Shane what had happened to her when she was twelve. He didn't think Abby would mind. She hadn't asked him to keep it to himself.

"Wow, tough break. I feel bad now. I thought she was just a klutz. You should tell Aunt Elsa. Maybe she'll back off. It sounds like Abby had her reasons for cutting ties with the Findlay side of her family. Too bad she didn't get a chance to know Liz though. I think they would've liked each other."

A week ago, Hunter would've had his doubts about

that, but not anymore. "This stays between you and me. If Abby wants people to know, she'll tell them. And whatever you do, don't treat her any differently now that you know."

"Sounds like you speak from experience. Can't say I blame you."

"Yeah, it's not easy to keep my mouth shut."

"I find that hard to believe since that's all you've done these past couple years. Sounds to me like Abby has gotten to you, big brother."

If he only knew. His brother smiled, and Hunter turned to see Abby running toward them, waving. Then she disappeared from view. The way people were leaning and reaching out, Hunter figured they'd saved her from falling on her face. She bounced right back and, with a wide smile and a wave, made her way toward them.

"Just once, could you walk where you're going instead of running?"

"I'm fine. Besides, I left you on your own long enough. Are you okay?" Her face fell when she looked at the table. "We didn't sell anything, did we?"

Shane turned with his phone in his hand, and Hunter figured his brother was putting out the word to stop by Honeysuckle Farm's tent. They'd soon have more customers than they could handle. He felt Winter looking at him and glanced over. She held up her phone and gave him a thumbs-up. "Most people are grabbing their lunch. Give them half an hour," he told Abby.

She probably thought he was psychic when, in exactly thirty minutes, they were swamped. When they looked up forty-five minutes later, there was only one blueberry hand pie left. "That's mine." Hunter claimed it.

Her arms went up, and he braced himself. She got that look in her eyes and that smile on her face that she always got just before she threw herself at him. But instead, this time she caught her bottom lip between her teeth and lowered her hands. Then she smiled. "I knew they'd be your favorite. I'll make you another batch when we get home." Her eyes went wide, and she looked around. He was going to assure her that it was fine when she jumped up from the chair. "We didn't have room on the table, and I have another three dozen cupcakes in the cooler."

They'd just gotten them out on the table when Winter came over and said something to Abby.

"Hunter, would you mind manning the mayor's booth and mine? The powwow is starting so it shouldn't be too busy. You can have a cupcake and read your book."

He eyed Winter and Abby. The last thing he wanted was the two of them together out of his hearing. "Where are you guys going?"

"Winter's leading the drumming session, and she's letting me take part. Isn't that exciting? I'm going to film it too."

Abby linked arms with Winter, who glanced over her shoulder at Hunter and mouthed *I like her* as they walked away. Hunter would've said *That's nice*, only he knew what the older woman meant. She liked Abby for him.

From the tent next to him, his aunt said, "She's not for you. Sloane is. She looks good, doesn't she?"

Hunter's pulse began to race as he followed the

direction of Elsa's gaze. Sloane and her mother stood across the green. They were talking to Granny MacLeod. He didn't know what she said but Sloane and her mother looked his way.

His aunt was right. Sloane looked good. She was a beautiful woman with long, dark hair and cool gray eyes. She wore her hair pulled back from her angular face in a low ponytail. She was tall with an athletic build and walked with an elegant, confident stride. But if he thought that either woman would ever forgive him, the look in Sloane's mother's eyes told him otherwise.

Chapter Sixteen

♥

Abby's excitement over the drumming session she'd captured on video fizzled as if someone had let the air out of a helium balloon when she saw Elsa sitting where she'd last seen Hunter. She'd been anxious to share her experience with him, and now he was nowhere to be found.

Elsa looked up from her book and came to her feet. "My nephew asked me to look after the table for him." She nodded at a half-eaten cupcake. "I took that in lieu of payment."

"That's fine. Please, help yourself." She glanced at Winter, who hovered outside the tent. She had a feeling the other woman knew more than she was letting on. "Is Hunter okay?" Abby asked his aunt.

She shook her head. "No. I don't think he is."

Winter came to stand beside Abby. "Sloane and her mother are here. He saw them, didn't he? Sloane is Hunter's ex-fiancée," the mayor explained to Abby.

"Oh, okay," Abby responded lamely.

She didn't know why she felt so much worse than

a deflated balloon now. It shouldn't come as a surprise that Hunter had been engaged. It would've been more of a surprise to learn he'd never loved someone or been loved in return. Without thinking, she pressed the tips of her fingers to her lips, remembering the mind-numbing kiss they'd shared earlier. She realized then the reason for the heavy, nauseating weight in her stomach.

If his ex was back in town, and Hunter had reacted as strongly as he had, there was only one way Abby saw this ending—the couple would soon be back together. Hunter wasn't the type of man you let get away. Which meant Abby wouldn't get another opportunity to explore her feelings for him or get another chance to kiss his warm, wonderful lips.

Maybe that was a good thing. She had a crappy history with men, after all. What was wrong with her? Elsa said he wasn't doing well, and all Abby was thinking about was herself, when Hunter was obviously hurting. Some friend she was.

"Did Hunter try and talk to Sloane?" Winter had barely gotten out her question when Shane ran into the tent.

"Sorry, Abby," he said as he brushed past her to confront his aunt. "I just heard Sloane and her mother are at the festival. Where's my brother?"

"He left as soon as he saw them. They were over there." Elsa pointed across the Village Green to the garden's entrance. "Even from here, you could see that they don't forgive him. Especially the mother. It was harder to tell with Sloane."

"And Hunter?" Shane asked.

"How do you think? This would've been the first

time he's seen Sloane since he ended their engagement," Elsa said.

"He didn't end it. He gave her a choice, and she chose to blame him for Danny's death. It's bullshit. Hunter didn't deserve that. He took a bullet to bring Danny home. It wasn't his fault he died. My brother's a hero." He dragged a hand down his face. "I'm sorry. It's just that I felt like he was coming back to us, and now this."

They watched Shane walk away. His aunt was the first to break the silence. "These past few years have been hard on Shane too." Elsa glanced at Abby. "For three weeks, we didn't know if Hunter was dead or alive. They were on a mission in Afghanistan, and all contact had been lost. Then Hunter came back but it was like he'd left a part of himself in Afghanistan."

"He can't forgive himself for losing Danny," the mayor murmured.

"He needs Sloane and her mother's forgiveness. I was hoping, after all this time, they'd finally find it in their hearts to offer it to him. I guess I was wrong about Sloane. I thought..." Elsa released a heavy sigh. "I think I'll close down early."

The day had lost its appeal for Abby too, and she moved to the table to pack up the last of the cupcakes, filling two bakery boxes.

The mayor hugged Elsa. "Don't miss tonight because of this. You need it."

Elsa nodded and pulled away. "You're probably right."

Abby offered them each a box of cupcakes. "I find sugar helps when I'm feeling down."

The mayor smiled. In the short amount of time she'd

spent in Winter's company, Abby had come to like and respect her.

"Thank you, Abby," Winter said. "That's very sweet of you. If you see Hunter, don't let him push you away. He needs to talk to someone, and I think the someone he needs to talk to is you."

"Granny MacLeod said the same thing," Abby admitted, and then, seeing the shock on the two women's faces, she held up a hand. "No, she didn't say it in that creepy prophecy voice she has. She said it in her sweet, nosy Granny MacLeod voice."

The mayor frowned and laid a concerned hand on Abby's arm. "Has Granny MacLeod prophesized your future?"

"She did, only it wasn't my future she saw. It was my past." Because they'd so readily shared with her about Hunter, she shared her story with them. And while she didn't do it for sympathy, she wanted Hunter's aunt to realize she wasn't the awful person she thought her to be. Abby had kind of hoped Hunter would do it for her, but that had been wishful thinking considering getting the man to talk was like pulling teeth.

Winter gave her a warm hug and thanked her for sharing her story with them while Hunter's aunt gave her a long, considering look. Then she nodded and said, "I may have misjudged you, Abby Everhart."

If Abby had worried that sharing her story with the two older women would result in them coddling and protecting her like Hunter had, she'd worried for nothing. Elsa accepted Abby's help packing up her tent and then left Hunter's cousins to cart it all away while Abby sat on a chair waiting for the man himself to arrive.

Three young girls packed up Winter's tent while she was off judging a competition. Abby had filmed the dancers and singers and would've liked to see who won, but she didn't want to miss Hunter's arrival.

Two hours later, after texting him for a third time and receiving no response, Abby had to accept the fact that she was on her own. She looked around for someone she could ask for help but everyone had either cleared out or was gathered around the stage.

Even though the sun had gone down an hour earlier, the lights from the stage and the bonfire made it appear lighter than it would normally be at this time of night. Or so she'd thought when she began her trek to the parking lot loaded down with two coolers. She took her time making her way across the uneven ground. At least the lot was well lit, she thought as she deposited the coolers in an empty space and then trudged back for the tables and chairs.

On her last trip back to the parking lot, she was just thinking how grateful she was that Hunter had insisted she wear sneakers instead of heels, when she stumbled. A hand shot out of the dark and saved her from falling.

"Thanks," Abby said once she'd regained her footing, turning to smile at her rescuer.

The woman was tall with long, dark hair pulled back in a low ponytail that showed off her gorgeous face and incredible light eyes. She wore a black tank top over a white one and a pair of well-worn jeans. She gave off a cool, confident vibe that Abby admired.

"Here. Let me help you," the woman said, taking one of the tables from her.

Abby smiled her thanks, then sighed. "You make it look so easy. You must work out. Oh my gosh, look at the definition in your arms. They're amazing." She stopped and leaned the table against her legs to flex her arms. "I've seen four-year-olds with more definition than me."

The woman gave her a closed-mouthed smile, reserved but not unfriendly. "Some people develop muscle easier than others."

"I guess I'm just one of the unlucky ones." Abby smiled as they reached the parking lot and nodded at her pile. "That's me. Thanks again," she said when the woman rested the table against the coolers and then took the other one from Abby and did the same. "I'm Abby, by the way." She offered her hand.

The woman took Abby's hand, and it wasn't until her cool, firm fingers wrapped around Abby's that she realized hers were sweaty. "I'm so sorry." She pulled her hand away to wipe it on her jumpsuit and made a joke. "I'm so out of shape that even my hands sweat."

The woman gave her another reserved smile. "It's nice to meet you, Abby." She looked around the lot. "Are you going to be okay here on your own?"

"My friend should be here soon. She just has to do her last drop-off at Three Wild Women Winery. Maybe you know her, Sadie Gray? If you don't know her, you'll definitely know her grandmother, Granny MacLeod. Unless you're a tourist. Are you—a tourist, I mean? Because if you are, Sadie and I are kicking off a great tour this weekend, and I'll totally hook you up for helping me."

With her head tilted to the side, the woman was looking at Abby like Hunter sometimes did. Abby sighed.

"Sorry. I have verbal diarrhea. I really did appreciate your help."

The woman glanced toward the other end of the lot when a truck door opened and a silver-haired woman stuck her head out. "Sloane, get a move on. I've been sitting here waiting for more than twenty minutes."

"Nice to meet you, Abby," the woman said, then turned to walk away.

Abby grabbed her arm. "Wait. You're Hunter's Sloane, aren't you?"

"Not anymore. Have a good night."

She needed to do something, to say something. All she did was talk; it was her superpower. She could talk to anyone but she didn't know what to say to this woman. "I don't know what happened between you and Hunter, Sloane. But he's a really good guy. I mean, don't get me wrong, he's far from perfect. He's the strong, silent type. I have a feeling you might be into that, but if you're not, trust me, it can get really annoying. He's a total alpha too, which I kinda get the impression you wouldn't like."

She touched her chest. "Confession time, I do. I know, I'm all girl-power and punching through the glass ceiling too but I seem to have a thing for a man's man. Who knew? But under his tougher-than-nails exterior is a man who is kind, caring, and considerate. He truly is one of the good guys, Sloane. And trust me, there's not a whole lot of them out there." She didn't think it would be appropriate to say that he also kisses like a dream or that he was one of the most gorgeous men she'd ever seen or that he had muscles that would make Michelangelo weep.

"I know he's one of the good ones, Abby. But—"

Across the parking lot, a dome of light went on in a truck, and the silver-haired woman yelled, "Sloane!"

Sloane drew in a deep breath through her nose, then said, "I have to go." She turned and walked across the gravel lot with a long, elegant stride, and Abby had never been more envious.

But for once in her life, Abby's envy had nothing to do with the woman's gorgeous face, incredible muscle definition, long legs, or easy grace. Abby was jealous because Hunter Mackenzie loved her.

* * *

An hour later, Sadie drove the tour bus up to the farmhouse and helped Abby unload the chairs, tables, and coolers onto the porch. "Just leave it there," Abby said, and she gave Sadie a grateful hug. "Thanks for driving to my rescue."

"Anytime," Sadie said. "We're partners now, right?"

"We are. But only for the next few weeks. Or at least until I sell this place."

"I hear you. I don't plan on running a tour company for the rest of my life. The summer is bad enough. Actually, that's not true. I'm kinda looking forward to it now with you onboard."

"Aw, that's so nice." Abby gave her another hug. "Thank you."

"No, thank you. You're the one with all the experience. I had no idea you had millions of followers on your You-Tube channel and were such a big deal in LA, Abby."

"I'm not anymore, and I'm definitely a very little deal here. It's your experience and connections that will be even more useful here than mine."

"Oh, wow, I forgot to tell you. I guess the news about Sloane blew mine out of the water." She glanced over her shoulder, looking at the yellow barn that shone like a beacon in the dark night. "It doesn't look like Hunter's around. Are you going to tell him that you talked to Sloane?"

"I think so." She chewed on her thumbnail, then looked at Sadie. "Now tell me your news."

"Well, when I dropped off the last of the tour guests at Three Wild Women Winery, Daisy, one of the owners, mentioned that Mallory Maitland booked rooms for a bachelorette long weekend two weeks from now, and she asked if the winery could organize it for her. Daisy recommended us because they do hikes and winery stuff, but nothing like what Mallory seemed to be looking for."

Sadie grabbed Abby's hands and bounced on her toes. "This could be our ticket. Mallory grew up in Highland Falls and married some gazillionaire from Atlanta, and from what Daisy said, it sounded like Mallory has a sky's-the-limit budget."

"Oh my gosh, this could absolutely be our ticket, Sadie. We have to come up with something incredible, something no other tour company does." And then she'd have to convince Mallory and her friends to let her film them. Abby tried to come up with something. But her brain was on empty, just like her body. "We'll sleep on it tonight, and brainstorm in the morning."

"Sounds good, and it sounds like someone needs to go outside," she said at the barking and scratching coming from the other side of the farmhouse door.

They hugged and said goodbye, shared a happy dance, and then Abby inched her way inside the dark house to pick up Bella. She looked around, disappointed that there was no sign of Hunter. He'd taken Wolf and didn't think to leave her a note or turn on a light. She refused to let her disappointment steal her excitement over Sadie's news.

"It looks like we might have our ticket back to LA, Boo." She picked up Bella's leash and snapped it on the collar before grabbing a sweater off the coatrack and heading back outside.

She turned on the flashlight on her phone and held tight to Bella's leash while shining the light on the patch of grass, looking for snakes. Frogs too. She didn't trust them not to be poisonous. Bella did her business but didn't show any interest in going back inside. Due to the swarm of mosquitos buzzing around her head, Abby was more than interested but felt guilty that Bella had spent most of the day inside.

"All right, we'll go for a walk around the house." She decided to stick toward the back of the house and the patio so she didn't have to listen to Bella whine when Abby refused to walk across the meadow to the yellow barn. It would be a wasted trip. Hunter wasn't there. Except if he wasn't there, why did she smell wood smoke?

She squinted at the dark forest, positive she'd seen a dancing ball of light. There it was again. It was too big to be a firefly or even a swarm of them. Abby strained to listen to the night sounds, almost positive she'd heard women's voices. But all she heard were the chirp of crickets, the croak of frogs, and the hooting of a great horned owl. She knew the exact type of owl it was because Hunter had pointed out its nest in the big pine tree. She also knew it could pick up her dog. So when Bella started barking, Abby decided it was time to go inside.

But just as she turned to round the house, a light breeze rustled the leaves on the trees and carried with it the faint sounds of women's voices. Curious, Abby brought Bella back inside and grabbed a flashlight. She tucked her cell phone in the pocket of her sweater. "I'll be right back, Boo."

She found a narrow path and followed it and the dancing lights through the trees. For someone who wasn't a fan of mother nature and the great outdoors, it was a little freaky, but Abby had a gut feeling that she had to keep going. As she got deeper in the woods, she counted at least seven lights, and orange sparks from a bonfire shot high into the night sky. The sound of women's voices got louder. She wasn't sure if they were chanting or singing but it was comforting to know she wasn't alone.

As the trees thinned, Abby got a clear view of the women, and her eyes practically bugged out of her head. She couldn't believe what she was seeing and dropped to her knees. Afraid they'd see her, she stretched out on the forest floor.

There was a semicircle of five standing stones. They were of varying heights; the taller ones looked to be nine feet tall and six feet wide. The smallest appeared to be as tall as her. The women danced among the imposing stones with their lanterns held aloft, singing softly. There was something about the scene playing out before Abby that seemed familiar. Some of the women looked familiar too. She recognized Granny MacLeod, Elsa, Winter, Eden, and Josie.

Abby reached for her phone and began filming. And as she looked through the small screen, she remembered exactly why the scene seemed familiar. It was just like the opening from *Outlander*.

There was a soft rustle from behind her, and she froze. She swallowed hard, tempted to look over her shoulder but terrified of what she'd see. Something lurked in the woods. She could feel the weight of its presence.

She strained to hear something that would indicate how close it was or what it was, but her heart began pounding so hard it drowned out all sound. But not hard enough that it drowned out the thoughts in her head, specifically Granny MacLeod's prediction. What if she really had seen Abby's future and got the date wrong? What if she was going to die in the woods tonight? Right here. Right now.

Her breathing tried to outdo the frantic beating of her heart. She'd either faint or hyperventilate if she didn't get herself under control.

You're being ridiculous! You don't have a superstitious bone in your body. This has nothing to do with Granny MacLeod. You're just nervous they'll see you, which they totally will if you don't calm the heck down. Your imagination is getting the better of you. No one is breathing down your neck. You're just—

A big hand clamped over her mouth.

Chapter Seventeen

♥

Relax. It's me," a familiar deep voice said against her ear as she fought to free herself.

Abby smelled whiskey on Hunter's breath. So instead of responding to her repeated texts, he'd chosen to go to a bar and drown his feelings for Sloane? Abby wanted to bite the hand he'd yet to remove from her mouth. Before she had a chance, he reached under her sweater, hauled her to her feet by the back of her jumpsuit, then proceeded to half-drag her down the path.

She told herself she didn't want to bite him because he'd hurt her feelings but because he'd terrified her. He was also ruining what she was positive would be the video that reignited her career.

As they moved deeper into the woods and the women's voices and the firelight began to fade, he nudged her along another path, his hand still firmly over her mouth. "I'm going to take my hand away but don't make a sound."

"You are—"

He clamped his hand over her mouth again, cutting

off her furious words. "If you think my aunt's a pain in your ass now, you don't want to know what she'd do if she discovered you filming them tonight."

His hot breath tickled her ear, and she shivered. His lips curved against her cheek, and she stomped on his foot, smiling when he muttered a curse.

After Hunter guided her along the path with one hand over her mouth and the other pressed to her lower back for what felt like an hour but was in all likelihood less than five minutes, they stepped into a clearing just up from the yellow barn.

As soon as he removed his hands from her mouth and back, she whipped around, about to tell him exactly what she thought of him, but the words dried up in her throat when he said "Strip" and began taking off his jacket.

She worked the saliva in her mouth to get the words out. "If you think I'm going to have sex with you after the way you manhandled me, you have—"

"Abby, I don't want to have sex with you."

"Why not?" she said without thinking, her eyes glued to his chest as he stripped off his shirt. Wrong thing to ask! Even though she really did want to know.

"Because you were lying in a bed of poison ivy."

Her eyes jerked from his chest to his face. "I was not."

But then her mind went someplace else entirely. It seemed she wasn't as concerned that he was telling her the truth and that she had been lying in a bed of poison ivy. What she really wanted to know was: Would he want to have sex with her if she hadn't been?

"Yes, you were. I'll take you back tomorrow, and you can see for yourself. But right now, you're going to take off your clothes and then put on my shirt. And you're not going to scratch, rub, or touch yourself in any way."

Maybe because it sounded a little dirty and Hunter was standing in front of her half naked in the moonlight, she shrugged off her sweater and began taking off her jumpsuit without first telling him to turn around. The memory of her conversation with Sloane quickly cleared up any *let's get down and dirty* thoughts.

"Do you mind?" she snapped, twirling her index finger.

She couldn't be sure but she thought his lips might've twitched before he turned his back on her. The man might be annoying but his back truly was a work of art, she thought while stepping out of her jumpsuit and then undoing her bra, mesmerized by the sculpted lines of his smooth, golden skin. Her eyes took a leisurely tour over all that masculine beauty before blinking to a stop at the deep purple pucker peeking above his jeans on the lower right side, and she gasped.

He whipped around. "What's wrong?"

"Hunter!" She crossed her arms over her bare chest.

He raised his eyes to her face and held up an apologetic hand. "Sorry. I thought you saw something that scared you."

"I did." She lifted her chin. "Your back. You were shot."

His face hardened, and he turned around. He crossed his arms and the muscles on his back flexed as if daring her to say anything more.

"I didn't notice the scar the other day ..."

"My tool belt covers it." He glanced at her over his

broad and muscled shoulder. "You've got five seconds to finish stripping and putting on my shirt before I turn around."

"You were shot when you tried to save Sloane's brother, Danny, weren't you?"

"I wondered how long it would take for the gossip to start after I left. I didn't get shot trying to save Danny. I got shot recovering his body." He turned and looked her in the eyes before walking past her. "That'll teach you to listen to small-town gossip, Abby. They never get it right."

She stood almost completely naked in the golden light of the moon, and he hadn't so much as sneaked another peek.

As she bent over to pick up his shirt, he said, "Leave your clothes on the ground. I'll get them later."

She squeezed her eyes shut, praying he hadn't turned around to deliver his mandate.

"Panties off too," he added, his voice gruff. "And your sneakers."

So much for that hope, she thought, and shrugged into his shirt. She was just about to set off across the meadow to the house when he called, "Abby, this way."

She turned to see him heading for the far corner of the barn and decided she might as well follow him. She couldn't afford to have poison ivy, especially now that she was about to get her new channel off the ground. If anyone would know how to take care of it, Hunter would.

He shone a flashlight at her feet, lighting the way to where he stood beside an outdoor shower made of cedar.

The water was already running, steam billowing into the cool night air. "Get in. Don't worry about the shirt. You can take it off when you're in there."

"Okay, but can you at least tell me why I'm having a shower outside in the middle of the night?" she asked as she got in and began peeling off his now wet shirt.

"You need to get the urushiol off you. It's the sticky oil from the plant that causes the allergic reaction. Here." He handed her a bottle of liquid detergent. "I'm going to get you some towels and a salve."

She held up the bottle and made a face. "You expect me to wash my hair with this?"

He looked at her like she was being a diva.

"Trust me, if you had crazy-curly hair like me, you'd understand."

"I've got some shampoo and conditioner you can use. But you have to wash your hair with dish soap first. It'll cut through the oil."

"Okay, I wasn't expecting that." She grinned at the thought of Hunter using conditioner and squirted the green liquid soap into her palm.

"Liz used me as her guinea pig. She was experimenting with shampoo and conditioner made with honey before she died."

His face had changed, and she felt bad for teasing him. "I'm sorry. I—"

"Duck," he said, just before she was dive-bombed by two bats.

* * *

After he'd finally convinced Abby the bats were gone
and it was safe to get out of the shower, Hunter took
her place and lathered up with the dish soap. He'd been
careful not to touch her anywhere the poison ivy might
have but wasn't willing to take the risk that he was
wrong. *Although it might've been worth the risk,* he
thought, remembering how she'd looked standing in the
moonlight. He'd never been one for curvy women. He'd
always been attracted to the strong, athletic type.

Through a cloud of steam, he glanced to where she
sat on a log in another of his shirts with a towel draped
over her head to protect her from bats, working her cell
phone. The woman was addicted to the thing. She'd just
about pitched a fit when he'd wiped it down. No doubt
she'd guessed his intention to delete the video she'd
shot at the standing stones. He would have if she hadn't
looked close to tears.

He knew he was in trouble the moment he spotted
her in the woods tonight, and his heart had stuttered to
a stop seeing her lying there. He'd panicked, and Hunter
didn't panic. But his mind had immediately gone to
Granny MacLeod's premonition. Abby's belief that the
prophecy was about her past and not her future hadn't
been enough to shut down the fear.

Once he realized she was all right, he'd panicked
for an entirely different reason. The emotions that had
stopped him cold were over the top for someone he'd
known for little more than a week. She'd gotten to him.
He felt something for her, something he'd vowed never
to feel for anyone else again. He couldn't completely
shut down his feelings for his family and longtime

friends, but he could and should shut them down for her.

As though sensing him watching her from the shower, she looked up and gave him a blinding smile. "So, Mr. Cranky Pants, Sadie thinks the *Outlander* attraction is a brilliant idea."

Mr. Cranky Pants. Seriously? That made him want to smile. He wished that was all it was, but it wasn't—it was her. Abby and her optimism and resilience, her wide smile, pretty green eyes, and flame-colored hair, and that body he couldn't stop thinking about.

He'd known from the moment he'd met her that she'd turn his world upside down. And if her plans for a tourist attraction with the standing stones playing an integral role came to fruition, things were going to get a whole lot worse around here.

"Stop glaring at me. It's a great idea. We're going to be rich. And even though you're being all negative and grumpy about it, I'll cut you in on the action. When I go back to LA, I'll pay you to manage the attraction. How does that sound?"

Like he'd be left running the show when she eventually headed back to her real life in LA. He wasn't sure why he resented the idea of her leaving more than he resented the idea of her staying and turning his quiet world into a sideshow. Yeah, right—if he needed a sign to show him just how into Abby he was, he'd just gotten it.

"Like you haven't heard a word I said. My aunt isn't exactly your biggest fan, Abby, and the standing stones are sacred to the members of the Sisterhood."

The owners of Three Wise Women Bookstore and Winter Johnson, the mayor, founded the group decades before. No one in town knew much about them or who belonged, but Hunter did. Mostly because he spent so much time in the woods and had come upon their gatherings. As he understood it, the Sisterhood was a group of women who celebrated their connection to each other and Mother Earth.

Little Miss Sunshine's face said it all. She saw only rainbows and pots of gold and had no interest in his negativity.

He turned off the shower and grabbed a towel off the back wall, thinking the day had gone from bad to worse. But as he stepped out of the shower, Abby gasped. He looked up in time to see her fall backward off the log.

Securing the towel at his waist, he went over to give her a hand up. "There was a reason I told you to sit over there." He nodded at the chair.

"You could've warned me you were getting out of the shower." She glanced at him from under her lashes while straightening the towel over her head.

"You act like you've never seen a man's body before. One that's mostly covered with a towel."

"The towel isn't that big, and you are." She glanced at him. "And, no, I've never seen a man like you naked before. But whatever. We can't all be like you and not bat an eye when we see someone mostly naked."

So that's where the attitude was coming from. "Trust me, I did more than bat an eye, Abby. I'm just really good at not showing it." It was the truth, but probably not one he should've admitted. But he'd sensed he'd hurt her feelings when he walked by her without reacting. Seems he'd been right, on both counts.

She smiled. "I didn't think you noticed…It doesn't matter. I didn't fall off the log because of you. I fell off because of me."

"Yeah, I've noticed you have a tendency to fall," he said, amused at her attempt to cover her reaction.

Her eyes narrowed. "I'm tired. It was a long day at the festival. Made even longer when the man I was counting on abandoned me, and I had to pack up on my own. In case you're wondering, I'm talking about you."

He crouched in front of her and rested a hand on her knee. "Abby—"

"No, I get it. You haven't seen Sloane since she broke your engagement so you went to a bar and drowned your sorrows. I wouldn't have wanted you to drive anyway. But the least you could've done is respond to my texts."

"I wasn't at a bar drowning my sorrows."

"You weren't?"

"No. Owen had a problem with Boyd Carlisle. He lives up the mountain and sells moonshine without a license. He doesn't like cops, especially Owen, but he does like me, so I went up to talk to him. And the only way Boyd will talk is if you drink with him. I didn't get your texts until I came down off the mountain." He gave her knee a light squeeze. "I'm sorry I abandoned you."

"It's okay. You went to help Owen so I can't really be mad at you." She glanced at her phone and then back at him. "But you know, it really was exhausting doing that all on my own, and I even helped Elsa pack up too."

That was a surprise, but what Abby was attempting to do wasn't. Earlier today, she'd been trying to get him on video. "If you're trying to make me feel guilty, it won't work." It did, but he wasn't about to tell her that.

"Oh, come on." She held up her phone. "One little interview won't kill you. And you don't even have to get dressed. We'll do it right now."

"You want to interview me in my towel?"

"Ah, yeah. Sex sells, and while I don't want it to go to your head, you look delicious."

He stood up and crossed his arms, trying not to smile. "Delicious?"

She wrinkled her nose. "That's not what I meant to say. Sexalicious." She groaned.

And this time he did laugh. "Thanks, but I think I'll pass." He turned to head for the barn. "I'll—"

"Edible. Delectable. Urgh."

"Abby, stop while you're ahead. I was never going to agree to an interview anyway. I'll be out in a minute to take you back to the farm."

Five minutes later, he came to get her, only to see that she'd fallen off the log again. "That's it," he said, frustrated and concerned at the same time. "No more overdoing it, Abby." He scooped her into his arms. "Are you okay?"

"Just embarrassed," she said.

"There's nothing to be embarrassed about."

"Dangerously sexy?" She sighed. "Now I get it right." She wiggled her feet. "It's okay, you can put me down. I can walk."

"I feel better carrying you." She felt good in his

arms—too good. Out of the two of them, it was Abby who was dangerously sexy.

"Why won't you let me interview you? I heard about the little boy you rescued at Willow Creek. Shane and your cousin said he would've died if it wasn't for you. Can you really talk to bears?"

He snorted a laugh. "No, I can't talk to bears."

"Then why did they say the only reason that little boy is alive is because you got between him and a bear?"

Someone must've spotted him with a long-range scope. "The bears know me, and I know them. I respect them, and they respect me. I can read them. She wasn't going to attack."

"Shane said the ranger would've shot the bear. So you saved two lives. Why won't you take the credit?" She played with the button on his shirt and murmured, "Because from what I've heard, you're more than happy to take the blame, even when it's not your fault."

Every muscle inside him tensed. He knew what she was talking about. "Sounds like you got an earful when I left. Remember what I said, Abby. They never get it right."

"Maybe it's you who's wrong, Hunter. Sloane doesn't hate you. From what I saw, she doesn't blame you for her brother's death. Maybe in that moment, she did. Grief can make you a little crazy. But I don't think she does now."

"You don't know what you're talking about." He lowered her to her feet at the farmhouse door, then went to turn away.

She latched on to his arm. "Wait. Listen. You need to hear what she said."

He turned around and moved into Abby, backing her against the door. "You need to stop talking."

She placed her palms on his chest, not to push him away as he expected, hoped, but to gather his shirt in her hands and hold him close. "She helped me carry the tables to the parking lot."

He closed his eyes, pressing his forehead against the door, wanting to leave, but something kept him there and it wasn't Abby's grip on his shirt.

"Her mother called her name, and I said 'You're Hunter's Sloane' and she said 'Not anymore.' She wasn't angry. If anything, she sounded sad. I heard it in her voice, and you might know the woods and bears and every poisonous plant and creature out there, but I know people."

"Stop."

"I said you were a good man." She shook him a little, as though to get him to look at her. "You need to hear this." He looked down at her, and she held his gaze. "She said 'I know he's a good man.' You don't say that about someone you hate or someone you blame for your brother's death, Hunter. You say that about a man who is good and kind and caring and—"

He kissed her to shut her up, and he kissed her because of what she said and how it made him feel. He didn't want to feel, and yet that's all he did around her. He was angry, and frustrated, and...scared. It nearly killed him to admit that, and it came out in his kiss.

This kiss was nothing like the one they'd shared that

morning. It was a searing kiss with a lot of tongue and heat. Abby let go of his shirt, and he braced himself for her to push him away. He wouldn't blame her if she did. He wanted her to.

But she didn't. She wrapped her arms around his neck and pressed against him, and all he saw was the vision of her stripped down to her panties in the moonlight. He wanted to lay her out on the porch and taste and explore every inch of her but he had to stop. He had to stop before it was too late.

He pulled back. "I'm sorry. I shouldn't have kissed you, not like that."

He turned and walked away.

Chapter Eighteen

♥

Abby had spent the better part of the night tossing and turning after the kiss she'd shared with Hunter. Apparently sexual frustration wasn't conducive to a sound sleep, which she should know because she'd spent more than a year of her marriage in the same state.

Her morning so far hadn't improved matters. She'd gotten up early for her first day on the job with Highland Tours, only to discover that the couples who'd booked the tour had gotten their days mixed up.

But in the end, it gave her and Sadie the opportunity to get the town onboard with their plan to turn Highland Falls into the destination of choice for lovers of all things Scottish, including hunky highlanders.

Abby subscribed to the *Go big or go home* way of thinking when it came to business. She just hoped her lack of sleep didn't mess with her head, because the mayor had suggested they hold the meeting at Three Wise Women Bookstore.

She parked the tour bus on Main Street. Other than the hardware store, the grocery store, Penelope's

Pet Emporium, and the Village Green, she hadn't seen much of the pretty mountain town. The street was lined with leafy trees and old-fashioned black lampposts from which baskets of cascading orange and fuchsia flowers hung. Wooden and wrought-iron benches for weary shoppers and people watchers dotted the sidewalk.

The street was warm and welcoming, just like the shop windows proudly displaying their wares from beneath colorful awnings. Brick storefronts were interspersed with wooden storefronts and Victorian homes with gingerbread trim. Three Wise Women Bookstore was housed in a stately white Victorian house with violet trim.

In her great-aunt's second journal, which Abby was currently reading, the bookstore had been just a pipe dream. But Liz had mapped everything out to the smallest detail. Abby saw similarities between herself and her aunt as she read. They were both driven and determined, and Liz believed in *Go big or go home* as much as Abby did. Her aunt hadn't had much money either, and yet she'd made her dreams come true. *With a little help from her friends,* Abby thought, looking up at the bookstore from where she stood on the sidewalk.

A white car with a blue Highland Falls logo pulled up behind the tour bus. Chief Campbell.

She briefly closed her eyes on a sigh and then turned to Sadie, who'd joined her on the sidewalk. They were both wearing their tour bus uniforms: white shirts, kilts, wool socks, and kick-butt black boots. "You know, Sadie, I think you should present our vision to the town. After all, they're your friends and neighbors."

"I can't. You have to do it. You're way more enthusiastic and convincing than me. Besides"—she lowered her voice—"I'm afraid I'll slip up about the you-know-what."

The last thing Abby wanted was for Elsa and members of the Sisterhood to get word of their plans for the standing stones. Even Sadie had no idea how elaborate Abby's plans had become. As she'd tossed in her sleep the night before, the ideas had kept coming, each one bigger than the last. And, she was positive, more lucrative.

"It's okay. I'll do it." Abby glanced to her right as the chief approached with his thumbs hooked into his gun belt.

"So what's this I hear about you cooking up a new get-rich scheme, Fancy Pants? It better not have anything to do with the farm or the barn, or this time I won't allow the Mackenzie family to sway me. I'll put you in jail and throw away the key."

Abby opened her mouth to tell him what she thought about his threat and to remind him the farmhouse was hers to do with as she pleased. Then she closed it. Like Elsa, Owen had featured heavily in her aunt's journals. He'd been Liz's biggest cheerleader and champion, sticking with her through thick and thin.

So while Abby had yet to see the characteristics that made her aunt love the man, she gave him a smile and the respect Liz would've expected her to give. "You'll hear all about it in a few minutes, Chief. And just so you know, I've cleared it with Hunter." Cleared it as in she'd been completely aboveboard with her plans, not that he'd given them a thumbs-up. Still, the chief didn't need to know that.

That got her a *harrumph* from Owen. But as he held open the door for her and Sadie, he asked, "How's he doing? I heard about what happened at Summer Solstice with Sloane and her mother. I was tempted to set the two of them straight, but he'd probably never speak to me again if I did."

And there it was, a hint of why her aunt loved this man. She gave the chief's arm a reassuring pat. "He's okay. And if he actually lets what I told him sink in, he'll be better than okay."

He frowned. "What did you tell him?"

Abby hesitated as several women, including Elsa and the mayor, looked over from where they stood in front of a sweeping staircase of polished honey-colored wood. The rooms on either side of the staircase had been opened up to reveal shelves upon shelves stuffed full of books. Small groupings of brown leather chairs sat on an oriental rug in the space to her left. At the back of the room on the right, an ornate wooden bar served as a checkout counter. A gilt-framed mirror with gold veining leaned against the red-painted wall behind it, creating a dramatic backdrop. As did the gold chandeliers.

Abby smiled at the women before lowering her voice to tell the chief what she'd told Hunter about Sloane not blaming him before he shut Abby up with a kiss that blew her mind. She didn't tell the chief that part, but she might as well have, considering his look of shock. At least it wasn't tinged with horror. And she knew that because he rewarded her with a half smile, waving Elsa over to share what Abby had just told him.

Hunter's aunt nodded as she listened to Owen, then

she surprised Abby by saying, "Perhaps my best friend knew what she was doing after all. Thank you for being there for our boy."

"It was—" Abby began before a panicked-looking Sadie waved her over. She was standing with her grandmother, the owner of Bites of Bliss, and another woman.

"Ina and my grandmother are pumping me for information about our new tour, Abby. So maybe you should get on with the presentation? I don't want to spoil anything."

"I'll grab myself a coffee before the meeting begins," Owen said as he walked away.

As Elsa headed in Granny MacLeod's direction, she moved three woman along, and Abby caught a glimpse of a round display. There, prominently featured among the stacks of books, were several copies of *Outlander*.

Abby picked one up, hoping to gauge just how much the bookstore owner knew about the series. "My friends back in LA are rabid fans of this show."

Elsa walked back to the table. "The television series was adapted from Diana Gabaldon's books. They were wildly popular before the show and are even more so now. I prefer the books myself."

"I'll have to give them a try," Abby said as she mentally edited all references to *Outlander* from her upcoming sales pitch. She'd focus not only on the busloads of tourists they'd bring to town but also on the free, national advertising they'd get from being featured on her YouTube channel.

"Let me know if you do, and I'll order them for you

in audio." At what must've looked like her blank stare, Elsa said, "You mentioned your difficulties reading so I thought perhaps you'd prefer listening to the books instead."

Abby looked around at the rows upon rows of books in either room. It was as if Elsa had opened up a whole new world for her. "Thank you. I never would've thought to ask. Until I moved here, I did whatever I could to avoid reading. But the way my aunt talks about books in her journal made me feel like I was missing out."

"Not anymore you won't. I'm making it my mission to guide you on your journey from book hater to book lover." She smiled and reached for Abby's hand, giving it a gentle squeeze. "Lizzie would be so happy to know her words inspired you to give reading another chance."

"She loved you and Owen very much, you know." Abby smiled as she glanced around the bookstore again. "This is exactly how she'd imagined it. She must've loved it here."

"She did, and I hope you come to love it too. Now, let's hear about this new tour you and Sadie are introducing."

* * *

Two hours later, as they walked back to the tour bus, Sadie said, "Can you believe how well that went? I'm still in shock. I mean, don't get me wrong, you made an even bigger believer out of me today. But I didn't expect Elsa and Owen to get onboard so easily. They actually seemed excited about it."

Even better to Abby's way of thinking, they seemed to have changed their minds about her. She didn't realize until today how much she'd wanted Owen and Elsa to like her. Maybe because they'd meant so much to her aunt, a woman Abby had grown to love through reading her journals. And now that she seemed to be growing on her aunt's best friends, Abby didn't want to do anything to upset them.

"So," she said as they got back on the tour bus and she slid into the driver's seat, "I think we're going to pare back some of the events at the standing stones. We won't have Hunter build any permanent structures there."

He probably wouldn't have agreed to anyway. She'd been thinking of having him build a replica of Jamie and Claire's cabin on Fraser's Ridge and also life-size stand-ins of the couple for people to stick their faces in and pose for pictures. She'd planned on stand-ins for Brianna and Roger too.

"Um, I didn't know about the permanent structures. But I'm onboard with doing away with them and paring down the events," Sadie said.

"Sorry, I forgot I hadn't mentioned them to you yet. We'll just do the one event at the standing stones and keep it low-key and respectful."

An hour later, sitting with Sadie at the farmhouse's dining room table on a Skype call with Mallory Maitland, discussing her expectations for the bachelorette party tour, Abby's earlier optimism began to fade. She was getting a funky vibe off the gorgeous blonde whose husband had reportedly left her a gazillionaire widow. Funky, as in it was beginning to feel like Abby's and

Sadie's hope that the bachelorette weekend would put them in the black was going up in smoke.

"Just so we're clear, instead of three nights, you're doing two, and you want to cancel the suites at Three Wild Women Winery on the Fourth and go with the sleeping-under-the-stars idea instead?" It's what Abby had suggested when it looked like they were going to lose the tour completely. "And you want to go with regular rooms at the winery on the Friday after the *Outlander* event?"

Keeping a smile plastered on her face and her eyes on Mallory's, Abby wrote *She's broke* on a piece of paper and slid it in front of Sadie.

"Are you kidding me?" Sadie said, and then got a deer-caught-in-the-headlights look on her face.

Geesh, and Abby thought she had a problem keeping her feelings to herself. She patted Sadie's hand. "I'm so sorry," Abby said, then looked under the table. "Naughty girl, Bella. No more humping Sadie. Sorry about that, Mallory. Little dogs. Now let's get—"

"You know, sleeping under the stars sounds fun and adventurous. Maybe we should just do it both nights? What do you think?" Mallory asked, looking desperate.

Don't do it, Abby. Don't do it, she told herself, but of course she did it anyway. "Please don't be offended, Mallory, but has something happened since you made the initial booking with Daisy at Three Wild Women Winery?"

Beside her, Sadie groaned, obviously seeing their future go up in flames. But the thing was, if Abby was right, she had a fairly good idea what Mallory was going through and felt sorry for her.

"Is it that obvious?" There was a sigh in Mallory's voice as if she was mad at herself for not doing a better job of hiding her distress. She looked tired and a little sad. "Harry died last fall, and his first wife contested his will. We tried to handle it through mediation, but now it's going to court."

"I'm so sorry. That must be really hard." With her eyes locked on Mallory, Abby wrote *Google* on a piece of paper and then *Don't react* before passing it to Sadie.

"It's horrible. Honestly, if I hadn't promised Harry on his deathbed that I'd give his niece the wedding he wanted her to have, I would've canceled. But Blair would never forgive me, and neither would Harry. He adored her."

"Um, do you adore Blair?" Abby asked.

She made a face. "Harry adored her enough for everyone."

Sadie nudged Abby's knee and turned the iPad screen. Mallory wasn't wife number two; she was wife number three. And from the photo in the gossip section of the *Atlanta Star*, she was a dead ringer for Mrs. Maitland the First, only thirty years younger. The headline above the article about the upcoming court battle said it all: TRUE LOVE ALWAYS WINS, and it wasn't Mallory's picture beneath the heading; it was Mrs. Maitland the First's.

Abby and Sadie shared a commiserating glance. They had to help this poor woman. "Don't worry, Mallory. We'll take care of everything for you. I'll send you the itinerary by end of day, and you can let us know if it works for you."

Sadie, who'd just taken a sip of her coffee, sprayed the

screen. So maybe she wasn't as sympathetic to Mallory's plight as Abby.

"Darn that Bella." She patted Sadie's back while waving goodbye to Mallory. Abby disconnected before Sadie blurted out her feelings for the other woman to hear.

"Abby! We can't take care of everything. We'll go broke." Sadie held up the itinerary they'd come up with for gazillionaire Mallory Maitland.

"We're already broke." Abby took the itinerary, thinking while money-wise she was broke, she didn't feel broke. Not like she had in LA. She and Bella were no longer living in a car. They had a roof over their heads (albeit one that needed to be replaced), food, a new friend, a job, a really good plan to get back on her feet (even if they had hit a snag), and a dangerously sexy man who'd kissed her senseless last night. And who was no doubt having morning-after regrets.

But she couldn't think about that now and smoothed the paper Sadie had crumpled. "We just have to tweak the itinerary a little and think of some really fun, free things to do. We've got the biggest event covered, and it's going to be awesome. We'll just stick with the *Outlander* theme and go from there."

"I'm still a little worried about the night at the standing stones. I know you say no one will find out about us being there, but I'm with Hunter on this. People talk. And now that we won't be paying actors to play the roles of Jamie and Claire and hunky highlanders, we can't get them to sign an NDA."

"We can. We just have to give them another incentive. For some people, appearing on YouTube might

be enough. So we have to get rolling on the videos."
Thanks to Sadie, everything was in place. They'd also
started working on a trailer to spur interest before the
channel went live. "You're from here—you must know
some hot guys."

"I left for college and only came back a couple times
a year to see my grandmother. Or to bail out my brother.
Most of my friends left town like me. So my connections
are with business owners and the chief of police."

"Your connections with the business community are
more important than ever now. We're going to need
donations for food and camping gear and a whole bunch
of other stuff. But if we spread out the requests, we
should be okay.

"And while Mallory's basically broke, the other
women in the party aren't. I checked out the list of names,
and every one of them is connected to major money.
We'll head to Main Street when they arrive, show them
around and take in the Fourth of July celebrations that
evening. Friday will be all things *Outlander*, and maybe
we can organize a fun, free outdoor activity, and a picnic
before they leave on Saturday. They can do the Unicorn
Hunt in the garden maze, and your grandmother can tell
her stories." Abby smiled, feeling better already. They
could totally pull this off.

"Minnie and Myrtle, the horse and the goat, aren't
available. But you won't be able to keep Granny away."

"Perfect." Abby scratched out Friday's spa treatments
at the winery and replaced it with all things *Outlander*
and a fun, free outdoor activity. She swapped Saturday's
trail riding and white-water rafting with a picnic at the

Village Green. She chewed on the end of her pen. "I think I can take care of the unicorn. Wolf would totally work."

"His owner would also work as the hunkiest of high-landers, but I don't see either happening."

"He would, wouldn't he?" she said, thinking of Hunter last night as he stepped out of the shower. She released a dreamy sigh and then grimaced at the intrigued expression that came over Sadie's face.

"Okay, what happened? And please don't hold back. I want every last detail. No. I *need* every last detail. It's been years since I've had sex. I mean, I've had sex, just not very good sex." She wrinkled her nose. "Now that I think about it, I don't know why I even bothered. That's not true. I wanted a baby, and I was willing to put up with mediocre sex, and a mediocre boyfriend, so I could have one." She gave Abby a half smile. "I've always wanted to be a mom, and it's beginning to look like that's not going to happen for me."

"You've got lots of time. We're around the same age, aren't we?" Abby had never had a burning desire to have children so she couldn't really relate to what obviously was very important to Sadie.

"I'm twenty-seven. So, yeah, I do have time. But I've decided as much as I want a baby, I don't want the daddy to come with it. They're too much work."

Abby thought Sadie's brother might have soured her on men but kept her opinion to herself. "You can adopt."

"I've already started looking into adoption and in vitro. But right now, financially, neither is an option."

"Then we better get back to work so that it is."

"Absolutely, but first you're going to tell me about you and Hunter."

"There's really not much to tell. We didn't have sex. Except his kiss really made me wish that we did." She shook her head. "It's better that we didn't."

"Because of Sloane?"

Oh, crap—how could she have forgotten about Sloane? "Actually, I meant because I'll be leaving by the end of the summer." She made a face at the sharpness in her tone.

Obviously she was way more into Hunter than she thought if being reminded that there was another woman in his life, one he actually loved, made her cranky. She was rarely cranky. She reminded herself that Hunter was, and it was a trait she didn't appreciate. Although he hadn't been cranky lately. He really needed to be cranky again.

"Sorry. I shouldn't have snapped at you."

Sadie gave her hand a gentle squeeze. "You're falling for him, aren't you?"

"Of course not. I…Maybe. A little. But it wouldn't work anyway. Like I said, I'll be leaving at the end of the summer."

"Summer flings are the best."

"I don't have time for a fling, and neither do you, so back to work. And good news, I've figured out how to handle two nights of sleeping under the stars with women who, I have a sneaking suspicion, aren't into roughing it: glamping."

"What's glamping?"

"Glamorous camping. We'll have Hunter build us

a couple yurts or tepees, and we'll go all out on the interiors with furs and throw rugs and furniture from the farmhouse. It'll be fun. All we need to do is mow my half of the meadow."

"Um, did you notice that Hunter seems to be playing a very big role in our new itinerary?"

Chewing her thumbnail, Abby nodded. "We're going to have to talk to him about it. Especially now that I've realized he's the one person who can help us round up some men to play hunky highlanders."

Sadie pushed away from the table. "Good luck with that."

"Wait, we're partners. We have to do this together."

Ten minutes later, Abby was walking across the meadow toward the yellow barn by her lonesome. Despite wholeheartedly disagreeing with Sadie that she'd have better luck on her own, she left Sadie to call on local business owners while Abby was off to bait the wolf in his den.

After last night, she was nervous to face Hunter. She'd pushed too hard to make him see that he was carrying a lot of guilt over something for which he had no control. She'd pushed just as hard to get him to see that Sloane no longer hated him.

In all likelihood, she probably never had. Grief and guilt made people do things they never would've thought themselves capable of. Her thoughts drifted to her father, and she wondered if, like Hunter had suggested, those were the same emotions that had driven him to abandon her and her mom. It seemed to her that Hunter had understood her father because he'd also let grief and guilt rule his decisions when he came back from Afghanistan. But if she wanted him to help her, she decided it might be a good idea not to point that out.

She drew in a deep, hopefully confidence-inspiring breath as she reached the barn. At the hollow thud of what sounded like an ax hitting a log, she cautiously rounded the side of the barn. Instead of a warm tingle, her womb combusted at the sight of a shirtless Hunter wielding an ax.

Positive from her own reaction that this video would go viral, she raised her phone. Hunter's hair was damp and dark and held back from his ruggedly handsome face with a leather thong. His biceps flexed, the heavy veins in his forearms standing out with the force of each blow. His muscles rippled and contracted under his sweat-slicked, sun-bronzed back.

She was so caught up in his powerful warrior's body that she didn't realize he wasn't just chopping wood; an animal was beginning to take form with each savage stroke of the ax. Sunlight glinted off the edge of the silver blade as he swung it over his shoulder, and she gasped when it sliced through the wood, perilously close to his thigh. He turned his head and pulled out earbuds, which explained why he hadn't heard her approach. Burying the blade of the ax in another log, he picked up a towel and wiped himself down. She didn't think it was a good sign that she found that as erotic as the way he wielded the ax.

It also wasn't a good sign that he now prowled toward her making a *give me* motion with his fingers. "Hand over the phone, Abby."

"I didn't film your work. I didn't even know you were carving at first."

"Really. So what were you filming?"

"Um, your muscles." She put the phone behind her back. "Please don't make me delete it. I promise, I won't promote it as muscle porn, although it totally is."

He looped his towel around her neck and, holding both ends, drew her against his still damp chest. She thought he meant to kiss her and tipped her head back, only for him to drop the end of the towel and snag the phone from her hand.

"Hunter, that's not fair. Give me back my phone." Her cheeks heated as he watched the video she'd filmed. She'd made noises while videoing him. How embarrassing. It sounded like she was watching porn. "That's the only one." She groaned when he kept scrolling.

She wanted to say something about it being private, but given that she'd just filmed him, she didn't feel like listening to him point that out and went to sit on the log to wait him out.

Her mouth dropped. The log was gone, and for a brief and painful moment, she wondered if it was a sign that he didn't want her there. But then she lifted her eyes and saw that, in its place, a swing now hung from the oak tree.

And seeing it there did funny things to her heart. He wanted her here, with him. A man who preferred to be on his own with just his dog for companionship had opened his space to her.

She turned back to him and, while blinking back tears, reached for her phone. "Let me delete it."

"If the video's that important that you're going to cry, you can—"

"It's not the video. You made me a swing."

"Abby, it's not a big deal. I had some rope and an old board lying around."

She smiled at the touch of panic in his gruff voice. "Don't worry, Hunter. I know it's not a sign of your undying love for me. But I love it. Thank you."

From the look in his eyes when she mentioned undying love, she decided to forgo the kiss she wanted to give him. Instead, she walked over and sat on the swing, noting the beautiful slab of polished wood before she did so. No matter how much he tried to make light of the gesture, he'd obviously put both time and thought into it.

She smiled as she wrapped her hands around the thick rope. She couldn't remember the last time she'd been on a swing. Before the accident and her stroke, when she was carefree and adventurous Abby, she'd soar so high that her mom's voice would squeak with panic when she'd call out to her.

"Abby." Sort of like Hunter's did now, only his voice was deep and gruff and hitched instead of squeaked.

She opened her eyes, laughing when she discovered why the memory felt so real. She was swinging so high that her head brushed the leaves of the tallest branch.

"Abby," Hunter muttered when she leaned back, crossing her legs at the ankles and raising her feet to feel herself fly. This was the first time in a very long time that she felt like the carefree girl she used to be. Hunter had no idea what an absolutely wonderful gift he'd given her.

Chapter Nineteen

♥

Heard about the boy you rescued from the bear. Is it true you're an animal whisperer?" the kid from the hardware store asked as he attempted to help Hunter unload the sheets of plywood from the back of the delivery truck.

And people wondered why Hunter preferred to be left alone. "No. I'm not an animal whisperer."

Yesterday morning, he'd gone into town to order the plywood, flashing, and ice and water barrier, but Ed had been waiting on a delivery of plywood, so Hunter had taken the day to work on the eagle that visited him in his dreams.

Except every damn time he got a glimpse of the log in his peripheral vision, he'd see Abby falling off it. So he'd made her a swing that made her cry. And while he might not understand why a piece of wood and some rope made her weepy, he could handle the tears. What he couldn't handle was watching her swing on the damn thing.

She'd gone so high he'd been afraid she'd fly off and break her neck. But did his concern bother her? Not one bit. The woman who'd fallen off a log not once but twice laughed at his concern. Worse, the smile that had lit up her face and the laugh that bubbled out of her with joyful abandon got to him.

If he'd had any doubt that she'd gotten to him, all he had to do was look at his phone. He'd captured her leaning back, her toes in the air and her head tipped back, with a look on her face that had stolen his breath.

As he'd taken her picture, he'd heard Owen's voice in his head, warning him about Abby using her fairy magic to steal his heart. Which might've been why he'd turned his back on her and returned to work on the eagle, hoping his passion for the project would temper his desire for the wood nymph on the swing.

"Wood nymphs and fairies, you've lost your ever-loving mind," he muttered at himself in disgust. Feeling someone's eyes on him, he glanced at the kid standing in the truck's bed.

His eyes agog, the kid asked, "Are you saying it's the wood nymphs and fairies that helped you with the bear?"

Hunter swore under his breath. It didn't matter what he said, the kid would tell Ed, who'd broadcast the news to his customers at the hardware store and the rest of the business owners on Main Street. Hunter figured the whole bloody town would know by dinnertime. And he knew exactly where to lay the blame: Abby.

"No. I—" He went to answer the kid in hopes of negating some of the damage, but he'd lost his attention.

Hunter turned to see what he was looking at, and there was Abby. Wearing fire-engine-red rubber boots that matched the mass of curls piled on her head, a pair of denim shorts, and a white tank top, she attempted to push Liz's old hand mower through the meadow. *Attempted* being the operative word.

As though sensing their attention, she turned and waved, then pointed at the mower. "I think there's something wrong with it, Hunter. Would you mind taking a look? After you unload the truck, of course."

The kid scratched his head. "Do you think she knows it's a push mower and not a gas mower?"

Hunter didn't get a chance to tell the kid he doubted Abby had seen a lawn mower before, let alone cut grass, because he'd jumped off the back of the truck. "You look like you've got this covered so I'll just go give her a hand," the kid said and loped off.

"If you're not careful, she'll bat her eyelashes and give you a big smile, and before you know it, you'll be mowing the entire meadow for her." All Hunter had to do was look at himself to see the proof of his warning.

"It's not her smile I'm looking at, if you know what I mean," the kid said over his shoulder with a wink.

"How old are you?"

"Older than I look." The kid laughed.

Hunter's visceral response to that laughter bothered him almost as much as it bothered the kid when Hunter beat him to Abby's side. "What are you doing?"

"Come on, man. Can't you see she's trying to mow the meadow?" The kid stuck his hand out. "Hey there, I'm Dylan. I can give you a hand if you'd like."

"No, you can't give her a hand. You're here to unload the plywood." Hunter might as well have been talking to the lawn mower for all the good it did him.

"That's so sweet of you to offer, Dylan. Thank you. I'm Abby," she said with her big, genuine smile before frowning down at the hand mower. "But I think there's something wrong with the blades. They're hardly moving at all."

"You actually have to push the mower to make the blades turn, Abby." Hunter demonstrated by cutting a small patch. "But what I want to know is why you're mowing the meadow in the first place."

"I, uh..." She chewed on her bottom lip as though trying to come up with a reason.

"I think it's a great idea." The kid sent Hunter a challenging stare. "You never know what's hiding in there. Snakes and—"

"Exactly!" Abby said, giving Dylan a grateful smile. "I'm almost positive I stepped on a snake last week." She shuddered.

"Probably got a bunch of ticks hiding in there too," the kid said, hooking his thumbs in the pockets of his jeans and nodding. No doubt hoping for another of Abby's grateful smiles.

Her eyes went wide. "Ticks? Oh my gosh, I never thought about ticks, but you're absolutely right." This time it was Hunter who was on the receiving end of her smile. "Would you maybe be able to help me out? My muscles don't even come close to yours." She flexed, and Hunter wished she was wearing more than a white tank top. "But just my side. Except maybe you can cut a little path for when I come to visit you? I'll make you berry doughnuts."

"I'm not afraid of a little work. I'll take care of it for you," the kid offered, puffing out his chest.

"I've got it," Hunter said and then silently gave himself crap for being outmaneuvered by Abby and the kid.

"Thank you." She moved as though to hug him but then looped an arm through Dylan's instead. "You look like you have muscles too, Dylan."

The kid was a beanpole. What the hell was she up to? Hunter wondered, at the same time thinking she'd better not squeeze Dylan's biceps like she'd squeezed his in the past. The thought brought him up short. He was jealous of the kid.

"Any chance you have a kilt and can play the bagpipes?" Abby asked Dylan as they began walking away.

"Yes to the kilt, and I can sort of play the pipes."

Hunter snorted, though not as loudly as he would've in the past because he was still coming to terms with the idea that he was jealous of the kid.

"That's wonderful. Now what about your friends? Do they have kilts and musical talents too?" she asked, leaving Hunter alone with the lawn mower.

Two hours later, he'd finished mowing Abby's half of the meadow. Although she'd yet to give him a legitimate reason why. He was positive there was more behind this than the excuses Dylan had provided her with. And the reason Hunter hadn't gotten a straight answer from Abby was because she'd spent the better part of the morning eating berry doughnuts with Dylan on the front porch.

It'd taken three barked orders from Hunter for the

kid to finally finish unloading the truck and head back to the hardware store. But not before Abby had gotten his number.

Hunter planned to have a few words with Abby when he finally found her. He cleaned the mower's blades, returning it to the shed before going in search of her. At the sound of tires on gravel, he came around the house to see Sadie pulling in.

"Hey, Sadie, do you have any idea where Abby is?" he asked when she got off the bus.

She held up a camera. "Around here somewhere. She just called to say we're going to film the video to kick off the YouTube channel. We're hoping to take it live tomorrow."

He wasn't sure what that meant, even though he was pretty sure Abby had talked to him about it before. "She had one of those channels in LA, didn't she?"

"She did. And fingers crossed this one is half as successful."

"So she did well with it?"

"Ah, yeah. She had over forty million followers and was making an easy seven figures a year."

He blinked, stunned. "I thought her ex was the one with the money."

"He was, but Abby was super successful in her own right until he sued her. If you have a husband like that, who needs enemies, right?" She looked at the plywood and smiled. "Sweet. You've already got the supplies for the yurts. I wasn't sure you'd be able to make them in time."

"Say again?"

"The yurts. You know, glamping. Sleeping under the stars. The bachelorette weekend. None of this is ringing a bell, is it? Abby never asked you, did she?"

He shook his head in the negative.

Five minutes later, Sadie had cleared up what Abby was up to with the meadow and with the kid.

"I can see by your face that you're not happy about this, and I get it. If I were you, I'd be less than thrilled at the prospect of eight women camping out here for a couple days, and I'm a little worried about invading the Sisterhood's sacred place for the *Outlander* event myself. But we'll only be there an hour at most, and we'll be super respectful. Plus, they won't even know we were there."

"Right, because gossip doesn't spread like wildfire in Highland Falls."

"Abby says we'll include an NDA and add enough incentives that the guys will go along with it."

Off the top of his head, he listed ten reasons their plan was destined to fail.

"Please, don't say any of that to Abby. She's desperate for this to work. And it's not just for herself. We're basically swallowing the cost because Abby felt sorry for Mallory. And I can't say anything, because honestly, Abby's doing this as much to help me as she's doing it to help Mallory and herself. I guess I shouldn't be surprised. She did the same in LA." Sadie held up her phone.

"I'm not following. She ran tours in LA?"

"No," she said with a laugh. "Abby helped women who were in need. Like if a woman found herself in a bad situation and it was late and she had no money, she'd call Abby to pick her up. She became the go-to Uber driver if you were a woman and down on your luck. It's all right there in her reviews." Sadie's phone *ping*ed, and she glanced at the screen and smiled. "Found her. She's going to the pond with Wolf and Bella."

"Ah, what's she doing near the pond?" he asked, getting a feeling he already knew.

"Reenacting her introduction to Honeysuckle Farm. Don't worry though, she doesn't expect you to appear in the video," Sadie said, walking toward the meadow.

"She can't seriously be thinking of throwing herself in the pond."

"No, of course not. She can't talk about her leech experience without doing her panic dance. Have you seen her dance?" Sadie did an impression of Abby dancing on the spot, then smiled up at him. "She's awesome, isn't she?"

He was glad she didn't wait for him to respond because, after hearing how Abby put herself out there for women in trouble, he would have to agree that Abby was, indeed, awesome—a remark that would've eventually make its way to his family's ears.

Instead Sadie continued. "You know, the last thing I wanted to do was to spend my summer in Highland Falls bailing out my brother, but it's been worth it just to hang out with Abby."

"It sounds like you've become friends," Hunter said, his eyes on Abby as she rounded the barn in the same outfit she'd worn the day they'd first met. Bella also had on the dress and bow she'd worn that day. Wolf, looking unimpressed, trailed after them.

"We have. It feels like we've known each other forever."

"Abby seems to have that effect on people. And seeing as you're her friend, you might want to dissuade her from reenacting her run-in with Wolf and the pond."

"Don't worry, you won't have to rescue her. She'll pretend she's falling in the pond, and then I'll edit the video to make it look like she did. We'll throw a few weeds on her then hose her down." She glanced at him. "If you'd agree to appear in the video and come to her rescue, I can almost guarantee she'd throw herself in the pond."

"Yeah, not happening."

"Abby said you wouldn't agree."

It didn't seem to matter if he'd agreed or not. On the fourth take, Abby's fake falling in the pond ended up being the real thing. "Sadie had better not be filming this," he muttered as he hauled Abby from the pond.

An hour later, she sat on the swing wearing one of Hunter's T-shirts and towel-drying her hair. "This shampoo smells so good, I want to eat it. My hair feels amazing too."

It also looked amazing, not that Hunter would share the observation with her.

She smiled up at him, placing the towel on her lap before accepting the glass of water he handed her. "Thank you, and thanks again for letting me use your shower and your shampoo. I think I might have to steal it from you."

"You forgot to thank me for rescuing you."

"I appreciated the help, but I could've climbed out by myself."

He figured she might not have been so blasé about it if leeches had used her for lunch, but they hadn't.

"You should be thanking me. I got Sadie to promise she'd delete you from the video." Abby sighed. "That's a huge sacrifice on my part, you know. Having you in the video would've guaranteed thousands of subscribers as soon as it went live."

"I'm sure Dylan would volunteer. He could wear his kilt."

She laughed. "He's cute, but not in the same league as you."

"Is that right."

"Don't let it go to your head, but it's the truth." She took a sip of water, then glanced up at him. "I know you don't want to appear in the videos, but would you consider—"

"No."

"Hunter! You don't even know what I was going to ask."

"I'm pretty sure I do, but it's probably a good idea that we clear all this up right now. I'm not making yurts, and I'm not wearing a kilt and pretending to be a high-lander, and I'm definitely not playing the bagpipes. I'm going fishing on the Fourth."

"Oh come on, please don't go. I can't pull this off without you. I won't ask you to play a hunky highlander, but I really need help with the yurts. There's no way this particular group of women will enjoy *literally* sleeping under the stars."

"Abby, do you have any idea how much it'll cost to build just one yurt?" When she shook her head, he told her, "Thousands of dollars."

"What about tepees? I saw a couple of them at the Summer Solstice Festival. They shouldn't be too hard or expensive to make."

"Good, then you and Sadie should be able to handle it, because I don't want any part of it." He turned to walk away.

"Hunter, wait. The bachelorette party probably doesn't sound like a big deal to you, but it's really important. Mallory Maitland, our client—"

"Mallory Maitland? You don't mean Mallory Maitland from Highland Falls, do you?"

"I think so. Sadie said she grew up here. Why?"

"Because the Mallory Maitland I know does her best to avoid Highland Falls. Her dad is Boyd Carlisle."

"The man you had to go talk to the night of Summer Solstice?"

Her voice dropped a bit at the end, and he imagined she was remembering why he'd left the festival and the kiss they'd shared that night. They hadn't talked about the kiss or what Sloane had said. It didn't mean he hadn't thought about it; he had. Even when he didn't want to, it was there.

"Yeah, the man who makes moonshine is Mallory's dad."

Abby moved back and forth on the swing. "It makes you wonder why she decided to have her niece's bachelorette party here, doesn't it?"

"Is that a rhetorical question?"

She rolled her eyes. "All right, I know you don't think this is a big deal. But Mallory promised her husband on his deathbed that she'd give his niece the wedding she dreamed of, and Mallory doesn't have the money because Mrs. Maitland the First is tying up the will in court. And it's not just Mallory this is important to, Hunter. It's Sadie. Highland Tours is having a horrible summer so far. Something I feel partially responsible for. And the bachelorette weekend is going to turn it around. Just FYI, you should feel a little bad about Sadie's lack of business because you're partially to blame too."

"You don't want to go there, Abby."

She made a face and began slowly pumping her legs. The memory of her soaring high in the sky yesterday had him moving behind her so he could control how high she went. He gave her a light push, and she laughed. "You can do better than that."

He made a noncommittal sound and then said, "You've told me why you want the bachelorette weekend to go well for Mallory and Sadie, but you haven't told me what's in it for you."

"It all ties in to my new YouTube channel. I'm hoping to gain a bunch of subscribers as well as get some great content. If everything goes the way I expect it to, by the end of the summer, I'll be back in LA living the good life."

"The money, the fame—that's important to you, isn't it?" He didn't know why that bothered him, but it did.

From the beginning, Abby had been open about who she was and what she wanted. But spending as much time with her as he had, he'd seen another side of her.

Or maybe what bothered him didn't have anything to do with her need to be rich and famous. Maybe what really bothered him was that she could walk away from the farm so easily.

"I can hear the censure in your voice, you know." She tipped her head to look back at him, and he retreated a couple of steps. "There's no way you can understand because of who you are. Everyone looks up to you, wants to be like you. You probably were voted most likely to be an American hero. I wasn't. I was voted most unlikely to succeed. So yeah, call me shallow, but fame and fortune are important to me. People treated me differently when I had money. They respected me. I mattered."

"You matter to . . . a lot of people, Abby." He'd caught himself before he said *me*. Because as much as he didn't want to admit it, she did.

Chapter Twenty

♥

Thanks for doing this, you guys. I really appreciate it," Abby said to her sisters via FaceTime.

"Are you kidding?" Haley said. "This is the best job ever. We're judging hot men in kilts."

This was the final audition for Hottest Highlanders, and Abby wanted a second and third opinion. Hunter was no help at all. He'd been grunting, snorting, and sighing from the top of her roof for a little more than a week, and she was positive she was as annoyed with him as he was with her. Although, since he was up there repairing her roof, she had a really hard time staying mad at him, especially when he'd also put up three tents for her last night. They weren't yurts, but she planned to glam them up.

So while it might be hard to stay mad at him after everything he'd done for her, it didn't relieve her hurt at his obvious attempts to avoid her for the past ten days. She didn't understand why he seemed distant. Still, there was a chance she was being overly sensitive and reading more into him not hanging around to chat. Maybe, like her, he was just busy. Between driving the tour bus, working on her YouTube channel and website and getting organized for the bachelorette party's arrival, she'd been a little overwhelmed herself.

Sadie was supposed to help at the audition today, but she was at the garage with the tour bus. They had less than twenty-four hours before they picked up the bachelorette party at the Asheville airport, so of course the bus would choose to start stalling while going up hills yesterday afternoon.

Abby prayed it was nothing more than a clogged fuel filter or they'd better hope the mechanic was willing to take an IOU. Between her and Sadie, they were swimming in a sea of red.

Abby's hair fell forward as she bent over to place Bella in the gated portion of the living room before turning on the TV. "I promise you won't have to stay in there for long, Boo."

As Abby had discovered, not all hunky highlanders were macho men who also loved dogs. Bella had terrified several of the contestants on day one of auditions last week.

"If you feel really bad about us giving up our morning to help you out, Abs, you can send us some of your shampoo. Your hair looks incredible."

"Haven's right. Does it smell as amazing as it looks?"

"It does, and I swear it's repairing the damage that dying it blond for all those years caused. I'll send you some, but it won't be much. There's only one bottle of shampoo and conditioner. My great-aunt made it so it's not like I can go out and buy more." Now that she thought about it, she'd give small samples to Josie and send some to Kate too. Maybe between them, they could recommend a similar shampoo to Abby.

"You said your aunt left journals. Maybe she wrote down the recipe? If she did, you could try making it yourself," Haley suggested.

"If she did, it'll be in the last journal. I know this sounds weird, but I don't want to skip ahead."

"No, I get it," Haven said. "Haley likes reading the ending first, but I don't. You'll get to it soon enough, so no worries."

At the speed Abby read, it would probably take her a year.

"Okay, ladies, let's get this show on the road." Abby opened the door to step onto the porch. "Just remember, they'll be able to hear you so keep your voices down." Abby smiled at the fifteen men in kilts who were gathered in the gravel driveway.

"Hey guys, thanks for coming out this morning. As you know, you're here because the subscribers on my YouTube channel, all one hundred thousand of them—yay—voted you to the final round!"

She still couldn't believe they'd hit a hundred thousand subscribers in under ten days and that her channel continued to grow by the hour. It was an incredible achievement, and one she couldn't take credit for.

She had Sadie, the citizens and shop owners of Highland Falls, the contenders for Hottest Highlanders, her sisters, Elinor, Kate, and He Who Shall Not Be Named—because if he ever found out his video went viral, he'd of things for her.

Elinor may no longer be wor[king in the] mansion, but she was close friends with the majority of housekeepers, groundskeepers, maids, and nannies, who—shockingly (at least to her)—were in Abby's corner, especially after the way Chandler had treated Elinor.

Abby waited for the high-fiving and backslapping among the men to stop before continuing. "Because tomorrow is the big day, and we have to make a decision right away, the subscribers won't be picking the winners. My sisters will." She turned the screen. "Say hi to Haley and Haven. And just FYI, they're as wonderful as they are gorgeous, and too young for all of you."

"Hey, don't lump us in with them." Dylan, who wore a red-plaid bandana tied around his head (his way to stand out in the videos, Abby was sure), said of himself and his two twentysomething companions, jerking his thumb at thirtysomething-year-olds, forty-year-olds, fifty-year-olds, and a sixty-year-old who made up the final contenders.

Abby didn't tell Dylan she trusted the older guys way more than she trusted him, but she learned via their clapbacks that she'd been right to keep the flirtatious say," he laughing, "but I can't hold my phone and video at the same time so I had to get a little creative." Besides a shower cap, the only hat Abby had been able to find was straw with a red daisy in the band, which she wore with her denim shorts, white shirt tied at the waist, and wedge sandals. She tucked the phone in the band, adding a piece of electrical tape at the top to keep it in place.

"Can you see all right?" she asked her sisters. They nodded, and Abby fit the straw hat on her head. Then she said to the men, "Okay, so I'll just go over how this is going to work one more—"

A familiar deep voice from up on the roof cut her off, and she bowed her head, nearly losing her phone.

"Jamie and Ewan, what are you doing down there when you're supposed to be up here helping me?" Hunter yelled at his cousins.

Catching the sheepish glances her top contenders exchanged—they were almost as hot as their cousin— Abby stepped farther out onto the path and tipped her head back to glare up at him. "Hunter, Jamie and Ewan are—"

He cut her off again, not by yelling this time but by laughing.

She knew what she looked like so she understood a smile or chuckle, but not a deep laugh that sent shock waves all the way to the tips of her toes. It was incredibly annoying that, even when Hunter was laughing at her, she found the man toe-curling hot. His hotness factor diminished somewhat when the other men joined in his laughter, all expect Dylan, who came to her defense.

"I don't know what you're laughing at. She looks hot. Doesn't she, guys?" He elbowed his laughing friend.

Abby groaned inwardly, praying that Hunter wouldn't decide to respond. Her sisters saved the day by squealing his name, clearly happy to see him.

"Hey, Haven and Haley," he responded, the rumble of amusement still in his voice.

"Why aren't you auditioning for Hottest Highlanders? Abby's followers love you," Haven said.

Crap! Abby lifted her hand to disconnect the call or at the very least mute her sister.

"Abby, take your hand away from the phone." There was no trace of amusement in his voice now, just a terse command that she couldn't seem to disobey. "And how exactly do Abby's followers know about me, Haven?"

"Don't you ever go online, man? You went viral. No accounting for taste, I guess," Dylan said, and everyone, including Abby, stared at him.

"Kid's got a death wish," Hunter's cousin murmured to his brother.

"That or balls of steel," his brother said.

She had to get ahead of this now. "It's fine, Haven. Hunter knew I was going to put the video online, eventually." She bit her bottom lip and glanced up, but he'd disappeared from view. She heard the rattle of metal against the side of the house and cringed. He was coming down the ladder.

"Okay, we better get going," she said, unable to keep a note of hysteria from her voice. If he yelled at her in

front of her sisters and these men, it would be all over
Highland Falls in minutes. His aunt would find out, and
so would his brother and Eden. Oh gosh, what if Hunter
made her take the video down?

No. He wouldn't confront her now. It wasn't his style.
He'd wait until they didn't have an audience. Anytime
he'd been ticked at her or someone else, he went off
on his own.

Still, she had to hurry this along and turned on her
camera. "All right, Haley and Haven, do you have any
questions for the guys that will help you make your
decision?" She'd suggested that her sisters study the
contenders' social media accounts last night to make this
morning's job go faster. The majority of men weren't
retired or on vacation and had to get to work.

"We do," her sisters said at almost the same time.

At the giggles in their voices, Abby thought Hunter
might not be the only one she had to worry about.

"We read a survey that said fifty-five percent of
kilt-wearing men wear underwear, thirty-eight percent
go commando, and seven percent wear shorts. So Haven
and I want to know if that's statistically accurate. Who
here is commando and who isn't?"

Abby had wondered the same about Hunter's brother
and cousins the day she'd first met them so she couldn't
blame her sisters for asking, but she didn't trust Dylan
and his friends' cheeky grins. Sure enough, the three
of them turned and mooned the camera while the rest
of the men shouted their answers. Abby now realized
her sisters were even more brilliant than she gave them
credit for. The video would go viral, and Dylan and his

friends were now out of the running. She didn't want her hunky highlanders mooning tour guests.

"Okay, let's move on to the pipers." It would help them weed out more contestants. Along with being hunky, she needed a couple of the winners to have musical talent. "The winner will be asked to perform at a very special event, but the rest of the finalists will have an opportunity to play for the ladies throughout the tour. So everyone's a winner."

She smiled, but none of them smiled back. They were looking beyond her. She glanced over her shoulder to see Hunter leaning against the post with his arms crossed over his chest.

From the top of her head she heard Haven whisper, "He really is the hottest highlander."

Before Abby could say anything—and what could she say since it was the absolute truth—a now-familiar sound came from the edge of the woods. She turned to see Owen Campbell in full Scottish regalia walking toward them as he began to play "Amazing Grace" on the bagpipes. But playing the pipes and the hymn like she'd never heard before. Certainly none of the contenders played half as well as Owen.

A ball of emotion swelled in her throat as the haunting music touched her. A glance around showed she wasn't alone. She followed the older man's progress as he marched proudly onto the gravel drive.

As the hymn came to a close, her sisters clapped, and Abby did the same, smiling when Owen took a small bow. She had opened her mouth to announce him as the winner when someone approached her from behind.

It was Hunter. He leaned in to whisper in her ear, "He might be the best piper you've got, but he's also chief of police and best friends with my aunt. Do you really want to risk letting him in on the *Outlander* event?"

She shivered, but it wasn't in reaction to his reminder; it was in response to his body crowding hers and the brush of his warm lips against her ear. Which went to show just how easily he messed with her head and how—thanks to stress and lack of sleep—she wasn't thinking clearly to begin with, because he was absolutely right.

"Thanks, but now what am I supposed to do? Look at him." The chief's gaze moved from her to Hunter, and his silver handlebar mustache twitched in what appeared to be a smug smile. He must've heard the other pipers practicing this week. Imagining his reaction to learning he wasn't her top pick, she almost groaned out loud. The last thing she wanted was Owen Campbell mad at her.

"Hey, that's not fair. The chief can't horn in at the end. He's not one of the contenders."

Thank goodness for Dylan, she thought. "I'm really sorry, Chief, but Dylan's right." Owen tried to hide it, but Abby sensed his disappointment. From what she'd heard, he was having a difficult time adjusting to the idea of retiring so she felt twice as bad for disappointing him.

Think, Abby, think. "Wait," she called to Owen when he went to walk away. "We've been trying to come up with a special way to welcome the bachelorette party to Highland Falls, and I think you'd be absolutely perfect, Chief. You could wait for us on the flower bridge and start playing as soon as we pass the town's sign."

"I'll check my schedule, but I think I can manage that," he said with another twitch of his mustache, and this time there was no doubt he was smiling.

"Okay, so I'm sure you're all anxious to know who—" Abby began, only to be cut off by Hunter again.

"Why don't you guys go into the kitchen and help yourselves to the cupcakes and doughnuts while Abby's sisters make their final decision? There's some lemonade in the fridge."

Abby's mouth opened and closed as the men trooped past them, some of them ducking around Hunter to say *hi* to her sisters and put in a good word for themselves.

"Hunter!" she said as the door banged closed behind the last of the men. "Those are for the bachelorette party. Now I'll have to stay up half the night making more." At the thought, she felt like crying.

His eyes narrowed, then his mouth flattened, and he took his phone from the back pocket of his jeans. "You're not staying up all night, and as soon as you get rid of these guys, you're going to take it easy." He tapped out a number and brought the phone to his ear. "You're beat, and don't bother denying it. Hey, Bliss, it's Hunter. I need to place an order for pickup later today. Yeah. Hang on a sec. What do you need?"

She reached up and covered the phone, whispering in case her sisters were able to hear, "I'm a little short on cash, Hunter. Sadie and I have—"

"I'm the one who told them to go eat, so I'm the one who's paying."

"No, you're right. I absolutely should've fed them. It's not like they're being paid—" Hunter cut her off with a finger on her lips as he placed an order that would cover them for the entire weekend and then some.

"Thank you," she said when he ended the call. "I'll pay you—What are you doing?"

He reached for the phone attached to her hat. "Finding out how to take down the video of me."

Chapter Twenty-One

♥

The truck's high beams cut a swath across the meadow as Hunter pulled up to the farmhouse later that same night. He blinked, positive he was imagining things. He leaned against the steering wheel to get a better look. He wasn't imagining things. The tents he'd lent to Abby had been painted: one soft pink, one butter yellow, and one baby blue. They'd also been decorated with flowers, rainbows, and what looked like a unicorn. So not only had Abby ruined three perfectly good tents, she'd also broken her promise that she'd take it easy in exchange for him not taking down the video.

The video hadn't been as bad as he'd expected. Other than a few people around here, no one would recognize him from his back or the back of his head. Most important, it didn't show his carving. It just looked like a guy chopping logs. So while he didn't care if she left it up, he'd needed the leverage. Not that it had done him any good.

If he hadn't been at Owen's surprise retirement party at Highland Brew, he would've seen to it that she did what he'd asked. He'd done his best to avoid spending one-on-one time with her over the past ten days, but that didn't mean he didn't know what she'd been up to. Except when it came to her online adventures. As he'd come to learn, she'd been as busy on there as she'd been here.

With the comings and goings of what at times had seemed like half the male population of Highland Falls, Hunter had been impressed he hadn't lost his ever-loving mind. He was close to losing it now and thought it might be best if he stored the cupcakes and muffins in the barn until morning.

These feelings, his desire for her, his need to protect her, were exactly why he'd kept his distance from her. He glanced at the farmhouse. But instead of his feelings for her diminishing, they'd only increased. He got out of the truck, leaning in to pile the bakery boxes in his arms. He shut the door with his foot. He didn't have to worry about waking her up. Nearly every damn light in the farmhouse was on.

He heard her talking to the rat through the screen door off the porch. "I'm sorry, Boo. I'm too tired to make us something to eat."

"Because you were too busy ruining my tents," he said as he walked inside.

"They're not ruined. I used water paint." Her voice came from behind the open fridge and freezer doors. "Thank you for the cupcakes and muffins. I hope you didn't have to leave Owen's party on my account."

He winced and put the boxes on the counter before crouching to pet Bella, who was dancing at his feet. "I thought it was just the guys, Abby. I'm sorry. I would've taken you had I known it was open to everyone."

"Everyone as in friends and neighbors. No one thinks of me that way, so I wouldn't have been invited anyway."

She tried to sound flip but he knew she was hurt. "That's not true. Quite a few people asked for you, including Owen. If it makes you feel better, he gave me crap and so did my aunt." And half a dozen other people, including the mayor and his brother and Eden.

"That's nice."

He only heard the smile in her voice because she was still hiding behind the freezer and refrigerator doors, and the only reason he could think of for that was... "Are you naked?" His stomach muscles contracted as his gaze traveled from her cherry-red toenails to her bare legs.

"No, I'm not naked. I'm wearing pjs. I'm just... hot."

She wasn't telling him anything he didn't already know, but he doubted she was referring to her looks. He walked over, and she let the freezer door go to duck her head into the almost empty refrigerator. And while she might not be naked, her pjs consisted of hot-pink silky shorts and a matching camisole.

"What's going on, Abby?"

"Nothing. Thanks again for the cupcakes and muffins. Enjoy your fishing trip." She waved her hand behind her.

"Good try. I'm not going anywhere so you might as well show me whatever it is you're trying to hide."

"I don't know what the big deal is. You didn't want anything to do with me for the past ten days."

He reached in, wrapped an arm around her waist, and

placed a hand on the back of her damp hair to pull her out of the fridge.

"You're so annoying!" she said as he turned her in his arms. "If you yell at—"

"What the hell happened to you?" The left side of her face looked like someone had knocked her around. When she went to pull away, he tightened his hold on her. "Just tell me. I won't yell."

She sighed. "I was glamming up the tents, and the air mattresses didn't fit my vision, so I decided to bring out one of the mattresses—"

"You carried a queen-size mattress down the stairs by yourself?"

"Umm, yeah, and let me tell you, that's not easy to do, which is probably why..." She grimaced as she brought her hand to the side of her face.

"Keep going." He reached around her to open the freezer door and take out a tray of ice cubes. Instead, he grabbed a bag of frozen peas that looked like they'd been in there for a year and handed them to her.

"I sort of fell down the stairs, and I, um, messed up your paint job too. I'm really sor—"

"Abby, go upstairs, lie down, and ice your face."

"You're mad at me."

"Yeah, I am. So unless you want me to yell at you, go upstairs."

"You know what, yell at me. I don't care. I'm hungry, and Bella is too, so go away." She sounded close to tears, and she went to turn away. "I'm sorry, that was rude, and you've been so good to me. I'm just really tired."

"I know you are, and that's why I made you promise

to take it easy for the rest of the night." He twisted a long, damp curl around his finger and gave it a gentle tug. "A promise you broke."

She'd used Liz's shampoo and smelled like honey and lavender, and she looked good enough to eat standing there in pjs that left little to the imagination. And he'd spent a lot of time imagining her in even less than what she had on. "Go upstairs, Abby. I'll make you something to eat."

Thirty minutes later, he joined her on the bed to finish up the last of the omelet she offered to him, declaring she was too full to eat the rest.

"Thank you. It was exactly what Bella and I needed." She leaned up to look over the side of the bed. "She's already out."

"You should be too." He went to get up, but she laid a hand on his arm.

"Don't go. I'm not tired yet, and if you leave, I'll think of something else I need to do."

"Abby."

She smiled and mimicked him saying her name before agreeing to his request. "I promise. No more glamming up the tents."

He placed the now-empty plate on the bedside table and noticed Liz's journal. He picked it up. "What number is this?"

"Two. I'm a slow reader."

"Do you mind?" he asked.

"No, not at all."

He missed his old friend. It would be nice to hear her voice again if only through her written words. As he opened the book, Abby snuggled in beside him, resting her cheek on his shoulder so she could see.

"Could you read out loud?" she asked.

He remembered her telling him she'd had to relearn to read and that even now it was difficult for her. His chest tightened with an emotion he almost didn't recognize, and his internal warning system went crazy.

He didn't need to be warned he was in danger; he'd known from the very first day he met her. But he was tired, tired of making excuses to keep his distance, tired of lying to himself. He wanted Abby, and if he wasn't mistaken, she wanted him. So maybe they should just give in to their desire. It wasn't like she planned to stick around or wanted a ring on her finger.

Abby interrupted his thoughts. "Do you think Liz was gay? Is that why her father sent her away?"

"I don't know. She never married, and Owen kept asking up until the day she died. She loved him, but I don't think the same way he loved her. She used to say we can't choose who we love."

"That would be so hard to love someone who didn't love you back, or who didn't love you as much as you loved them." She worried her bottom lip between her teeth, then looked at him. "I'm sorry. I didn't think."

"I'm not sure what you mean."

"You and Sloane. You're still in love—"

"I'm not in love with Sloane."

"You might be. Once you move past the anger, the guilt, and the grief."

"Trust me, I've moved beyond the anger, Abby. It's been more than two years."

"What about the guilt and the grief?"

"The grief will always be there. But it eases as the years pass." He knew where she'd go next and changed the subject. Plus, he wanted to know the answer. "What about you? Are you still in love with your ex?"

"Well, no, but that's not the same. You and Sloane had something special. You had one of those grand love affairs that you only see on the big screen. Everyone says so."

He laughed, something he'd never thought he'd do when it came to him and Sloane and their breakup. But Abby's assurance a couple weeks back that Sloane didn't hate him or blame him for Danny's death had gone a ways to helping him heal. He hadn't realized it until now.

"We were just like any other couple, Abby." He thought back over the years. "That's not quite true. We weren't ever just a couple. Danny was always with us. I honestly can't remember asking Sloane to marry me. It was just assumed we'd marry so we went along with it." Until that night at the pub when he'd told her about buying the land and shared his plan for their future. He didn't think he even noticed it then, but looking back, it was obvious his vision and Sloane's weren't the same.

"Are you okay?"

"Yeah, I am. Better than okay," he said, and put the book aside to kiss her. He feathered his fingers over her bruised cheek. "But you're not."

"No, I'm really good. Better than good. Or I will be," she said, pressing her body against his side.

He kissed her. "Hold that thought. I'll be back. I'm just going to pick up Wolf and lock up for the night."

Hunter made it back in record time, stripping off his clothes as he took the stairs to the bedroom two at a time. He hoped Abby had left hers on. He wanted to strip them off her himself. He walked into the room to discover that wasn't something he had to worry about. Abby was sprawled comatose on the bed.

Hunter sighed and crawled in beside her, casting her a hopeful glance when he nudged her over and she released a small sigh. Instead of waking up, she snuggled in beside him. And if he thought he was in trouble before, it had nothing on how he felt now when merely sleeping with Abby put a contented smile on his face.

Chapter Twenty-Two

♥

Apart from the pink headband decorated with white fluff and two penises that Granny MacLeod wore on her head, she was dressed in the Highland Tours uniform: a white shirt, a kilt in the MacLeod plaid (yellow with horizontal and vertical black stripes and thin red lines), and kick-butt boots, the same as Abby and Sadie.

Unlike Abby and Sadie, she was holding a microphone in her red-gloved hand and entertaining the bachelorette tour party they'd picked up an hour and half ago at the Asheville airport. Abby was behind the wheel of the tour bus while Sadie sat in the seat behind her, filming. No doubt inwardly cringing as her grandmother continued with her repertoire of penis jokes. It had been clear when Sadie picked up Abby earlier that morning, that her grandmother was a surprise addition to the tour, and not a welcome one in her granddaughter's eyes.

"How many knees do men have?" Granny MacLeod asked, looking for a target. Her gaze landed on Mallory, who sat looking pained beneath the penis headband.

Harry Maitland's widow of a year had already been

the butt of several of her niece-by-marriage's jokes. Abby got the feeling this was nothing new. Harry's beloved Blair made it painfully obvious how she felt about Mallory, who was as nice in person as she'd been on Skype.

The only reason Abby could see for Blair to dislike her aunt as much as she clearly did was jealousy. Mallory, with her sun-kissed blond hair, golden complexion, and blue eyes, was as head-turningly beautiful as Abby's sisters. She also appeared to be the same age as Blair and her six bridesmaids.

"Enough with the penis jokes, Granny," Sadie said, coming to Mallory's rescue.

"No, we love her penis jokes," Blair called from the back of the bus with a Southern Belle accent. "Come on, Mallory. Don't be a poor sport, give it a go. I'm sure you were acquainted with a few men and their penises before you married Uncle Harry."

Then, in a whisper clearly meant to be heard, Blair shared with her giggling friends that Harry had been rendered not only sterile but impotent from his cancer treatments before he and Mallory married, and not even a little blue pill had helped. Abby could almost see the thought bubbles appearing above the bridal party's heads with the words *Gold Digger* aimed at Mallory. Which was no doubt exactly what Blair had intended.

Abby glanced at Mallory, who'd turned her head to look out the window—her cheeks a bright, fiery red.

The dark-haired bride-to-be with her debutante hair and fake violet eyes reminded Abby of every mean girl in high school and the Bel Air Bs combined. So instead of swerving to avoid the large pothole up the road, she pressed on the gas and hit it head-on. The bus sailed through the air before landing with a hard bounce.

At the screams coming from the back of the bus, Abby glanced in the rearview mirror and smiled as several of the women bounced so high that they bumped their heads on the ceiling, and Blair fell off the seat.

But Abby's pleasure was short lived when the women helped Blair off the floor and Bridezilla met her gaze in the rearview mirror in such a way that suggested she knew exactly what Abby was up to, and she would get even.

You idiot, Abby berated herself. Once again, she'd acted without thinking of the consequences, and this time the blowback wouldn't hit just her. She'd put Highland Tours and the bus at risk, not to mention video for her YouTube channel. The entire bridal party, including Mallory, had signed waivers that video and photos from the weekend could be used for promotional purposes, including on Abby's YouTube channel.

"I'm so sorry," she called to Blair and her posse. "This is exactly the reason I've started a petition for seat belts on buses. I promise, I'll make it up to you when we get to town. We'll stop at Highland Brew before we hit the Village Green for the Fourth of July celebrations. Drinks are on me."

Blair nodded, looking slightly mollified, but Sadie stared at Abby with wide eyes.

"I know," Abby whispered over her shoulder. "I'm so sorry, Sadie. I didn't think. I was just so ticked off at Bridezilla—"

"I don't care about that. I would've done the same. I just wish you'd opened the emergency door and Blair and her posse fell out," Sadie whispered back. "But, Abs, we can't afford to buy rounds for them. We—"

Mallory, who leaned forward as though checking out the scenery, said from the side of her mouth in a low voice, "I'm covering their bar bill. No," she continued when Abby opened her mouth to argue. "I'm not broke, honest. I just didn't want to make a big dent in my nest egg by throwing Blair a ten-thousand-dollar bachelorette weekend. We can talk about it later, but I'm paying for meals, drinks, accommodations, and whatever else. You've already saved me thousands with your glamping idea."

Behind her, Abby felt Sadie sag with relief and did the same. She wanted to pay back at least some of what she owed Hunter and Ed, the owner of the hardware store, right away. She also needed to buy some special treats for Bella, who was once again stuck at home on her own. Still, Abby needed to be sure Mallory had thought this through. Abby and Sadie had been paying close attention to Atlanta's gossip mavens on Twitter and Instagram, and it was looking like Mallory would lose the court case.

"So you'll be okay if the judge finds against you?" Abby asked. They didn't know each other well, but she didn't want to think that Mallory would have to go through what she had.

"I'll be okay. If I thought it's what Harry wanted, I would've let Marsha—that's his first wife—have it without a fight. But no matter what she says or what Blair or the press does, I don't believe he did."

If Blair backed the first wife, Abby thought Mallory was either a saint or an idiot for going ahead with the bachelorette weekend. She was just about to ask her about it when she realized a set of penises was missing. "Sadie, where's your grandmother?"

"I knew it was too quiet!" Sadie cried. "Granny? Granny, are you okay?"

"Three. A left knee, a right knee, and a wee-knee!" came Granny's voice from behind a seat in the middle of the bus.

Abby, Sadie, and Mallory shared a laugh, which drew the narrow-eyed attention of Blair. Great, now all three of them were on the woman's radar. Abby smiled. "Blair, would you mind giving Granny MacLeod a hand up?"

"Good try." Sadie laughed as she put the camera down to go to her grandmother's aid.

Blair, no surprise, pretended she hadn't heard Abby.

"She's not wearing her red gloves as a fashion statement," Sadie said. "She's wearing them because I insisted. We noticed her gift of prophecy doesn't work quite as well in the winter. At least when someone shakes her gloved hand." Sadie gave Abby an apologetic shrug. "She hates wearing them in the summer, and I'd forgotten to check if she had them on the day we met you at the grocery store. That's why I ran back to the car."

Sadie's apology led to Abby explaining about Granny MacLeod's prophecy to Mallory, which in turn led to Abby explaining why she wasn't worried about her death sentence. At Mallory's insightful follow-up questions in regards to her stroke, Abby asked, "Are you in the medical field?"

"I'd just completed my first year of medical residency when Harry and I married. We learned his cancer had come back days before we left on our honeymoon." She lifted her shoulder. "I didn't finish my residency."

"Will you finish it?" Having spent months in the hospital and then in rehab, Abby had a deep respect and affection for doctors and nurses. She had fond memories of the care and kindness she'd received. She credited her doctors and nurses with instilling in her the belief that she'd one day talk and walk again.

Mallory rubbed the side of her face with an elegant, manicured hand. "I should. The way things are going I'll most likely need to bring in a paycheck in the not-too-distant future, but... This sounds incredibly selfish, but I nursed Harry for years, and then there's been all of this drama with Marsha and Harry's family and... I just need some time for me." She grimaced. "I've never said that out loud before. It sounds even more horrible than in my head."

"What it sounds like is you're burned out." After years of being Abby's primary caregiver while also trying to keep a roof over their heads and the wolf from the door, Abby imagined her mother would understand only too well what Mallory was going through.

She glanced over her shoulder to make sure Bridezilla and her posse weren't trying to listen in. "If the rest of Harry's family are anything like Blair, I can only imagine how horrible the last year has been for you. Personally, I think it's great that you recognize you need some time for yourself, and I hope you take it. As women, we tend to put everyone else's needs before our own. Although

Blair doesn't seem to have that problem," she said at the woman's hyena laugh.

"She doesn't. But she's not entirely to blame. She was the only girl in the Maitland family and a late-in-life baby at that, so everyone spoiled her rotten. Harry most of all. Mainly because he had the money to do so."

"You can tell me to mind my own business, but Blair's not exactly nice to you, so why are you doing this for her?"

"Blair's mother has stood by me through everything. She's the only one who welcomed me into the family, and she hasn't been well this past year."

"Oh my gosh, you're looking after her too?"

"As much as she'll let me. But she's doing much better now." Mallory glanced over her shoulder at the women taking selfies in the back of the bus. "I thought that would improve my relationship with Blair, but it hasn't." She smiled at Sadie, who was having a heart-to-heart with her grandmother in the middle of the aisle, and then said to Abby, "Blair didn't appreciate all the time I spent with her mother. She accused me of trying to take her place. Just like she accused me of doing with Harry. I've—"

"Are you talking about me to the *bus driver*?" Blair came to her feet with what looked like every intention of storming down the aisle.

"Yes, she was." Abby gave Blair her best fake smile. It was a smile she'd perfected after having to spend time with Juliette Devereux at the company's many social functions. "Mallory was telling me what a gorgeous bride you'll make, and how much your uncle had wanted to be at your wedding."

"Oh, well then." Blair fluffed her hair as she took her seat, returning her attention to her friends until Granny MacLeod clapped her hands.

"Lassies, we're fifteen miles from Highland Falls so we need to stay alert."

"Alert for what?" A couple of the bridesmaids looked nervously around.

With her eyes on the road, Abby leaned back in her seat and Sadie moved forward. "She's not going to tell them about the poisonous snakes and spiders, is she?" That was all they needed.

"No. I told her to point out the waterfalls as we drive by, then to tell them about the rumors that Jamie and Claire Fraser from *Outlander* fame were not a figment of the author's imagination, but that the couple actually existed and that Fraser's Ridge was based on Honeysuckle Ridge."

Abby glanced in the rearview mirror at Granny MacLeod, who was peering out one of the windows. "But not about the you-know-what, right?"

"No way, I—"

Sadie's grandmother cut her off with a gasp. "There. In the woods. Can you see him?" Granny MacLeod asked with what sounded like panic in her voice.

"Who?" three of the women asked in anxiety-riddled voices.

"Hunky highlanders!" Abby blurted in an attempt to break the nervous tension on the tour bus. "You can't go anywhere in Highland Falls without running into—"

"Bigfoot," Granny MacLeod said, then went on to tell of the reported sightings of the man-beast in the woods that surrounded Highland Falls. "You can Google it," the nonagenarian said at Blair's snort of disbelief. "There are Bigfoot societies and a Bigfoot festival in the next county."

"Is she serious?" Abby whispered. Both Sadie and Mallory grimaced, then nodded, reminding Abby that the elegant blonde was from Highland Falls and Boyd Carlisle's daughter. Hunter had seemed surprised that Mallory had picked Highland Falls to host the bridal shower. Abby had a feeling Mallory might not have been behind the decision after all.

So as Granny MacLeod answered the bridal party's curious questions about Bigfoot, Abby said, "Mallory, what made you decide to host the bachelorette weekend in Highland Falls?"

"It wasn't my idea. It was Blair's," she said with an expression that implied she wanted to be anywhere but here.

Crap. Abby's gut told her Blair was up to no good. Unless...She cut off Granny MacLeod and the brides-maids, whose conversation had somehow made its way back to penises. Abby was confiscating every one of those headbands before they walked into Highland Brew.

"So, ladies, tell us what made you choose our lovely town to host your bachelorette weekend." She smiled at herself. Lovely town indeed. Somehow, without her realizing it, she'd begun not only to feel a part of the town but to recognize its natural beauty as well.

Her question was met with silence. "Our beautiful

blue mountains? Bountiful waterfalls? Hiking paths? Fishing?" She shouldn't have mentioned fishing, not only because, like her, these women weren't the type to fish but it made her think of Hunter and how much she wished he'd stayed home. Now that was weird. When had she begun to think of Honeysuckle Farm as home?

She pushed the thought aside for another time. She had a mystery to solve. "I know," she said when the women remained stubbornly silent. "Our abundance of hunky highlanders and mountain men."

The posse shared a glance with Bridezilla, who smirked. Double crap, Abby was almost positive she was right.

Sadie mustn't have noticed the women's silent exchange and leaned across to retrieve the microphone from her grandmother. "It has to be for the shopping, then. Highland Falls might be a small town but our locally owned boutiques are high-end and unique, and you won't find a prettier Main Street than ours. And there's nothing we like to celebrate more than our highland heritage, isn't that right, Granny?"

Perfect. Sadie had gotten her grandmother off Bigfoot and on to sharing the town's history, real and fictional. Abby glanced in the rearview mirror at Granny MacLeod's mention of *Outlander. Woohoo,* she silently cheered. Four of the women were as fanatical about the television series as Tiffany and the Bel Air Bs. Abby decided, from now on, that should be the first question they ask potential tourees.

Behind her, Sadie breathed a sigh of relief while Mallory looked out the window, appearing lost in her thoughts. Abby glanced at Blair and vowed to do whatever she could to protect Mallory. First thing she'd do is share her fears with Sadie that Blair was out to embarrass Mallory, but right now Abby had to pay attention to the upcoming curve in the road.

Abby didn't know what Granny MacLeod said, but all of a sudden the women were chanting *Highland Brew*. "Ten minutes, ladies," she called back. "First I want to drive across our gorgeous flower bridge and over Highland Falls to the sound of 'Amazing Grace' played on the bagpipes. You're in for a very special—"

They drowned her out by chanting, "Highland Brew. Highland Brew."

Sadie shrugged. "You might as well give them what they want."

"But Owen—he'll be waiting on the bridge." The turn-off for the old stone mill in which Highland Brew made its home was right before the WELCOME TO HIGH-LAND FALLS sign.

"From the sounds of it, he won't get the reaction we were hoping for. We'll text him to join us at Highland Brew," Sadie said.

Five minutes later, they were getting settled at Highland Brew. Blair and her posse grabbed a table close to the stage, which was when Abby discovered the draw. A sign announced that Shane and his band were performing at two. Granny MacLeod must've shown the women the band's publicity photo; either that or the Highland Games poster with Shane front and center. A good sign, Abby decided. At least they knew handsome men in highland garb were a draw.

Abby took a seat with Sadie and Mallory at a table toward the back of the bar. To the right was the coffee side of the brewery—the smells of exotic brews wafted through the open stone archway. She also knew from Eden that they sold sandwiches, baked goods from Bites of Bliss, and gift baskets. The staff on both sides wore white T-shirts and what Sadie had informed her was black watch plaid. The brewery part of the old mill was polished wood and brass, with an older man and a younger man tending the bar. But one person was noticeably missing.

"Where's your grandmother?" Abby asked Sadie.

Sadie looked around and pulled out her phone, tapping on the keys as she brought it to her ear. "Granny, where are you?" She listened and then nodded. "Okay. Wait for him in the shade." She disconnected. "She's waiting for Owen."

"All right, tour ladies. We're ready for our drinks now," Blair said in a Southern drawl.

Sadie looked wide-eyed from Blair to Abby. "Does she seriously expect us to wait on her?"

"I'll do it." Mallory pushed to her feet, her chair bumping into the man sitting at the corner table behind them. "Sorry," she apologized, releasing a tiny gasp when the man turned to smile at her.

"No problem," he said in a deep voice that held a touch of New York. Abby had picked up an ear for accents while driving for Uber. And if she were Mallory right now, she might've fainted at the look in the man's watchful gray gaze. With his thick, wavy dark hair and scruff-shadowed, chiseled jaw, he'd give the Highland Falls hotties a run for their money.

Exactly what Mallory needed to take her mind off her problems: a weekend fling with a hot man. "I've got this. You sit and...chat." Abby smiled at the man, but he only had eyes for Mallory, whose gaze was locked on his. It was like a moment in a rom-com movie when the couple first meets. Sadly, it was interrupted by the ringing of his cell phone.

Sadie fanned herself with the menu and said sotto voce, "Okay, I'm totally jealous. I bet Bridezilla is too." She made a face and apologized to Mallory. "Sorry, I shouldn't call her that."

Her cheeks pink, Mallory waved off her apology. "Don't worry about it. Once this wedding is over, I'm done with Blair."

"Hopefully she'll be done with you too," Abby said, unable to shake the feeling that Blair was up to something.

"She would've been out of your life for good if I'd been driving the bus," Sadie said with a laugh. "Hit the pothole, open the emergency door, and out she goes. No one the wiser." Sadie's phone *ping*ed with incoming texts, and she glanced at the screen, responding with sharp taps on the keys. Another text followed and then another. Sadie was clearly unhappy with whoever was sending the texts.

Blair stood up and raised her hands. "Hello, bus driver. We're waiting. Drinks on the house, remember?"

"Okay, guys, I'm not joking," Sadie said. "She is getting on my last nerve, and my brother has eaten up most of my patience, so she better knock it off or I'm going to knock her off."

At the table behind them, Mallory's admirer stopped talking on his cell phone long enough to turn his narrowed gaze on Sadie.

"Um, you might want to keep talk of murder on the downlow," Abby murmured with a furtive nod at the table behind them. She had a feeling Mallory's admirer was either military or some sort of law enforcement.

As though to prove her right, the older bartender delivered a beer and burger to the table. "On the house, Chief."

"Appreciate it, but I don't officially take over from Owen until next week." Mallory's admirer accepted the beer and burger with a smile.

Blair suddenly appeared at their table. "Did I hear you correctly, sir? Are you the law in this pretty little town?" she asked all Georgia peach–like.

"Not yet, ma'am." He smiled politely at Blair, who clearly didn't appreciate being *ma'am*ed.

It looked like it took some work to keep her smile in place but she did and held out her hand. "Blair Maitland."

"Gabriel Buchanan." He nodded and turned back to his burger.

She seemed disappointed he didn't recognize the name. "This is my aunt Mallory." She placed a hand on Mallory's shoulder as if to keep her from bolting. Soon-to-be Chief Buchanan shifted in his chair, his gaze holding Mallory's, who lowered hers, color sweeping up her neck to her cheeks. "She's originally from here, you know. Her daddy still lives around these parts. Boyd Carlisle. Isn't that right, Mal?"

The spark of attraction Abby had noticed in the man's gray eyes when he'd looked at Mallory earlier seemed a shade cooler as he regarded her now. Mallory looked like she wanted to crawl under the table.

Abby shot to her feet and took Blair by the arm. "We should let Mr. Buchanan get back to his beer and get you those drinks I promised. I hear they have great pub fare too. We'll get you guys—"

Blair shook her off. "If you don't recognize the name, you soon will. He's the town drunk and makes moonshine. Isn't that illegal?"

Sadie stood up. "Not here it isn't. All you need is a license. And just FYI, Mr. Carlisle isn't the town drunk, he's the town's hero. He saved two boys last winter." She went to take Blair's arm, but given how she was looking at the bride-to-be and how the soon-to-be chief was looking at Sadie, Abby intervened.

"Look, Shane and his band have arrived." She nodded at the men entering the brewery. "Let's get you settled before they start the show. Trust me, you don't want to miss this."

An hour later, Abby wished they had. She imagined Shane and his band did too when the slightly tipsy, penis-headband-wearing bridesmaids joined them onstage and the bride-to-be got up on a table to perform with Owen's bagpipes. While Sadie tried to get Blair off the table in a manner that no doubt reinforced Highland Falls' future chief of police's impression that she was going to murder the woman.

Chapter Twenty-Three

♥

Abby spread out the blankets on the grass while a choir performed a patriotic sing-along at the bandstand. "Okay, ladies. Grab a place to sit. The fireworks are going to start any minute—" She looked around. The bachelorette party was gone.

Sadie and Mallory approached, loaded down with the iced teas, corn on the cob, and hotdogs that Blair and her friends had ordered. "Where are they?" Sadie asked as she put down the cardboard trays packed full with food. Mallory followed suit.

"I have no idea. They were right behind me a few minutes ago," Abby said.

"I'll text Blair," Mallory said, looking stressed.

"I saw the soon-to-be chief of police checking out the MAMA—Mountain Area Medical Airlift—helicopter. What do you want to bet she's over there chatting him up?" Sadie said. "I'll go check."

Mallory paled at the mention of Blair chatting up Gabriel. Abby didn't blame her after what had transpired at Highland Brew, but given how Sadie felt about Blair, the last thing Abby wanted was her hunting them down. "Now that I think about it, one of the bridesmaids wanted to get closer to the bandstand for the sing-along, so they probably went with her. I'm sure they'll be back any minute now. Let's sit down and get comfy."

They slid off their shoes and sat on the blanket. A few minutes later, the fireworks started, and the bachelorette party had yet to show up or respond to Mallory's texts. Abby had talked to Eden, Josie, and Winter earlier in the evening and texted to see if they had seen Blair and her friends. They hadn't, which she relayed to Mallory and Sadie.

Sadie handed her a hotdog and an iced tea. "Forget about them. They're adults. Let's just enjoy the fireworks."

So that's what they did. They *oohed* and *aahed* over the dazzling display of red, white, and blue fireworks lighting up the sky. And they talked and laughed and ate until their stomachs were stuffed and their sides ached.

"That was the best Fourth of July I've had in I don't know how long," Mallory said, as they stretched out on the blanket looking up at the night sky as everyone around them gathered up their chairs and blankets.

"You gals might want to pack up before the rain starts," an older man suggested.

An hour later when it began to rain, they were still waiting for the bachelorette party. "We have to call the chief," Sadie said.

The last thing Abby wanted to do was tell anyone they'd lost their tour group, but it couldn't be helped. "Let's put out a group text to the Hottest

Highlanders contenders first. Maybe one of them has seen the bachelorette party." Ten minutes later, they had their answer. Blair and her girlfriends were at the local pool hall.

Pulling blankets over their heads, they ran for the tour bus to set off for the pool hall. They missed them by five minutes.

Abby saw more of Highland Falls that night than she had in the entire time she'd been there. Just as they were about to give up and call Owen, Mallory got a text from Blair arranging a pickup. Their relief that they'd found the women ended the moment they pulled up to the farmhouse.

"I will not sleep out there," Blair said, and her friends wholeheartedly agreed. "Take us to the hotel now."

Abby couldn't say she blamed them. The water paint she'd used to glam up Hunter's tents hadn't survived and was puddled outside. "All the hotels in this area are booked." An out-and-out lie but she didn't want Mallory to get stuck paying for their accommodations. "You can sleep in the farmhouse instead."

It was almost midnight by the time they'd finished hauling the queen-sized mattresses back into the house under tarps and got the bachelorette party settled for the night. A wet wind tugged at the umbrellas Abby, Sadie, and Mallory held over their heads as they ran for the tents in the rain-soaked meadow.

Abby looked around. "You guys don't have to sleep out here. Sadie will drive you to a hotel, Mallory. And Sadie, you can go home."

"No way. We're in this together," Sadie said. "But

you don't have to stay, Mallory. You've already done more than—"

"I'm staying. I'm the one who got you into this mess so I'll do whatever I can to make it up to you. Unless you want to cancel the rest of the tour. I'd completely understand if you do."

"We can handle them. Plus, we're getting some great video for my YouTube channel, and Sadie's been monitoring their social media and most of them have been happy with the tour so far. It's really only Blair who's been complaining, but even she's been posting some great pics of Highland Falls. But Sadie and I talked about it, Mallory, and we understand if you want to cancel."

"I'd be lying if I said I want to subject myself to more of Blair's abuse. But it's been fun hanging out with you guys, and I haven't had fun in a while. So if you're okay to continue the tour, I'm happy to." She glanced at them from under her lashes.

"I feel exactly the same way," Abby said, feeling a bond with these women that she'd never felt with the Bel Air Bs. Sadie and Mallory wouldn't care about her net worth, or what she looked like and wore, or whose party she was invited to and whose party she wasn't. They were the kind of women who'd have your back and not abandon you when times got tough.

"The weather's supposed to clear up early tomorrow so we'll have a great day at Bust-Yer-Butt Falls." Bella popped up from inside Abby's raincoat and gave her chin a lick. "I think that's my cue. I'll see you guys in the morning. Sleep well."

They managed a group hug despite the umbrellas, then

Abby walked them to their respective tents, holding the flashlight as they each crawled inside. Then she crawled into the one a few yards from Sadie's.

Abby's efforts to glam up the interior of the tents had fared about as well as the outside. Along with the mattresses, she'd returned the throws, lamps, and side tables to the farmhouse. She'd left what she could in the other two tents, but all that remained in hers was a semi-deflated mattress, a thin blanket, and an overturned crate that served as a nightstand.

"It's just for two nights, Boo. And they're not calling for rain tomorrow." She took off her boots and rain jacket and got settled on the mattress with Bella, glad she'd found a sweatshirt Hunter had left at the farmhouse to pull on over her T-shirt and leggings. She'd found a pair of thick wool socks too.

Tucking the blanket around them, she lay down. As she did, she got a hint of Hunter's familiar scent. His sweatshirt smelled of mountain air and cedar. She buried her nose in the fabric and inhaled. She missed him.

He'd done so much for her these past couple of weeks—actually, pretty much since the day she'd arrived in Highland Falls—that she hadn't had the heart to ask him to stay when he'd stopped by before heading out of town this morning. He'd delivered one last parting lecture on not overdoing it and then wished her luck with the bachelorette party before heading out the door. Without a goodbye kiss. She wondered if he'd been thinking of kissing her as much as she'd been thinking of kissing him.

After last night, things seemed to have changed

between them. If she hadn't fallen asleep on him, she thought they might've become friends with benefits, and she really would've liked to share some benefits with him. Still, no matter how much she wanted to kiss him before he left for his weekend away, she worried she'd misread his feelings for her last night. So the last thing she wanted to do was ruin whatever this was between them.

"It couldn't hurt to send him a quick hi, could it, Bella Boo? I know, I'll send a selfie of you and me saying how much you miss Wolf." Bella gave a little *yip*, and Abby snuggled her close. "Aww, sorry to remind you he's away for the weekend, Boo. But they'll be back soon. And let's be honest, they deserve a break from us. We're not exactly low maintenance. Here, we'll take the picture and maybe Hunter will call and let you talk to Wolf."

Picturing Hunter's face if she said that to him, Abby laughed as she held up her phone. She gave a practice smile first, then took the picture and sent it to Hunter. Along with a text about how much Bella missed Wolf and how badly the tour was going so far. Then she told him not to worry about them and to bring home lots of fish. She added a kissy-face emoji, then erased it, added it and erased it, until finally she closed her eyes and hit Send.

She fell asleep with the phone in her hand waiting for a response, only to awaken later with a start. She didn't know how much time had passed or what had awakened her. She glanced at her phone, checking to see if Hunter had responded. He hadn't.

The rain had slowed to a soft pitter-patter on her tent,

and beside her Bella lightly snored. So if a text from Hunter and thunder and lightning hadn't awakened her, what—She cut off the thought with a panicked *eep* at the sight of the dark shadow moving outside her tent. Bella sat up and got out two barks before Abby managed to cover her mouth. "Shh, Boo," she whispered, trying to get her own panic under control.

There was no snuffling or growling, and the animal's movements didn't seem bearlike. Except Abby had never had a run-in with a bear so she couldn't be sure one wasn't currently prowling around her tent.

She made herself smaller on the mattress. What if Granny MacLeod hadn't been kidding about Bigfoot sightings in the woods? At the sound of the tent's zipper being unzipped, Abby's eyes went wide, and she clutched the covers to her chin.

What now? she silently cried.

The only thing that came to mind was what she'd heard to do when approached by a bear. She threw the covers over her and Bella and played dead. Remembering the heavy flashlight, she reached out from under the blanket and grabbed it, clutching it to her chest just as something very large and wet entered the tent.

Then she heard a human snort of amusement—a deep, manly snort that was all too familiar. She pushed back the covers to see Hunter crouching beside her with Wolf at his side. Instead of giving him grief for scaring her half to death, she threw herself at him. His hair was wet, and his jacket was rain-slicked and cold, soaking through her clothes, but she didn't care.

"I'm so glad you're here. I missed you so much," she

cried, hugging him tight. At that moment, she didn't care that she'd given her feelings for him away.

He wrapped his arms around her and held her close, rubbing his cheek against her hair. "I missed you too."

At least that's what she thought he said but she couldn't be sure because he'd murmured the words against her hair. She leaned back. "Did you say you missed me too?"

Before she kissed him like she'd been dying to kiss him, she had to be sure he felt the same as she did. She sensed the wariness in his gaze that held hers, felt his shoulders tense beneath her hands, and she went to pull away.

He sighed and then told her what she wanted to hear. What she needed to hear. "Yeah, I missed you."

If he hadn't sighed, she might've let it go at that. "How much did you miss me?" she asked, but even as she did, she pressed closer to him and grinned. "You're very happy to see me."

His lips twitched, and then he lowered his mouth to hers, and he kissed her like he had the night of Summer Solstice. Only this time he wasn't kissing her out of anger and guilt and frustration. This time the only emotions she felt from him were desire and need. He wanted her as much as she wanted him, and she would've cheered if his warm, firm lips weren't devouring hers and his tongue wasn't tangling with hers. She nearly cried when, moments later, he broke the kiss, leaving her panting.

"I'm happy to see you. I'll be even happier when you're naked and in my arms," he said, his voice a rough rasp.

"Will you be naked too?" She shivered as his heated gaze slid over her and his fingers caressed the strip of bare skin where the sweatshirt had inched up.

He lowered his head to give her a teasing kiss that got deeper and hotter when his hands moved from the strip of bare skin at her waist to tease the band of her bra, and she cursed herself for not taking it off. She'd been afraid one of the bachelorettes would need her in the night.

She pressed closer to Hunter, telling him with her body what she wanted him to do, groaning in frustration when he pulled back instead of undoing her bra. He nipped her bottom lip. "As soon as I do something about our audience, I'll get naked with you."

She followed his gaze to where Wolf lay on the tent's floor while Bella jumped around him, kissing and teasing with little nips. Oh my gosh, Abby thought, briefly closing her eyes—Bella was her and Wolf was Hunter. She was head over heels for the man, and he... Well, he wanted her. She supposed for a man who hadn't wanted or needed anyone in his life for the past couple of years but his dog, that was a pretty big deal.

But she wondered if he was as ready to take this next step as she was. Maybe he didn't attach the same meaning to making love as she did. A lot of women didn't attach the same meaning or emotions to making love as she did, and more power to them. But she'd never been a one-night-stand kinda girl. She didn't have sex unless she was in a relationship, and the last thing she wanted was to be in a one-sided relationship. Been there, done that, and hated that she had the T-shirt. She wouldn't put herself through that again.

She'd fallen in love with Hunter. She'd known it for a while now. And deep down she knew, if they made love, that would be it for her. There'd be no turning back. And if there was no turning back, that meant there was no going back to LA.

He cupped her chin with his hand, turning her face to him. "What's up? Second thoughts?"

"No, I want you. I want this."

"Good. You had me worried." He kissed her, slow and deep, and then pulled away as he went to stand. But he must've seen something on her face because he once again crouched beside her. "I'm sensing a *but*. You're not done, are you?"

She smiled. There were many things she appreciated about Hunter but his ability to read her and the way he listened, really listened, to her were the traits she appreciated most. Still, it didn't make it less uncomfortable to leave herself vulnerable to rejection. "I need to know that you're as into me as I'm into you. You want me, don't you?"

"I think that's pretty obvious, isn't it? I'm here."

"For more than sex, I mean. This, us, means something to me. I—"

"I wouldn't be here if you didn't mean something to me, Abby. I was looking forward to getting away."

"Be honest. You were looking forward to getting away from me and Bella. You needed some peace and quiet."

"I was looking forward to being out there with just me and Wolf. Only I kept thinking about you. I missed your laugh. I missed your smile. I even missed your hundred and one questions." He frowned, rubbing a strand of her hair between his fingers as if the admission surprised him. Then he smiled and tucked her hair behind her ear. "Don't let Wolf fool you. He missed Bella too."

"So you came back because of Wolf?"

"I came back because my brother, Owen, and my aunt decided I needed updates about what was going on with you and your tour group every ten minutes. I'm guessing they weren't into sleeping under the stars."

"No, but I am." She wound her arms around his neck, seeing the answer to her question in his eyes. "As long as you sleep under them with me."

"It's too wet to sleep under the stars tonight. We'll do it another time. Right now, I'm just as happy to stay where we are." He laid her down on the air mattress and then straightened to take off his boots and windbreaker.

"What about Bella and Wolf?"

He reached for the blanket and tossed it over them. "They'll have to get used to it." He stretched out on top of her, raising himself up on his elbows to look down at her. "Now, where were we?"

"Getting naked."

"Right. Let me help you with that."

Chapter Twenty-Four

♥

The next morning, Hunter sat behind Abby on the tour bus. "Slow down. Don't roll your eyes at me, Abby. I'm serious. You're driving through the gorge, which means you're driving on the edge of a cliff."

He curled his fingers around the bar separating him from the woman who had their lives in her hands. He was beginning to think agreeing to join her on the tour this morning was as bad an idea as having sex with her last night had been. This wasn't morning-after regrets. He'd experienced those before, and this was far from the same.

Up until an hour ago, he'd thought having sex with Abby had been the best idea he'd had in years. Until he overheard her telling Sadie about her plans for the future as they loaded up the tour bus for today's trip to Bust-Yer-Butt Falls.

Abby wasn't leaving Highland Falls. She was settling down at Honeysuckle Farm to build her future, and from the sweet smile she'd sent his way, that future included him. A future, if he wasn't mistaken, that eventually included a ring on her finger and 2.5 kids.

She met his eyes in the rearview mirror. "Stop pretending you're terrified."

He wasn't pretending. Years before, he'd planned a similar future with Sloane, and then a land mine had blown those plans sky high. He couldn't give Abby the future he saw in her pretty green eyes. She deserved to have her dreams come true. He wished he was the man he used to be and he could give her what she wanted. But he wasn't.

He glanced at the two women sitting across from him, laughing. "Sadie, stop filming me. If you use that on Abby's YouTube channel, I'll sue." He bowed his head at the sight of an oncoming semi and muttered, "Never mind, we probably won't make it." He gritted his teeth as the semi sped by with an inch to spare.

"Fitbit," Abby said, then cleared her throat. "Ijit. Idiot!"

Her jumbled words told him that, underneath the bravado, she'd been nervous too. He imagined his attempts at backseat driving hadn't helped. So five minutes later, when they reached their destination alive, he leaned forward as the bachelorette party began to disembark.

"Abby, I—" He broke off when several of the bachelorettes crowded around him and one held up a camera to take their picture with him. He knew it was important to Abby and Sadie—Mallory too—that the tour went well so he smiled when the dark-haired woman prompted him to. He wasn't as accommodating when she asked to squeeze his biceps.

"Let's go, ladies. Another tour bus will be arriving soon, and we want to scope out the best tanning spots before they do." Sadie ushered the women off the bus. She glanced from Abby to him with a frown and then said, "Hunter, would you mind bringing the picnic baskets and blankets?"

"Sure. No problem." He reached for Abby's arm when she went to follow them. "Hang on a minute. I want to talk to you."

She wouldn't look at him, and he tugged on her hand to bring her closer. "I'm sorry. You were nervous, and I made it worse."

"I wasn't nervous."

"Come on, Abs. Fitbit? Ijit? I know you were upset about the cracks I made about your driving."

"You can doubt my driving skills all you want, but I don't. That's not what upset me. I was mad at myself, and I was mad at you."

Don't ask why. Just let it go. He had an uneasy feeling she'd seen through him, and this was the moment of reckoning he wanted to avoid. Because, as terrified as he was of her dreams and expectations and his inability to be the man she wanted, he wasn't ready to lose her.

"I promise. I won't say anything on the way back to town." Before she could argue that that wasn't the problem, he curved his hand around her neck and drew her close. Then he bent down to kiss her, some of his tension easing when she softened and leaned against him, kissing him back with as much passion as he kissed her.

"Abby . . . Sorry. I didn't mean to interrupt," Sadie said from the top step of the bus.

"It's fine." Slightly breathless, Abby straightened and glanced over her shoulder.

He took it as a good sign that she didn't pull completely away from him, leaving her hand on his chest.

"What's going on?" she asked Sadie.

"Dylan and his friends are here, and they're dropping hints about tonight's *Outlander* event."

"I should've known he'd be a problem. He wasn't happy that Haven and Haley didn't choose him and his friends for Hottest Highlanders. But how did he know where we were?"

"I think Blair or one of her bridesmaids mentioned it last night at one of the bars, but we have more to worry about than them. Owen just pulled up with the soon-to-be chief of police. He said he's showing him the ropes, but I think it's more than that."

Ten minutes later, Hunter found out Sadie was right. She had much bigger problems than Dylan and his friends. Only Hunter couldn't warn her because he'd just been sworn to secrecy by Owen.

"You're putting me in a difficult position here, Chief." He leaned against the white SUV, watching Abby as she laid out the blankets and picnic baskets on the flat rocks at the base of the waterfall with the help of Sadie and Mallory. Dylan wore a plaid bandana on his head and whooped it up as he slid down the rocks with his buddies, performing for the bachelorettes who sunbathed nearby.

Gabriel Buchanan, the former detective from New York City who would replace Owen next week, was also watching the three women. Unlike Hunter, his attention was on Mallory.

"It's for Sadie's own good. Abby's too, now that she's

involved with Highland Tours. Gabriel says his contact in the DEA doesn't believe Sadie knew what her brother was up to, but the men he is, or was, involved with don't fool around. Word is he left town with their money and product."

"I'll keep an eye out. Nose around some."

Owen nodded. "Wouldn't hurt if you stuck close for a while."

Hunter looked over at the sound of Abby's laugh, and his eyes nearly fell out of his head. She'd taken off her tour guide outfit to reveal a red bikini that left little to the imagination and had him remembering their night together in vivid detail. If he didn't soon take his eyes off that lush body of hers, he'd embarrass himself. He hadn't been planning on swimming today, but it looked like he'd be spending most of his time in the chilly pool at the bottom of the falls.

Owen laughed. "Told you she'd work her Findlay magic on you." He clapped Hunter on the back. "It's a good look on you. Happy for you, son. Liz would be too."

"It's not what…" As though she felt his eyes on her, Abby looked over and waved. Hunter smiled, and instead of telling his old friend he'd misread the situation, he thanked him.

Owen patted the hood of the SUV. "Let's go, Gabe. Dot's got pancakes on for us."

The other man offered Hunter his hand. "Good to meet you. I'm sure I'll see you around." He went to walk toward the passenger-side door but then stopped and turned. "Do you happen to know anything about the circumstances of Harry Maitland's death?"

"No. Why?" Hunter asked, surprised by the question.

"Just something his niece said last night at the Village Green. Probably nothing."

"I wouldn't put much stock into anything Blair Maitland has to say about Mallory. From what I've heard, the woman has it in for her."

"Yeah, that was my impression too," he said with one last look in Mallory's direction.

Chapter Twenty-Five

♥

I really am sorry that you had to sell your Louis Vuitton bag to cover the bill at the winery, Abby. Once I get everything straightened out with the bank, I'll buy you another one. I promise." Mallory had looked defeated when her credit cards were declined at Three Wild Women Winery earlier that afternoon but a little wine and girlfriend time had helped.

Just like they'd caved to Blair's demands to visit the winery, Abby had caved to her offer to pay the bill in exchange for Abby's pink Louis Vuitton bag. She would've preferred to sell it to anyone other than Blair, but she didn't want Hunter to cover the charges for the wine tasting, and she didn't want to run up another tab at a local business as Daisy had kindly offered.

"You know what? I'm glad I sold it," she said, surprised to discover she wasn't just trying to make Mallory feel better. Somehow it felt right. "I carried my pink Vuttie wherever I went, just like I carried my past. But I'm not that girl anymore, and I'm not going back to LA."

She was making a life here, with the man she loved. She ignored the tiny warning blip in her brain that people she loved always disappointed her and traded up. Her mind even offered the moment earlier today on the drive to the waterfall as evidence that Hunter might be having second thoughts. But throughout the rest of the day, he'd more than proved he was as into her as she was into him so she pushed the negative thoughts aside and raised her glass. "A toast to our futures."

"*Sláinte*," Sadie said as the three of them clinked wineglasses.

Her friends didn't appear as optimistic about their futures as Abby. Without the stress of selling the farmhouse and returning to her old life in LA weighing her down, she felt freer than she had in years. Which was why she suggested to both women, "Why don't you guys just sell everything and move back here?"

Sadie held up a finger as she read the many messages coming in over her phone, pushing back from the table when it began to ring. "Sorry, I've got to take this," she said and walked toward the living room.

It was just the three of them at the farmhouse. Hunter had reluctantly volunteered to drive the women for a last-minute shopping spree. He'd probably sensed Abby was on the verge of a meltdown at the bachelorettes' demand to be taken into town.

She had to finish making dinner and preparing for the *Outlander* event with Sadie, who wore a white blouse, long drab skirt, and a lightweight dark cape for her role as Claire Beauchamp Fraser. Hunter's cousin Jamie had won the role of Jamie Fraser.

Mallory swirled the red wine in her glass and gave Abby a wan smile. "The way it's going, I might not have anything left to sell."

Abby wished she didn't, but she agreed with Mallory's assessment. Today's incident with Mallory's credit cards was just one more piece of evidence that Mrs. Maitland the First was probably going to win the court case. The older woman had power and influence.

Chandler, Abby's ex, had power and influence and a team of lawyers led by the manipulative Juliette Devereaux at his beck and call. And he'd wielded all that power and influence like a battering ram, smashing Abby's glamorous life in LA to smithereens.

"You're probably not going to want to hear this right now, and I don't blame you. But I want you to know that if the worst happens and all you're left with is your nest egg, Mal—"

"I'm not sure it even counts as a nest egg."

"It doesn't matter. You'll be okay. The main thing is you're not alone. You have me and Sadie, and it sounds like you have Blair's mother in your corner too. But here's the part you might not want to hear, because I didn't want to hear it when my ex's housekeeper said it to me, but sometimes things really do happen for a reason. Something good will come out of all of this, and if you don't believe it, just look at me."

"Thank you, and you're right, at least about this weekend. I dreaded the thought of coming back to Highland Falls and spending three days being tormented by Blair and her friends, but in the end, I wouldn't change a thing because I met you and Sadie."

"Aww," Abby said, leaning over to pull her in for a hug.

"But as much fun as it would be to live close by, I couldn't face coming back here. My dad... Anyway, if I do lose the court case, it would be better job-wise for me to stay in Atlanta."

"But then you'd have to put up with Blair and her friends."

"I wouldn't exactly be traveling in the same circles."

"Why do you think Blair's trying to make you look bad?"

Mallory shrugged. "Maybe she believes Marsha will leave her everything."

"Why would she think that?"

"My husband and Marsha remained close after their divorce. Harry's second marriage was messy and volatile, and Marsha was afraid ours would be the same. And while she may have thought she was looking after Harry's best interests, she caused a lot of problems for us, using Blair to do some of her dirty work. Marsha isn't getting any younger, and she doesn't have children of her own."

"Oh my gosh, no wonder she's trying to cause problems for you. She doesn't want you to inherit. One day you'll marry again and have a family of your own, so that money would be lost to her."

"If that's what she believes, she's wrong. I have no intention of marrying again or having children."

Sadie rejoined them and picked up her glass of wine.

"Everything okay?" Abby asked.

"Yeah, I've just been getting a lot of hang-ups on

my cell phone. A couple of weird texts too. I tried to look into it but I'm not getting anywhere. It's probably nothing."

Abby put down her glass of wine to check on the Slow-Cooked Chicken Fricassee that was tonight's main course. She'd designed the entire menu around recipes from *Outlander Kitchen,* by Theresa Carle-Sanders.

Abby felt bad that she'd ordered the cookbook online instead of getting it from Three Wise Women Bookstore, but she didn't want to arouse the curiosity of Hunter's aunt. The book had been a godsend. Sadie had created a script for their Highland Falls Jamie and Claire by adapting some tidbits about the literary couple's fictional life from the book.

Blair had vetoed Abby's plan to dine in the woods so they were dining alfresco on the patio instead. Along with the main course of chicken fricassee and bannock buns, she was serving Beer-Battered Corn Fritters for appetizers. For dessert they were having Black Jack Randall's Dark Chocolate Lavender Fudge. The man might be Jamie's tormentor in the series, but his fudge was to die for.

"Abby, I almost forgot. While I was checking out the hang-ups, I got a bunch of inquiries about the tour. The video from the Fourth of July celebrations and Highland Brew are getting lots of attention, and so are Shane and his band. You've gained two thousand more subscribers and a couple of inquiries from advertisers."

"That's awesome. What about the tours? When do they want to book?"

"Several for the fall, one that I'm not sure what

they wanted. It was kinda weird. And there was one for next week during the Highland Games. She seemed to know you." Sadie swiped her screen. "Here it is. Tiffany Grimes for a party of six. What's wrong?"

"Remember the Bel Air Bs?" Abby asked as she retrieved her phone from the kitchen counter and placed a call to Elinor.

"*That's* Tiffany? Okay, I'll get back to her right now and tell her we're booked for the next five years."

"Hi, Elinor," Abby said as soon as the older woman picked up. If she hadn't already spoken to Elinor earlier in the week, she would've taken the time to catch up. As it was, she quickly explained the situation. "Great, thank you. I really appreciate it. I'll have a room ready for when you and Kate visit this fall." She said good-bye and disconnected. "Okay, as far as Elinor knows, Chandler and Juliette have no idea about my new YouTube channel. But she'll make some calls and get back to me."

"Our reprieve is over," Sadie said at the sound of the bachelorettes laughing and calling Hunter's name.

"I think they like their new bus driver better than they like me," Abby said, turning at the heavy clump of boots on the porch, followed by the click of heels.

"Too bad, because they're stuck with you. I quit," Hunter said from behind the boxes and bags he carried inside. He stomped into the living room and tossed everything on the couch. Then he stomped back through the kitchen, ignoring the bachelorettes patting him and thanking him.

Abby followed him out the screen door, trying not

to laugh. But Blair's "We couldn't eat a single thing. Hunter took us to Sweet Basil Bistro and then to Udderly Delicious Creamery for dessert!" cleared up her laughter and her smile.

"Hunter, how could you?"

"If you want to blame someone, blame the business owners on Main Street. They were practically doing back flips to get them in their stores. What was I supposed to do?"

"Say Abby's slaved in the kitchen for three hours making your dinner for tonight."

"I'd have more sympathy for you if I hadn't been stuck with them for three hours." He dragged a hand through his hair. "I've spent enough time dealing with giggling, flirty women to last me a lifetime."

"What about me?"

"You, I can handle." He tipped her chin up for a kiss, then went to walk away.

"Hang on. I didn't slave over a hot stove for nothing."

* * *

Hunter sat outside eating Abby's chicken fricassee and bannock buns by the open fire while keeping an eye on the bachelorette party on the patio across the meadow. The sun had set more than an hour ago, and stars littered the night sky. Voices carried, and for the last hour, he'd listened to Sadie and Abby tell some bullshit stories about life in the mid-1700s on the ridge.

They stopped talking and picked up lanterns. Supposedly Sadie, who had taken on the role of Claire

Someone-or-Other, was going to travel through the stones to the man who visited her in her dreams.

Hunter shook his head. He'd be glad when this part of the tour was over. He was worried someone—namely his aunt—would find out what was going on tonight.

To his mind, too many people already knew. It was only a matter of time before word got out, and he'd be in the middle of it.

"Your mama's a pain in my ass," he told the rat, who sat by his side on her leash. "She's lucky she's beautiful and can cook, and has the best laugh this side of the Continental Divide."

He watched as the lanterns wound their way along the trail. Then came the low drone of the bagpipes and the dry whine of the fiddles as they prepared to play "The Skye Boat Song." He would've known the song even if Abby hadn't told him. She'd given him a rundown of what would take place that night. The music faded, and the bobbing balls of white light disappeared in the dark woods. A half-moon shone down from above, and nearby an owl hooted.

Hunter sat back to enjoy some well-deserved peace and quiet. He got to enjoy it for all of fifteen minutes before headlights cut across the meadow and a familiar white SUV made its way down the hill.

He muttered a curse when Owen pulled in front of the barn. He wasn't alone. Hunter got to his feet and tossed the rest of his food in the fire so the dogs wouldn't get it before heading toward the SUV. He had to keep them in the truck and send them on their way as quickly as possible.

Too late. Buchanan was already out of the SUV, and Owen was rounding the hood. Something was up.

"Sorry to bother you, Hunter. But I got a call from an agent at the local DEA's office, and I could use your help. Owen says if anyone knows what's going on in these woods, it's you."

These days, thanks to Abby, that wasn't completely true. "What do you need?"

"DEA thinks Sadie's brother is in the area," Owen said, then frowned at the sound of raised feminine voices coming from the woods. "What the hell is that about?"

"Probably a couple girls going skinny-dipping at the springs," Hunter said. "As to Elijah Gray, I haven't seen any sign—"

From deep in the forest, he heard Abby scream his name.

He took off at a run with Owen and Gabriel chasing after him.

Chapter Twenty-Six

♥

Abby ran down the path toward him wearing a white blouse and long skirt, tripping on a tree root just before she reached him. He grabbed her before she fell. "Hunter, Blair—" She broke off as Gabriel caught up to him, a winded Owen trailing behind. Out of the corner of his eye, Hunter caught movement. If he wasn't mistaken, someone was hiding behind a tree several yards away.

"How could you?" Abby cried, regaining his attention.

He put his hands on her shoulders. "I didn't call them. Now tell me, what happened?" Up ahead lights bobbed in the woods as men and women shouted Blair's name.

"She's missing. We've looked everywhere, and we can't find her."

"I'll call it in." Owen pulled out his cell phone.

"No, wait. She has to be close by. It's only been minutes. Ten at most. Please, Owen, Hunter will find her. I know he will."

"Abby, there's more..." He trailed off when Gabriel gave him a warning look and the detective pulled out his phone.

Hunter took Abby by the hand. "Come on. Tell me what—"

She hung back, pleading with Owen. "Please, you don't understand. If Elsa finds out we were at the standing stones, she'll turn everyone against me like she did when I first moved to town."

"Sorry, Fancy Pants," Owen said. "But I don't have a choice here. There's a dangerous—"

Gabriel cleared his throat as he followed Hunter to the standing stones.

"The woods can be a dangerous place," Owen corrected himself. "Just ask Hunter. His brother died when the old gem mine collapsed not far from here. Robbie was only ten, but he knew the woods better than most men three times his age. Accidents happen."

At Abby's devastated expression, Hunter shot Owen a glare. She didn't need to hear something like that now just so Owen covered his ass, and Hunter didn't need to be reminded of losing Robbie.

Gabriel saved Hunter from having to say anything to Abby. "Was Ms. Gray with the group when Ms. Maitland disappeared?" It looked like Owen planned to let Gabriel take the lead.

"I'm not exactly sure when she disappeared." Abby gestured to the clearing, where six women stood with their hands pressed against the standing stones. "We noticed she was missing after Sadie had gone through the standing stones."

Gabriel cocked his head.

"She didn't really go through the stones, but that's what

we said. We distracted the bachelorettes with our hunky highlanders, who were running through the trees."

Gabriel rubbed the back of his head. "Okay, so we have hunky highlanders running through the woods. And where would they be now?"

"Looking for Blair, I think."

"What are they doing?" Gabriel pointed at the women with their palms pressed to the standing stones.

"Umm, they think Blair traveled back in time, and they want to go too."

"Welcome to Highland Falls," Hunter said when the other man looked at him like they'd entered the twilight zone. "Now, if you're finished questioning Abby, I'm going to tell everyone searching for Blair to return to the clearing. You can question them while I see if I can pick up Blair's trail. If I don't pick it up within the next ten minutes, we'll talk about calling in SAR." Search-and-rescue.

At Gabriel's and Owen's nods, Hunter cupped his hands on either side of his mouth and yelled for those who were searching to stop and reconvene at the clearing to await further instruction. "I want to talk to Blair's friends before I start looking. It might save us some time," he said as he took Abby by the hand, glancing back at the trees. The moon wasn't overly bright tonight so he couldn't be sure, but he'd caught a glimpse of what looked like fair hair and a flash of plaid. "Any chance that Dylan and his friends were out here tonight?"

"Not that I know of." She cast a worried glance at Gabriel, who walked to where Sadie and Mallory were huddled on the edge of the clearing. "He can't think Sadie and Mallory had anything to do with this, can he?"

"No. He's just trying to get answers," Hunter said as he went to question Blair's friends. "Stay with me, and we'll get to the bottom of it."

"You think Dylan is involved?"

"Maybe." After his talk with the six women, Hunter believed he was on the right track. He signaled to Gabriel that he was going to start his search as he tightened his grip on Abby's hand. He wasn't letting her out of his sight.

He knew which way to go from where the women's eyes went when he asked where they last saw Blair. Their physical responses were automatic, unlike their verbal responses, which were clearly rehearsed. He needed to find Blair before Gabriel spoke to them and they shared their suspicions that Mallory, and possibly Sadie, were involved.

"Hunter." Abby tugged on his hand as they left the clearing.

He stopped to look down at her. "What is it?"

"I'm sorry about your brother." She wrapped her arms around his waist and pressed her cheek to his chest.

"Thank you, but it was twenty-seven, almost twenty-eight years ago that it happened." He kissed the top of her head.

"Still, it must've been awful. Were you with him?"

"Yeah, me and Shane. We shouldn't have been there. My dad warned us not to go near the mine. But telling that to a kid is like waving a red flag at a bull." He stepped back and took her hand to continue the search, looking for signs that someone had walked this way.

He and his brothers had crossed this same trail. It was almost three decades before, but he remembered the day Robbie died like it was yesterday. The smell of fall had been in the air, and the leaves were starting to change color, a reminder that their daylong adventures in the woods were coming to an end and they'd soon be stuck in school. They'd decided to celebrate the end of summer with the biggest adventure of all and set off early that morning.

"Robbie went in ahead of me. I told him we had to wait for Shane to catch up, but he was impatient. A couple of men from town were thinking about reopening the mine as a tourist site. Robbie was determined to find the emeralds he'd heard my dad talking about. Robbie told me I could wait if I wanted to—he wasn't waiting for anyone." Hunter stopped at the rustle of leaves and the snap of a twig ten yards away. Just as he was about to head in that direction, he spotted the reason for the noise. A racoon skittered through the underbrush.

"What happened then?" Abby asked.

"Shane had fallen, and I went back to get him," he said as he scanned the woods up ahead. "Then that was it. All I remember was a loud bang, and I was blown off my feet by a cloud of dust and debris. Shane ran to get help. I should've gone with him, but I had to get to Robbie. He called for me, at least I thought he did. Shane got lost, and by the time my dad came looking for us, Robbie was gone. He died in my arms, just like Danny."

At her hiccupped sob, he looked down. He hadn't

meant to say the last part out loud. "Don't cry, Abs. Come on, please."

"How can I not? No little boy should have to go through that, no man either." She hugged him tight before lifting her head to look at him. "But as hard as it must've been for you, it must've brought some comfort to your family and Danny's knowing that you were with them at the end. They didn't die alone. They died with someone who loved them holding them in his arms. It would've been a comfort to your brother and Danny too."

He cleared the thick ball of emotion from his throat. "I never thought of it that way."

"You wouldn't. All you'd see is that you failed to save them, but you can't save everyone, Hunter."

He nudged her to get her moving. He'd told her too much, more than he'd told anyone else. "We don't have time for this, Abby. We have to—" He spotted a couple of broken branches on low-lying shrubs and let go of her hand to walk a few feet ahead. He crouched to survey the forest floor. "We're on the right track." There were two sets of footprints. One he suspected to be female given the imprint of a heel. And from what Hunter could tell, no one had dragged the woman away. She'd gone of her own volition.

He straightened, about to share his observation with Abby, but she was staring at him with so much compassion in her eyes that he couldn't help himself.

"You're wrong. I could've saved Danny. Granny MacLeod prophesized that he'd die in my arms like Robbie. Two days before we were set to come home from our last tour, he did. I didn't believe her, and I laughed at Sloane when she said we should tell him. I could've saved him, but I forgot about it. Completely put it out of my head. And because of that I lost Danny and Sloane."

The Sinclair family had moved to Highland Falls a few weeks after Robbie died. Hunter didn't know how he would've survived that year without Danny and Sloane.

He cupped Abby's face with his hands. "I won't make the same mistake with you. You need to be careful, Abby. No more going into the woods." Next week would be a month since Granny MacLeod had delivered her prophecy.

"I promise. I'll be careful, Hunter. But nothing will happen to me. Granny MacLeod saw my past, not my future."

He kissed her with a desperation that shocked him. He knew then that Abby had stolen his heart. He couldn't bear the thought of anything happening to her.

"Is someone there? Please, help me." A few feet ahead of them, Blair stumbled onto the path. She was blindfolded with a plaid bandana, her hands tied behind her back, a ragged piece of cloth that had probably been used as a gag hanging around her neck.

"Oh my gosh, Blair," Abby cried out as she and Hunter ran to the woman's side. He removed her blindfold.

"Thank God, it's you," Blair sobbed. "They kidnapped me, but I got away." Her dry eyes narrowed on Abby. "You knew, didn't you? You knew Mallory paid them to kidnap me."

"No, of course not. But Mallory would never do something—"

"Do you know who kidnapped you?" Hunter asked, turning the woman around to untie her hands. As he did, he mouthed to Abby that it would be all right. All he had to do was break Dylan and his friends.

"No, it was too dark to see their faces."

All hell had broken loose by the time they made it back to the clearing with Blair. Half the town had arrived, including his aunt and members of the Sisterhood.

Owen spread his arms to keep Elsa and her friends back. But he couldn't stop them from yelling as Sadie was led away in handcuffs, along with Mallory. "They should be taking you away in handcuffs too, Abby Everhart! You're the worst offender of them all. Your aunt left you the farm to honor her legacy, not to make a mockery of it for fame and fortune. Do you hold nothing sacred?" Elsa yelled, as some of the locals egged her on. "Is fame and fortune the only thing you value?"

Chapter Twenty-Seven

♥

Abby was almost positive the Sisterhood had put a curse on her, Sadie, and Mallory. Life had certainly taken a distinct turn for the worse since Blair faked her own kidnapping last week. Hunter had gotten a confession out of Dylan later that same night but even that hadn't exonerated them in the eyes of Highland Falls and the press.

Sadie and Mallory were released from jail early the next morning, but the damage had been done. Yesterday, the *Atlanta Star* reported on Mallory's night in jail. Her lawyer believed that the incident in Highland Falls wouldn't help her court case. Abby felt horrible for the part they may have played in giving Mrs. Maitland the First more ammunition against Mallory.

Here in Highland Falls, Abby and Sadie were persona non grata thanks to Hunter's aunt Elsa. Although Sadie was less non grata than Abby, as Granny MacLeod was her actual granny and a founding member of the Sisterhood. But those events weren't the reason Abby believed they'd been cursed. As the week went on, things got progressively worse.

Someone stole the tour bus. Its burned-out shell was found ten miles from Highland Falls, and poor Sadie got hauled into the station again. The rumor in town was that her brother had staged the theft in hopes of claiming the insurance. The problem with that theory was that Highland Tours' insurance had lapsed two weeks earlier, which was news to Sadie. All Abby could think was that they were incredibly lucky nothing had happened on the bachelorette tour—aside from Blair's fake kidnapping.

But that wasn't the end of their bad luck. While some people in Highland Falls thought Elijah might have died in the fire, Sadie and Abby had discovered he was very much alive. Two days ago, he'd called Sadie demanding money. When Sadie refused, on account of the fact that she didn't have any, Elijah hijacked Abby's YouTube channel.

He knew about the channel and his sister's involvement from hacking into Sadie's computer. Apparently, Elijah was a world-class hacker, and as Abby watched Sadie try to outmaneuver her brother online, she realized that Sadie was equally skilled herself.

She prayed that Sadie soon figured out a way to beat her brother at his computer games and regain control of the YouTube channel before he ruined Abby and Sadie's best opportunity to earn a living.

Abby sighed and returned her attention to her sisters on FaceTime. They'd called earlier in the week to let her know they wouldn't be making it to the Highland Games as planned. As today was the big day, they were feeling bummed that they weren't here and, if Abby wasn't mistaken, guilty too.

"No, I know you wanted to be here, but you can come to next year's Highland Games." Abby worked to keep a wide smile on her face. She could've used a visit. "Mom's right though. You're getting the keys to the town next month so it wouldn't look good to refuse the mayor's request to judge the pies at the fair."

"Cutest dog too," Haven said.

"You might want to get out of that one," Abby suggested. "The last thing you want to do is tick off the doggy mamas of Shady Mills."

"Not a chance the mayor will let us pass it off. He claims we're unhateable. I'm not sure that's even a word. Anyway, that's why we got the job. That and we're not up for re-election," Haley said.

Abby wished she was unhateable like her sisters. She wasn't looking forward to attending the Highland Games, where approximately fifty percent of the people were mad at her. The other half were tourists. Abby prayed Tiffany and the Bel Air Bs weren't among them.

When Sadie informed Tiffany that they couldn't fit her in this week, she'd thanked Sadie for getting back to her and said they'd find someone else. Abby, Sadie, and her sisters had been stalking the Bel Air Bs' social media for any sign they had. So far everything was quiet— almost too quiet.

"I have to go, guys," Abby said when a horn honked outside the farmhouse. Sadie was picking her up for today's opening of the games. Abby had expected to go with Hunter, but he'd left for the field before she woke up. He had to help with last-minute setup. At least that's what he'd told her when she'd texted him earlier.

She was feeling a little less than confident in her relationship with Hunter these days. She knew it was her old insecurities getting the better of her, but knowing where the doubts came from wasn't exactly helping. They weren't spending as much time together as she would've liked. Hunter told her she was being ridiculous when she'd complained about it last night. Since he'd more or less moved into the farmhouse and they slept together every night, he had a point. Still, with everything that had happened in the past week, she was feeling particularly vulnerable. She just needed something positive to happen to correct the downward spiral she felt she was in.

"Abs, are you sure you're okay? You don't sound like yourself."

"Everything's great. Promise. I gotta go before Sadie leaves me behind."

"Okay, don't forget to send pictures. Go Clan Farquharson!" The Findlays didn't have their own clan. They were a sept of Clan Farquharson.

Abby didn't tell her sisters that she wasn't sure if the Farquharsons still wanted her after the drama at the standing stones. Instead she blew them kisses with a fake smile on her face and disconnected. As though sensing she was feeling down, Bella licked her leg.

Abby picked her up. "I'm sorry I can't take you, Boo. I could really use you on my side today, but Hunter said you had to stay home." She gave Bella a cuddle and then gave her a treat and a toy before slipping on a

pair of sneakers and picking up a backpack she'd found
at the cute vintage clothing store on Main Street before
she realized she was broke again. She'd also bought the
outfit she had on—a red T-shirt paired with a short kilt
of Farquharson plaid in dark blue with red and yellow
diagonal lines.

She gave Bella another quick cuddle before heading
out and locking up. She turned to the 1950 white Chevy
sitting on the gravel drive. It was Granny MacLeod's
pride and joy and known around town as the unicorn
mobile due to its unicorn seat and steering wheel covers,
the unicorn flag flying from the antenna, and the sparkly
unicorn decals on the doors. Abby was relieved to see
Sadie wasn't wearing her pink-and-gold unicorn headband, which Granny MacLeod insisted she wear at the
store. Sadie had been working at I Believe in Unicorns
for the past three days.

"Sorry. Granny insisted I take it to the field today.
But I've got an awesome surprise that will make it
worthwhile."

"Oh my gosh, you genius! You beat your brother, and
we're back in business?" She wouldn't tell Sadie, but
she'd begun to doubt that they'd ever get the channel
back up and running.

Sadie grimaced, and Abby's heart sank. Then Mallory
leaned forward in the backseat to wave out the open
window. "Sorry, I'm the surprise."

"Don't be sorry! You're the best surprise ever. I'm
so glad you're here." Abby stuck half her body in the
window to give Mallory a hug.

"Sit up front, Abs. I had to put the equipment in the

backseat. I couldn't get the trunk open." Sadie nodded at the video equipment on the seat beside Mallory. "I'm not giving up, and neither should you. We'll get some amazing video at the games, and companies will be begging to advertise on your channel as soon as we get it back online," she said as Abby slid into the passenger seat.

"You're the best. And it's our channel." She leaned over the console to hug Sadie. "You've given as much time and energy to it as me. No"—she shook her head when Sadie opened her mouth in what looked to be protest—"don't argue. I've given it a lot of thought. Besides, I have an ulterior motive. I'm hoping you'll reconsider moving back to Highland Falls." She straightened and looked back at Mallory. "I'm still hoping you'll change your mind and move back too."

"As much as I'd love to hang out with you guys every day, I took your advice to heart, Abby." Mallory's face lit up with a smile, and she looked happier and more beautiful than ever. "When all this is over, I'm going to spend a month in Europe. I've always dreamed of going to France and Italy. Harry and I were supposed to go on our honeymoon, but we learned his cancer had come back the day before we were to leave, and then he was never well enough to travel. If Marsha wins, the trip will put a huge dent in my nest egg, but I've already got a job lined up and a place to stay. One of Harry's old friends has offered me free room and board in exchange for taking care of his wife."

Abby and Sadie shared a glance, obviously coming to the same conclusion: The last thing Mallory needed was to take care of someone else. She was burned out from her

years of taking care of Harry and, more recently, Blair's
mother. But neither of them wanted to put a damper on
her excitement so instead they asked her about her travel
plans. Abby had been to Italy and France many times
and shared some of her favorite places and experiences
with Mallory. She was telling her about attending the
Formula 1 race at Monte Carlo and getting to drive with
one of her favorite race car drivers, Ferrari's Sebastian
Vettel, when Mallory made a face.

"Why are you making a face? Sebastian Vettel is
awesome. He—"

"I wasn't making a face about him. I was making it at
him." Mallory lifted her chin.

Abby followed the direction of Mallory's chin lift.
Gabriel Buchanan was directing traffic into the farmer's
field across the road. Officially chief of police now, he
wore his uniform of navy pants and shirt with a shiny
badge and a big gun.

"Okay, so I get that you haven't forgiven him for
arresting you on suspicion of kidnapping Blair—" Abby
began.

"I don't care about Blair. I understand why we were
under suspicion—well, not entirely, but it was him questioning me about Harry's death. He implied I was a gold
digger who had married Harry for his money."

"Yeah, because that's what Blair's friends said. He
apologized, right?"

"I guess," she admitted grudgingly.

"And you have to admit he's the hottest single guy
in Highlands Falls...Scratch that, in the entire state,"
Abby said as he rested his arms on the roof of a car,

smiling and chatting with the group of women inside. "And there's definitely a spark of interest every time he looks at you." At that moment, Gabriel glanced their way, and Abby knew the second he spotted Mallory in the backseat. "Just like that."

Mallory slouched down when he headed their way. "Don't you dare say anything, Abby."

"I promise. I..." Abby trailed off when the carload of women moved forward, and she had a clear view of the entrance to the field and a man wearing Mackenzie plaid who was even more gorgeous than Gabriel Buchanan.

Hunter was leaning against a fence post talking to an equally gorgeous woman who wore her long, dark hair scraped back from her face in a ponytail. Abby's heart dropped to her feet. Hunter was deep in conversation with Sloane, and it looked serious. Seeing them together was a blow to her ego. They were the perfect couple— equals in every way.

Knock it off, she told herself. Hunter had never given her any reason to be jealous. He'd told her he was no longer in love with Sloane, and she knew from experience he didn't lie. Like she'd told Sloane, he was one of the good guys. This was a positive development. Sloane and Hunter needed to talk. They needed closure. They needed...Her inner pep talk died in her throat when Hunter straightened and gathered Sloane in his arms.

Abby must've gasped because Sadie glanced at her and Mallory sat up in the backseat. "What's wrong?" Sadie asked. She turned her head. "Oh, I...I'm sure it's not what it looks like, Abs. This is probably the first time they've talked since the day Hunter came home and told Sloane about Danny."

But was it? Abby wondered. Hunter had been busy all week helping prepare for the games. Chandler's excuse for not spending time with her had been he was busy with the company. Only she'd later learned that he'd been busy with Juliette.

Chapter Twenty-Eight

♥

His brother walked over to where Hunter waited to take his turn at the caber toss. The caber was a seventeen-foot hundred-pound pole trimmed at the end to fit in a man's hand. It was Hunter's first time taking part in the event in four years. "I hear you smoked everyone on your first toss. The Douglases aren't thrilled to see you back." His brother grinned, flipping off Ronan Douglas.

Then Shane turned back to him, and Hunter knew exactly what his brother wanted to know. He figured it would only be a matter of time before word reached his family that Hunter had spoken to Sloane. "So...Sloane?" His brother raised an eyebrow.

"We talked. And what's with the face? I thought you'd be happy we did."

"I am. The question is, is Abby happy you were hugging your ex-fiancée?"

"Why wouldn't she be?"

"Okay, let me rephrase that. Is your girlfriend happy you were seen making out with your ex-fiancée?"

"Come on, Shane. We weren't making out. Abby

knows I'm not in love with Sloane. She knows that I'm..." No, Abby didn't know he was in love with her because he hadn't told her.

And now that his brother mentioned it, she hadn't been her sweet, bubbly self when he caught up with her, Mallory, and Sadie at the bagpipe competition earlier. He'd put it down to his aunt and her cronies giving Abby the cold shoulder at the event. He'd had a word with Elsa, but it hadn't seemed to help matters.

Then again, Abby hadn't been herself for the past week. Lately she seemed worried about where she stood with him...Okay, so his brother was right. This wasn't good. Not that he'd tell Shane.

"Do you remember telephone tag when we were kids?" his brother asked.

"No. I didn't play telephone tag."

"Well, let me enlighten you. By the time the gossip reaches Abby's ears, you and Sloane will have been making out in the back forty like a couple of horny teenagers."

He cursed under his breath.

"You're better at telephone tag than you think. That's exactly what they'll be saying you were doing next."

"Mackenzie, you're up." He heard Shane betting on him against one of the Douglases as he walked onto the field. He could've told him to save his money. Hunter's concentration was broken. He lifted the log easily, took a short run, and then tossed the caber. He knew he overshot the mark before the pole landed and his brother groaned.

"You should've thought about what you just told me

before betting on me," Hunter told his brother, then hailed Owen. "Have you seen Abby?"

Owen grinned. "She's at the hammer toss."

"As in she's watching the hammer toss, right?" Hunter said.

"Nope, she's all signed up. Seems to me she's competing with Sloane. Any idea why that would be?"

"Told you," his brother said.

"Not helping, Shane," Hunter said as he made his way through the crowd.

"Incoming! Heads up!" someone yelled just as a hammer went sailing through the air. Everyone scrambled to get out of the way, and the hammer landed without incident in front of his aunt's tent.

"Sorry! I'm so sorry." Abby ran to pick up the hammer, her cheeks as red as her hair. "It slipped out of my hands."

"Abby," he called to her. "Abby, hold on a sec." He jogged after her. He put out a hand to stop her when she kept walking. "Hey, what's going on? Didn't you hear me?"

She wouldn't look at him and walked to where it appeared Sloane was taking her final throw. "I don't want to miss my turn," Abby said and went to move past him.

"Honey, I, ah, think that was your turn." He took the hammer from her. "It's not easy to do. It takes practice, you know."

She wasn't listening to him. She was biting her bottom lip as she watched Sloane take her throw.

"A hundred feet. We have a winner. Sloane," the judge began, to much applause. He announced the names of second and third places. Abby sighed halfheartedly and clapped.

Sloane walked over with her medal and smiled at Abby. "They should've given you a second chance. That would've been a great throw if it hadn't slipped out of your hands."

"They probably were afraid I'd take out Elsa next time. Are you doing the five-mile run?" Abby asked.

"Yeah, I was just heading over there now. Are you doing it?"

"For sure. I love to run."

"Since when?" Hunter laughed and realized how badly he'd stepped in it even before Abby turned to give him a look.

Sloane grimaced. "Okay. I guess I'll see you over there." She walked away, giving him a look that said *You screwed up big-time, buddy*. And even though he knew he had, it felt good receiving the familiar look from Sloane.

He realized he was smiling and knew exactly what that smile might look like to Abby. "It's not what you think." He handed her back the hammer.

"You have no idea what I'm thinking. If you did, you wouldn't have given me the hammer."

He laughed, moved into her, and brushed her hair from her cheek. "You have nothing to be jealous of, honey. I…" He glanced around and decided it wasn't the time to tell her he loved her. "Shane told me what people are saying. It's not true. Sloane and I talked. That's what you wanted, wasn't it?"

"You did more than talk, Hunter," she said, then walked over to return the hammer. She chatted with the judge, smiling when he teased her about her throw.

His brother joined him. "So how did it go?"

"I think I'm lucky I didn't get a hammer in the head. She says she's doing the run up the mountain. I don't know what she thinks she'll prove. There's no way Abby can compete with her. Sloane's in better shape than—" He broke off at the look on his brother's face.

"Hey, Abby. Nice throw. I don't know why they didn't count it. You would've won." His brother looked from Hunter to Abby. "I'll just go and eat some haggis now."

"Hunter! Hurry up, man." His cousin waved at him. "You're tied for first place in the caber toss with Ronan Douglas."

"You better go," Abby said. "Who knows, you and Sloane might end up king and queen of the games."

"I'll be right there," he yelled at his cousin, who kept shouting his name. "Come on, don't be like that."

Abby crossed her arms and lifted her chin. "Like what?"

"Jealous of Sloane. You don't have any reason to be." He drew her into his arms and kissed her. "Please do me a favor and don't run in the race. I don't want you to hurt yourself. You haven't been sleeping well."

"I hate that you think I'm weak. I'm not, you know."

He blew out a breath. They weren't going to get anywhere, and there was no way he'd win this argument with her. "All right, just don't hurt yourself competing with Sloane. I have plans for tonight."

"What kind?"

"The best kind. We're going to sleep under the stars. There's a meteor shower tonight." He didn't ruin the moment by telling her there was also the chance of rain.

She smiled. It wasn't the wide smile he was used to and loved, but he'd take it. "Don't hurt yourself either," she said with a teasing grin that had the tension releasing from his shoulders.

* * *

Four hours later, the tension in Hunter's shoulders was back and magnified times ten. He couldn't find Abby. He'd been competing in several events and hadn't noticed how much time had passed until he looked up to see Sloane cheering on the sidelines of the tug-of-war between the Mackenzies and the MacRaes.

After he shook hands and took some good-natured ribbing about losing, he walked over to Sloane. "Hey, when did the race wrap up?"

"I think the last of the runners came in around an hour ago. Why? What's wrong?"

He dragged a hand through his hair. "I haven't seen Abby. Did you see her?"

"No, but I'm sure she's okay. She's probably talking to someone. She's very friendly." Sloane smiled and patted his arm. "I like her. She's good for you. Danny would've liked her too. He never thought we should get married, you know."

"I didn't know. He never said anything to me."

"He thought we just went along with what everyone expected because it was easy. That we were afraid of losing what we had, so we settled," Sloane said as they walked toward the mountain.

"What do you think?" he asked.

"I think he was right."

"Maybe he was. He was a smart guy."

"Not smart enough to listen to Granny MacLeod's prophecy."

"What do you mean? I didn't tell him. Neither did you."

"Yeah, I did." She raised a shoulder at his incredulous look. "He was my brother, my twin—that trumped fiancé."

His knees buckled, and she reached for him. "Hunter, what's wrong?"

"Abby. Granny MacLeod. The prophecy. She told Abby she was going to die in the woods in a month. Today. It's a month today."

"Okay, don't panic. Just breathe," she said as they reached the foot of the mountain. "Have you called her?"

"Yeah, it goes straight to voice mail."

"Try again," she said as she flagged down one of the volunteers and asked to see the list of runners. Abby's name was on the list without a check mark beside it. "Did you see her come down the mountain?" Sloane asked, giving the man Abby's description.

He shook his head and then looked from Sloane to Hunter, who was on his phone. "Is there a problem?"

Hunter followed the muffled ring tone to a black-and-red knapsack. His heart was in his throat as he unzipped it; he prayed he was wrong even when he knew he wasn't. "It's Abby's phone. She wouldn't leave it."

"Yeah, we have a problem," Sloane told the volunteer. "Abby Everhart's missing."

Chapter Twenty-Nine

♥

Hunter stood alone in the mountain's shadow. A tornado of emotions had threatened to rip him apart when he first realized another of Granny MacLeod's prophecies had come true and Abby was gone. Now there was nothing left inside him.

He heard people calling her name as the search got underway. A command post had been set up where hours ago she'd taken part in the hammer toss. He should've told her he loved her when he'd had a chance. He should've begged and borrowed until he had enough money to send her away before the month was up. He should've moved heaven and earth to get her out of Highland Falls and back to LA. And now he'd never see her smile, or hear her laugh, or hold her in his arms, or tell her she'd become his sun and moon and stars.

He heard their whispers, the sound of their approach. His family and friends were coming for him. He wouldn't go. He'd held his dying brother in these woods; he'd held his dead best friend on the side of a road in Afghanistan after an IED blew up his Humvee. He couldn't face finding Abby's body, looking into her lifeless green eyes, knowing it was his fault she'd died.

A heavy hand fell on his left shoulder. "Hunter, they want you to lead the search," his brother said.

He shook his head. "No."

Another hand came to rest on his right shoulder, and Owen said, "You need to find her, lad. One way or another, you need to bring her home."

He opened his mouth to say no but then he remembered what Abby had said to him that night in the woods when they were looking for Blair. She'd talked about the comfort he'd given to his brother and best friend and their families by being with them at the end. She'd expect that of him. And no matter that it would kill him, he could do nothing less for her.

Each word felt like a razor blade scraping his throat as they came out of his mouth. "All right."

"You won't be alone this time. Come what may, we'll be by your side," Owen promised.

* * *

Abby had run from a black bear. It was a mistake. She'd known it from the second the thought went from her brain to her feet and she'd started to run. She'd heard her father's voice in her head. *Don't run from a bear. Their natural instinct is to give chase. They're faster than you think.*

It had been his constant refrain every time they went for a walk in the woods. But he hadn't walked in the woods with her for fifteen years. And as she'd tripped over the undergrowth and branches slapped at her arms and face and the sound of the bear's heavy grunts came closer, she'd admitted a truth she'd kept buried for all that time—she missed her dad.

As though the admission unlocked a treasure trove of memories that she hadn't thought about in years, the answer had come to her at the same time as her breath had seared her throat and she'd gotten a cramp in her side. She needed to go down. She'd veered to the left, grabbing on to a tree branch when her feet slipped on a bed of pine needles. Behind her the bear had crashed through the trees. So close she could've sworn the air had warmed the back of her neck.

Run!

She ran, slipping and sliding down toward the forest floor. She'd managed to stay upright. She didn't look back. She didn't have to. She could tell by the sounds of tree branches breaking that, bottom heavy, the bear had slammed into rock and trees as he rolled down the mountain.

She'd reached a small stream, and swerved to her right. She'd kept running, weaving and bobbing. Fear and adrenaline had kept her going. On and on she'd run until her legs gave out and sweat blurred her vision. She'd practically crawled toward a rock bathed in sunlight and collapsed. Panting, she'd pulled her shirt from the waistband of her skirt and wiped her hot, sweat-drenched face.

A faint smile had tugged on her lips. She'd done it. She'd saved herself. At least from the bear. Because now, she was well and truly lost. She'd broken her dad's cardinal rule: stay put. She didn't have a choice now. She had to find a way back to the farmer's field.

She should've listened to Hunter. She never should've entered the race. It was laughable that she thought she could compete with Sloane. Abby was pretty sure she saw the woman coming down the mountain before Abby had even made it to the quarter-mile mark. Sloane didn't look like she'd broken a sweat, whereas Abby had been hot and dripping wet. But her lack of athletic ability wasn't to blame for her slow progress or how she'd ended up lost in the woods.

At the quarter-mile mark, she'd stopped mid-stride, frozen at the sight of one of the runners near the back of the pack with her. The woman was Tiffany's identical twin, and she was running with three women who looked exactly like the Bel Air Bs, albeit with some recent face work and one boob job. But when Tiffany's twin broke into a familiar high-pitched laugh and turned her head, Abby ran into the bush. Terrified that she'd seen her and would come looking for her, Abby, like an idiot, kept running.

Because she'd been afraid Tiffany and the Bel Air Bs would find out her luxurious mountain hideaway was a farm still in need of work, and that she was still close to broke. But they'd also see that, despite her fears earlier today, she had her very own hunky highlander, who didn't care that she was clumsy, couldn't read all that well, and mixed up her words.

All Hunter had tried to do today was keep her safe, and she'd acted like an insecure biatch. She was glad he and Sloane had finally talked. Despite Sloane being the kind of woman Abby could only dream about becoming, she really liked her. Now Abby just had to figure a way out of the woods so she could finally sleep under the stars with Hunter and tell him how much she loved him.

She took in her surroundings and panic bubbled up inside her as she remembered everything that crawled and slithered on the forest floor. She drew her knees to her chest, curling inward. *Don't panic. Stay calm.* She whispered her father's words. Then more words: fire, water, food, shelter. *Remember the girl you used to be,* she told herself. Fearless, confident, up for anything. She was there, somewhere inside her. As with her dad's voice, all she had to do was reclaim the memory, reclaim that part of her that she'd buried deep inside.

Pushing to her feet, Abby searched for a big stick to carry before setting out on her journey back to the man she loved, and it wasn't only her dad's voice that she heard as she walked through the woods, it was Hunter's.

Three leaves, leave it be. Blue, black, purple berries mostly safe. Only pick mushrooms with tan and brown gills, white, tan, and brown caps. Don't drink out of a stream unless you have no choice. Dig a hole a foot deep and wait, strain the muddy water through a cloth.

She walked for hours, foraging and listening for the sounds of people, cars, water. The already dark forest grew steadily darker as day turned into night. Above her, the sky lit up, and thunder rumbled. She needed to find shelter. A flutter of nerves weakened her knees, but she fought past it. Up ahead, she spotted a rocky outcropping and moved toward it. She'd have to climb up a steep ridge to get to it. *You've got this,* she told herself.

Abby awoke hours later stiff and cold, itchy from bug bites, and prayed the night was over. She pushed herself upright and stuck her head out. A shaft of early morning light shone through the leafy canopy. She'd done it. She'd survived a night alone in the woods. She, the woman who'd been terrified of anything and everything when she first arrived in Highland Falls, had made it despite being surrounded by creatures of the night. She hadn't died; she'd thrived. The thought filled her with confidence and hope.

But as the day wore on, her confidence began to dwindle. She sat on a rock to regroup, and that's when she heard it, the roar of water in the distance and the faint sound of voices. She followed the sounds, picking up her pace as the voices got louder. She heard cars, and then through the trees saw flashes of silver and white whizzing by. She stumbled out of the woods. A man parked on the side of the road looked over, startled.

"You're the woman who went missing yesterday, aren't you?" he said, coming to her side.

She nodded, tears of relief spilling down her cheeks. He patted her shoulder and smiled. "They've set up a command center at the games. I'll take you there. The paramedics can check you over." He got her settled in his van and then handed her a bottle of water. Ten minutes later, they arrived at the field. The man ignored the officer telling him to stop, powering down his window to yell "I've got the woman you're looking for."

He drove across the field, honking his horn to get

people out of the way. As soon as he stopped, the vehicle was swarmed. A woman helped her out while calling for the paramedics. Someone else wrapped a blanket around her. Then she heard someone on the radio letting search-and-rescue know she was safe. Word spread quickly that she'd been found, and the area was soon crowded with familiar faces. Owen and Elsa rushed over, followed by the mayor.

Abby answered their questions and thanked the man who'd driven her there. Somewhere to the far left of the crowd that continued to grow, she heard Hunter demand, "Where is she?" He sounded like he was going to tear someone apart, and he didn't sound like the Hunter she knew and loved.

"Here. Hunter, I'm here." She stood up, letting the blanket fall to go to him. She hadn't moved more than a foot and he was there, in front of her, and she knew from the haunted look in his eyes that this wouldn't be the reunion she'd dreamed of.

"What the hell were you thinking?" he yelled, taking her by the shoulders to shake her.

Shane pushed through the crowd to put a hand on his brother's arm. "Hunter, take it easy. She's okay."

It was as if Shane weren't there. Hunter didn't take his eyes off her. "How many times did I tell you to be careful? To not go in the woods alone? You promised. You promised you'd be careful." His eyes searched her face as his hands left her shoulders to fall to his sides. "I thought you were dead." His voice was a dull monotone.

"I know. I didn't think, Hunter. Please, let me explain."

He shook his head. "We're done. You need to leave. You need to go back to LA."

"You don't mean that," she whispered, suddenly aware that the crowd had gone completely quiet and still.

"Yeah, I do," he said to the ground, then he nodded and turned to walk away.

She stared after him, knowing that everyone was watching her. She blinked back tears, trying to hold it together. But it was as if the Universe decided she hadn't been tested enough, and a voice from her past called her name. Through a veil of tears, she saw four women standing before her. It was Tiffany and the Bel Air Bs. Abby hadn't been imagining things. They really were here.

She stiffened her spine. She could get through this. If the last twenty-four hours had taught her anything, it had taught her that she could handle whatever life had to throw at her. She'd embraced the fearless, adventurous girl she used to be, and she wasn't going to bury her again for anyone.

"We're so glad you're okay, Abby. We couldn't believe it when we heard you were the one lost in the woods. We thought you were a goner for sure. I mean, you're the ultimate city girl. You do not do the woods. Now here you are, right as rain after being missing for more than a day. You're our new shero—isn't she, girls?"

Abby didn't feel like a shero. It was hard to after watching the man she loved walk away from her. She hadn't done it on purpose, but she'd made him relive the worst moments of his life, his greatest fear. He thought another of Granny MacLeod's prophecies had come to pass. Yet he'd gone after her, even while thinking he'd find her dead in the woods.

What he didn't know was that he was right and so was Granny MacLeod. A part of Abby, the fear and shame that had been her constant companions since her accident, had died in the woods yesterday. They'd no longer rule her life or play a role in every decision she made.

"And this place, it's exactly how I dreamed it would be," Tiffany continued. "We subscribe to your new channel, and we love it. So much better than the last one. Which is why I'm about to make your dreams come true. I want to buy the farm from you. We stopped by earlier hoping to see you and had a look around. I hope you don't mind. But it's the perfect vacay property. So what do you say, seven hundred and fifty thousand?"

Abby blinked. Tiffany's offer was incredible, more than Abby had dreamed of getting for Honeysuckle Farm. Actually, that wasn't quite true. On the drive to the farm, that was the number she'd mentioned to Stan. It was more than enough money to pay off Sadie's brother and rent a place for herself and Bella in a good neighborhood in LA. She saw what her life would be like in high definition. In no time at all, she'd be rich and famous again. But everyone crowded around her— Mallory, Sadie, Granny MacLeod, Owen, Hunter's family, Winter, Josie, Sloane, Ed, and Walter—they weren't in that picture. And neither was the man she loved or the dog she and Bella loved.

And there'd be no standing on her front porch enjoying the cool mountain air while listening to the sound of the gurgling stream. She'd miss the sunrise and sunset visits of the owl, the eagle, and the deer. She'd miss sun-warmed tomatoes and berries and the meadow of rainbow-colored flowers.

"Okay, you drive a hard bargain," Tiffany said. "I can go to eight hundred thousand, but no higher. Does that work for you?"

Abby smiled. "I appreciate the offer, but I'm not selling. The farm is my great-aunt's legacy to me, and I think it's about time I did something with it." She looked at Owen and Elsa. "I might need some help though."

"You'll have all the help you need," Elsa and Owen promised at almost the same time. Then Elsa added: "With my nephew as well as the farm," and the rest of Hunter's family agreed.

Tiffany and the Bel Air Bs—*Babes*, Abby corrected in her head—hugged her. "I wish I could take back that day in the kitchen, Abby. But if I did, you wouldn't be here, and it's clearly where you were meant to be. I'm happy for you." Tiffany grinned. "A little jealous too."

Mallory and Sadie waited until the end of the long line of people to hug her, and so did Sloane. "Don't give up on him, Abby. He loves you." Sloane glanced at the mountain. "I've never seen him like that. He was terrified he'd lost you. He thought he had. Give him some time. There are things he needs to work through that don't have anything to do with you."

Abby nodded. Hunter had to deal with his ghosts and his guilt once and for all.

Chapter Thirty

♥

It took ten days for Hunter's nightmares to stop. He worked out the dreams that haunted him in his carvings—his guilt, his fear, his shame. Abby had gotten lost because of him. She'd had to save herself because he'd failed to find her. They were the stories he told himself until Abby set him straight.

She didn't come to see him on the land where he now lived—she wrote him a letter. And knowing how hard that was for her touched him as much as her words. She loved him, and she promised to wait for him for as long as Owen had waited for Liz. Honeysuckle Farm was his as much as it was hers. When he was ready to come home, they'd be there waiting for him.

He'd moved out of the barn the day he'd walked away from her and signed over his half of the farm to Abby. He'd planned to live in his brother's garage until he figured out where to go, but Sloane had found him hours later. She'd signed the property on Mirror Lake back to him. She'd also returned the money he'd been sending to her every month for the past two years. She'd never touched it, and neither had her mother.

Their reasons for not doing so weren't the same. Her mother would never forgive him. Sloane never blamed him. She'd been angry at him and at Danny, and she'd lashed out. Same as he'd lashed out at Abby the morning she'd walked out of the woods.

Abby knew that. She'd absolved him of his guilt in the letter Owen had delivered yesterday. His old friend had delivered a message of his own: Either Hunter wanted Abby in his life or he didn't, but the time for him to decide was up. While he'd been wallowing—as Owen put it—another load of crap had landed on Abby.

The day before Owen had delivered Abby's letter and his ultimatum, Hunter had already realized that being without Abby was more painful than living with the fear of losing her. She'd brought light and laughter back to his life, as his latest carving proved. He no longer saw the faces of wild and ferocious beasts in the wood; he saw her. He removed the tarp from his latest work and stood back, glancing over his shoulder at the rustle of grass.

His brother stood with two mugs of steaming coffee in his hand, staring at the carving. It was Abby. Her hair was streaming behind her as she swung high in the sky with a smile on her face, confident that he would always be there to catch her. In three days, he would prove to her that she could depend on him. He wouldn't let her down. She'd never doubt his love for her again.

"I know you don't think of yourself as an artist, but, brother, that belongs in a gallery."

He smiled, accepting the compliment and the mug

from Shane. "It's the one piece I'll never sell. Did Eden hear back from her friend?"

"She did. The money will be in your account by end of day Friday." He looked around. "Where's Wolf?"

"He's gone home."

* * *

Wearing her white beekeeper suit, Abby gingerly removed the lid, leaning it against the hive. Owen, wearing a suit identical to hers, handed her the smoker. Once she'd applied smoke to the hive, she handed it back to him. She waited two minutes for the smoke to do its work before removing the frame.

"You've got company," Owen said, taking the frame from her. He shook his head at the question in her eyes. It wasn't Hunter. She worked to keep her disappointment from showing. Owen had been angry when Hunter didn't come back to the farm yesterday. He'd expected him to come as soon as he'd read Abby's letter. She had too.

As she walked back to the house, she removed her gloves and the hood with the veil. She smiled at Wolf, who'd risen from where he'd been stretched out on the porch with Bella soaking up the sun. His arrival had taken some of the sting out of Hunter's rejection. She held on to the hope that soon his master would follow his dog's lead.

"Abby!"

Her gaze shot to the gorgeous, leggy blondes getting out of the black sedan parked on the gravel drive. She dropped her hood and gloves. "Haven! Haley!" she cried, running into their open arms. "Oh my gosh! What are you guys doing here?" She hugged them again. "I'm so glad you're here."

Someone cleared their throat, and Abby looked around her sisters. "Don't I get a hello and a hug?"

"Mom? What's going on? Is someone sick?" Her hand went to her throat. "Is Tim okay?" she asked after her stepfather.

"He's fine," her mom said, and gathered Abby in a warm hug. "Your sisters got a text yesterday that you needed them. And I thought that if you needed them, you needed your mother too. So what is it? What's going on?"

The only person who would text her sisters was Hunter. She didn't think it boded well that he'd sent them instead of coming himself. She swallowed the lump in her throat and forced a weak smile. "You're probably going to want to sit for this. So let's get you settled in first."

An hour later, as the four of them sat on the patio with glasses of honey-sweetened iced tea, Abby told her mother what her life had been like for the past year. She would've just as soon left it in the past, but it played into the latest drama that was set to unfold at the farm that Saturday.

Her mother stared at her, then stood up.

"Mom, where are you going?" she asked

"To get something stronger to drink." She returned moments later with a bottle of wine and two glasses. She put them on the table beside her chair, then sat, her lips pressed together.

When she looked away, Abby's sisters shared *what's going on?* glances with her.

She was as much in the dark as they were until her mother brought her gaze back to Abby, her eyes shiny. "I don't know what I've done that you've felt you needed to keep this from me. No." She raised her hand when Abby went to protest. "It's not the time. Not when Juliette and Chandler are threatening the life you're making here. But later, Abby. Later you and I will talk."

She leaned over to take her mother's hand. "We'll talk, but I just want you to know, it wasn't you. It was me."

"Abs, that's not true," Haley said. "It was all of us. We let you put distance between us, and we're not letting you do that anymore. Are we, Haven?"

"Nope, we're not. We've talked to you more since you moved here than we have the entire time you lived in LA, and we realized how much we've missed you."

"I haven't," their mother said.

"Mom!" the twins cried.

"What? I've hardly talked to her at all. You kept stealing my phone and having long FaceTime calls together, and you never included me." She sniffed and crossed her arms. "Tell your sister your news."

"See, Mom, that is one thing you need to stop doing. You brag about us all the time. Every time we talked to Abby, you'd go on and on about us," said Haley, the sister who didn't mind conflict.

Her mother frowned. "But that's why she phones. She wants to hear about you girls. She doesn't want to talk to—" She shifted in the chair to pour a glass of wine.

"Oh, Mom, I'm sorry if I ever made you feel like I didn't care about you or want to talk to you." At the sound of the screen door opening, Abby wiped her eyes.

"Abby—" Owen began as he came around the corner. He took one look at the four of them crying and said, "I'll get more wine."

Two hours and a bottle of wine later, Abby and her mother and sisters had moved on from crying to laughing to plotting.

With no malice intended on Tiffany's part, she had shared about her visit to Highland Falls and her offer to buy Honeysuckle Farm with Chandler and Juliette. And, as Elinor had learned and shared with Abby, Chandler was in desperate need of money, no matter how small the amount. He'd already refinanced the mansion in Bel Air.

Since their divorce had been finalized in June, Abby didn't understand why this had anything to do with her. But Juliette, in her desperation to save Chandler and his cosmetics company, had been looking for a loophole and found it. Abby had claimed her inheritance twenty-four hours before their divorce was final, which made Honeysuckle Farm matrimonial property. Which now included the barn and surrounding property, because Hunter had signed it back to her.

Abby had consulted with Eden as soon as she received the registered letter from LA, and learned there was nothing she could do to stop them. She had two options. First, buy Chandler's half of the property, which had been valued at six hundred thousand dollars—not only did she own the land with the standing stones, she owned the gem mine too. Second, the property would be sold at auction. Even with everyone offering to pitch in to help her buy the property, they couldn't come up with the funds, so Honeysuckle Farm would be sold at auction this Saturday.

"I understand that Hunter's aunt believes she can keep the people in Highland Falls and the surrounding county from bidding on the farm, but how can she stop everyone else?" her mother asked.

"Elsa apparently has a long reach. Plus, she and the mayor have ensured that notices of the sale have been buried. The short turnaround time for the auction is also playing in our favor."

"From what you've told me about Juliette, I can't see her agreeing to anything that works in your favor," her mother said.

"You're not wrong. They're bringing their buyer with them. Tiffany. What they don't know is I've already talked to Tiffany, and she's going to lowball her bid."

"How did you get her to do that?" Haley asked.

"Let's just say Juliette isn't who they thought she was, but more than that, I promised the Bel Air Babes free room and board during next year's Highland Games and starring roles in a couple of my videos." She returned her sisters' high-fives. "Now, what was your news?"

"We're not going to Stanford. We're going to UNC so we can be close to you."

"You're kidding? I mean, I'm thrilled. But you had free rides at Stanford."

"We have enough money in our college accounts that

you set up for us to cover a couple years, plus there are scholarships we can apply for next year," Haley said.

"Mom, are you and Tim okay with this?"

Her mother nodded. "We like that you're only a couple hours away if they need you and they can come see you on the weekends. And it'll be nice that we can see all three of you when we visit."

Haven and Haley talked about their plans and the school all through dinner, which relieved Abby's concern that they'd made the decision for her. It would be fun having them close by, and they began to make plans for September. None of them mentioned the possibility that Abby wouldn't have the farm. She refused to let her mind go there.

Later, as she and her mom did the dishes together, Haven and Haley came into the kitchen carrying one of Liz's journals. "Abs, don't be mad at us. We know you wanted to read your aunt's journals in order, but—" Haven began.

"It's my fault, Abs. We ran out of the shampoo, and I thought if we found the recipe, we could make some while we're here." Haley held up the book. "There's something you need to see."

Abby wiped her hands on the dish towel and walked over to the table where they placed the book. "What is it? Is the recipe there?"

Haley nodded. "And a letter for you from your aunt. Your dad too."

"Girls, let's leave Abby to read them on her own," her mother said as Abby pulled out a chair at the table. Her mother put her arms around her from behind and kissed the top of her head. "It wasn't all his fault, Abby. He'll take the blame for not coming to see you, but I didn't make it easy for him. I was angry. Angry he'd left us and left me to deal with the bills and a little girl who missed the daddy she adored."

Her mother was right; her father took the blame. Hunter was right too; the guilt had eaten away at her dad. He'd blamed himself for the accident and couldn't bear to watch her struggle to walk and talk again. But he didn't love her any less—if anything he loved her more. At the time he wrote the letter, he expected to see her again. He had no idea he would only live for another year.

As much as life isn't the same without you, I've come to love the farm. Your great aunt too. She's a spitfire, just like you. I hope one day your mom can find it in her heart to forgive me, and she'll let me bring you to Highland Falls. You'll love it here as much as I do, firefly. I know you will. Liz and I are making up a room for you so you can stay the summers if you want. I hope you'll want to, but I'll understand if you don't. I love you, firefly. I always will.

She wiped her eyes and then tucked the letter back in the envelope. It had been returned to sender. They had moved to Shady Mills by then.

While her dad's letter had made her cry, Liz's letter made her gasp in shock. She hadn't planned to leave

Abby the farm. She'd been going to leave everything to Hunter. But she'd changed her mind six months before she died. She loved Hunter like a son and worried that he'd live the rest of his life alone so she'd left the farm to both of them in hopes they'd fall in love. She'd followed Abby online and decided she was just what Hunter needed, and that he was what Abby needed. She'd instructed Eden to wait until around the time Abby's divorce would be finalized to send the letter. She hadn't wanted Abby to lose the farm in the settlement.

Chapter Thirty-One

♥

Three days later, Abby was sick with nerves as she watched people wander in and out of the house and the barn. The auction was scheduled to begin in fifteen minutes. Owen was standing on the porch beside her, keeping his eye on things out here while her mother, sisters, and Elsa were keeping an eye on people inside the house.

Abby wrapped her arms around her waist. "I didn't expect there to be so many people."

"There's one person I expected to see, and he damn well better show up or I'm going to go over and drag him from his lean-to."

"He'd hate this, Owen. He'd...Oh my gosh, it's Elinor and Kate." She ran down the steps and walkway to greet the older women who were getting out of the car. "Stan." She laughed when he came over and shook her hand. He wished her luck, then moved away to make room for Elinor and Kate.

"I can't believe you're here." She'd barely finished hugging them when Shane, Eden, and Hunter's mother and sisters and cousins arrived, followed by just about everyone from town that she knew. She'd just told them to help themselves to the cookies and cupcakes in the kitchen when Sadie arrived with Mallory.

Abby talked and texted with them at least once a day. Last week, Sadie had shared the news that Granny MacLeod had been right not just about the kidnapping charge; Sadie was pregnant.

"You're glowing," Abby said to the mommy-to-be as she went to hug her. She couldn't say the same about Mallory. Yesterday, the judge had found in Marsha's favor, and Mallory's world had been turned upside down. Abby hugged her. She wanted Mallory to come and stay at the farm for a couple weeks until she got back on her feet but as positive as Abby was trying to be, she had to face the possibility that she could lose the farm today.

"Abs, I think you-know-who has arrived," Sadie said.

She turned to see Chandler and Juliette, both of them outfitted in black and designer shades with Tiffany hurrying to catch up to them wearing a pair of four-inch wedge sandals. Abby almost laughed, remembering the day she'd arrived at Honeysuckle Farm wearing a similar pair of shoes.

"Abby." Chandler nodded. The North Carolina sunshine shone down on his shaved head, giving his tawny brown skin a gorgeous glow. He'd always been prettier than she could ever hope to be.

He removed his black-and-yellow-gold aviators that Abby knew for a fact cost more than she'd made in the past eight months. "You look good despite having to rough it out here in the middle of nowhere. At least you'll be able to move back to LA once we've sold this place."

"Why would I? Everything and everyone I love is here."

Juliette gave a snort of derision as she pulled an official-looking document from her purse. "That's good, because none of the money from the sale will be going to you."

"What are you talking about, Juliette?" Chandler asked as Abby stared on in shock.

"She broke the terms of our agreement by starting a new YouTube channel. If she doesn't turn over her half of the proceeds from the sale of Honeysuckle Farm, then I'll bury her in lawsuits."

Abby waited for Chandler to say something. Surely he couldn't be that cruel. But when the auctioneer pounded his gavel to open the auction, Chandler cast her a sheepish glance and then offered Juliette his arm to head across the meadow to the podium.

"Wolf!" Abby called, hiding a smile when Chandler and Juliette sent panicked glances around the meadow. Sadie and Mallory smothered their laughter behind their hands.

Shane and his cousins, catching on to what Abby was up to, called for Wolf too. Owen obliged by letting him out of the house.

Chandler and Juliette caught sight of him and cried, "Oh my God, it really is a wolf. Wolf!" and began to run. Juliette's spiked heel got caught, and she fell. Chandler looked back, saw that Wolf was chasing him, and kept running.

Juliette looked up, her sunglasses askew, and her eyes narrowed at everyone laughing. "Chandler, you idiot. It's not a wolf!"

"Actually, Juliette, he is. Half at least," Abby said when the couple, adjusting their clothing and sunglasses, joined everyone gathered in front of the auctioneer.

When the man opened the bidding at a hundred thousand, Tiffany cried out the agreed-upon amount. "Two hundred thousand."

Chandler and Juliette turned to stare at her.

"Two hundred and fifty thousand," a man called out.

Tiffany glanced at her, and Abby gave a furtive nod. "Two hundred and seventy-five thousand!"

"Three hundred thousand," a woman shouted.

Abby's heart sank as more people got involved. They couldn't afford to go any higher. At five hundred thousand, Tiffany glanced at her, and Abby shook her head. The auctioneer raised his gavel. "Going once. Going—"

"Five hundred and fifty thousand," a familiar deep voice called from the back of the crowd.

Abby turned and went up on her toes, searching for Hunter. Instead her eyes locked on a ridiculously handsome man with copper-streaked chestnut hair, piercing blue eyes, and a clean-shaven masculine jaw. And while he didn't look exactly like the man Abby knew so well and loved so much, the warm, tingly feeling she got in her stomach gave him away.

And for a minute, she just stood there staring at him, basking in the knowledge that he was here and that he loved her and that he was bidding on… *Wait a minute. He can't bid on the farm. He doesn't have any money!*

"Hunter—" she began, only to be cut off by a flurry of shouted bids.

"Five hundred and fifty-five thousand!"

"Five hundred and sixty thousand!"

"Five hundred and seventy-five thousand!"

"Six hundred thousand," Hunter called out, the crowd parting to let him walk to her side.

"What are you doing?" she whispered, taking the hand he offered her and squeezing tight. "You can't afford to pay—"

Before she could finish, the auctioneer raised his gavel. "Going once. Going twice." Their family and friends were holding their collective breaths, praying that no one would bid against him, while Abby was worrying no one would and he'd get in trouble for his fake bid. "Sold to the man with the pretty redhead."

"No! This is fixed. This is not right. The property is valued at one-point-two million. It can't have sold for only six hundred thousand. Where's the sheriff in this town? I demand this be investigated."

While several people, including the auctioneer and Owen, explained to Juliette how auctions worked, Abby turned to Hunter. "I love you for trying to save the farm, but I don't want you to get in trouble."

"How am I going to get in trouble?"

She went up on her toes to whisper in his ear, "When they cash your check and it bounces, that's how."

He smiled down at her, reaching up to tuck a strand

of hair behind her ear. "It's not going to bounce, honey. The farm is ours."

"I don't understand."

"You were right. People will pay a small fortune for my carvings."

"You sold them? You sold your beautiful carvings for me?"

"No. I sold them for us. I want us to build a life together here. I know it's not the life you dreamed of. I can't offer you fame and fortune. But I—"

"I don't need fame and fortune, not if I have you. I love you, Hunter Mackenzie."

"And I love you, Abby Everhart." Hunter lifted her off her feet to kiss her. It wasn't a long kiss or a deep kiss; it was a perfect kiss. A kiss that promised a lifetime of star-filled nights.

"Now I see how it is. Your boyfriend bought the farm so you think your life can just go on as if you haven't ruined Chandler," Juliette screeched. "Well let me tell you, I'm going to bury you in court. I'm going to—"

"Juliette, that's enough," Chandler said, taking her by the arm to lead her away. Then he stopped and turned. "I'm sorry. For everything, Abby. I'm not suing you."

Juliette jerked her arm away. "If you don't sue her, you and I are over, Chandler. Six hundred thousand is a drop in the bucket. It won't save the company. A million would've—"

"Enough, Juliette. I can't do this anymore. It's not worth it."

"Neither are you," Juliette said, then called out to

Tiffany, who was talking to Hunter's cousins. "Come on. I'm done here."

Tiffany smiled. "I'm not. Have a good trip back to LA. I'll hitch a ride with Chandler."

Chandler winced as Juliette stormed off.

"The two of you can get a ride to the airport with us," Elinor offered as she and Kate joined them.

Chandler hugged his longtime housekeeper, who'd been more of a mother to him than his own had ever been. "I'm sorry. I never should've let her convince me to force you into retirement."

"You were under a lot of stress. But I can't say I'm sorry she's out of your life."

"Is it as bad as Juliette said?" Abby asked Chandler.

The last couple years hadn't been good between her and Chandler. But even if he hadn't had an affair, Abby didn't believe their marriage would have survived. Still, there'd been a time when she'd loved him, and she knew he was a good man despite doing some pretty awful things.

He nodded. "When I get back, I'll have to start closing down operations."

And all those people would be out of work. "What if I told you I have a miracle shampoo and conditioner, and I'd give you the recipes? I'm not making it up, Chandler," she said as he stared at her like she'd lost her mind. "Ask Kate, and Josie." She waved Josie over. "They've used it. So have me and my sisters. It repaired the damage to my hair in less than a month."

Family and friends crowded around them as Kate and Josie shared their experiences with Chandler, and Abby saw a flicker of excitement and hope come into his eyes.

Then he looked at her. "But why? Why would you give me the rights to it after everything I've done? You could make a fortune."

Abby looked up at Hunter. "I've already got everything I've ever wanted. I shouldn't have outted the company for animal testing the way that I did. It hurt more than just you."

"You paid for that, Abby. No matter what Juliette says."

"I know, and I do have an ulterior motive. I'll give you the rights, and I'll promote you on my new YouTube channel, if you draw up an agreement giving ten percent of every sale to the Liz Findlay Foundation."

"What's the Liz Findlay Foundation?"

"It's a foundation I'm starting in my great-aunt's name. The recipes for the shampoo and conditioner are hers. The money will go to help women who are homeless get back on their feet."

An hour later in the farmhouse kitchen, they'd ironed out the details with Chandler's lawyers via Skype. Eden represented Abby and agreed to take on the legal work for the foundation.

The rest of their family and friends stayed late into the night. Owen and Elsa were the last to leave. Before they did, Hunter's aunt leaned in to Abby and whispered, "Welcome to the Sisterhood."

"The day couldn't have been more perfect," Abby said as she stood on the porch with Hunter waving goodbye to Owen and Elsa.

"I wouldn't bet on that," Hunter said and took her by the hand.

"Where are we going?"

"To sleep under the stars."

Abby looked up at the thousands of stars twinkling in the inky black North Carolina sky as she walked with Hunter to the meadow. Elinor had been right—only in the dark can you see the stars, and Abby had to walk through the dark to find herself and her light, a man she loved with all her heart, and this place she now called home.

When her stepsons' antics land them in jail, Mallory Maitland comes face-to-face with the tall, dark, and incredibly handsome chief of police in Highland Falls. But Gabriel Buchanan has his hands full with three young boys of his own. However, when the families find themselves caught up in a whirlwind of holiday activities together, they might find that no one is immune to the magic of Christmas.

Please turn the page for a preview from *Christmas on Reindeer Road*, coming in Fall 2020.

Chapter One

♥

Mallory Maitland hummed along with the Christmas carols playing on her car's radio as she took the long way home the day after Thanksgiving. Despite her best friend living there, she wasn't anxious to return to Highland Falls, North Carolina. For years, Mallory had done her best to avoid the town in which she'd grown up. Except now she no longer had just herself to think about.

She glanced in her rearview mirror at Oliver and Brooks, her late husband Harry's sons, who were no doubt silently plotting how to get back at her for ruining their lives. If they knew how difficult it had been for her to accept the job offer from the mayor of Highland Falls, they might take some pleasure in today's move from Atlanta to the small mountain town.

Instead of blaming her and burning holes into the back of her head with their resentful stares, they might want to take a good, long look at themselves in the rearview mirror. They were the reason she'd lost six of her seven clients at Aging Awesomely, her newly formed senior care company. They were also the reason her landlord presented her with an eviction notice last week.

But did she tell them they were to blame? Remind them how often she'd warned them what could happen if she had to keep leaving her clients to meet with their over-bearing principal? Or how often she'd told them that, the next time they invited half the school to their apartment when she wasn't home, they'd get kicked out and good luck finding another one without a reference?

No. She didn't blame them or give them an I-told-you-so lecture. She wanted to, but she couldn't bring herself to do it. And the reason she couldn't was that, no matter how difficult they'd made her life these past two months, she understood why they hated her and acted out. They needed a scapegoat for the crummy hand life had dealt them, and she was it.

Their mother, Harry's second wife, had given up her parental rights in exchange for half of Harry's fortune when Brooks, the youngest, was born. Mallory hadn't been around then. She'd been fifteen at the time. Harry wouldn't make the fateful decision that forever cast Mallory in the role of stepmonster until the lead-up to their wedding. He'd sent his sons to boarding school two weeks before the big day.

Oliver and Brooks had no idea how hard she (a woman who hated conflict) had fought to change their father's mind, and she'd never tell them. She wouldn't do anything to diminish Harry in their eyes. She'd gladly shoulder the blame to protect them. She knew what it was like to grow up feeling abandoned and unwanted.

Yet despite her understanding and empathy for her

teenage stepsons and the many weeks she'd spent applying every piece of parenting advice she'd gathered from podcasts, books, and friends, she'd reached the depressing conclusion that establishing a loving relationship with Oliver and Brooks was a lost cause. They'd never be a family no matter how hard she tried or how much she wanted them to be.

Abby Everhart, her best friend, had told her not to lose hope, that love was the answer. Mallory knew better. Love wasn't enough to heal broken hearts or guarantee a happily ever after. Her own experiences had proven that to her time and again. Except, deep down, beneath all the hurt, beat the heart of an eternal optimist. She couldn't seem to help herself. She always looked for the bright side of life, the light at the end of the tunnel, the good in the bad.

And thinking of finding the good in the bad, she forced a smile in the rearview mirror and tried to make eye contact with Oliver and Brooks in the backseat.

Her stepsons could pass for British royals William and Harry. Almost sixteen-year-old Oliver, with his sandy blond hair providing a curtain for his eyes, looked like William. While Brooks, with his curly ginger hair and freckles, looked like Harry—the prince, not his father.

The boys also had British accents to go along with their royal good looks, which only served to make Oliver's superior attitude sound even more superior. He had a way of making Mallory feel like a downstairs maid in an episode of *Downton Abbey*. Why on earth Harry had thought it a good idea to send the boys to boarding school in England, she'd never know.

When smiling and staring at Oliver and Brooks in the rearview failed to get their attention, she cleared her throat. "Only ten minutes until we arrive in Highland Falls!" she said with fake cheer. She continued in the same over-the-top, upbeat voice despite the boys' chilly blue stares. "Abby checked out the house on Reindeer Road, and she says we'll love it." She actually said the house needed some TLC, but the backyard was a nature lover's paradise. Since Oliver and Brooks weren't exactly lovers of the great outdoors, Mallory didn't think that would help her cause.

The boys shared a mutinous glance that made her nervous. Sometimes it felt like they could communicate telepathically, and whatever they shared mentally never boded well for her.

"Okay, I get that you guys are unhappy about the move. You've made your feelings perfectly clear. But let's be honest, you haven't exactly been happy in Atlanta either. It'll probably be easier for you to make friends in Highland Falls."

At their insulted glares, she realized she probably shouldn't have implied that they didn't have friends. But it was true. They didn't. Not real friends. "I mean better friends."

They shared another look before Oliver said, "We need to use the loo."

"We're not far from...okay." She folded like an accordion at Oliver's pointed stare. "There's a truck stop up the road."

She reached for her Christmas-spiced latte and took a restorative sip as she continued on Highway 64 with

Mariah Carey singing "All I Want for Christmas Is You" on the radio. All Mallory wanted for Christmas was for Oliver and Brooks to give her a chance. To give *them* a chance.

And right then, with the smell of Christmas in Mallory's nose, the taste on her tongue, and the sound in her ears, the answer came to her: She knew exactly how to solve her stepson dilemma.

Love wasn't the answer; Christmas was.

She need look no further for evidence than two of her favorite childhood holiday reads: *A Christmas Carol* and *How the Grinch Stole Christmas*. The holiday had changed Ebenezer Scrooge into a kind and generous man, and the Grinch's tiny heart grew three times its size that day.

But proof of the holiday's power wasn't found only in fiction. During World War I, soldiers on the Western Front called a ceasefire to celebrate the holiday. Surely if Christmas could change the hearts and minds of sworn enemies, it could change her stepsons' minds about her.

Her optimistic heart beat a little stronger as she turned off the highway and into the truck stop's parking lot. "Do you need me to come in with you?" she asked as she parked the car.

Oliver rolled his eyes. "I think we know how to go on our own."

"That's not what I meant. I just thought—" He shut the passenger door on her explanation.

Brooks scrunched his nose as he watched his brother walk toward the red clapboard diner. Then he turned to her. "Me and Ollie are starved. Can you give us some money for crisps?" he asked, referring to potato chips.

"I gave you guys your allowance last week. Surely you haven't spent it already." The move had taken a big chunk out of her nest egg, and she had to watch her pennies. But while she knew the value of a dollar and was fiscally responsible, her stepsons didn't and weren't.

"Ollie's mates needed a loan."

Needed a loan, my eye. It was probably a shake-down. As much as she wasn't thrilled to be moving back to Highland Falls, she was relieved Oliver and Brooks would be away from the juvenile delinquents they called friends. *Mates,* she corrected herself.

"All right, but this has to last until next week." She reached for her brown leather satchel on the passenger seat and withdrew a ten-dollar bill for each of them from her wallet. "I'll order pizza for dinner, so just buy a bag of chips. *Crisps.*"

"Thanks." Brooks pocketed the money and took off to join Oliver, who waited for him. When he reached his brother's side, Oliver opened the door, and both boys glanced her way. She lifted her hand to wave. Oliver shoved his brother inside.

With a sigh that came straight from her exhausted soul, she picked up her latte and settled back in the driver's seat to wait for the boys. As the minutes ticked by, she glanced around the packed parking lot and decided she had time to indulge in her guilty pleasure. Nothing relaxed her more than a good love story. She credited romance novels for getting her through the past few difficult years.

She pulled up the audiobooks app on her phone and connected it to her Bluetooth. She was already three quarters of the way through the book. She'd left off at the part where the hero was trying to sweet-talk the heroine into his bed.

Mallory couldn't believe the woman was playing hard to get. She wouldn't have to be asked twice. She'd be dragging the handsome small-town sheriff into *her* bed. Then again, the heroine wasn't a twenty-nine-year-old widow who couldn't remember the last time she'd had sex. Sadly, now that she'd inherited two teenage boys, she didn't see any sexy times in her future. Unless she counted living vicariously through the heroines in her romance novels.

She leaned back and let the story take her away, smiling at the heroine's attempts to deny that she'd fallen in love with the hero. Mallory knew it was only a matter of time before the woman realized he was perfect for her in every way. They were meant to be. She was silently cheering the hero on when she happened to glance at her phone, shocked to see that Oliver and Brooks had been gone for twenty minutes.

She glanced at the diner's window, but a giant blow-up Santa swaying in the breeze made it difficult to see inside. She powered down her window to stick her head out. The crisp mountain air smelled of wet leaves and wood smoke and brought back childhood memories of the holidays.

She wouldn't let her mind take a trip down memory lane. Like her life, it never ended happily. Instead, she focused on her stepsons. They were either making her wait on purpose or had decided to have a burger and fries at the lunch counter. She figured it was the former. Still, she couldn't see them being much longer and went to turn off her book.

All she'd need was for Oliver and Brooks to catch her unawares and overhear the literary couple in the throes of passion. Besides, it wasn't like she could get caught up in the fantasy while worrying the boys would suddenly appear.

A flash of white light in her side mirror caught her eye. She looked up to see the midafternoon sunshine glinting off the shiny chrome grill of an SUV pulling into the truck stop. Noting the blue Highland Falls police logo on the side of the vehicle as it drove by, her shoulders tensed.

Please don't let it be him, she prayed, and slid down in her seat. Only she forgot she had her latte in her hand as she did so and her elbow hit the console, spilling Christmas spice coffee down the front of her white shirt.

"Son of a nutcracker." She grimaced as the words came out of her mouth. It was one of her client's favorite curses. He said it so often to Mallory as she tried to help him age awesomely, she wasn't surprised it stuck.

She returned the latte to the cup holder, then reached once more for her bag and pulled out a stack of neatly cut paper towels and a purse-size stain remover. In her job, she could never be too prepared—aging wasn't always awesome. As she dabbed at the stain with the paper towel, she looked to where the SUV had parked. This prayer, just like all the others, had gone unanswered.

The tall, dark-haired man who was coming around the front of the SUV wore a pair of aviators, a hint of scruff on his chiseled jaw. From where she sat, she couldn't see the shallow dimple in his chin. But he filled out his navy uniform as magnificently as she remembered.

For one brief and shining moment last July, the Highland Falls chief of police, Gabriel Buchanan, had been the man of her dreams. Days later, he had become the man of her nightmares.

She pulled out her cell phone to text Brooks. He didn't seem to hate her quite as much as his older brother did.

Hey, sweetie, what's taking you guys so long?

Waiting for a response, she cast a nervous glance at the door. The last thing she wanted to do was go inside and risk Chief Buchanan seeing her. But as the minutes ticked by, she didn't have a choice. Something could've happened to the boys. At the thought, every horrible thing she'd ever heard about truck-stop restrooms came to mind, and she practically leaped from the car.

Her heart fluttered like a caged canary. As the past two months had proven, she wasn't equipped to deal with teenage boys. Seniors, she could handle: Being married to a man decades older than her had left Mallory well equipped to deal with golden-agers.

She zipped up her burgundy leather jacket to hide her stained shirt in an effort to look presentable. Dealing with Oliver and Brooks while packing up what little was left of her old life had taken a toll. She lifted a self-conscious hand to smooth back the strands of hair that had escaped from her ponytail as she approached the diner's door, then peeked in the window to get an idea of the layout.

She backed away when a barrel-chested man opened the door, offering him a smile as he stepped outside. "Do you know where the restrooms are?" she asked.

"To your right and down the hall on your left. Word to the wise: Buy gas or some food, else Dot, the owner, will tear a strip off you."

"I will, thank you."

He touched the brim of his ball cap and headed for a big silver rig.

The smells of hamburgers, fries, apple pie, and coffee greeted Mallory when she walked inside, and her stomach rumbled. She couldn't remember when she'd last eaten. The air was warm, filled with the sounds of people talking and a waitress yelling out an order. Somewhere in the diner a man called hello to the chief. Mallory froze midstep.

"How's it going, Walter?"

Gabriel Buchanan's voice was even deeper and sexier than she remembered. It was also close, like he was sitting at the lunch counter. And she was standing mooning over his voice, drawing the curious attention of the customers—none of whom were her stepsons—lined up at the cash register. As soon as they paid and moved away, Gabriel would see her. He'd also see her if he stood up, as she was nearly six feet in her high-heeled boots.

She bent at the waist to brush a piece of imaginary lint off her jeans while walking toward what looked like a hall on her left. It was. She spotted a sign for the men's restroom midway down the hall and hurried for the door.

She knocked. "Oliver, Brooks, we have to go." Thinking her stepsons might not have heard her over the banging of pots and pans, she tried again.

When there was no response to her second attempt, she said, "Guys, this isn't funny anymore. Come on." Pressing her ear to the door, she jiggled the knob. It was locked.

Someone cleared their throat. She looked down the hall to see an older man watching her with a bushy white eyebrow raised.

"It's not what it looks like," she said with an awkward laugh. "My sons are in there."

With her lips pressed to the door, she knocked and called, "Do you hear that, boys? There's a nice gentleman who'd like to use the restroom."

The way the man was looking at her made her as nervous as the absolute silence coming from the other side of the door. "I'm really sorry," she apologized while attempting to force the knob to turn. She used both hands but it wouldn't budge. "I'm sure they won't be..." She turned to tell the older man they wouldn't be much longer, but he was no longer there.

She bent down to look under the door but couldn't see anything from that vantage point. With a quick glance up and down the hall to ensure no one was around, she got down on her hands and knees. Her cheek touched the tile as she tried to get a look under the door. She grimaced at the gritty feel beneath her face, imagining how many pairs of boots and shoes had walked over the floor today.

"Oliver, Brooks, I'm not fooling around anymore. If you don't get out here this second, I'm going to..." *What? What was she going to do?* "I'm going to break down the door?"

She sighed. She hadn't meant it to come out as a question.

"Or you could simply ask for the key," a deep and familiar male voice suggested from behind her.

About the Author

Debbie Mason is the *USA Today* bestselling author of the Christmas, Colorado, Harmony Harbor, and Highland Falls series. The first book in her Christmas, Colorado series, *The Trouble with Christmas*, was the inspiration for the Hallmark movie *Welcome to Christmas*. Her books have been praised by *RT Book Reviews* for their "likable characters, clever dialogue, and juicy plots." When Debbie isn't writing, she enjoys spending time with her family in Ottawa, Canada.

You can learn more at:
AuthorDebbieMason.com
Twitter @AuthorDebMason
Facebook.com/DebbieMasonBooks

Fall in love with these charming contemporary romances!

SUMMER ON HONEYSUCKLE RIDGE
by Debbie Mason

Abby Everhart has gone from being a top L.A. media influencer to an unemployed divorcée living out of her car. So inheriting her great-aunt's homestead in Highland Falls, North Carolina, couldn't have come at a better time. But instead of a cabin ready to put on the market, she finds a fixer-upper, complete with an overgrown yard and a reclusive—albeit sexy—man living on the property. When sparks between them become undeniable, will she be able to sell the one place that's starting to feel like home?

PRIMROSE LANE
by Debbie Mason

Olivia Davenport has finally gotten her life back together and is now Harmony Harbor's most sought-after event planner. But her past catches up with her when she learns that she's now guardian of her ex's young daughter. Dr. Finn Gallagher knows a person in over her head when he sees one, but Olivia makes it clear she doesn't want his companionship. Only with a little help from some matchmaking widows—and a precocious little girl—might he be able to convince her that life is better with someone you love at your side.

Find more great reads on Instagram with @ReadForeverPub.

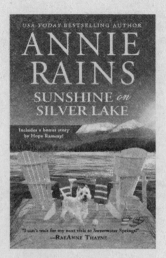

SUNSHINE ON SILVER LAKE
by Annie Rains

Café owner Emma St. James is planning a special event at Sweetwater Springs National Park to honor her mother's memory. Which means she'll need the help of the ruggedly handsome park ranger who broke her heart years ago. As their attraction grows stronger than ever, will Emma find herself at risk of falling for him again? Includes a bonus story by Hope Ramsay!

STARTING OVER AT
BLUEBERRY CREEK
by Annie Rains

Firefighter Luke Marini moved to Sweetwater Springs with the highest of hopes—new town, new job, and new neighbors who know nothing of his past. And that's just how he wants to keep it. But it's nearly impossible when the gorgeous brunette next door decides to be the neighborhood's welcome wagon. She's sugar, spice, and everything nice—but getting close to someone again is playing with fire. Includes a bonus story by Melinda Curtis!

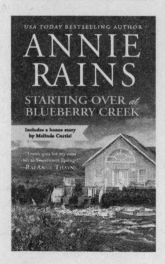

RETURN TO MAGNOLIA HARBOR
by Hope Ramsay

Jessica Blackwell's life needs a refresh. So while she's back home in Magnolia Harbor, she's giving her architecture career a total makeover. The only problem? Jessica's new client happens to be her old high school nemesis. Christopher Martin never meant to hurt Jessica all those years ago, and now he'd give anything to have a second chance with the one woman who always haunted his memories.

CAN'T HURRY LOVE
by Melinda Curtis

Widowed after one year of marriage, city girl Lola Williams finds herself stranded in Sunshine, Colorado, reeling from the revelation that her husband had secrets she never could have imagined, secrets that she's asked the ruggedly hot town sheriff to help her uncover. Lola swears she's done with love forever, but the matchmaking ladies of the Sunshine Valley Widows Club have different plans...Includes a bonus story by Annie Rains!

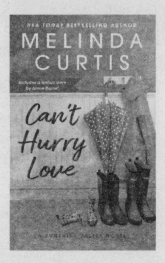

THE SUMMER HOUSE
by Jenny Hale

Callie Weaver's too busy to think about her love life. She's invested her life savings into renovating the beach house she admired every childhood summer into a bed-and-breakfast. But when she catches the attention of local real estate heir and playboy Luke Sullivan, his blue eyes and easy smile are hard to resist. As they laugh in the ocean waves, Callie discovers there's more to Luke than his money and good looks. But just when Callie's dreams seem within reach, she finds a diary full of secrets—with the power to change everything.

PARADISE COVE
by Jenny Holiday

Dr. Nora Walsh hopes that moving to tiny Matchmaker Bay will help her get over a broken heart. When the first man she sees looks like a superhero god, the born-and-bred city girl wonders if maybe there's something to small-town living after all. But will Jake Ramsey's wounded heart ever be able to love again?

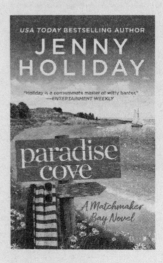